COUNTY OF LENNOX & ADDINGTON P. L.
36494900240931

THE GATES OF ATHENS

Conn Iggulden is one of the most successful authors of historical fiction writing today. He has written three previous bestselling historical series, including Wars of the Roses, as well as *Dunstan*, a stand-alone novel set in the red-blooded world of tenth-century England, and *The Falcon of Sparta*, which saw him return to the epic Ancient World. *The Gates of Athens* is the first novel in his brand new Athenian series.

T0204778

Also by Conn Iggulden

Dunstan
The Falcon of Sparta

THE WARS OF THE ROSES SERIES
Stormbird
Trinity
Bloodline
Ravenspur

THE EMPEROR
SERIES
The Gates of Rome
The Death of Kings
The Field of Swords
The Gods of War
The Blood of Gods

THE CONQUEROR
SERIES
Wolf of the Plains
Lords of the Bow
Bones of the Hills
Empire of Silver
Conqueror

Blackwater
Quantum of Tweed

BY C. F. IGGULDEN
EMPIRE OF SALT SERIES
Darien
Shiang
The Sword Saint

BY CONN IGGULDEN AND HAL IGGULDEN
The Dangerous Book for Boys

BY CONN, ARTHUR AND CAMERON IGGULDEN
The Double Dangerous Book for Boys

BY CONN IGGULDEN AND DAVID IGGULDEN
The Dangerous Book of Heroes

BY CONN IGGULDEN AND
ILLUSTRATED BY LIZZY DUNCAN
Tollins: Explosive Tales for Children
Tollins 2: Dynamite Tales

ATHENIAN

THE GATES OF ATHENS

Conn Iggulden

MICHAEL JOSEPH
an imprint of
PENGUIN BOOKS

MICHAEL JOSEPH

UK | USA | Canada | Ireland | Australia
India | New Zealand | South Africa

Michael Joseph is part of the Penguin Random House group of companies
whose addresses can be found at global.penguinrandomhouse.com.

First published 2020
001

Copyright © Conn Iggulden, 2020

The moral right of the author has been asserted

Set in 13.5/16 pt Garamond MT Std
Typeset by Jouve (UK), Milton Keynes
Printed and bound in Great Britain by Clays Ltd, Elcograf S.p.A.

A CIP catalogue record for this book is available from the British Library

HARDBACK ISBN: 978–0–241–35123–9
OM PAPERBACK ISBN: 978–0–241–35124–6

www.greenpenguin.co.uk

MIX
Paper from
responsible sources
FSC® C018179

Penguin Random House is committed to a
sustainable future for our business, our readers
and our planet. This book is made from Forest
Stewardship Council® certified paper.

To Simon Broome. A great teacher.

'He spoke to me – his words had wings.'
– Homer

'Quick, bring me a beaker of wine,
that I may wet my mind and say something clever.'
– Aristophanes

Lennox &
Addington
LIBRARIES

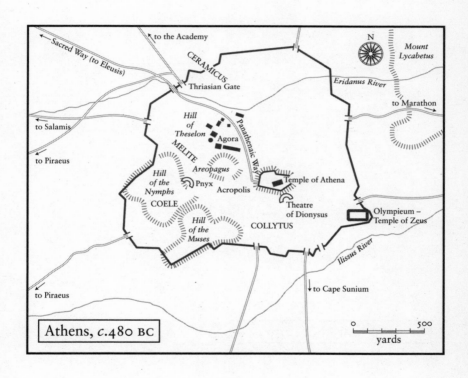

to the Academy

Sacred Way (to Eleusis)

N

Mount
Lycabetus

CERAMICUS

Eridanus River

Thriasian Gate

to Salamis

to Marathon

to Piraeus

Hill
of
Theselon

MELITE

Agora

Panathenaic Way

Hill
of the
Nymphs

Areopagus

Pnyx

Acropolis

Temple of Athena

COELE

Theatre
of Dionysus

Olympieum –
Temple of Zeus

Hill
of the
Muses

COLLYTUS

Ilissus River

to Piraeus

to Cape Sunium

Athens, *c.*480 BC

0   500

yards

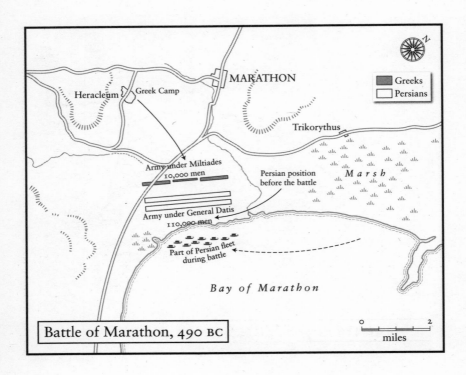

Heracleum · Greek Camp

MARATHON

Greeks
Persians

Trikorythus

Army under Miltiades
10,000 men

Persian position
before the battle

M a r s h

Army under General Datis
110,000 men

Part of Persian fleet
during battle

Bay of Marathon

Battle of Marathon, 490 BC

0   2
miles

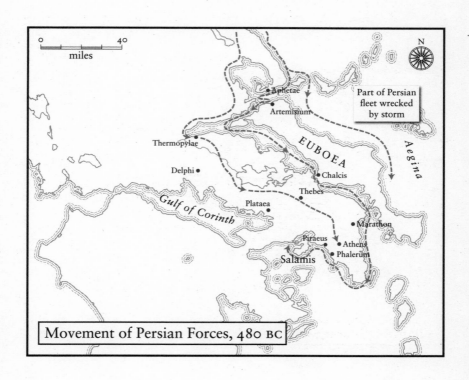

Movement of Persian Forces, 480 BC

Pronunciation

Military terms

	Ancient Greek	Ancient Greek Pronunciation	English Pronunciation	Meaning
archon	ἄρχων	ark-own	<u>ark</u>-on	Ruler, leader.
epistatai	ἐπιστάται	ep-ist-at-eye	ep-<u>ist</u>-at-eye	Second row in phalanx, behind the protostatai.
epistates	ἐπιστάτης	ep-ist-at-airs	ep-<u>ist</u>-at-eez	Chairman in the Athenian Assembly.
keleustes	κελευστής	kel-eu-stairs	kel-<u>you</u>-steez	Trireme officer.
phalanx	Φάλαγξ	fal-anks	<u>fal</u>-anks	Body of heavily armed infantry.
protostatai	πρωτοστάται	pro-toss-tat-eye	pro-<u>toss</u>-tat-eye	First row in phalanx, in front of the epistatai.
strategos	στρατηγός	strat-air-goss	<u>strat</u>-egg-oss	General, commander.
trierarch	τριήραρχος	tree-air-ark-oss	<u>try</u>-err-ark	Commander of a trireme.

Underlining indicates stressed syllables.

Locations

Agora	Ἀγορά	ag-or-a	ag-<u>or</u>-a	Open place, market.
Areopagus	Ἄρειος πάγος	a-ray-oss pag-oss	a-ree-<u>op</u>-ag-ous (as in danger-ous)	Rock of Ares. Hill in Athens used as a court.
Ceramicus	Κεραμεικός	ker-a-may-koss	se-<u>ram</u>-ik-ous/ ke-<u>ram</u>-ik-ous	Potters' district of Athens.
Eretria	Ἐρέτρια	e-ret-tree-a	e-<u>ret</u>-tree-a	Greek town in Euboea.
Marathon	Μαραθών	ma-rath-own	<u>ma</u>-rath-on	Fennel plain on the east coast of Attica.
Plataea	Πλάταια	plat-eye-a	pla-<u>tee</u>-a	Greek town in Boeotia.
Pnyx	Πνύξ	p-nooks	p-<u>niks</u>	'Packed in'. Hill. Meeting place of the Assembly in Athens.
Salamis	Σαλαμίς	sal-a-miss	<u>sal</u>-a-miss	Island off Athens.

Characters

Agariste	Ἀγαρίστη	ag-a-rist-air	ag-a-<u>rist</u>-ee	Wife of Xanthippus.
Ariphron	Ἀρίφρων	a-ri-frone	<u>a</u>-ri-fron	First son of Xanthippus and Agariste.
Aristides	Ἀριστείδης	a-ris-tay-dairs	a-<u>rist</u>-id-eez	Strategos, eponymous archon 489 BC.
Cimon	Κίμων	kim-own	<u>ky</u>-mon	Son of Miltiades.
Cleisthenes	Κλεισθένης	clay-sthen-airs	<u>cly</u>-sthen-eez	Athenian lawmaker.
Eleni (Helen)	Ἑλένη	hell-en-air	e-<u>lay</u>-nee	Daughter of Xanthippus and Agariste. (Never named in ancient sources.)
Epikleos	Ἔπικλέος	ep-i-kle-oss	ep-i-<u>klay</u>-oss	Friend of Xanthippus.
Heracles	Ἡρακλῆς	hair-a-klairs	<u>herr</u>-a-kleez	Mythical hero famed for strength.
Miltiades	Μιλτιάδης	mill-tee-ad-airs	mill-<u>ty</u>-a-deez	Military leader, father of Cimon.
Pericles	Περικλῆς	per-ik-lairs	<u>per</u>-ik-leez	Son of Xanthippus and Agariste.
Pheidippides	Φειδιππίδης	fay-dip-id-airs	fy-<u>dip</u>-id-eez	Marathon runner.
Themistocles	Θεμιστοκλῆς	th-mist-o-clairs	th-<u>mist</u>-o-cleez	Eponymous archon 493 BC.
Xanthippus	Ξάνθιππος	ksan-thip-oss	<u>zan</u>-thip-ous	Strategos, leader. Husband to Agariste.
Xerxes	Ξέρξης	kserk-seez	<u>zerk</u>-seez	King of Persia.

Additional words

Athena	Ἀθηνᾶ	ath-air-na	ath-<u>een</u>-a	Patron goddess of Athens.
Eupatridae	Εὐπατρίδαι	eu-pat-rid-eye	you-<u>pat</u>-rid-eye	Hereditary aristocracy of Athens.

Ten tribes of Athens

Erectheis	Ἐρεχθηΐς	e-rek-thair-ees	e-<u>rek</u>-thay-iss
Aegeis	Αἰγηΐς	eye-gair-ees	a-<u>jee</u>-iss
Pandionis	Πανδιονίς	pand-ee-on-iss	pand-ee-<u>own</u>-iss
Leontis	Λεοντίς	le-ont-iss	lee-<u>ont</u>-iss
Acamantis	Ἀκαμαντίς	ak-am-ant-iss	ak-am-<u>ant</u>-iss
Oeneis	Οἰνηΐς	oy-nair-ees	ee-<u>nee</u>-iss
Cecropis	Κεκροπίς	kek-rop-iss	kek-<u>rop</u>-iss
Hippothontis	Ἱπποθοντίς	hip-oth-ont-iss	hip-oth-<u>ont</u>-iss
Aeantis	Αἰαντίς	eye-ant-iss	eye-<u>ant</u>-iss
Antiochis	Ἀντιοχίς	ant-i-ok-iss	ant-ee-<u>ok</u>-iss

Prologue

The dust of mountain flowers lay thick on the air, like perfume or boiled varnish. Living things panted in the shade. Goat's-thorn grew on all sides, with scrub grass and bare rocks too hot for anything alive to rest upon. Crickets creaked and sang in the branches of pines that clung to stone and somehow endured.

Into a stillness as old as the hills around them music sounded as a faint thread on the air, swelling into something that rang with brass and voices raised in song. Lizards scuttled out of sight as the king's dancers reached the crest, making the air tremble with cymbals, pipes and drums. At a single order, they halted, panting, dripping with sweat.

The king himself came forward on his stallion, dismounting with a hint of the grace he had known as a young man. Darius tossed the reins to a slave and clambered onto a huge flat stone to stare over the plain. From that height, he could see the scars of the land, the marks of war and fire. He frowned, moved by both the distance and the closeness of the past. He had stood in that same place thirty years before. In that moment, it seemed as if he could take a single step and be there once again, with his father at his side and his life all ahead.

Ruins lay where the city of Sardis had been. The flames had died down long before, though when a whisper of breeze rose, Darius thought he could smell char on it, a scent of burned bricks or perfume, or rot. There were people too, in the distance. The air was so clear, Darius could see the sparks of cooking fires, with thin trails of smoke rising above. No doubt some of them had run, only to return when the conflagration had died down, or perhaps they had come to loot the ruins, searching for beads of gold that had once been coins.

The funeral pyre of a city could never be a small thing. On that day, from the height and distance of the mountains, it was hard to imagine entire streets and parks and districts consumed in flame. The watchtowers along the great wall had fallen, Darius saw, spilling their stones. Roads too stretched away from the walls, clearly marked. The steps of families had carried ash and soot, making dark trails like the veins in an old man's arm. The king knew pestilence would stalk there now. Those who had survived cared nothing for the dead, not without leadership. Flies crept over corpses – and the living hurried past, desperate not to see.

The Great King did not wince or shake his head at the thought. He had known death before, many times. He knew his workers would have to bury the fallen in vast shallow pits outside the city before they could even begin to rebuild.

Darius turned at last, looking to include his young son in his deliberations. Xerxes sat some way back from the front ranks, one leg tucked beneath the other as he balanced on the shoulders of a young bull elephant. Darius saw the boy was distracted by something, perhaps one of his pets. Xerxes could always find some creature to train and amuse him. The most recent had been a cricket, the one before a tiny blue lizard that held food in both hands to devour it. The Great King had never felt the need for such things himself. He worried the boy was not concerned enough with the empire he would inherit. He sighed. The cares of a father were legion.

The royal procession had come to a halt at his gesture.

Having climbed steadily all morning, relief shone in their faces. Behind the king stood sixty thousand men, back and back, reaching so far down the trail he could not see an end to them. Darius had come prepared for war, but found only ashes.

Ahead, the dancing women rested, quivering in their exhaustion. One of them had fallen just that morning, dropping to the ground in loose-limbed delirium, then shrieking as carts and men behind passed over. Only the royal elephants had stepped around the broken girl, fastidious in what they chose to crush.

Darius knew he didn't have to say a word to his seneschal. Ashar's grim countenance and faint blush was evidence enough of his shame. The mistress of the dancers would certainly be beaten that evening, perhaps bound to a tree and simply left, for lions and wolves to find. The others would see her fate and know not to shame the Great King in the honour he did them.

Darius was no longer the vital young warrior he had once been. As he contemplated climbing down from the rock, he suppressed a wince at the twinge in his hips and lower back. There was a time when he would have leaped down, delighting in his strength. His servants knew him well, however. Steps had been brought as he'd stood and looked out. He walked down then, back straight, his expression perfectly calm.

Xerxes watched warily as his father approached, wondering if he would be punished for something only the king could possibly have noticed or cared about. Seated on a pad of stuffed silk, the boy wore just sandals and a kilt of leather studded in gold. Bare-chested, he was a living reminder of youth that could only sour his father's mood further.

Servants sprinkled dried lavender and myrtle on the dusty path as the Great King approached his son. It was an insult

3

for Darius to be made to look up, but Xerxes seemed frozen in his seat high on the elephant. The enormous young bull swung its head to eye the man at its side. Both boy and beast were at the most awkward of ages. With a gesture, Darius waved the petal servants away. They trembled on the edges of his vision, ready to make the ground fragrant once more, for steps that shook the world.

'Come down from there, Xerxes,' the Great King said softly.

His son nodded and put out one hand so that his elephant could see. The trunk curled round and he stepped onto the muscled length, brought to the ground in perfect smoothness. The boy seemed proud of it. Darius showed no reaction to a trick more suited to the markets or the logging camps. He put his arm around his son's shoulders and walked with him to where he should have been standing, waiting on his father. There, Darius rested one hand on the great stone, feeling its warmth.

'You see that city?' he said. 'Dark with ash?'

Xerxes made a show of peering in the distance before he nodded, still unbending. Darius found he was proud of the young man who would surely follow him, if Ahura Mazda, the Lord of Wisdom, allowed it. It did not pay to be too sure of the future, aloud or in the most private thoughts. The God of Light heard all.

'It is Sardis, the capital of this entire region,' he said. 'Or it was. It was sacked by an enemy and burned, including the great temple that had stood for two thousand years. This is why I brought so many soldiers, Xerxes. By tomorrow, every home and temple will be cleared to the foundations. We will rebuild it all.'

'Who would dare attack one of our cities?' Xerxes asked.

'Men of Athens, men of Eretria,' his father replied. 'The

Greeks. I thought . . . They sent ambassadors here a dozen years ago, asking for friendship. I thought they had agreed to become one of my chosen — my beloved subject peoples. They gave earth and water to my governor and they went home, across the sea. I confess I hardly thought of them after that.'

The king smiled and tried to ruffle his son's hair. He hid his hurt when Xerxes pulled away.

'This is the edge of the world, Xerxes. The sea lies not two days from here — and beyond it, lands which have never known the blessing of our laws, our soldiers.' He waved an arm over the plain. 'I rule here, from the slave markets to the gold mines. Every pot and cup is mine, every coin and beam and child. Yet we are a long way from civilisation, from the heartlands. Perhaps I have been too gentle with them, too forgiving. I trust too easily. It has always been my weakness.'

He saw his son shift uncomfortably and smiled.

'No man can say I am without honour, Xerxes. Can you accept that? If I give my word, I keep it, though the world falls around me. If I forgive an enemy, if I welcome him as a child into my house, he knows there will be no more anger from me. Even the Greeks know this. Oh, they may shout and struggle, but for those who are men, who are willing to put aside their pride and offer me tokens of earth and water, I will be always a forgiving god.'

'But why? Why would you forgive the men who did this, who burned Sardis?'

Darius leaned closer to his son. Though a hundred servants and slaves waited on his slightest whim, though two naked and kohl-eyed women peeped from the curtained litter that adorned his elephant, he was alone still, with his heir.

'I speak now as a king, Xerxes. Hear me. My word is unbroken because when a man takes the field against my

5

armies, I want him to look in fear on his allies, to wonder if they will desert him, even in the heat of battle. I want him to know, as he knows his own name, that if he surrenders to me, if he takes the taste of dust onto his lips and offers me water from his cupped hands, I will honour him as an ally to the end of the world, without rancour, without vengeance. Because he will be a living example of my mercy. Do you understand?'

Xerxes shook his head a touch, closing his eyes as the wind picked up, easing the great heat of the day. In that moment of silence and peace, he suddenly saw it. His eyes opened and his father smiled to see the gleam in them.

'Trusting you weakens them all . . .' Xerxes said, in something like wonder. 'It means brother will turn on brother as we approach, friend against friend. But the cost, father? To your honour? You lose vengeance – is it not too high a price to pay?'

'No. There are forty nations in my empire – Media, Assyria, Lydia, India – by the god that binds, men like silver fish in the ocean, all subject to my throne, my crown. If I were a trickster, a liar, they would have fought much harder to keep me away. Instead, their leaders are given palaces and lands. In their quiet times, they might wonder if they have been conquered at all.'

'But they have,' Xerxes said.

His father nodded.

'Yes. So it is with these cities, this "league of Ionia". They look to their forefathers the Greeks instead of us. Perhaps they thought I was too far away to care what they did on the very borders of the western seas. They called to Athens for help in their betrayal – and those Greek whores sent ships from Eretria and their hoplite soldiers to roam this coast, to murder and terrorise peoples that are mine. They talk now of throwing off the yoke I have placed on them, of the "out-rage" of our rule.'

The king laughed, though there was little humour in it and his eyes remained black and shadowed by his brows.

'In the destruction of my garrison, the Greeks set the reed roofs of Sardis aflame. It spread like the wind itself until all was consumed, even the temple to Cybele, Great Mother of the World. That is hard to forgive.'

The king stood looking into the distance for a time. His son did not dare interrupt his thoughts. Nor did he resist when his father placed a hand on his shoulder again.

'I will rebuild for a season here. The armies I have brought will enter all the towns and cities of this Ionian league and exact punishments as I see fit. They will take men's hands, so they cannot carry a spear or blade again. The most beautiful children will find their way to our markets. The old men and women will be thrown on the fires. I sometimes think that is a mercy in its way – to those who would have been burdened by them. You see? Even in the furnace of my anger, there can be wisdom. I am no tyrant, Xerxes. When I move, when the mountains move, it is a trembling greater than the tread of a thousand kings. You will know the same, when I am gone. All men are slaves; all kings are slaves to us.'

His son's face lit with pleasure at the words. Xerxes reached up with his left hand and touched the fingers resting on his bare shoulder. His father's wisdom had built an empire of such extraordinary wealth and power, it was as he said: the world bowed to him. Xerxes thought even the rain would fall at his command.

'And what of the Greeks, father?'

'They have gone back in their ships, like children asleep in innocence. They have butchered my garrisons, after all. They believe the work is done. They are mistaken. The work has begun! I will see them again, when I am finished here.'

The king looked over his shoulder to the ranks of his bodyguard standing in white panelled coats. The heat must have been oppressive, but they stood in perfect stillness, as if carved from stone. The general who commanded them came forward at that single glance, prostrating himself full-length and raising both hands to his eyes as he lay on the ground, as if blinded. When he rose, dust stuck to the oil of his equipment, giving him the air of a soldier on campaign rather than mere ornament. Darius thought it was a fine omen.

'Fetch me my bow, General Datis.'

The royal weapon was unstrapped from its case and strung in instants, while the king stood with his hand outstretched. Darius accepted the weight of it, a weapon almost as tall as he was himself, though it shone with oil and sunlight on the gold bands wrapping the grips.

'Arrow,' Darius said.

He fitted one to the woven string and drew as easily as any man who had practised every day since childhood. The muscles on his arm, shoulder and chest grew taut and he let it fly into the distance, soaring for an age as the ground dropped away to the plains below.

'I send this shaft as my vow,' Xerxes heard his father murmur. 'God, let me punish the Athenians as they deserve.'

He handed back the bow and crooked a finger to his wine slave. Though the slender young man had served the king for all his twenty years, earning authority in the golden court, he dropped to his belly without hesitation, sensing his master's mood.

'Mishar, you have a new task, from today. Rise now and accept it from my hand.'

The eunuch rose smoothly, standing with eyes downcast

as father and son regarded him. His silks had not fared well on the dusty ground and Xerxes grimaced at patches of sweat. There was no excuse for poor standards, not when there were slaves to bathe and change a man's robes, as many times a day as he could desire. If Mishar was even a man. Xerxes had made the guards hold him down once, so that he could examine the old injury and the shrunken little sack there, dark as a bruise. Mishar had wept like a woman then. It was odd that a slave might understand his life was not his own, yet expect to keep some semblance of dignity – a part owned as surely as the labour of his hands! Xerxes thought his father allowed some of the servants too many liberties, perhaps through long association. He would not make the same mistake when his turn came. He smiled at the thought.

'Mishar,' the king went on, 'you are to approach me each evening, as I sit for dinner. You will interrupt me, without fear of punishment. You will say this: "Master, remember the Greeks." Do you understand what I have said to you?'

The wine slave tried to nod, though he trembled so violently Xerxes thought he might be ill. Mishar too had noted the black ruins of Sardis. He had not known how the king would react. A trickle of sweat showed as a bright line on his forehead, slipping into the creases by his painted mouth.

'I . . . I do . . . I understand, Majesty. It will be as you say.'

'It will indeed, Mishar. If you forget, I will have that fine tongue I own torn out. Now leave us – and find fresh silks. Those you are wearing are fit only for the fire.'

The eunuch bowed and dipped away. Xerxes watched his father in anticipation, seeing the wolf in him, the destroyer of nations.

'So,' the king said, 'I will not forget the debt I owe the Greeks, my son. Not until it is paid a thousand times over. They are a small and scattered people. I will purchase ships from the Phoenicians and march some of my lazy western garrisons to this place. There are too many palace officers here, Xerxes, men fat and soft, living lives of ease. A little campaign would do them good, I think. Perhaps I will see how my Immortals fare on the open sea. It would amuse me to watch men like General Datis heaving their breakfast over the side!'

The king laughed at the thought, his grim mood vanishing. He turned to his son and Xerxes managed not to flinch.

'Now, have your horse brought up. I would see you ride out with the scouts as we reach the plain.'

'I would prefer . . .'

'It would please me, Xerxes,' his father said softly.

The boy bowed his head immediately.

'Very well.'

With that settled, the king smiled.

'Good. The men should see you ride. When the sun sets, I will expect you at the feast for my officers. My generals and I will make plans to punish these Ionian cities who quake before us.'

Xerxes bowed once more. He had hoped for some time to himself, without his father directing every hour before sleep. Still, the rewards for his obedience would come. Though he could not imagine a world that did not have his beloved father in it, one day, the empire would be his. His command would turn the clouds back then, or dim the sun in his father's memory. It was a good thought.

PART ONE
490 BC

I

Xanthippus stood very still, breathing through his nose, murmuring instructions to the slaves working around him. The three men responded with slight dips of their heads, intent on their tasks. All of them had served his wife's family since childhood. A stray thought came to him that every Spartan had seven slaves whose task it was to ready him for war. Perhaps Athenians were more efficient. Xanthippus neither smiled, nor voiced the thought aloud. His mood was restless, impatient. He was thirty-eight years old and he knew he might die that day.

He could no longer hear the uproar in the city, though he doubted it had lessened. His wife's home was huge, an estate with olive and fig orchards. The room where Xanthippus stood to be armed was right in the centre, far from outer walls that would not have disgraced a fortress. Columns of white stone ringed a central space around him, open to the blue sky above. There was peace there, far from the tumult and fear of war. Around that quiet heart lay a dozen rooms on two floors. Past the outer wall, the house gates opened onto the road to Eleusis, standing to the north-west of the centre of Athens.

Xanthippus had been woken by shouting in the darkness, long before the sun had risen. Runners from the house had been sent into the Agora, to the bronze statues of heroes that represented the ten tribes of Athens. The council of the Areopagus had mounted sheets of fine papyrus there, under each statue. Slaves with torches stood to lend a flickering light to anyone who needed it. Every tribe was called, every deme of the city and the lands around. All they feared had come.

Xanthippus grunted as his greaves were pressed into place. Moulded to the exact shape of his shin and knee, they needed no straps or thongs, but were held secure by the natural spring in the metal. They gleamed as if made of gold, shining with the same blessed oil that had been rubbed into his limbs.

'Hold a moment,' he said.

The men stood back and he dropped into a low lunge. The greaves remained in place and he nodded. As he rose again, one of the men reached around him to fasten a kilt of white linen. His thighs would remain uncovered. It was one thing to run or train naked in the heat of summer. Battle was different. Xanthippus had learned from his father how useful a bit of cloth can be, when sweat or blood is in your eyes.

Bare-chested, Xanthippus eyed his breastplate as it was raised up. The inner layer was of bleached linen, sewn thick and strong. Over that was a greater weight of bronze scales. He knew he would feel it every step he marched away from the city. Yet for all its heaviness and ridiculous expense, it was the skin of war. Some of the other strategoi preferred a solid plate of bronze or leather. Xanthippus disliked the feeling of restriction. He had seen a man who could not tie his sandals without removing his breastplate, helpless as a fish on land. In comparison, his scales made him feel invincible. As his greaves had been shaped to him, the breast-piece was the work of a master smith. Bronze was a warm metal when it touched his skin. Everything about it pleased him.

He nodded and muttered as the armour was fastened, with two straps over his shoulders and a cinch at his waist. Two smaller plates – the wings – hung down over his groin, protecting the great vein at the top of each leg. With his shield

14

raised, an enemy would see only bronze greaves, round shield and helmet – a man of gold. The thought was good. His arms were left clear of all obstruction and he clenched his hands and swung them, loosening stiff shoulders and checking he had full movement.

His studded sandals were tied securely and he added a cloth headband above his eyes. It would soak up sweat and help cushion the weight of his helmet. Xanthippus felt his heart quicken as a second group of slaves brought in the weapons of a hoplite. These had not been bought for him by the wealth of the Alcmaeonidae, his wife's family, who traced their line back to the adventures of Homer's *Iliad*. No, they showed the years of use, in scratches and dents and even a small patch of brazed repair by the helmet nose-piece. Each part of his gear had saved his life at some point. Xanthippus looked upon the collection with pride and affection, as a man might pat the head of a favourite hound.

'Where is my shield?' he said.

The hoplon shield had not been carried in with the rest. The others looked to the most senior man there to answer. Manias bowed before replying, more serious than usual on such a day.

'The mistress asked to be the one to show it to you.'

'I see. Agariste has had it repainted.'

It was not exactly a question, but Manias dipped his head even so, flushing under the cold gaze of the master of the house. As slave to the Alcmaeonidae, Manias had served the household in various roles for every year of the mistress's life. He was fiercely loyal to Agariste, as only one who had carried her on his shoulders when she had been a little girl could be. Yet that moment was one of silent communication between two men, regardless of their different stations.

Xanthippus said nothing more, though anger radiated from

15

him, making the other slaves clumsy as he checked his spear for cracks along its length. There were none. On impulse, he waved them back and whirled the great weapon around his head and body, making it sing through the air. As long and half again as he was tall, the weight of the iron-leaf point was perfectly balanced by the bronze spike at the other end – the lizard killer, as young epheboi hoplites called it. The length of Macedonian ash felt good as he twisted it in his palms. He could feel the marks of tools in its planes, the memory and sweat of older craftsmen as they worked on it. He had killed men with that dory spear. It felt right to hold it.

Xanthippus ran a hand through the horsehair plume that formed the crest of his helmet. There was no dust and the massed bristles were neatly trimmed and new. Satisfied, he placed it at his feet and unsheathed his sword, checking the iron blade for imperfections. Some things could not be left to slaves, no matter how experienced. The sword had been well cared for since the last time he had drawn it on behalf of the city. It too shone with olive oil, unmarked by stubborn black spots of rust. Sheath and belt were buckled to his waist and he began to feel heavier, armoured.

Agariste came out of the shadowy cloister beyond the sunlit room. Slender as she was, she bore the weight of his shield, the heaviest part of his kit – and the most important. The bronze circle was covered in a white cloth. He thought he knew what image would be there even so.

'Leave us,' she said softly.

The slaves vanished into the gloom around them, skilled in their ability to follow her orders. This was her house, after all, her father's before her. Her uncle Cleisthenes would have stood where Xanthippus did now, the man who had re-designed democracy in Athens, who had chosen the names of the ten tribes. Hers was a famous line. Xanthippus felt the weight of it at times. Yet he knew she loved him in all her unmarked youth, the green spring of her life. They had married when she was sixteen and he thirty, just embarking on his political life. Eight years had passed and if he had risen, it was in part due to the support of her family. Yet she had come to a grown man in her first bloom, and still feared his disapproval. A single angry word could bring tears to her eyes, he knew. It was written in every line of her as she approached, terrified Xanthippus would not like what she had done.

'Show me, then,' he said. He still held his spear in his right hand and reached out with the left, his fingers splayed.

Mute, with her lower lip held under her teeth, she pulled away the cloth, letting it flutter to the tiles.

He had expected some aspect of a lion the moment he'd heard she had repainted his shield. The dream had tormented Agariste for years, coming again and again to disturb her sleep. He'd heard every detail a dozen times. Yet it did not have the feel of prophecy, at least to his ear. Though he indulged her to keep the peace, Xanthippus thought the gods would not have trusted his foolish young wife with a true vision. He thought instead that it sprang from her worry for him, or for the children. He could not banish a pang of dread at losing the simple old eye on his shield, however. It had glared out at every enemy he'd ever faced, but now it was gone, made blind by her.

'It is very fine,' he said.

'You like it? Truly?' she said, looking into his eyes. 'No. You don't like it.'

'It is beautiful,' he said in perfect honesty. In truth, the artist was very skilled. The lion roared out of the centre of the shield, all head and teeth and rage. It was a fine image, though he would still have preferred the old unblinking eye to watch over him.

'In the dream where I gave birth to a lion,' she said, choosing to fill the silence with a stream of words, 'I thought at first it had to be the baby. As I was full of child, what else could it be? But then I saw your shield and I thought . . . what if *you* were the lion? What if I could help to make my Xan the lion of Athens?'

'I cannot say which is right, not today,' he replied.

The conversation demanded more of him than he wanted to give in that moment. He needed to be still and grim and silent, with the tools of war in his hand and battle ahead. Yet she continued to draw him out, breaking the cold hardness in him. It was not always welcome.

There were no slaves in sight as he looked around, though he knew they would be within call.

'Agariste . . . what will happen today . . .'

'Oh! The children! I must bring them out to see you off.'

'*No*, Aggie . . .' but she had gone, vanished in a few steps, so that he stood alone in the beam of sunlight under the blue sky. The sun was rising and he was suddenly eager to go. He almost strode from that place, but he heard the voices of his children, the sound catching him like a briar.

Ariphron was the eldest at seven, the boy's six-year-old sister Eleni approaching in his wake. They came in like little geese, looking with awe at the sight of their father gleaming oil and gold, like a living god. Agariste held the hand of the youngest, stumbling at her side. At five years old, his youngest son seemed close to tears.

Xanthippus laid down his spear and knelt.

'Come to me, little ones. You too, Pericles. It's all right. Come.'

The three of them ran to him, thumping their father in the chest and running their hands over the bronze with wide eyes.

'Are you going to kill Persians?' Ariphron asked.

Xanthippus looked over to his eldest son and nodded.

'Many Persians, yes. Hundreds.'

'Will they come here to kill us?'

'Never. Every man in Athens is arming himself to face them. They will regret ever coming here.'

To his irritation, his daughter Eleni suddenly started to weep, a process that began with her face crumpling and continued with the issuing-forth of wails and sobbing of extraordinary volume. Xanthippus winced and regretted that he had allowed the moment at all.

'Perhaps you could take your sister and brother to the kitchens, Ariphron. Find them some fruit, or whatever the cook has on the spit. Would you like that?'

His oldest son nodded solemnly, understanding that he was being trusted with a task of responsibility. Xanthippus could not prevent another embrace, but then the children were gone, Ariphron leading the others.

Agariste reached down to pick up the spear. It looked strange in her hand and Xanthippus took it quickly. There had been too many strange omens that day already – weeping children being the last of them. He had lost the eye on his shield and he did not want her to drop his weapon, for fear of what that might mean. His hand closed over hers and he could feel the warmth of her and smell the perfume she used, a paste of rose and lavender and musk. It filled his nostrils and he wondered if he smelled the sweet oils of his own funeral pyre.

'Agariste, if we lose . . .'

'Don't say it, Xan. You will invite the disaster. Please.'

'It has to *be* said. I have to know you understand.'

'Please . . .'

He thought she might turn and run from him. In reply, he felt anger surge. In some ways, she was still an innocent. He gripped her wrist, hard enough to make her cry out.

'If we lose and they come here, you must kill the children.'

'I can't do that,' she whispered.

She would not look at him and twisted almost unthinkingly, trying to remove his grip. He held her even tighter and he did not relent, though tears ran down her cheek.

'You are the mistress of the house, Agariste. You *will* do that. If you cannot wield the blade yourself, give it to Manias. Do I need to tell you what Persians do to children they capture? Will you force me to describe the horror of it? They are a plague in the world, Agariste. I have seen the results of their . . . attentions. I have seen the corpses. If we lose, they will make an example of Athens. The city will die and there will be no safe place. It is not like the battles of before, when an army of Sparta came to stand beneath the Acropolis, or the horsemen of Thessaly fought against us. We are Greeks and we know the limits of war — and when there are none. The Persians . . . they are too cruel, my love. And they are many, like grains of sand. If they win, you must save the children and yourself from what will come.'

'If it is your command, husband, I will do as you say.'

She bowed her head, though when she met his gaze, he realised he was not certain she told the truth. Her family had been wealthy and powerful for centuries. It gave them a sense of confidence, not least in their ability to survive. He could see that in her. He could only pray — to Ares, to Zeus, to Hera the goddess of marriage — that Agariste would be spared, that she would never have to discover how fragile the world truly was.

He kissed her then, without passion, but as a farewell and a promise.

'If I can, I will come home,' he said.

He did not tell her how small a chance he judged it to be. Those Greeks who thought they could win the battle had never seen the armies of Persia. They had been like black locusts in Ionia – and that was said to be just one small part of the whole. Xanthippus had fought then against their garrisons, supporting Greeks who merely wished to live free. He had witnessed Persian vengeance, carried out on innocents. It was rare for him to sleep without some picture from that time coming back to throw him out of slumber. His wife's doctor had told him the dreams would fade in a few more years, but it seemed he would not be given the time he needed. He had to go to war on Greek soil, a man who had watched Sardis burn.

Xanthippus took up his helmet and pushed it hard onto his head. His hair had been drawn into a knot that served to cushion him from a blow. The lining was old enough for him to recognise the smell of sweat and rancid oil the moment he shoved it down. His view was a crosspiece, like a sword hilt. It brought back memories of all the other times he had worn it and he felt his mood darken. Reverently, he took up his spear and shield, testing the grips for strength. There would be blood sacrifices made on the gathering field by the Academy. As a senior man of the Assembly, he could easily be chosen to slaughter a ram to the gods for their good fortune. He would certainly be called upon to kill men.

'You will come home,' Agariste said, suddenly. 'In glory, with your lion shield. I see it, Xan. I see it now.'

He could not kiss her while he wore the helmet, but she embraced him once more, clinging to his armour. He saw the slaves and staff had gathered. Some fifty of them had abandoned their work to see the master leave for war. Cooks and elderly gardeners knelt as he passed. Horse boys stared at the man in golden bronze who would fight for them and for the city.

Out beyond the walls, in the sun, the road was surprisingly

quiet. Xanthippus had expected crowds of refugees trying to get out. It seemed the people of the city understood what his wife would not. There was nowhere to run. The Persians had landed. If they were not thrown back into the sea, it was the end.

Xanthippus murmured thanks to his groom for bringing his horse. He nodded to the two who would run alongside him out to the gathering ground. Both Xenias and Theos were free men, though they had earned that freedom in trade and skill. They too wore serious expressions and he had a sense of falseness, of wrongness. On the one hand, his wife and her slaves stood to see him off. The children had crept out, of course, clambering up to peer over the wall at him like little owls. Xanthippus nodded to Ariphron. It might almost have been a normal day.

On the other hand, a dark gulf yawned before him. Xanthippus could already sense the silence to come, just moments off. He and his two seconds would leave the estate behind and go to a place where the whole army was gathering, to destroy or be destroyed.

He had to go, to leave his family behind. The fear and seriousness of it lay heavier than armour. He passed his shield and spear to his seconds and mounted his horse, taking up the reins. Xenias and Theos fell in beside him, shining with oil and early sweat. As Xanthippus turned his back on all he loved, the high voices of his children called after him, dwindling with every step. He did not look back.

2

The Academy had been created as a gymnasium for the young warriors of the city. When it had first been laid out, around a sacred grove of twelve olive trees, it had been a place of great beauty, with statues and a running track alongside the river banks. Over a hundred years, it had been poorly maintained, with the track now more moss and crabgrass than ashes and fine stones. Without proper care, the groves and walkways had returned to clay and patches of weeds. It was a symbol of hopelessness and Xanthippus glowered as he rode through to the gathering ground. His two seconds loped along with him, taking their mood from his.

Beyond the Academy, Xanthippus took some heart from the massed ranks assembling. Only the gods or the Spartans could have moved faster to war than his people. Though it was barely noon, Xanthippus could see banners from all ten tribes of the city. He found his tribe of Acamantis easily enough. He could have named many of the thousand men he would command, certainly those from his home deme of Cholargos. There were just a hundred of those and each one knew Xanthippus well.

He greeted them with clasped arms as he passed along the line, stopping to exchange words with the smaller number he called friends. Each of them was similarly garbed in helmet, breastplate and greaves. With sword, spear and shield, the cost of the entire kit represented anything up to a year's wage. Most had been inherited, or won on the field of battle.

'*There* he is!' said a voice Xanthippus knew.

The one who spoke had been present in Ionia for the Sardis campaign. Epikleos was a wealthy man in his own right, though his family had made most of their fortune trading oil and figs rather than from the spoils of war. One of four brothers, Epikleos had drawn the short straw, as he described it, forced to train as a soldier from a young age rather than something more worthwhile, like politics or writing poetry. In truth, Epikleos was as skilful at the Pyrrhic dance as any warrior Xanthippus had ever met. He had not been made for a merchant life, nor counting beats in a line of verse. Sparring with him had almost certainly saved Xanthippus' life, more than once.

'I like the shield,' Epikleos said. 'A lion is better than that old dead eye of yours. Agariste, was it?'

Xanthippus found himself flushing.

'Yes. She dreamed of a lion.' He preferred to change the subject. 'What news here?'

His friend was still oiling himself and stretching muscles. Epikleos wore a bronze breastplate, accepting the penalty in weight for the gleam of a thing that made him look like a young Heracles. Or because it made the younger warriors look at him, Xanthippus thought. Epikleos could be astonishingly vain. He had once carried Xanthippus' spear, a boy following his hero in bronze. It was a strange thing to see fine lines around his eyes.

'They're buzzing like wild bees over there,' Epikleos said, inclining his head.

Xanthippus looked over the field to the massive stone altar, surrounded by men in armour. Plumed helmets rested on the ground, with shields and spears much like his own. Xanthippus recognised the laughing figure of Themistocles instantly. He was a man who seemed to stand out in any

24

group, perhaps aided by the mass of dark blond hair, tied into a club at his neck. No doubt Agariste would have seen the resemblance to her lion in Themistocles when he left his hair unbound, Xanthippus thought.

To one side of Themistocles, the man Xanthippus respected above all others was, strangely, far easier to overlook. Aristides was as much one of the leaders in Athens as Themistocles, yet his manner was quieter and more thoughtful. Men leaned close to hear when Aristides spoke in the Assembly. It was said that Themistocles would be the first to call for a glorious charge, but Aristides would send it in the right direction. The Athenians valued both men, though the rumour was that they detested one another.

Slaves and runners sprinted to and from that great altar, so that Xanthippus nodded at the image of angry bees. He could see the tribes still forming in squares and ranks, ready to march. He swallowed, his throat suddenly dry.

'Water here,' he called.

One of the passing boys skidded to a stop and a skin was pressed into his hands. His bladder squeezed as he drank, making him feel the blood-warm liquid was going straight through. Ten thousand bronze-clad men of Athens was the entire army. It seemed both an extraordinary number – men who had to be equipped and watered and fed – and yet nowhere near as many as they needed.

'What of Sparta?' he said as he tossed the skin back. 'Are they coming?'

Epikleos shook his head, his expression sour.

'I heard they have one of their festivals. The rumour is they cannot march while it goes on.'

'Perhaps we should wait, then,' Xanthippus said.

Epikleos gave a short laugh, though it was a bitter sound.

'Yes, they would love that, to have Athens wait for them.

Can we not go to war without their permission, without them holding our hand? By Athena, no!' He saw Xanthippus was still sceptical and shook his head. 'A thousand men of Plataea have come – see them there, with their general, Arimnestos. Why not? We saved them once, when they were threatened. Good men remember what they owe – and pay it back when they can. Good men of Plataea!' His smile skewed into bitterness then. 'Yet there are other debts ignored today. No one else stands with us. Still, we know what we face. Our scouts have come back and they are not dismayed.' He spoke with laughter in his voice, for anyone who overheard him. It did not reach his eyes.

'The Persians have already landed up the coast,' Epikleos said, leaning closer. 'Perhaps twenty thousand, perhaps thirty, with as many oarsmen on their ships. Across the water, they say Eretria is gone – still burning. No, Xan. We need to go *today*. We need to hit them before they come too far inland. Before they build fortifications. We have one chance to throw them back into the sea. So we're not waiting for the Spartans. Let them come when we've won. I'll enjoy seeing their faces then!'

'At least it means no cavalry,' Xanthippus said.

Epikleos shook his head.

'They have landed horses from the ships.'

He and Xanthippus shared a glance of worry at that. Any man who had stood in a square, with flutes wailing and drums beating time, knew to fear horsemen on the field. They were just too fast.

'Where have they landed, then? How far off is it?' Xanthippus demanded. He could feel his heart thumping, not in excitement or fear, but . . . anticipation. He would march with his people, with ten thousand hoplites in bronze. They were the elite soldiers of Athens. They would not fail.

26

Epikleos rested the point of his spear on the dusty ground.

'On the plain where the fennel grows, by the sea. I think . . .'

He broke off as the archon – the most senior strategos of the Athenian force – called the tribes to attention. Miltiades was heavily bearded and wore a panelled coat studded with polished nubs of iron, more Eastern in his personal style than Greek. His arms were bare and powerful, with thick black hair on his forearms, and hands that looked like clubs. It was hard to imagine the man caressing a lover. His fists were made to crush and strangle.

Themistocles and Aristides commanded two tribes apiece in the centre, under his orders. As archon, Miltiades had authority over the hoplites of Plataea and all ten Athenian strategoi in battle. His place was the left wing, his own tribe at the heart of it. Xanthippus swallowed. The tribe of Acamantis would be in that wing. Every man there would know those around him, from school and training, from work and the Assembly. They carried shields with the symbols of their houses and their fathers. They could not run, not with those eyes and those spirits watching them. Not with the men of Plataea looking on! There would be no stories of Athenian cowardice to tell all Greece afterwards. This was why they trained. This was why they built fitness with thousands of mornings on the gymnasia running tracks. For days like this.

At the stone altar, Miltiades threw one leg across to stand astride a massive black ram, gripping its head from behind, though it struggled mightily. As Xanthippus watched, precious maps were rolled up and bronze bowls set out for blood and the liver. Two soothsayers stood ready to read the future. Silence settled on them all, so that Xanthippus could hear banners snapping in the breeze.

Miltiades cut the ram's throat with a sawing motion. As life fled, it kicked out and struck the altar stone, so that all the bowls trembled. Themistocles stepped in to help, gripping the ram's fleece and guiding the stream of blood into the bowls. After a time, the two men opened the dead animal up in a great gash down the centre. Blood marked them to the elbows and spattered their faces. The soothsayers completed the task of cutting out the shining liver, placing that into a bowl for the most senior of their caste to examine.

'He will be delighted,' Epikleos said in a murmur at Xanthippus' side. 'He will never have seen such a good omen as this one.'

The words were spoken as the chief priest of Athens pointed to some aspect of the liver's shape and beamed. The group of generals relaxed and Xanthippus nodded to himself, though he was annoyed at Epikleos for his irreverence. It did not do to mock such things. Xanthippus was reminded again that he had lost the eye of his shield. He found himself muttering a prayer to Apollo that he would keep his sight. The thought of being made blind filled him with fear as death itself could not. Perhaps it was because he could imagine being blind, while the reality of death was still beyond him.

Miltiades offered prayers and any idle talk died away as he began to lead the oath of Athenian hoplites. The men of Plataea stood with their heads bowed and their hands clasped in silent respect. Ten thousand voices spoke the words along with Miltiades, and Xanthippus felt his heart fill.

'I shall not dishonour my spear and shield, nor leave the line. I will defend the sacred, and return the land stronger than I found it. I shall listen to those who command me – and obey the laws of my city. If anyone attempts to abolish them or threatens me, I shall not give way. I shall never give way. I honour the cults and the faiths. My witnesses are the gods: Ares and Athena, Zeus, Thallo, Auxo, Heracles. My witnesses are the boundaries of the land, and her wheat, barley, olives, figs and vines. My witnesses are those who stand with me today.'

They roared then – and those of Plataea joined them. When the last echoes of that great cheer had faded, Miltiades came to stand with the commanders in the part of the line that would become the left wing. Horns blew and the archon nodded to Xanthippus in greeting. Miltiades would march with them, the hoplites of his city. Scouts and messengers went out on horseback, ahead of the main column. The camp followers formed up behind, with servants and armourers, carts and waterskins and musicians. They would travel light and fast, with supplies to last for a single meal that evening, enough for those who lived. As for the rest, they would march on foot, together, towards the coast and the plain of Marathon.

3

They marched east, with mountains of ochre and green scrub on their left, winding towards the coastal path as the sun reached noon and seemed to hang. Scouts raced ahead, heading out on foot or riding snappy little animals as wiry as themselves. Those men reported back to Miltiades as archon, then the other strategoi down the column. Xanthippus watched the lads coming in hard, dismounting to walk alongside the generals and pass on all they had seen. It was not skilled work and some were little older than boys. He thought they might burst with excitement or at their own importance. Had he been as young once? Sometimes the memories were so close to the surface, they could have been from just that morning. On days like this, he could hardly remember the innocence, or the confidence and strength he had assumed would be there for ever.

Miltiades headed the column, with banners and drummer boys marching alongside him. Weathered and stern in manner, he walked easily enough for a man in his fifties, at least while slaves carried his shield and spear. Even those were an affectation. Miltiades would not hold a battle line with his deme, but remain apart, directing them. The other strategoi would fight in formation, but there had to be at least one cool head on the field.

Another man Xanthippus did not know well walked at Miltiades' side. Callimachus was the official polemarch, war leader, appointed to the advisory role by the Assembly – their eyes and ears on that march. He wore no armour, Xanthippus noticed. Callimachus strolled along in cloak, tunic and sandals, as if on a country walk. The authority he had been granted had not even survived leaving the Academy field. Without personal experience of war, Callimachus had deferred immediately to Miltiades, almost as if he'd had a choice.

Watching Miltiades bend to listen to his runners, Xanthippus was consumed by the desire to hear the news. He could not stroll ahead. His duty was to stay with the ones he would lead in battle. Of course, Epikleos suggested loudly that he should go and see what was going on, with a hundred others listening. Xanthippus did not reply. The strategoi were not gossiping market traders to be gathering around one of their number. No, he would wait – as Epikleos knew very well he would. He saw the gleam of amusement in his friend and half-cursed him under his breath as he marched on, waiting to whistle to the next boy racing down the line with news. He did not want to be overlooked. Men like Epikleos or Themistocles never seemed to be. They caught the eye.

Xanthippus lowered his head a touch as he strode along, knowing he was glowering. His mood was a dark one, but given what lay ahead, what did they expect? When one of the others offered some comment on the distance they had covered, Xanthippus almost bit his head off, speaking far more harshly than he had intended. He regretted it when he saw the flash of anger on the other man's face, but he could not take it back and he had learned not to apologise. It did not matter if the men feared his temper, his political power – even the wealth of his wife's house that could be used against them. As long as they held the line when he told them to stand, or marched into sling-stone and arrow when he told them to advance. That was what mattered. That was what would keep them alive to see the sun set. Marathon was just five hours' march from Athens, a hundred and sixty stades at most, with each one called out as they put another two hundred paces behind. The road was no more than a dirt track beneath their feet, but it was dry in the summer month of Metageitnion. The longest day of the year was past, but they would still reach the Persian landing place with light enough to act. Miltiades and the strategoi would decide then if they should attack or withdraw to a safe camp.

Xanthippus watched sourly as Miltiades continued to grill the scout walking at his side, as if they had all the time in the world. Did the older man have any idea how the rest of his column yearned to know what was happening? Not that they showed any sign of it, he realised. Discipline was good in the men of Athens. They had all left their homes that morning, just as he had. They wore the same bronze and carried the same spear and sword. Perhaps they understood the stakes just as well. It was a fine thought and it comforted him.

Men like Themistocles and Aristides were in the midpoint of the marching column, where they could turn and form the centre of a battle line. They could not hear reports faster than Miltiades. When Xanthippus glanced back, he thought he saw Themistocles glaring at him, the man's big frame and lighter hair drawing his attention amongst all the others. Again, Xanthippus did not smile. There was just no room on the march for the petty rivalries of the Assembly. Themistocles was a braggart, but he was a born leader of men in a way Xanthippus found difficult to understand. They responded to something in the big man, as he laughed and confided in them and gripped them by the shoulder. It should have made them contemptuous of him, as the officer trainers sometimes warned of leaders who courted favour with their men. They were all old soldiers, made of gristle and oak and impressed by nothing. Yet they had smiled like boys when Themistocles inspected them; Xanthippus had seen it. It was a mystery. Men needed to see strength, distance, a stern demeanour. Not to be sent staggering by a strategos who carried a wineskin and laughed until the stuff came out of his nose.

Xanthippus shook his head at the thought. Enemies of Themistocles liked to portray him as a buffoon, too often given to levity. The truth was more subtle, Xanthippus believed. His ambition was there to be seen. There was both callousness and amusement in Themistocles, as if nothing in the world had to be taken quite seriously. It was hard to know what to make of such a man. Xanthippus was pleased they would not fight directly alongside one another. Themistocles was a stone dropped into still water. Yet with Miltiades in overall command, the responsibility of the ten strategoi was to obey, to stand and to crush the enemy.

Xanthippus found his throat had dried once again and called for water. The boy who looked around and raced back to him had been close by Miltiades. It seemed natural enough to ask 'What news?' as men did when they met in the Agora. The boy flushed with pride as he handed over his waterskin, already flatter than it should be. Water was precious, with so little of it to be found in the land. They would all be gasping like crows by the end of the day. Xanthippus had seen it before.

'The scout says there are at least ten thousand horse and twice as many men again.'

Xanthippus waved that away, though the men around him stumbled over their own feet as they tried to lean close enough to hear. Large numbers were notoriously difficult to judge – it was hardly a skill that could be taught or practised. Yet Xanthippus had seen single garrisons on the Ionian coast as large as the ranks of hoplites he marched alongside – and those on the very edges of the Persian lands. Men they had captured boasted of heartlands with a million men under arms, of massed regiments each ten thousand strong, numbers so great he could only pray it was a lie, designed to strike fear into the hearts of enemies.

'Anything else?' he said, eyeing the lines ahead. Like Themistocles, Xanthippus was taller than most of his countrymen. The gods awarded height to the sons of fishermen and the wealthy, so that it set them apart. Xanthippus could see over their heads to where the scout was making his way back. Another was already with Miltiades, he saw, the lad deep in earnest conversation as he cut shapes in the air with his hands, describing what he had seen.

'They say the ships came round the coast from Eretria. The scout said some of his mates went up into the hills and saw smoke from the port there.'

Xanthippus nodded, though his heart sank. Lies and wild rumours flew when war was in the offing. Yet it seemed Epikleos had been right. Eretria was around the coast from Marathon, on a vast spit of land across a stretch of open sea. That long branch of ancient hills was part of the natural protections that sheltered Athens from Poseidon and his rages. Eretria was a wealthy port and some thirty thousand had lived there. If the Persians had hit that spot, there would have been horrors beyond imagining, perhaps still going on. Xanthippus clenched his jaw. He hated them, in their arrogance and appalling cruelty. The Persians made him a darker man than he would have been without the visions they brought to torment him. He sometimes thought he had seen too many things to ever sleep well.

'Take water to those further back, lad,' he said.

His tone had been harder than he had intended, so that the boy looked confused and hurt. Xanthippus tried to reach out and ruffle his hair, but he ducked away and ran down the line, the waterskin gurgling on his shoulder.

The actual scout had remounted to carry back what he

had learned. Full of his own importance, he did not seem to notice Xanthippus until the strategos raised his right hand, calling him over. Even then the man hesitated. When Xanthippus looked over his shoulder, he could see Themistocles was also gesturing briskly for him to approach. The strategos had no patience! They were barely two hours on the march. They hadn't covered half the distance to the enemy and, at that moment, they were heading closer to the sea to skirt a range of hills that loomed above them all and cast a shadow on their path ahead. Xanthippus cursed when he saw that. Was it another omen? After the missing eye on his shield, he did not want to walk through cold shade just before a battle. It was too much like a premonition of death.

With the sun warm on his neck, he glanced over the sea as it appeared to widen before him – and missed a step, knocking into the man ahead, so that he cursed and stumbled. Some of the others were already pointing and drawing attention to the ships out there. Xanthippus swallowed drily, wishing the water boy had not gone running back.

There was a fleet out on the dark waters. They were not the sleek vessels of Eretria and Athens, nor even the lesser craft of Sparta. For any man who had grown up in a seaport, the ships were instantly strange, alien. The flags that streamed from them bore odd symbols and letters none of them knew. They moved in sluggish beats, with rowers heaving at their stems on both sides. The dimensions too were wrong, with heavy, wide decks. Xanthippus thought they would handle poorly in a swell, though perhaps they avoided the four months of winter when only madmen and suicides ventured out onto the deep. Most traders kept the coast in sight even in the summer months. Yet these were warships, carrying an army. There were just too many for them to be anything else.

The path the column marched took them close to the edge

of the sea-cliffs before it began to wend its way back. Xanthippus tried to count more ships than he had ever seen before. His eyes were good, though the vessels shifted and blurred into the distance, making it impossible. It was like asking a boy to count soldiers, he thought wryly. How many of those tiny specks were triremes heading away from dropping armed men? How many were heavy-laden still? Were they landing horses for cavalry? Stone blocks for fortifications, weapons for the men? The ships moved, confounding every attempt to count them – and then the marching line was heading away from the sea, the sense of scale vanishing as they wound their way inland once again, step by step.

Xanthippus felt the drop in temperature as he passed through the shadow of the cliffs, but it went almost unnoticed. The chatter and nervous laughter in the column had fallen silent as every man there considered what such a vast fleet must mean. They were two hours or so from encountering the army those ships had dropped, fresh from victory and violence in Eretria, across the strait.

Xanthippus felt those around him looking over. Men needed to be reassured, or their nerve could fail. He considered his own dread. Perhaps he needed it too. It was one thing he had seen Themistocles do well. The thought made Xanthippus smile for the first time that day. No. He would not laugh and pound his friends on the back as Themistocles did. He would not call them appalling names that might have led to knives being drawn for anyone else. That could never be his style. Yet Xanthippus still sensed their eyes on him. He knew Aristides would have spoken to them, calming their nerves. They were not the golden automatons said to serve in Olympia, creations of metal made to cater to every whim of the gods. No, these were ordinary men, with fear coiling in their stomachs as if they had swallowed a viper.

'I saw the Persians fight, in Ionia,' Xanthippus said. He spoke clearly, making his words carry. He had a good voice, so Agariste had told him. She had called it rich and dark and strong as a man's voice should be. He used it then.

'They favoured the sling and archers, bringing large numbers of those – and as many foot soldiers. Their lords and generals are both clean and brave; I have seen it. The rest, though . . . they are poorly trained. They run, when a battle goes badly. They break, like rotten wood. I have seen the backs of those we encountered in Ionia. I will see their backs again today.'

He paused and was rewarded with an appreciative chuckle from men around him. It was not ideal – who gave speeches on the march, actually while moving? The noise of tramping feet and creaking armour meant that only the closest ranks could hear him. Yet he continued, seeing the effect. He raised his voice further, making it carry.

'All those who serve the Persian king are slaves. Beyond his family and a few chosen favourites, the rest mean nothing to him. He spends them like they are worthless. Remember that. We are free men, of Athens. We are bronze – we are gold and silver. The greatest warriors in Greece, descendants of Theseus, beloved of Athena, who brought us the olive. Against us, no untrained slaves can know victory. We are fitter, faster, stronger than anyone they can put in the field. Remember that, when you are asked to hold the line. They will grow weary, like panting dogs – and we will be there, still standing, fresh and ready.'

It was true of him, true of all the strategoi. He was not certain every one of the hoplites of Athens had put in the hours in the gymnasia they had sworn to. Still, they seemed pleased. Not more than two in ten that day had encountered Persians before. Some of them were twenty years younger

37

than him, just beginning their two years of army training after eighteen. If the veteran strategos said they could be beaten, it strengthened their resolve.

'Those are fine words,' said a voice to one side.

Xanthippus looked across and blinked in surprise at the sight of Themistocles, walking along the edge of the marching rank. Of course the man had not considered himself bound to remain in one spot, as Xanthippus had. The rules did not apply to Themistocles! In that, he resembled Agariste, Xanthippus realised. Her uncle had created the underpinning structures of Athens, throwing out centuries of traditions as he did so. A man of vision, his structures had been welcomed as binding threads that drew new men into the Assembly, to serve on juries, to decide their own laws. There was nothing like Athenian democracy in the world – and yet in private, Xanthippus knew his wife considered her family above the laws, immune from the will of the people in a way he could hardly understand.

Themistocles had the same strange confidence when it came to the rules of men. Xanthippus wondered if he even feared being ostracised – the ten-year exile that required just six thousand votes from the people of the city. It was designed to stop the rise of tyrants, but it would stop one like Themistocles just as easily.

'Thank you, strategos,' Xanthippus said, realising he had been staring in thought for too long.

'You have the most experience of anyone, except perhaps Miltiades. You should be at his side, to advise him. That Callimachus will be no help at all.'

'I serve in his wing,' Xanthippus replied. 'That is enough.'

Was the man trying to flatter him or just lead him into saying something that would be reported later? It helped that he did not trust Themistocles. Xanthippus took his manner from Aristides in that. He would not be tempted to smile or laugh, or be drawn into a rash opinion without considering it from all angles. His was a defensive style, but it stood as a wall against the quick mind of one who watched him with gleaming eyes.

'Still, I am glad you have seen the backs of Persians,' Themistocles said. He turned his head as he spoke, Xanthippus saw, including men of a dozen ranks as his audience. It was an interesting technique. 'We will see such a thing again, perhaps before the sun sets today. You know, I was furious at first when I heard the Spartans were not going to march. To hear of them sitting there, waving their smoking myrtle branches, while we defend the coast? It was an insult! What festival could be more important than the mother of all cities? Will the Persians march by the Peloponnese because the Spartans are waiting for the new moon?'

Some of the men laughed, but Xanthippus frowned, uncomfortable at hearing the other strategos skirting what sounded almost like blasphemy. The gods were too easy to offend, as he knew very well.

'But then,' Themistocles went on, 'I thought of what a pleasure it will be to have those Spartans come late to a battle we have already won!'

At that, Xanthippus looked to Epikleos. The younger man was grinning to hear his earlier sentiment echoed.

Themistocles chuckled and shook his head.

'I have spent the morning thinking what I might say to them in such a circumstance! Can you imagine their faces? I tell you, I would rather fight with my brothers around me, the men of Athens, our hoplites . . .' His voice had hardened subtly and grown louder, bringing more and more of them in. Xanthippus found his heart beating faster, despite his reservations. '. . . our victory. I would not trade my place in these lines for a palace in Sparta, or anywhere else in Greece today. I swear by Ares and Apollo, the victory will be ours — the glory will be ours! We won't share any of it with Sparta, Thebes or Corinth, not today. Because we are one. We are Athens. One people, one language, one culture!'

To Xanthippus' surprise, the men actually cheered. He saw Themistocles glance in his direction, as if to see how a performance had been judged. Yet the man had provided something of value. They'd all felt a cold clutch in their innards at the sight of such a vast fleet darting across the waters like insects. Yet Themistocles had raised their spirits and put the spring back into their step. It was not a small thing, Xanthippus realised. He dipped his head in acknowledgement and saw Themistocles blink in surprise and something like pleasure at the response. Then the big man was off, clapping younger hoplites on the helmet with the flat of his hand, making them nod and laugh as he passed further down the line.

Xanthippus watched in silence as Themistocles spotted one of the other strategoi and did the same thing again, completely unabashed that those behind could still hear. It might have been embarrassing, but Xanthippus saw men close by were smiling and craning their necks to listen. He shook his head in wry amusement. Themistocles was a vital part of their forces, but he could not like him, not when he was so easy to like. A man like that could never be trusted. Xanthippus wished briefly that Aristides would also come down the line, to show the men proper dignity. Of course, he would never do such a thing, so all the men would remember it had been Themistocles who walked at their side and spoke to them.

4

The wide bay was perfect for their purposes, General Datis thought. Gulls called overhead and the air was sharp with salt and the smell of the sea. Some of the other Persian officers detested deep waters. Datis could understand their fear. After all, it did not matter if you had learned to swim as a child or not. If a man in armour fell overboard, the weight of his kit carried him to the bottom, regardless of his efforts or his strength. No one who fell into the sea was seen again, until their bodies washed up somewhere further down the coast, borne by unseen currents. Yet General Datis had grown to manhood without ever seeing the great blue vastness, a thousand shades of movement and a sky as wide as the empire itself. Not that he would have dared say such a thing aloud. The empire could not be encompassed, so the priests of Ahura Mazda said. Its borders could not be walked in a lifetime, its scope beyond the imagination of mere men.

Datis breathed deeply, enjoying the smell of salt and seaweed. The king was said to be pleased with the campaign so far. The fleet had been purchased and built over two years. With a free hand from the royal treasury, anything was possible. The empire had made a mere province of Lydia after all, a kingdom that was itself a byword for impossible wealth. Gold, silver and gemstones were mined wherever the Great King was loved. It was as nothing to him to employ tens of thousands at a time, to build and craft and beat on the forge.

The Greeks had brought a pitiful little force to free the cities of Ionia from the empire. In burning Sardis, they had stung like an angry wasp and then gone home, believing they had mortally wounded their enemy. Instead, they had only awoken him. General Datis smiled at the image, wondering if it was safe enough to repeat at the officers' banquet that evening. Probably not. Someone would decide the empire could not sleep and report him. He'd lose his pay or be docked a rank, or perhaps much worse if his enemies whispered poison in the right ear. The Great King Darius heard only a fraction of the news in the empire. His satraps were like little gods, acting in his name. No man who served was beyond criticism, not even the senior commander of the greatest sea invasion the world had ever known. Or rather, General Datis had reached his exalted position in part because he had a fine sense of when to say nothing.

A week before, the Persian general had landed the fleet at Eretria. It could not have gone more smoothly and Datis recalled the sack of the port with enormous pride. Darius himself had looked on, at first from the safety of his royal flagship, then later from an enormous pavilion raised on the shore.

They had killed male Greeks over the age of fourteen, as well as all the women who were past child-bearing, diseased or too ill to work. The rest had been herded onto transports and taken back to the coast of Ionia. From there, they would travel overland for months, to the heart of the empire. Those who survived would be sold as exotics, to rich men like Datis, who had never seen the sea.

There had been wealth, too, to be found in their temples. The offerings of centuries had been there for the taking. General Datis had not been able to interest his king in those spoils, but that did not mean they were left behind. Gold was gold and silver was silver, regardless of the image hammered onto it. Most would be melted down and recast, changed by the passage of fire – just as free men could be branded by hot irons and made slaves.

The general showed no satisfaction as the last of the horses were brought up alongside the ships that waited for them. The vessels had been rowed at speed straight onto the sandy beach, their keels cutting a trench as they came to rest, then leaning over. Dozens still lay like shells, though with walkways stretching down. The animals and their riders had been given a chance to ride and breathe on solid land again, after too long afloat. Datis was only too aware that the proud steeds could not vomit, no matter how they suffered. Instead, they grew sicker and sicker in the ocean roll, until their eyes blanked and they began to die. The same could not be said for their riders, he thought. It was wise to stand upwind of a cavalry ship after a week or two at sea.

Datis could see the grim faces of the men walking mounts back onboard, into foetid holds with their stalls and filth and rat-infested gloom. Yet they did not complain, nor hold back. The wide, flat beach surrounded by mountains and a marsh had been a perfect place to rest and ready the next strike. Invasion took a toll, on men and equipment alike. Still, they had sacked Eretria easily enough. Once the army had embarked and the ships had been towed out once again, they would sail round the coast to Athens, blockading the city and landing forty thousand veteran soldiers. It was a good thought. In oar-slaves alone, the Persians outnumbered the Hellenes. They would make a fine pyre of their Greek temples, just as those at Sardis had burned.

General Datis smiled as the last of the horse-transports began the laborious process of refloating. Ropes grew taut as they were carried out by small boat to other ships, ready to harness the strength of oars and men and drag the wooden keels off the beach into deep water. It was a delicate task and

43

a nervous one. It was not unknown for entire ships to turn over in the shallows, drowning all those aboard. Datis looked down the sands to where the king watched from the shade and comfort of his pavilion. He sent a prayer to the angels to hold the last ship upright. The Great King was troubled by bad omens, so it was said.

Datis found he had been holding his breath until the last pair of horse-transports rolled precariously in the surf. It was not too far for him to hear angry voices raised amidst the whinnying of horses, but he breathed in satisfaction as the oars settled and began to sweep the ships out.

With the horse transports all safe, the task of embarking the waiting regiments themselves could begin. Sleek triremes circled like sharks, with decks that could be packed with men. Some of them were already coming in, their captains tired of waiting with just the creak of wind and wave and sullen oar-slaves for company. Datis felt himself relax as the first ranks drew up on the beach in formation, ready to go on board. That piece of coast was a perfect natural harbour, protected from the ocean waves that turned men's stomachs. Datis had seen only gentle waters there since they'd landed the evening before. His men had eaten well and rested, checked equipment and weapons, tallied all they had taken from Eretria and sent back the new slaves. All in a single night, he thought. The empire was efficient. Datis wondered if the Great King would allow him to build a house there, when all Greece had been brought to heel. The view would make a fine prospect on waking.

His gaze was inland, to the plain that stretched away from the coast, blurring into mountains that rose against the horizon. As a result, he was one of the first to see a snake of gold and dust shimmering between the hills from the west. Datis shaded his eyes as he stared into the afternoon sun. He cursed softly as the lazy scouts caught sight at last of the marching force and blew their horns.

The men waiting on the beach grew still. Even the oars of the boats froze, so that waiting warships lolled and drifted closer in the surf, in danger of being broken to pieces. Datis saw his officers sending runners to where he stood. He had to make a decision, under the very eye of the Great King. Every moment of hesitation brought the enemy closer and reduced what he could achieve. His cavalry was lost; Datis saw that immediately. He could not call those ships back and land them, not before the enemy was in range to attack. Datis bit his lip as the first running slaves threw themselves to the sand at his feet, waiting for orders, chests heaving. He looked again at the forces stretching across the beach. He had twenty thousand soldiers, with the ten thousand Immortals as the heart and shield of them. As many archers and slingers again, men of Ethiopia who carried bows of great power. In all, forty thousand veterans of Persia stood on the beach at Marathon, ready for his word. He made his decision, even as the king's royal herald came running towards him.

'His Majesty, God-King and Father to the World, bids me ask what orders you will give the men,' the herald said.

He did not prostrate himself, but merely bowed. Datis disliked the man, but liked his own life too well to risk offending him. He bowed in return.

'Please tell His Majesty that my orders are for the men to advance and engage. I will not decline battle. There is no time to embark our army, not before these Greeks are close enough to harry the last of us.' He rubbed his chin as he thought, then nodded to himself. 'We cannot fight on sand, nor with the sea so close to our backs. The ground is dry and steady ahead. We will march and form up, to make ready for them. Archers and slingers on the wings, Immortals and other

45

regiments in the centre. Please suggest to His Majesty King Darius that there is rising ground to the east of the plain. He might wish to find a place there to observe the battle.'

The herald smiled on one side of his face, as if something about Datis amused him. He bowed again without a word and jogged away, his footsteps vanishing beneath the smear of seawater, hissing white over the sand.

5

Xanthippus swallowed nervously as they rounded low hills on either side. 'Marathon' meant 'overgrown with fennel' and the plants did indeed grow well on the red earth. Crushed by sandals, he could smell the scent thickly on the salt air.

The speed of the march increased almost imperceptibly, driven by the desire to get to where they were going. Pace by pace, the sky widened, green hills giving way to the plain of low scrub bushes, straggling trees like sentinels – and the dark sea beyond. They could see ships still swarming there. Every step revealed more detail, with the scouts and runners racing in and out, visibly excited. Word spread back down the line and the news brought jubilation at first.

'No cavalry!' Epikleos repeated in a shout when he heard.

A cheer went up at that, spreading right along the column. The men of Athens had been in trouble when they'd fought Thessaly a few years before. Horsemen could not break a tight phalanx formation bristling with long spears, but neither could that phalanx advance at any speed. It led to little islands of hoplites, pinned down on the battlefield while their enemies roamed freely and arrows rained down, taking them one by one.

The numbers they faced were another matter. Estimates were wild, as scouts tried to count moving men in different formations and marching lines. Xanthippus could hardly believe how many Persian soldiers were coming up from the beach. At that distance, they appeared as a city wall. He shook his head to free it of the image, narrowing his eyes and trying to think like a strategos. Were the Persian ships still landing forces, or taking them off? It was impossible to say, but he thought back to the description of cavalry from earlier that day. False reports were common, but it would be hard to mistake thousands of horses for anything else. He wondered if the quick march east from Athens had interrupted the Persians taking the army back to sea. There was no such thing as luck. For just such an outcome, they had sacrificed and made an oath to the gods.

Xanthippus heard Persian ram horns blown and saw silken banners shimmer as they began to form up. The sight and sound stilled talk and nervous laughter in the ranks around him. Every man who had left home that morning knew the stakes. The Persian soldiers would be killing Athenian women and children that night, unless they were stopped in that place. There was no one else to do it, no other authority.

Miltiades stepped out from his position in the line. His personal herald, Pheidippides, kept pace at his side. The herald had already run far that day, carrying orders and keeping the strategoi informed. The man shone with oil or perspiration, though he breathed long and slow. Two younger men carried banners of cloth bound to long spears, so that all others knew where the archon stood. Xanthippus felt his heart thump almost painfully as a jolt of fear and rage shot through him. The march had been no harder than a training run to that point. He was loose-limbed and warmed up, breathing well. What would come next had no equal, however. It would be the most exhausting, terrifying and exhilarating experience a man could know. Yet he would not have refused to stand there with his people, not for a kingdom.

'Column to phalanx! Pha-lanx!' Miltiades roared. 'By tribe! On strategos! Column to phalanx formation!'

He had the voice for it, Xanthippus thought. With the other strategoi, Xanthippus took up the order and elaborated on it, cracking out commands to the officers who answered to him. Every man of ten thousand represented the people of the Assembly, the city of Athena. The thousand hoplites who had come from Plataea would stand in their midst, accepting the command of Miltiades rather than fighting as independents. That had been the condition of joining the greater force. They wore the same armour and carried round shields, with different images painted on the skin. For all they were men of Greece, they could never be of Athens.

Xanthippus sensed the mood darkening around him, men filled with earnestness and hate. Golden shields and greaves reflected the sun as they moved. Their shadows writhed before them on the ground, as if in submission. It was a good thought.

'This is it, then,' Epikleos said from the side of his mouth.

Xanthippus came out of his reverie and dipped his head once, as if he made an oath. He and Epikleos broke rank with the others of the left wing, not a dozen yards from Miltiades himself. The column became a rabble in instants, men jogging to new positions and looking for strategoi to tell them where to stand. Xanthippus could hear Themistocles and Aristides bellowing to the mid-column, herding them into central squares. Their tribes of Leontis and Antiochis led a block of four as the unbreakable heart of the hoplite formation, eight ranks deep. On the right wing, another formation of three tribes matched the three on the left with the Plataea thousand. It was all slow and clumsy to Xanthippus' eye. Yet when they were done, ten tribes and eleven thousand men stood in neat ranks, in wide battle formation, spears raised like the quills of a porcupine. It was hard not to feel the thrill of it as they lurched forward, though each step across the plain brought a clearer sight of the enemy host.

Dry-mouthed, Xanthippus stepped over a thick, crushed shrub, feeling stems crack like bones under his sandals. He licked his lips and looked for the water boy again, though he was nowhere to be seen. Why was his mouth always like cloth before a battle? He wished he had brought his own flask. His two seconds had fallen back with the baggage, of course, as soon as the enemy was sighted. No doubt they were drinking and idling back there. Some of the men carried pottery flasks on a single shoulder strap. Xanthippus tore his gaze away from those. It was poor form for a man who hadn't brought any to ask for water from one who had.

They walked loosely in step, falling into rhythm as pipers and drummers struck a tune. It was the 'Theseus March' and it brought its own memories, of youth and strength. Xanthippus felt fresh sweat break out, as well as an old ache in his right knee. He had dug a spear-point out from under his kneecap, a dozen years before. It had not seemed like much at the time, but the pain kept returning, something else to endure on a long march.

There was marshland on their left-hand side, hills to their right, enough to limit the width of the Persian front. Xanthippus could hope for that, at least. For the rest, he could see a dark mass of slingers whirring their weapons, far out of range but loosening muscles ready for the fight. Perhaps they hoped to intimidate, he did not know. Archers, too, were unmistakable on the wings, black men striding back and forth without armour, bending bows in and out and waiting, waiting to send precious shafts down their throats. Xanthippus had never seen so many.

Miltiades had not forgotten his overall responsibility, he saw. Just a few paces away, the man was glaring down the lines, checking and adjusting the phalanx formations as they formed. The men tended to cluster too tightly at first, so that they could hardly march without stumbling. It was just an instinct, but it had to be avoided while the enemy were two thousand paces away, closer with every moment.

Xanthippus could see the archon biting his lip as he compared the length of their front with that of the enemy. The marshland had not constrained the Persians as much as they'd hoped. It was clear enough that with forty or fifty thousand on the field, the enemy would immediately overlap the Greek wings, as soon as they came into contact. Xanthippus noted how Miltiades was sweating in his armoured coat as he considered what to do. No answer was ideal and Xanthippus was not sure what the older man would order. He waited, his heart crawling slowly up his gullet with every step. Sixteen hundred paces – eight stades. Twelve hundred – six stades. He could just make out individuals in the enemy line as their banners rippled across the face of their army, an impossible number of them.

'Strengthen the wings!' Miltiades called at last. 'Centre tribes rear four – ease right and left. Eight ranks deep on the wings. Four in the centre.'

Xanthippus breathed, relieved a decision had been made. It had surely been the correct order, though it didn't seem to please Miltiades. The very heart of their strength was that the tribes fought alongside one another in tight formation, standing with men they knew. Male pride was a powerful thing to harness. The Spartans went even further, with each rank representing a year graduating from their training, so that young men stood behind the year ahead – and in front of those who looked up to them. They could not run. Shame was the other side of the same coin – and at least as powerful as pride.

With just eleven thousand, Xanthippus knew they would always struggle to prevent the wings being overrun. The phalanx formations were bronze hammers – dense blocks with shields overlapping. They could not widen the lines without a cost, not without more men. All they could do was strengthen those wings to withstand the assault that would come. The long spears would hold them off. He nodded, accepting. At worst, they would be a golden stone dropped into a flood. It would be a hard day, but there was no turning from it.

Xanthippus saw Themistocles send runners to query the order was accurate – the closest the strategos would come in battle to refusing. Miltiades sent those men back to their master with red faces and the centre formation shifted as they had been ordered. Themistocles looked furious, though Aristides seemed unruffled, as calm as ever. Xanthippus was proud of him, pleased a man he admired was acting with dignity. The battlefield was no place for petty emotions, nor the ego of men like Themistocles. Victory lay in cooperation and complete trust.

Ahead, Xanthippus saw the enemy halt and make ready. Eight hundred paces separated the two armies – four stades. The sea was behind the Persians. They had come up fast from the beach and found firm ground under their feet and room to manoeuvre. Xanthippus grimaced, knowing they would be wanting to use their missile men from as far back as possible. Slingers and archers were no more use than wasps in the churn and heave of battle. Their task was to ruin an enemy before he could ever get close enough for a spear-thrust. Yet they faced armoured hoplites, with equipment and tactics designed to counter their advantage.

Xanthippus gave the order for his tribe of Acamantis to ready shields, which was echoed up and down the lines. He swung his own shield on its cord, from his right shoulder onto his left arm, gripping the leather and feeling the comfort it brought. His entire forearm disappeared into the deep wooden bowl with its bronze skin, so that it felt a part of him. The lion's glare would be bright against the gold, he knew. He brought his spear low, held underarm, ready to stab with the men of his line. Sweat trickled down his face and he felt fear, but also a sort of joy. He was very strong. He was fast and fit and clad in bronze. He would kill the first man to stand before him that day. He would kill the second as well. What happened after that lay with the gods.

The rest of the tribes brought shields to the 'ready' position alongside Acamantis, as if Xanthippus had ordered it. It was just a coincidence, but it was a good feeling even so, though he saw Themistocles watching him. The man took anyone else's foot over his line as a personal insult. Xanthippus knew from training days that Themistocles was quite capable of approaching him with a complaint after the battle. If they both survived.

On the left, Xanthippus saw Callimachus arguing briefly with Miltiades, before stalking over the field to join the right wing. The red-faced polemarch seemed to have found a shield and spear, at least. Perhaps Callimachus had annoyed the more senior man, Xanthippus could not tell.

Behind him, left in sole command, Miltiades raised his arm. Xanthippus thought he might still order a brief halt, perhaps to make the enemy waste their first stones and shafts. It was a hard thing to endure, but the men knew how to hold shields. They had practised and drilled, so that the sudden bronze shade was something they all knew. Still, the reality was different. Men rarely died in formation practice.

Instead, Xanthippus heard Miltiades bellow a different command.

'Left wing . . . slow advance! *Slow* advance! Centre and centre right . . . *engage*!'

The order was repeated by Xanthippus at full volume, though he could not see the reason for it. The marching tribes on the left wing halved their pace immediately, as the centre and the right wing surged.

'*Steady!* Steady, left wing,' Miltiades roared over their heads. 'We need reserves — and you are it. Slow pace now.'

Xanthippus nodded. Perhaps it made sense against so many. He saw Themistocles looking back over his shoulder and gesturing for them to keep up, but that was the point of having one man in command. Miltiades was responsible for the entire field, not just the left. Xanthippus felt a cold spot appear in his stomach as he considered how it might look to Themistocles. Half his men taken away, the centre made weak, then one of the wings hanging back as he was sent in. It looked a lot like . . . Xanthippus shook his head, feeling sweat sting one of his eyes despite the cloth band beneath his helmet. No. Archon Miltiades was loyal. The alternative was to suspect everyone. Though it was said the Persian king spent gold like water and always, *always* rewarded those who pleased him. It was easy to imagine some who might choose wealth and comfort over loyalty and poverty. The Great King's generosity was the stuff of legends. Could a man like Miltiades have been bought . . . ?

'Epikleos!' Xanthippus called.

His friend ran to him, looking serious.

'Yes, strategos.'

'Give my regards to Miltiades and tell him Acamantis tribe stands ready to support the centre.'

'Yes, strategos.'

Epikleos vanished from sight as he went to pass on the comment. Xanthippus watched as Themistocles and Aristides crossed the invisible line that meant they were in missile range. The insect shine of the enemy shifted as thousands released some sharp thing designed to break or pierce. The Persians went too early in their eagerness, but then shot again and again, formations rippling like breaths. Their missiles flew too fast and high to be seen or dodged, whining in the air like the call of birds. That was the most terrifying thing. A piece of lead no larger than a finger could break a man's shoulder when it came whirring down out of the clear air. An arrow could rip his life right out of him.

The barrage cast a flickering darkness across the Persian lines as they shot into the afternoon sun. Xanthippus hoped that was an omen – that they made their own defeat, their own shadow. It reminded him of the hornets' nest in an oak tree he had disturbed when he was a small boy. On a dare, he'd thrown a bucket of rancid olive oil into the cleft and run. He hadn't understood how many were still coming back or how they would hunt him. He swallowed in memory, pleased he was not in range. He'd thought the hornets would kill him that day in their rage and spite. They had filled the air with pain and followed him all the way home.

Gold flashed as four ranks in the centre and eight more on the right raised shields overhead like scales. Stones and lead shot rattled in a great hail off the surface, though cries of pain sounded too. Some of the arrows passed through the skin of bronze shields to wound arms or shoulders beneath. One or two bodies appeared out of the back of the marching phalanx, twitching or trying to stand and rejoin. Xanthippus found he had chewed his lip bloody. He stopped only when he recognised the taste of salt and iron.

The whole centre block under Themistocles and Aristides had pulled ahead of the left wing, easing ahead even of the right. Thousands and thousands of Persians were still pouring everything down on their heads, while the Great King's centre readied themselves to meet them hand-to-hand. Iron swords flashed on the Persian side, catching the sun.

The Immortals were all warriors in their prime, wearing long panelled tunics that reached past their knees. They wore beards in thick braids and clubs, folded and twisted up to make them harder to grab. Gold bands bound their brows, as if each man wore a crown. They used no helmets, but relied on armour and skill with swords. They were the elite soldiers of the empire, the best the Great King could bring to the field. On their own, they numbered as many as the Greek force. Xanthippus felt fear increase as their drums and strange horns began to rattle and whine, the tunes discordant and wrong for that place.

Ahead of him, Greek pipe-players redoubled their efforts. They could not hope to match the volume of the Persians, yet the tune they chose – 'Athena' – was taken up by thousands of voices. The Greeks began to sing the promise she had made when the city was founded. It settled and bound them as they trudged forward under a hail of stones and shafts. Xanthippus swallowed, his bloody mouth like sand. He could see more than a few faces turn to see why their left wing had abandoned them. Shields jerked as those in the rear gestured, calling them in.

Epikleos returned to his side, looking flushed. The pace of the slow advance had not altered, so Xanthippus knew the answer before he spoke.

'Archon Miltiades was unmoved, strategos. He says we are best used as the reserve. Wait for the order to halt and then hold position.'

Xanthippus swore under his breath, surprising his friend. Before he could think of a proper reply, the order came down the line and the left wing was made to halt. Over four thousand stood with Miltiades, drawn clear of the battle as it began. Xanthippus said nothing, firming his resolve. Discipline lay in obeying the archon, in holding the line. Trust was accepting the orders of the one appointed by the Assembly to give them. He thought of his wife and what she would say. Agariste didn't seem to understand his respect for senior men. She said Miltiades was a fool and that he had wasted a family fortune on silver mines in Thrace – mines that had been lost to the Persian king.

Xanthippus and Epikleos watched in frustration as the Greeks under Themistocles and Aristides lowered spears and locked shields. All the Persian Immortals could see were men of gold: helmets, shields and greaves beneath, spears like a forest of iron leaves.

Xanthippus stared at Miltiades, willing him to give the order to join the attack. With Callimachus absent, the older man stood as if enjoying a debate in the Agora, one foot slightly ahead of the other, his head tilted to one side as he leaned on a spear. His shield was still in the hands of a slave. Xanthippus told himself to wait, to be patient. The orders had been clear. Men of Plataea watched, frowning, not understanding why they had come so far only to stand apart. Xanthippus *had* to obey, or shame his deme, his tribe – and his wife. Agariste would never forgive him if he came home in disgrace. That much he knew. If the choice was losing his life with dignity and respect, or leaving his honour on the field, he knew she would prefer him to die. He growled under his breath, an animal sound of frustration.

6

Themistocles took his place in the front rank. The plume on the helmet his second handed to him was black and white, marking him out. He had considered wearing a cloak like the Spartans did, though of a different colour. He had not made the decision when the call had come to assemble and now he regretted it. The men had to *see* him; he understood that in his bones. If he ever hoped to lead Athens, his life had to be wagered first as a token on the board. That was simply the truth of it. He had no family wealth backing him like Xanthippus, nor could he make a fetish of poverty and the simple life the way Aristides did. Themistocles enjoyed his water and wine too much for that!

As the two armies closed, he heard prayers muttered beneath the singing voices. They fell silent then, concentrating on perfect lines. Themistocles could not resist a glance at the strange pavilion that had been erected to one side of the Persian forces. It could only be their king, the position on a rising bluff of land giving him a good view. Perhaps a thousand men surrounded him there, so he was not particularly vulnerable. Any force turning to attack him would expose their flank to the Persian Immortals. Darius would watch without having to risk his own life, like the crowds who came to see dramas in the theatre of Dionysus in Athens. Themistocles felt his lip curl. On that day, the God-King was no more than an audience. *They* were the players.

The Immortals readied swords, but Themistocles could already see fear in their twitching heads, looking back for new orders as they understood the threat coming towards them. The long spears had that effect when they came down together.

'Ready, Leontis!' Themistocles called to his tribe. He called further to those around him. 'Ready, *Athens*!'

They were all his people. He did not care what some uncle by marriage to Xanthippus had decreed was his tribe. He was Athenian! He had run those streets as a boy and skipped over sewage trenches that overflowed whenever it rained. He had slipped and fallen in once or twice as well. He chuckled at the memory. He had trained every dawn for many years, learning by watching, growing so strong and fast that other men paled to see him step into the fighting rings. Boxing or wrestling was all one to him. He liked to fight – and everything he was had been made by his own hand. Themistocles felt pride soar in him. Aristides could keep his dignity and cold logic. Xanthippus could keep his sense of superiority, though he had married all his fortune. Themistocles was the new Greece – and he was strategos alongside them that day. He laughed aloud at the thought and the men around him responded with grins.

'Look at their *fear*!' he called over their heads. 'Ready spears! Ready pipers!'

The new rhythm would drive the iron points forward, fast and vicious. It was one of the wonders of the age, how music affected the hearts and strength of men. To fight with music blaring raised the spirits – and guided the arm.

'You see the enemy? Do you? Can you see their fear? Then charge!' Themistocles called, baring his teeth.

The other strategoi matched his bellow. The Greek hoplites broke into a run. The steady pace of before was lost as they closed. Arrows passed right over them as archers misjudged their speed.

The lines crashed together and long spears punched through

armour and flesh. Heaving them back bloody, the Greeks locked shields and roared, drummers rattling and pipes screaming high. Their spears stood out as far from the shields as a man was tall, thick as hairs. The Immortals tried to knock them aside, but iron leaves found them even so, stabbing relentlessly, jerking in and out of flesh, too many to dodge.

The slaughter was instant and brutal. The long dory spears were driven with desperate strength, held by men who had trained to hit gaps no larger than a man's fist. They jabbed at thighs, faces, anything they could see. Not every blow was aimed well, but they struck with the rhythm of dancers, of drummers and pipes, again and again. Their own shields were so wide they could be overlapped. The Persians saw no weaknesses, just helmets with trimmed plumes, then huge shields, with greaves of bronze stamping below.

The long Immortal coats were not proof against spear-heads that struck and twisted and withdrew to strike again, twice with every pace. The Persians fell back, lives spurting red from wounds, or just trying to find space to counter the forest jabbing at them.

There was no respite. The phalanx formations drove on, giving the enemy no chance to breathe or counter. The Greeks pressed forward and if one of their number went down, he was passed over and guided to the rear, his space taken instantly by another. The pressure forward was crush-ing. As the advance slowed, the front ranks could hardly withdraw their arms to jab, so great was the weight of shields behind. They had to go on or fall – and Themistocles went with them.

'Dress that line!' he shouted suddenly, looking displeased.

He lunged his spear under the shield of the man on his right, feeling the solid thump and shudder that meant he had found living flesh. Good. With the lines so clustered he was not sure which of the bloodied Persians ahead had taken the wound. His line pushed on and when they reached Persian bodies, the ranks marching behind drew daggers and cut the throats of dead and still living alike. There would be no feigned death in that line, no mercy. These were invaders who had come to make slaves of Greece. Themistocles bellowed his next words just to be heard.

'What, are you Thebans, to be so sloppy? Are you foreign metics? Are you slaves? I will not die of shame today, in front of these! Make a better show, would you? By Ares, would you embarrass your leader? Would you shame me in front of Aristides?'

He knew he tended to rattle on when he was nervous. Themistocles was not sure his exhortations and criticism were any use to the men, though some of them smiled. He had heard himself quoted afterwards, though, by those who had survived. It was appreciated then, when their lives were not counted in heartbeats, spears slippery in sweating hands.

It could not last; nothing could. Spears were wrenched from the grip of hoplites. Some snapped near the hilt or were hacked aside and weakened by some Immortal blade, so that they shattered on the next impact. The perfect bristling wall of spears sprang gaps as the Immortals fought to contain the advance. Their king watched from the shade of his pavilion, not even a mile from the heaving lines.

Those Greeks who lost their spears drew swords and used them, standing alongside brothers in arms. The shields stayed locked in close formation, each man protecting the one to his left, protected in turn on his right. Blades jabbed out at anyone who tried to wrench that line apart.

The Persians were used to destroying tribes who could not even stand against their archers, never mind hold a battle line. As individual Immortals struggled past the long spears, they could only hammer at shields and helmets of bronze, while all the time, men of Athens cut low and high, gashing them across the head and stabbing at their feet, anything vulnerable. The gold bands the Immortals wore seemed to attract high overhand blows.

Despite terrible losses, the Persian lines settled and recovered. New orders were passed on from General Datis. Those who got inside the long spears ignored swords or wounds to strike on either side, cutting as many spears as they could before they were killed. It was an astonishing tactic and it cost them hundreds of men, especially when Themistocles saw what they were doing and growled new orders. Those Persians who stepped forward then to throw their lives away were killed the moment they turned to hack at shafts.

The battle heaved and swung and the right wing held well with eight ranks, while Themistocles saw Persians streaming around on his left. The right flank was always weak where the shields ended. It made sense to keep it strong, even at the expense of the centre and left. That he could grudgingly appreciate. Yet how long had it been? He had no way of knowing. It seemed as if he had been fighting for an hour or more, but the sun hung like it had been painted.

He cursed as a rattle of new stones and arrows brought cries of pain from the men of the centre. Where was Xanthippus, with his stern disapproval of everything that made life worth living? Where was Miltiades, with his coat straining to cover his paunch? The left wing had been held back and the result was this boldness of Persian archers and slingers. They had withdrawn down to the shore as the main forces clashed. Seeing the Greek left holding back, they crept in again like flies to ply their trade. It was not yet the massed volleys of before, but every moment brought more of them into range.

Themistocles blocked a high blow with his raised shield and risked his life to look over his shoulder. He could see the left wing waiting there, stopped – actually *stopped* on the sandy earth, while the rest of them fought and bled. In the image that flashed across his vision before turning back, he'd thought he had seen Miltiades standing like a whore on a corner, waiting for customers. Themistocles prayed then that they would come, or that he would survive the battle to bring them down. If Xanthippus had betrayed him, it would be because he feared a popularity he would never understand. If Miltiades had done . . . it would be for gold. There had always been greed in the older man, Themistocles knew it. There had been rumours of Miltiades losing his family wealth. Some men coveted power, some gold; Themistocles understood that much. The easy life was just too tempting, especially for those who had once known hunger. He had experienced more than his share of that himself . . .

Themistocles lost his train of thought as his spear was dragged from his hand, wrenching his fingers. He swore and drew his sword.

'Hold the line now!' he called to them. Aristides was some-where on his left, with Antiochis tribe. They were edging back and, to his horror and fury, Themistocles saw his own men were wavering as well. They could not raise shields against arrows and stones and keep the formation intact. Fear swelled in them and they took hesitant half-steps back, shuffling. Themistocles cursed, so loudly it made someone laugh.

'On my mark and not before!' he bellowed. 'We'll take a breath – and we won't leave one drop of our honour on the field, not to men such as these. Six paces back and re-form. On my mark and not before! *I see you, Xias!* Take one more step before I give the order and I will make your wife say please and thank you.'

The threat was outrageous and yet it settled the retreating line. They held position and the rest of the centre anchored on them, with Themistocles at the heart. It was a moment he thought he would remember, the air like wine.

'Six paces – now!'

He counted aloud as they went. It kept them steady, though the Persians howled victory and drove them on, convinced they were winning.

'And *hold* the line! Hold!' Themistocles bawled. 'Lock shields. Make them pay for those six, lads. Think of them marching into Athens and grabbing your daughters by the throat. Hold your nerve. Pick up spears if you find one. When you have settled, we will replace the front line. Epistatai ready? Well, are you? Second line! Those-who-stand-behind. Answer me, you lazy whoresons, would you?'

The second rank of epistatai roared an angry response to him, right across the centre, as the fighting went on in a frenzy of noise and rage and terror. He grinned at them.

Themistocles paused in the constant rattle of orders. The lines had steadied. Aristides had taken the opportunity to come back with him, he saw. It would have been that or be overwhelmed. The Immortals were every bit as determined as he'd heard. They should have been crushed by the phalanx line, but they'd somehow hung on. Athena alone knew how many of them had been killed, however. The ground was littered with dead Persians and stained in their blood, so dry it drank them in. Themistocles shuddered at the image. He did not want the ground to drink him in. He loved the sun too much.

'Ready, epistatai second line! *Ready*, protostatai first line!'

Themistocles was getting hoarse, but he heard Aristides copying the order. No doubt his tribe were as exhausted as the front rank of Leontis. Themistocles took a deep breath. The move was dangerous in the middle of a battle, though the rewards were high. Of course, if the Persians spoke Greek, there was a chance they were all about to be slaughtered.

'First rank protostatai, fall back! Second rank epistatai, advance. Aaand . . . *lock* shields!'

It was slower and more chaotic than he would have liked. In that moment, Themistocles was genuinely pleased the Spartans were not there to sneer at them. The Immortals heaved forward and killed some of those who dared to turn away from them and try to slip through the rank coming forward. Themistocles saw men he knew well hacked down, but then the front line re-formed, fresh and furious.

'On my mark! Six paces back! Six paces on my mark. Ready spears,' Themistocles bellowed over their heads.

It was a hard order to hear. They did not want to step back again, not then. They fought in a frenzy, killing panting Immortals who thought they had been close to breaking.

'Six paces . . . now!'

With something like a shout of anger, they pulled back. The Greek line disengaged faster the second time, stepping away without looking behind, keeping their eyes on Persians who found themselves swinging iron through empty air in confusion. The hoplites drew clear as Themistocles counted off the steps. The shields came up – and some picked up spears from where they lay on the ground. The forest of thorns rose once more.

'Now *advance*,' Themistocles roared at the top of his lungs.

No one stood in sword range of him, though the damned archers and slingers were taking their shots again, picking off his men, his people. Where was Miltiades? The Persians had no reserve, not beyond the royal guard. They'd thrown everything on that beach at the Greek formations. More, they were winning, a victory bought in gold and treason. There was no other explanation.

7

Xanthippus watched as Themistocles and Aristides rallied the centre, pulling off a disciplined retreat and then re-forming the phalanx. It was well done, though they'd lost half the ground they'd taken in the first charge. Neither were they still fresh and unmarked. Both sides stood battered and visibly weary. Fighting exhausted the fittest of men. The sun had moved in the afternoon sky and the blood of hundreds had already been spilled. Yet the Persian forces still teemed and their king watched from his pavilion, his guards standing at perfect attention as if it was no more than a display and not a battle for the survival of a city – and a people.

'See there?' Epikleos said. 'The Persian archers are coming back.'

He stood in the front line with Xanthippus. They were all edging forward, straining to see every detail. The slingmen and archers had retreated as soon as battle joined, when their missiles were as much danger to their own as the enemy. Yet with the entire left wing drawn up and halted, they had begun to creep back. In full view of Xanthippus and Miltiades, they were loosing shafts and stones once more. It left the archers vulnerable and Xanthippus itched to charge them.

His line shuffled another pace, as those behind pushed and craned to see what was happening. The shorter men could see hardly anything, from just a rank or two back. It meant they were shoving and swearing, more desperate with every passing moment.

Xanthippus looked up in relief as Pheidippides came running across the face of the left wing, clearly aiming at his position.

'About time,' Epikleos said.

The herald of Miltiades bowed his head. Xanthippus thought the man looked less urbane and relaxed than usual.

'Gentlemen, Archon Miltiades asks that you dress your line. Your indiscipline has been noted. You will hold the position. He asks that each strategos acknowledge his orders.'

Xanthippus did not reply. Instead, he stared at the long-limbed herald in silence, while the man's brow creased in confusion.

'Strategos?' Pheidippides said, a little uncertainly.

'Wait,' Xanthippus said between clenched teeth.

He looked past the man to the ranks of archers stealing back onto the battlefield, then further to the centre as it heaved with hoplites and Immortals, its left flank horribly exposed. In the end, Xanthippus stared along the lines to where Miltiades himself was watching him speak to the herald, the face of the archon dark with anger.

'Tell Miltiades I accept his order to advance,' Xanthippus said.

Epikleos laughed and clapped him on the shoulder as the herald gaped.

'Strategos?' the man stammered. 'Th-that is not . . .'

Whatever else he might have said was lost as new orders cracked out along the lines. Epikleos roared one of them right next to the herald's left ear, so that the man flinched and retreated.

Ahead, a larger group of Persian archers came up at a run. They were keeping a sideways eye on the stationary ranks of Greeks, wary of them. They were the first to see the left wing jerking into motion, following Xanthippus and the

67

Acamantis. The Plataeans came with them, relieved at last to be fulfilling the promise of honour they had made. Athens had saved them years before. They had come to pay their debts, not be witnesses to a tragedy.

The Persian archers pivoted their attention and drew as a second group arrived. Xanthippus cursed. He hated archers almost as much as he hated cavalry. His attempt to confuse the order from Miltiades had resulted in real confusion. Not all the tribes on that wing were moving, and those that were marched in a ragged line. The forces around Miltiades seemed to be half-advancing, half-calling for orders. No doubt the archon himself was at the heart of the conflict, demanding to know what his strategoi thought they were doing.

'Damn it!' Xanthippus shouted. 'Acamantis! Plataea! Ready shields!'

The groups of Persian archers and slingers had become a flood, emboldened by the success of the first ones to return. If the Greeks did not move, they could shoot at will. It must have been too tempting for them, Xanthippus thought, as he strode forward. He gave up on those behind. His attention was on all the archers and slingers turning in his direction. He swallowed as the first ones let fly, a ragged volley. Every archer there knew he was exposed. They were all turning to face Xanthippus and the chaotic Greek advance.

Xanthippus found himself panting, his mouth gummed. Four hundred paces separated him from bank on bank of Persian archers. His lines were broken and without the overlapping shields held overhead, they could be slaughtered. It was the archers' dream, which was why some of them were *still* running back, determined to take advantage. They were forming up two stades from where he marched. There was only one thing to do, though in the heat and in bronze armour, he did not know if it was possible. Four hundred paces, filled with death.

He took a flask of water from the next man in line, grunting his thanks as he wet his lips.

'Charge, Acamantis! Advance, Athens! For Athena! Charge!'

Xanthippus raised his shield clear and pelted towards the enemy. He was looking at thousands of archers and they all seemed to be aiming at him. He caught sight of Epikleos racing at his side. They were fit enough to sprint in armour, though Xanthippus felt his knee sending increasing spikes of pain up his leg.

Behind him, the rest of the left wing saw Acamantis tribe break into a run. It was too much for them. They roared in support and sprinted across the sandy ground, closing the distance as fast as they could. The weight of greaves and shield and sword and spear began to tell on them. They grew flushed and shone with sweat, but they did not slow.

Arrows passed overhead as the massed archers hit the ones who had lagged behind, misjudging the speed of the mass of armoured men coming at them. They were used to hammering slow-moving targets, not spear-wielding maniacs, howling as they came on.

Xanthippus lowered his shield once more as he reached the archers. He used it as a battering ram, with Epikleos at his side. The smallest unit of the Greek army was its pairs – men who had mentored and trained together for years. They and their families were friends and Xanthippus was pleased Epikleos was there to die with him.

The lines of Acamantis and Plataea crashed through the archers like a feast-day sacrifice. They cut a bloody swathe and routed them in short order, so that they ran, back to the others on the beach who would know better than to rejoin the battle. Xanthippus found himself laughing in something like relief as the Acamantis phalanx re-formed around him.

Their presence had not gone unmarked, by either side. The closest Persians were twitching their heads again, looking for fresh orders or some way out. The Greeks in the centre were calling tribes they knew, as much in anger as welcome. There was work to be done and Xanthippus waited as the men settled and shields were overlapped. Miltiades had come with them, he saw. The archon did not even look in his direction, though he was as red-faced as anyone, as if the sun had burned him. Perhaps it had, while he'd stood and watched. Xanthippus wondered if Miltiades would risk complaining about his strategos. If he did, Xanthippus vowed he would make his own accusation. They had remained too long on the wing doing nothing. If that had not been treachery, it might as well have been.

The left wing moved forward as one, all divisions and rivalries forgotten as they hit the Persian flank with a roar. Even then, as Xanthippus and the rest crashed into the enemy and took the first lives with their spears, he was not certain. No. He was. In his heart, he knew Miltiades had been bought.

Battle was joined across the full line, with only the marshes preventing the whirling, hacking, bloody front spreading too far. Xanthippus fought in grim silence as the light changed with infinite slowness to the paler colours of early evening. He loved that time of day above all others, when the air cooled. He stood with the men of his city and he killed with them, though his knee felt like it was on fire and he could not trust his full weight to it.

Themistocles and Aristides fought well in the centre. On the left, Xanthippus and Epikleos cut Persians down with dark delight, with spears and then blades, going forward in formation to stab and withdraw and take another step. Lunge, pull, block with the shield, go forward. Those who fell under their heels were crushed and gashed until they could not rise again.

The Persians broke, though their king watched them. Xanthippus saw the pavilion coming down before he felt the shift, so that he could not have said which caused the other – whether the king had decided to retreat to his ships and so stolen the heart from his men, or whether the imminent rout forced the Great King to run before he was trapped on the beach.

The battle became a brutal slaughter. Xanthippus found his voice had gone completely, so that Epikleos had to relay his orders to keep discipline. The Immortals could feel the sea at their back as they retreated. In their panelled coats, they could not swim. When they felt waves lapping at their feet, the fighting became utterly desperate. It was then that holding the line of shields proved its worth. The sea frothed with red as Persians fell, slowly tumbling in the waves. A ship accepted their king into its hold and was hauled into deep water. His personal guard stood three deep as it was heaved off the sand, determined to allow him to get free, though they had no ship themselves.

Xanthippus saw Miltiades among the officers who pressed them while they stood in the shallow waters, cutting and battering until the king's guards had fallen with the rest. He thought the Persians had lost the will to keep fighting by then or they might have done better against weary men. His citizens of Athens fought for more than just a king. Perhaps that was it.

Themistocles took his centre tribes forward in a block to butcher the remaining slingers and archers. They were hard men, Ethiopians and Egyptians with knives and clubs. Yet

71

they died like lambs to hoplites in bronze armour. The killing went on until darkness came – and then Aristides set the last beached ships on fire so they could see. No Persian would be left alive to rob, rape or kill innocents after they had gone.

Bodies bumped against one another as the sea grew calm, like apples on the surface. In the end, it was done, with the moon rising high in the summer evening. Miltiades set guards and sent his herald Pheidippides running back from Marathon to Athens with news of the victory. There would be celebration in every house that night. The women and the elderly, the lame and the sick and the children would give thanks to the gods for being saved.

Bonfires lit the beach, with great bushes of fennel thrown onto them to sweeten the air. Xanthippus spent time checking the men of Acamantis were safe and not bleeding from wounds. There were bandages with the baggage train that came up. Gashes were sewn by the light of the fires, washed out with wine. The dead would have to be tallied in the morning, when there was light. Most of the survivors just sat or knelt where they stood, exhausted and stunned by all they had seen, all they had done.

8

Xanthippus stood with his eyes closed in the darkness. Orange gleamed through the lids as the bonfires crackled and snapped. Sleep had been impossible, though he ached in every joint and his knee was almost useless. It had swollen to twice its usual size and he had to concentrate not to make sharp sounds of pain whenever he moved. It was easier to stand and let Epikleos throw him a skin of watered wine that was probably half and half, at least. Xanthippus hadn't asked how his friend had found such a thing, with every man and officer wanting the same. The wine had slowed his thoughts, like a net thrown across a river to catch fish. Even in his exhaustion he could not drift away, not with every scene of the day to play out, over and over.

He had wandered down the shore for a while, hoping to find peace in the wash and hiss of the surf. Too many things still tumbled there, making him shudder. He thought he'd heard something thrashing further out and he had visions of beasts rising from the deep to snatch the dead. There had been no peace in that place and he'd returned to where his tribe had camped and Epikleos had collected his greaves, shield, spear and sword. The lion on his shield had taken a battering. Even in the firelight, Xanthippus could see it had been raked right across in stripes that gleamed bright. Yet he had not taken a wound. He would remember to tell Agariste the lion had taken his cuts for him. She would be pleased.

The ground was more sand than earth where Acamantis tribe rested. Xanthippus could hear the snores of weary men lying on their backs with their mouths open. Others were still talking in quiet groups, discussing the day. He knew them all. He had bought grain from some and invested with others. He had listened to speeches and arguments in the Assembly from many more, nodding his approval and proposing votes. Some of the eighteen-year-olds had already recovered enough to walk the battlefield in the darkness, perhaps to find a few coins or rings, or those intriguing gold headbands the Immortals had worn. There were fortunes to be found wherever the Persians made war, so it was said.

Xanthippus knew the men of his own generation better, of course, but on that day, they were all Athenian. They gathered in the same part of the Agora in time of war – and they knew one another. Sometimes, that was all it was. When Xanthippus had been a beardless youth, he recalled men in their forties and fifties. The oldest lay like the dead after a battle, with backs and knees and elbows swollen, or wounds that drained them of life like a leaky old skin. Yet they had marched and fought even so, grizzled and patch-bearded old bastards to a man. They had come because they were needed, sometimes to oversee the ones they had trained, like Xanthippus himself. He had done the same for a few young lads who'd hardly known one end of a spear from the other. That was the compact between them, the honourable labour.

He frowned at the thought. It had not escaped his notice how many had been gasping like birds after that long charge in armour. Their fitness was not what it could be – what it should have been. Above all else, his old trainer had told him. If a man could remain fresh for longer, while an enemy bent to vomit, or clutched his knees and grew red, he would win. Fitness meant speed and speed meant victory.

Xanthippus remembered the old words with a smile and felt something ease in him. He would train Acamantis. With a little luck and perhaps the support of Aristides or even Themistocles, he would institute a new training regime. Many more races in armour for a certainty, over long and short distances. That wild sprint to hit the archers had nearly ruined half the men.

Lost in his thoughts, Xanthippus did not hear footsteps approaching. The first he knew of it was Epikleos stepping out of the shadows and bringing a knife to the throat of the stranger, making him grunt and freeze in place.

'Why, I've caught myself a Persian,' Epikleos said.

The messenger swore. 'No you haven't, as you know very well. Strategos Xanthippus?'

Epikleos jerked his head to Xanthippus, putting his knife away. The messenger regarded him sourly as he rubbed his neck.

'Archon Miltiades waits upon you. If you'll follow me, I will lead you to him.'

'Shall I go with you?' Epikleos said. He tapped his belt, his fingers resting against the hilt of his knife.

Xanthippus understood the signal, but shook his head.

'I imagine the archon wishes to congratulate me on our victory,' he said. 'I will be perfectly safe, Epikleos.'

'Are you sure?' Epikleos said. 'I could call up an honour guard, quick as thought.'

His jaw was tense, though he forced a smile. The messenger was already angry at him for the scare. The man spoke with acid in his tone.

'The enemy are in the sea, sir, I believe you'll find. The strategos needs no guards, not tonight.'

'Is that a rebuke?' Epikleos snapped. 'I know very well where the enemy are. I should, I killed enough of them.'

The messenger decided against provoking the man further and merely waited, his eyes bulging slightly. Xanthippus took a deep breath. His leg was throbbing in time with his heartbeat, which was odd. He eyed his spear and Epikleos understood and brought it to his hand.

'Take me to Miltiades, then,' Xanthippus said.

He tried not to limp at first, making the sort of young man's vow that he would not show weakness, no matter what it cost him. Yet the knee was so swollen, it thumped against the other and made him stumble, so that he had to lean on the spear.

'Are you all right?' the messenger said, looking back. The man was hurrying through the camp, passing light and shadow where the fires had burned down to embers.

'I'm fine, thank you. Take me to your master,' Xanthippus said, nettled by the man's tone, or perhaps just his concern. He was weary himself. After being certain he could not possibly sleep, it was suddenly stealing over him and making his eyes heavy.

The messenger took them past the lines of sleeping men, past the few who were still awake. That fragile excitement was fading too, so that more and more of them lay down.

Xanthippus felt a prickle of alarm as he realised he had come through the outer lines. The sentries challenged him there and he gave his name and praised them for their alertness. The ground began to rise then and he struggled, leaning on the spear and feeling his knee had something sharp wedged between the bones.

He recalled the Persian king had raised a pavilion to watch the battle. The ground had risen there and Xanthippus found he was relieved when it levelled out once more. A single brazier sat atop the ridge, with Miltiades standing alongside. He had removed the studded coat and wore a loose white tunic with bare arms that emphasised his strength. Xanthippus was surprised to see the man had developed a stomach. It

76

pressed against the soft material like the womb of a pregnant woman. In that moment, Xanthippus was glad Epikleos was not there to comment on it.

'Strategos!' Miltiades said. 'Thank you for coming. You are limping? Are you injured? I am sorry, I was not told.'

'It is nothing – and I am no longer strategos, Miltiades. The long day is over. All the appointments of the Assembly are at an end.' Perhaps it was the pain in his knee and the fact that he'd been called to walk on it that made him add, 'Nor are you archon any longer.'

Miltiades' expression grew stiff and he nodded to himself, as if he had confirmed something.

'It is strange, Xanthippus. I have spoken to a few of the strategoi from today. Poor Callimachus did not survive the fighting. He was not made for war, not as some are. Yet Themistocles came to me, as did Aristides. Arimnestos of the Plataean thousand bent a knee to me and asked if their debt was discharged.'

'They fought well,' Xanthippus said. 'I hope you told him it was.'

Miltiades made an exasperated sound.

'There it is again – that concern for proprieties, the rules of the Assembly, the titles. I released the Plataeans from their debt, Xanthippus, because that was the path of honour, after today. My point, though, was that all those others congratulated me on our victory. Each one of them took my hand in greeting and offered wine. Yet from you, who stood in my own wing, I am lectured on the rights and wrongs of titles? You are a strange man.'

Xanthippus thought he sensed movement in the shadows to his left. He could not run, not with a bad leg. With that chance removed, he let all tension slide from him and stood easily. If Miltiades wanted his life, he would take it.

'Your silence is . . . strange, strategos,' Miltiades said.

'I am a free man of Athens, Miltiades. That is all I am.'

'And no longer strategos, yes, you have said. Yet you are a Marathonomachos – a man of Marathon, just as I am. You fought amidst the fennel and the sand and salt. More, you are one of the Eupatridae, the landowners. As I am. And an Athenian, as I am.'

Xanthippus regarded the man before him, trying to discern his intent. Miltiades was sweating, he saw. Many men did sweat more after a battle, sometimes for hours. Or it could have been evidence of a weak heart. He had seen men fall the day after, sometimes recorded in the rolls as the last to die, though they clutched their chests and dropped under a different sun. In Miltiades, though, he thought it was both guilt and fear that drew wet lines from scalp to chin.

'What do you want, Miltiades?' he asked. 'Is it just my congratulations on the victory? I am glad we won. I thought . . .'

He hesitated, unwilling to share an intimacy with a man he thought had betrayed them. Xanthippus had still not decided what to do about that. Battle was chaotic – orders could be misunderstood. Yet if there had been treachery, it was a crime so vile that it made his stomach clench.

'What is it . . . ? What did you think?'

By Athena, the man was like a lover Xanthippus had known, a woman who wanted to know what thought lurked behind every change of expression.

'I thought we would not win,' he said with a sigh. 'They were so many – and the Immortals wouldn't break with their king watching.'

He saw the tension go out of Miltiades in a great sigh, and it was suddenly too much. Xanthippus knew the dangers of the time after great exertion. He knew not to make a purchase, or get too drunk, or draw his knife in anger. His blood was still too rich with rage, as the old officer trainers used to say. For some men, the best thing to do was sit with trusted friends and say nothing until they had slept and woken again. Yet instead, he had been dragged across the camp with a sore knee and questioned by Miltiades, who thought he was a lot subtler than he actually was.

'I thought, too, that you had been bought by the Persian king,' Xanthippus added.

He could have cursed himself the moment the words were out, but it was too late. Miltiades watched him from under dark brows, his wrestler's hands flexing. Xanthippus felt a thrill of fear and pressed on, preferring not to be made a coward on that night. Let the truth be heard, he thought.

'I recalled you had lost your family fortune on silver mines – in Thrace, was it? And there we were, held back while Themistocles and Aristides were being battered by the Persians. You sent orders to hold, just when we were needed.'

Somehow, he stopped himself from going on. It all sounded so weak now that he had said the words aloud. Miltiades seemed to agree, as he smiled and shook his head.

'I sent those orders when we needed a reserve, Xanthippus. I held the wing back to lure in their archers and slingers. Was I wrong? Did we not carry the day?'

Xanthippus could have let it go. He understood by then why Miltiades had called for him, then dismissed his slaves. The man was afraid of an accusation. He wanted to know if Xanthippus was his enemy, or if he could return to Athens as a hero. If he had been twenty, perhaps Xanthippus would have bowed his head and gone along. Yet he thought the man before him was a traitor. He could not swallow all the bile that rose in him.

'We carried the day because I disobeyed your order to

79

stand, Miltiades. The men followed me – and we charged the archers, not at your order, but in spite of your orders. How is it then your victory?'

Miltiades shook his head again and Xanthippus saw spite and fury in his expression.

'You are mistaken. I held a reserve until the moment was perfect. You never heard my order to attack, it seems. Perhaps I should report your disobedience in the heat of battle to the Assembly. I wonder how your wife's family would receive that news?'

Xanthippus felt his grip tighten on the spear, so that he became aware it was a weapon he held. He had killed men with one just like it, that very day. He felt anger rise and he crushed it, ruthlessly. Accusations would hurt them both, he realised. If he was made to give an oath of honour, he could not deny he had disobeyed an order. It would not matter if he claimed the results had been vital. The Assembly would make an example of him. So too, for Miltiades. The glory of his victory at Marathon would be tarnished if one of his own strategoi called him traitor.

They could destroy one another, if they chose to. The awareness of it crackled in the air between them. Xanthippus felt the anger drain once again, so that he felt exhausted.

He had wrestled too many bouts to recall each one, in gymnasia around the city and in private grounds. It was a hard and bloody sport, as were the boxing matches favoured by men like Themistocles for fitness. Yet the Spartans would not train in either discipline – because each bout ended with one man's surrender. Spartan trainers said they did not want to accustom their people to giving up, that surrender had to mean death. Xanthippus sensed the philosophy was flawed, even as he admired it. Yet he was Athenian. He *could* take a loss – and wait for another chance.

'The midst of a battle is a confusing place,' he said. 'Perhaps I mistook your intentions.'

His voice grated, but he saw instant relief in the older man. Xanthippus saw how much Miltiades needed his victory — and it was a victory. He struggled with a pang of regret, a thought that he should have fought harder for justice. On that night, the air smelled of blood and fennel and he was just too weary, too numb.

'I am glad you understand,' Miltiades said. 'It was an extraordinary day. We are Marathonomachoi, now and for ever. Whenever I taste fennel seed, I will think of this place.'

Xanthippus bowed to him, giving him honour he did not deserve, then limped back down the slope to where his friends lay and snored. He did not think he would sleep, but he did.

9

The herald, Pheidippides, had carried the news of victory the night before, making the run back to Athens along the coast in record time. As he reached the Agora, he had cried, 'Rejoice! Victory is ours!' then sat on a bench as the cheering spread, rubbing the centre of his chest as if it pained him. When they thought at last to bring him wine, he was dead, his great heart still.

That small tragedy could not mar the celebrations of a city. When the hoplite column came into sight, it was met by children running along the road and what looked like all Athens turning out to greet them. There were women everywhere and they had draped themselves in flowers to kiss the returning soldiers. Slaves had been given a day free of labour on such an occasion and even the metic workers of foreign states turned out to witness men of bronze coming back from such an extraordinary victory.

Xanthippus wondered how many of the cheering crowds had slunk back in from the hills when they discovered their hoplites had won. He'd seen a stream of people and carts leaving the city as news spread of the Persian landing. Many would still be heading away, unaware the warriors of Athens had crushed the invasion and removed the threat.

He had woken early, so stiff he'd had trouble just sitting up. Despite the discomfort, he'd joined the younger men in runs along the beach and simple balances to stretch out his bruised limbs. It was astonishing how many times he'd been scraped or bashed without noticing it. His chest and right arm were mottled and there were odd welts on his thighs as if he'd been raked with claws. Half the bodies in the bay had vanished overnight, though there were others still bumping along in the shallows, held down by weight of armour. The smell was already growing stronger and Miltiades had declared burying the dead was not labour for hoplites. They had done their work the day before. Digging tombs, recording the weapons and valuables, could be handled by the seconds and slaves from the baggage carts. They had lazed their way through the battle, after all.

Though it was true the strategoi had lost the formal authority granted by the Assembly of Athens, the fiction of it was still in place, at least until they passed the walls of the city. Miltiades and Themistocles, in particular, seemed to expect complete obedience from the men. They were everywhere as the sun rose, giving orders, bringing structure to those who were still stunned, hardly able to believe they lived. In the process of counting the dead, Miltiades had chosen a dozen men to remain on the beach and complete the tally. No one who had seen the gold bands worn by the Immortals argued they should be left to rot. There were fortunes lying on the sand. It would be hard enough to stop boys from the city coming out and spending the next few days camping there, lost in fantasies and digging for rings and coins. Someone too had to be left to watch for ships returning, perhaps making a raid for slaves. They had lost children before in exactly that way – and there were still Persian vessels out there, somewhere. No one thought they would dare return, but who knew the minds of Persians? They were strange folk.

The column that came back to Athens was smaller by almost a thousand hoplites. Some four hundred of those still lived, but were too wounded to march with the rest. Their greaves, shields and spears were piled on carts, along with the equipment of the fallen. For the six hundred Athenian dead, those things would have been the most valuable items they possessed. Each was marked with a family stamp. They would be returned to the tribe, deme and individual heirs – to be sold, or perhaps worn with pride by another generation.

All those things were behind, as Xanthippus walked in the sun with Epikleos at his side. On such a day, it was simply good to feel it on the back of his neck, to know he was alive. He wondered if he would ever smell fennel again without thinking of the battle in that place.

The sound of cheering could be heard some way off. It raised his spirits as the crowds caught sight of them. He had not returned from many campaigns – and never before from a battlefield almost in sight of the city. Truly they were Marathonomachoi, as Miltiades had said. Men of Marathon. He wondered if it would be the defining day of his life and whether he would always be satisfied with his part in it. Memory was a difficult path at times. Already, he knew the previous night's conversation with Miltiades would weigh on him. His time in the front line was there in bright flashes. Xanthippus recalled his throat had been dry the whole day. Parts of it had lost their connection to the whole, so he could not remember the exact order of events. Yet his suspicion of Miltiades was as fresh and certain as ever.

The crowds adorned Miltiades with wreaths of crocus and amaranth, the eternal flower that never lost its deep red, even when dried. The archon was even persuaded to carry a branch of it, thick with blossom. With green vines woven around his right arm, he walked proudly at the head of the column. The men with him smiled and waved, their shields worn on their shoulders so they could embrace anyone who

84

dared to dart out and kiss them. Xanthippus tried not to frown, though he saw Epikleos glancing aside, amused at his expression.

'You have never liked this . . .' Epikleos shouted over the noise of cheering. 'The crowds of Athens, the people. See Themistocles there! He adores the attention.'

It was true, of course. Themistocles was strolling alongside Miltiades, beckoning for more blooms and allowing one young woman to take as long as she liked winding a green vine from his shoulder to his wrist. He was laughing with her and let his hand drop casually to her waist, pulling her closer as he bent his head and said something that made her blush.

Themistocles at least claimed the adulation of the city with no embarrassment. Xanthippus could only shrug at that. The man had led his tribe and the centre with cool bravery, rallying them under pressure and breaking the heart of the Persian Immortals. Themistocles deserved the acclaim.

The route they took would lead through the city to the Agora, with the hill of the Pnyx and the Areopagus to the south and west of it. Those outcroppings of bare stone were where the Assembly and the council met to discuss and vote. Such places were made sacred by their purpose. No doubt there would be speeches and sacrifices offered to Athena for their deliverance. Xanthippus would have to endure some of it, but he had a house nearby, where there would be cool water and silence. Agariste and the children would find him there, but perhaps not until he had let stillness and quiet seep back into him. He needed it, after so much clamour and noise, beating at him like wings. He needed to be alone, at least for a time. Men like Themistocles seemed to grow larger and brighter with the touch of hands, the weeping of grateful women. Epikleos too seemed delighted by it. Perhaps

Theseus and Heracles had been the same, Xanthippus thought.

He could see Aristides ahead, wearing a simple robe. He at least looked like an archivist or a scholar, out strolling through the markets. Aristides had played as vital a part in the victory as Themistocles, but there was no vainglory in him. It made Xanthippus proud to see the man's dignity. Themistocles was touching every outstretched hand, his teeth showing as he laughed and cheered with the rest.

It was all lead, all tin, Xanthippus realised. They had offered their lives on the field of battle, something only those who had been there would ever truly understand. It actually made Miltiades his brother, he realised. Perhaps that was part of the reason he had not spoken out. The man could make his counter-accusation of disobedience, of course, but he thought it was more than that. Xanthippus told himself it was – and suddenly he was choked and tears stung his eyes. He could not understand where the emotion had arisen and he longed more than ever for a place away from the noise and the heaving mob.

He felt Epikleos pat him twice on the shoulder, returning him to the world.

'Come on, Xan,' the younger man said, his concern clear. 'I've seen you like this before, after a battle. You need to rest, with a little wine and some simple food. Or a lot of wine.'

Xanthippus smiled and nodded. He endured the crowds all the way to the Agora, where they were greeted by still more. Every road had filled with them, every open space crammed. More men and women than he could possibly count had come out, showing how much they appreciated what had been done. It should have been a glorious occasion, though Xanthippus felt the sun beating on his neck and arms and he felt dry-mouthed and grubby. Themistocles was somehow untouched by filth, though he had fought and sweated as hard as anyone. Or had the man changed his clothes? He had certainly found a cloak of pale blue from somewhere, Xanthippus noted. With flowers wound around his neck and arms, it made him look like a king, or the god of some sacred grove.

Little by little, the column of returning soldiers drifted into the mass of people. They were greeted by tribe and deme as well as loved ones. There was weeping then for those who had not returned. Sobbing women and children were led away from that place, given space by those who understood their loss, taken home by sisters and parents. Around those small islands of crushing sorrow, the other citizens of Athens rejoiced, pounding the victors' arms and shoulders in jubilation.

In the Agora, Xanthippus saw Miltiades raised up on the shoulders of his tribe, so that he sat above them all and lifted his hands further, acknowledging their shouts and cheers. Xanthippus saw too that Themistocles had noticed the man's rise in status and adulation. He did not seem delighted about it. Xanthippus watched the victor of Marathon – and Miltiades seemed to sense his gaze, looking across the crowd. The noise had lessened and Xanthippus knew if there was a time to speak, it was then.

He saw Miltiades embrace a youth lifted up alongside. His son, Cimon. The young man was no more than sixteen or seventeen and gazed on his father with reverence. It was not too hard to imagine one of Xanthippus' sons looking at him with such pride when they were older.

Xanthippus made a final decision. Nothing was certain in a battle, nor in the hearts of men. He had no proof. He nodded to Miltiades. If the man noticed, he gave no sign of it.

It was Themistocles who spoke first to the crowd, of course. Xanthippus raised his eyes to the heavens as the man's voice boomed across the Agora. The sky was clear and dark blue and the sun beat down on a summer afternoon. Xanthippus felt tension vanish as he breathed out and out at last. There was a moment of perfect peace. He closed his eyes and drew in air and life and sound once more.

'We give thanks to the gods for a great victory,' Themistocles was saying, 'for without their aid and their strength, we could not have triumphed.'

He paused and Xanthippus wondered how much of the credit Themistocles would reserve for himself. It was an unworthy thought.

'You will hear a thousand stories in the days and months and years to come – of all we did. We drove the army of the Great King into the sea and made it run red as wine.'

The silence was absolute then. Xanthippus heard an intake of breath at the image. The crowd who had not been there hung on his words. Themistocles was witness.

'I give thanks to the men who stood with me, as brothers, as Athenians. As Hellenes. We are Greeks – and we are victors.'

Themistocles spoke almost sadly, Xanthippus realised, though whether it was artifice or exhaustion, he could not tell. The man looked across at him, as if he had heard the thought.

'I give thanks for the strategoi who ordered the battle: for Aristides, who held the centre with me; for Xanthippus on the left wing, who raised the hearts of the men. For Miltiades, who kept us steady – and sent in the reserve at exactly the right moment, so that they smashed the Persian lines, all while their king watched.'

The crowd cheered, the sound echoing across the entire city in ripples – those too far back to hear a single word nonetheless roaring their encouragement. He knows, Xanthippus realised. Themistocles knows exactly what happened, or at least he suspects. Perhaps he too had seen the way the crowd adored Miltiades, how they reached for his hands, just to say they had touched him! The man is beyond all criticism after such a victory. Whatever lies beneath, that is the truth.

Miltiades had been lowered to stand once again. He stepped forward, though to Xanthippus watching, it did not look as if Themistocles was ready to give way. Nonetheless, he did so with good grace, leading the renewed cheers for the hero of Marathon.

Miltiades beamed at them, basking in the approval. He did not let it go on for too long, choosing caution over vanity and patting the air for silence. Even then, the roars died away reluctantly. Xanthippus wondered what it had been like, waiting with slaves and metic foreigners to hear whether the army returning to Athens would be Persian or Greek. It was a reality – an agony – he had never known. He shrugged at the thought. Some men changed the world; some endured it. He knew he would always choose his fate, not let others choose for him! That was his right as a man – and a citizen of Athens. He put such thoughts aside as Miltiades spoke.

'I was blessed to lead us. Only we and the brave men of Plataea answered our call . . . just eleven thousand against four or five times as many, against slingers and archers and Persian Immortals – the best soldiers of their empire. Against war crews and hard-faced oar-slaves. Against their king, watching us. The day has gone. It is already a memory. Yet we who are Marathonomachoi know the only truth that matters. In that hour, we were enough.'

The hush lasted a full beat as the crowd stared almost in reverence, then erupted once more. Someone had taken up drums and pipes and the noise of those competed with the crowd, making Xanthippus' heart race at the sound of a battlefield, so fresh in his memory.

Miltiades had to wait a long time to speak again.

'Some of you may have heard the Great King was accompanied by Hippias, traitor and tyrant of Athens,' he said.

The sound of the pipes died with a squawk at that. A murmur of astonishment went around the crowd. Xanthippus too pricked up his ears, exchanging a glance with Epikleos at his shoulder. They all knew that name. Hippias had been forced out of the city years before, after attempting to overthrow the reforms that had given them the Assembly in all its noise and clamour. It was a debt they still owed the Spartans, for entering Athens at their request and surrounding the forces of Hippias on the Acropolis, forcing him to leave the city.

Xanthippus remembered that day well, though he had been just a youth of eighteen. The Spartans had wanted to remain, of course, claiming some rights over the city they had liberated, though they had been invited in as guests. Word they would not go had taken wing and, without speeches, without a vote even, the streets had suddenly filled with every young man of Athens, surrounding them. Perhaps the crowds that day had been shamed by their inability to stand against the tyrant and his soldiers. It did not matter. They had found their courage in the end. They would not be ruled by tyrants ever again! Even the Spartans had realised they could not prevail against so many determined men. They had looked like wolves confronted with armed sheep. Yet that had been the day Xanthippus thought that democracy might actually survive. He had not known there were so many who cared about it as much as he did, before that day. Yet if there were men willing to die for it, if they loved it more than life, perhaps it was worth something.

Xanthippus frowned. He had heard no rumours of Hippias in the battle, nor seen his banners, nor any Greek shields in the Persian lines. How could Miltiades have learned such a thing? There had been prisoners taken and interrogated, of course. They had suffered before being killed, some of them. Perhaps they had told Miltiades more than he had revealed the night before. Even so, suspicion flared.

'Before the battle,' Miltiades went on, 'I had word Hippias would return from the palaces of Persia to accompany the Great King. A traitor to all Greece, to be aiding our enemies in such a way.'

Miltiades paused while a growl swept through the crowd. It was a sound of true anger, and if Hippias had stood before them then, Xanthippus thought they would surely have torn him apart.

'Much of their fleet survives, with their cavalry and thousands of soldiers. They remain a threat to us – with Hippias among their number. So I ask no victor's wreath from you for yesterday, not for me, nor for the men who held the line. We know what we did – and we know it was enough. All I ask is to be given a fleet, to hunt down the Persian survivors, to seek out Hippias wherever he has gone to ground. If the Assembly votes today, to allow me construction of ships and men to crew them – as well as the silver from our treasury to pay for their service – if you can do this, I will bring back a greater sum in Persian silver, and I will exact our vengeance on Hippias: long, *long* overdue.'

As the crowd erupted once again, Epikleos leaned in very close, so that his lips almost touched Xanthippus' ear.

'At least he will be away from Athens for a time,' he said. 'If the gods are willing, we may never see him again.'

Xanthippus nodded, watching as Miltiades was lifted once more onto the shoulders of his friends and supporters. The man had held back the wing to give the battle to the Persians, Xanthippus was certain. If he had succeeded, the people who cheered would have wept in chains that very day, bought and sold on the slave blocks. It did not matter that Miltiades had failed, only that he had not been punished for his attempt. There was an injustice there and it burned in his breast.

'I am for home,' Xanthippus said to Epikleos, repeating it more loudly when the man cupped a hand behind his ear and looked blank. 'The house in Cholargos deme.'

Epikleos nodded. He knew his friend detested crowds. His duty had kept him there, to hear Miltiades and Themistocles speak. Yet the pressure of eyes wearied him.

Xanthippus and Epikleos waited only long enough to raise their hands in the public vote. Even then, Xanthippus might have kept his down. Epikleos tapped him on the elbow.

'Never let the deer see your bow,' he said into his ear.

Xanthippus breathed long and slow and raised his arm with the rest to be counted. Miltiades noted it, he saw. Amongst all the others, he seemed to spot Xanthippus in that instant. The man missed very little as he looked across the people he would have betrayed, tears shining in his eyes.

Xanthippus breathed in the smell of clean new wood as he watched ribs of pine and oak being shaped and lowered into place. The keels of forty new triremes had been laid in cradles all along the shore of the port of Piraeus. All but three had been finished through the winter months, ready for the spring he could already smell in the air. The work was almost at an end and with it came a sense of anticipation. Some of the new fleet were out, the crews training to work together, to learn commands roared in the heat of battle, to stop and turn in just a few lengths, astonishing anyone who saw them move. They would be able to defend themselves against any Persian warship. More, they would be hawks to them.

When the last ones were ready, there would be a final launch, with all the rest in formation on the sea. Galleys of pine, oak and bronze would surge out then, past the sheltered shores and into the deep. Ninety oars to a side in three banks of thirty, sweeping the dark waters of the Aegean. Free men rowed the ships of Athens, men who bore arms and could defend their ships from being boarded. They had surprised enemies before with that simplest of tactics. Chained slaves did not fight like free Greeks. Though they had to be paid, it was honourable work for those who wanted to play a part but had no armour or weapons. They too had a vote in the Assembly – and they wanted to defend the city.

Athens lay behind him as he watched the carpenters at their labours. Xanthippus smiled when he realised the beat of mallet and chisels made his ears ring, yet left him perfectly calm. There were different kinds of noise, it seemed. The shaping of wood and shouts for nails and glue did not trouble him. In comparison to arguments in the city, mere physical labour was a balm.

The port lay just thirty stades or so to the south-west of the city walls. Xanthippus could run to the shore in half an hour and he enjoyed having a destination. Some of the serious young men of the Assembly pounded laps at the gymnasia, lost in a sort of dreaming state as they poured with sweat. Xanthippus preferred to aim at a place – and he had an interest in the ships being constructed.

The city could not afford them, not really. The richest families had all been approached to do their part and provide vast sums of silver. Two of the keels taking shape in sections on the shore had been financed by the Alcmaeonid family. A piece of his wife's wealth – *his* wealth! – would travel with Miltiades when he set out in the spring.

Xanthippus had no responsibility for the ships, not once the payment had been made. He had heard one would bear a likeness of Agariste on the prow, but that was a whim of his wife and a side arrangement with a master carver, not any recognition of the payment. Xanthippus sighed to himself. The simplest design would be an eye painted on either side of the ram – to see the way to the enemy. As with his old shield, simple was often best.

He walked slowly along the quayside, where unfinished skeletons lay in cradles of grey oak, held away from the sea by wooden doors and great baulks. When the time came, when they were ready, the waters would be allowed to pour in, raising the triremes in their new element. They would be towed out then, for sea trials.

He watched in fascination as a ram was fitted to one that was almost ready. The massive bronze ship-killers were fearsome things, sheets of metal nailed onto wooden beams for the perfect combination of lightness and strength. Long and wide, they looked blunt, though he knew the reason for that. Rams were meant to break a hull and then allow the living weapon of the attacking ship to withdraw and seek another target. Anything like a spike would remain stuck. These rams were hammers. At full speed, with the weight of a ship and two hundred men behind them, they could smash through anything afloat. It was a kind of warfare that appealed to Xanthippus.

He stood naked, letting the sea breeze dry his sweat. His knee was hurting, of course. He missed the days when he had been able to complete a little run like that a dozen times if he'd wanted, without a week of stiff muscles and an aching lower back. He sighed. The years were cruel. At least the day was clear, after three of solid rain.

From among the triremes further down the line, he saw two men walk out together. Xanthippus swore under his breath as he recognised Themistocles, the taller man's head bent in conversation with Aristides. No doubt they were fulfilling their duties for the Assembly and checking each nail and tool and silver coin. There could be no waste, not with a fleet of this size. Seventy ships was a huge undertaking, a good share of the wealth of Athens sent out onto the waves to be fortune's plaything. There were some who said Miltiades should never have been granted his request, but he had picked his moment well.

Xanthippus turned to go, but of course in that instant Themistocles felt his gaze and looked up. The big man raised his hand and called out his name. There was a single heartbeat when Xanthippus might have pretended he had not heard, but he hesitated and the moment was gone. The pair strolled over to him. Both wore simple robes and carried scrolls of papyrus under their arms, marked with images and tally lists. Xanthippus groaned to himself, but he would not retreat. Instead, he forced a smile and stood, feeling sweat drip down his back. Had he grown so unfit since Marathon? He had trained harder than ever, but age stole all in the end. He imagined getting so soft he grew a stomach, as some men did in their middle age. The idea filled him with horror and he resolved to run hard on the return, knee or no knee.

Themistocles eyed him as he drew up.

'You are looking well, Xanthippus,' he said. 'I thought I recognised you. Have you come to see your ships?'

'They are not mine,' Xanthippus replied immediately. How was it that Themistocles always seemed to nettle him with just a word? It was frustrating. He saw Aristides looked calm and unruffled and understood in that moment how the man irritated Themistocles above all others.

'It is good to see you both well – and your concern for the new galleys,' Xanthippus said.

Aristides smiled gently.

'We all have an interest, Xanthippus,' he said. 'We three stood with him at Marathon. We bear the scars of that day. It is my duty to see Miltiades launched and launched well. It is the will of the Assembly, after all.'

Xanthippus dipped his head. He thought he saw Themistocles roll his eyes behind him but he did not look past the Assembly member.

'I heard of your appointment as eponymous archon, Aristides. It is much deserved.'

To his pleasure, Aristides waved away the compliment.

'Such things matter not at all, Xanthippus, as you know very well. At best, they are temptations to vanity. At worst, they are a worm in the soul! Should it matter to me that the Assembly of the people voted my name as the name for the year? There were other candidates. Were they somehow less worthy of honour? Themistocles could have been named to the position just as easily. A single vote might have separated us – would I then be eaten with envy? Would my worth be less, or his, more? Of course not. It is all trivial, Xanthippus. You understand, I know.'

Xanthippus felt himself flush. He was delighted to be included in the intimacy of equals, regardless of the truth of it. There could only be one eponymous archon elected each year. The year of Aristides would be the pillar on which all events were set. 'That was three years after Aristides,' men would say, perhaps for centuries. Xanthippus believed the older man cared little for such honours, but he knew he was not so detached himself. Neither, he suspected, was Themistocles.

'I am heading over to see the dockmaster,' Aristides said. He reached out and Xanthippus took his hand, feeling a firm, dry grip. 'I have found discrepancies in his accounts.'

'Criminal, or incompetence?' Xanthippus asked. He found the presence of Aristides made him want to be serious and thoughtful. The man set a high standard.

Aristides weighed his answer before replying, given that a man's life would hang on it.

'I believe it is the latter, but I will judge his reaction. If necessary, I will bring him before the Assembly to be judged.'

'Is there a chance of violence?' Xanthippus said. 'I have no sword, but I could accompany you. It would not do to have an archon assaulted in his duties.'

Aristides looked away in thought, then shook his head. He had no physical fear at all, Xanthippus had noted before, as if the threat of mere injury or even death were of no concern.

'I don't think so. I am well known here. If he did lash out,

97

there are a dozen carpenters and slaves who would restrain him. Thank you for your concern, Xanthippus. You are a good man.'

Xanthippus felt himself flush again as Aristides turned and walked down to the docks. It was tempting to go with him. He sensed Themistocles watching with raised eyebrows. The atmosphere was different, as if they had both stepped off the stage and could be themselves. Aristides had done that, Xanthippus realised. Or his admiration for the man had.

'I have spent the morning with our new archon,' Themistocles said. 'A morning I will not get back.'

Xanthippus glowered, unwilling to be drawn in and wary of criticising Aristides in any way.

'He is the best of us,' he said firmly, ignoring a snort from the other.

'For some, perhaps,' Themistocles said. He shrugged when Xanthippus looked over to him. 'Some men are ruled by greed and stupidity and lust. They would steal a drachm from their own mother, or stamp on the fingers of another man to stop them rising. They are like children in their spite.'

'You are not talking about Aristides!' Xanthippus said, turning to face him in his astonishment.

'No, of course not. Men like those *need* men like Aristides. They need to see that there are those who could be left guarding a room of gold coins and not steal a single one. More, they would starve to death and not lift a crust of bread that was not theirs. Aristides is such a man, I know it. You know it as well. His will . . . his honour – it is like iron. He could run this port of Piraeus, or the whole city, and it would work like a phalanx in perfect formation.'

Xanthippus looked suspiciously at him.

'You admire him then . . .' he said. 'As do I. We need men like . . .'

'But it would be a dead city, with men like Aristides in charge of the laws,' Themistocles went on. He turned to watch the small, slight man making his way to the dockmaster's office. 'Oh, it would run well enough, as a ship can be made to move against the wind. The rowers give their labour and the entire vessel cuts the waves, carrying us all. Aristides can make that happen.'

'Why then a "dead city"?' Xanthippus demanded, growing angry. How was it that every conversation with Themistocles seemed to go this way? The man had the most extraordinary ability to prick at him.

Themistocles shrugged again.

'Men need more than bread and wine, more than lovers, more than gold.'

'You mean the gods?'

To his surprise, Themistocles chuckled.

'I do not. How interesting your mind is, Xanthippus of Cholargos! No, men need ambition. Those like Aristides would be content to maintain, to conserve what we have.'

'That does not seem such an ill thing,' Xanthippus replied.

'The world changes. If you merely repaint and rebuild, the cracks will show eventually. You have seen ruins, my friend, of temples and gates. There are peoples gone before us, who would not change. Who did not have the ambition to stand up and say, "We will make a mark that will *never* be forgotten."'

He had taken on a strange intensity that was almost uncomfortable to witness. Xanthippus watched the gleam of it fade from his eyes. Themistocles shook himself as if waking.

'Either way, I would not want him at my dinner table. He kills laughter with that sour expression of his.'

Xanthippus nodded uncomfortably. In that moment, he was weary of Themistocles.

99

'Well,' he said. 'I am going back to the city. I promised myself I would put in a hard run today.'

Themistocles eyed him, seeing the long limbs and powerful muscles of a man who trained every day in the skills of war.

'May I run alongside, or would you prefer to be alone?'

Xanthippus heard the challenge and he smiled.

'I would be happy to have company, but I warn you, I set a hard pace.'

Themistocles shrugged out of his robe and sandals, pulling his tunic over his head so that he stood naked. Xanthippus was reminded this was a man who loved to wrestle and box. He gleamed with health and Xanthippus wondered if he had overreached. He was no longer young and his knee was already aching. He showed nothing of that.

Themistocles arranged his belongings in a small pile, then whistled down the hill. A slave came trotting up from the docks in answer.

Themistocles nodded.

'Lead on, Xanthippus. I will do my best to keep up with you.'

They set off at an easy lope, each man aware of the other and determined not to lose, even if they died in the attempt.

11

It was the knee that let him down. Xanthippus and Themisto-cles had almost burst their hearts racing all the way back. With the city wall in sight, they'd both broken into a sprint, pound-ing the earth road and spattering drops of sweat as they went. Xanthippus had felt his knee give way as if an iron spike had been driven through it. He'd lost speed, reduced to a hobble. He'd forced himself on even then, though Themistocles had pulled ahead without looking back. Some of those taking ox-carts from the port to the city had even cheered the heroes of Marathon, no doubt recognising Themistocles.

The two men ended up panting wildly at the city gate, watched by Scythian archers on the wall. Those metics were employed by the Assembly to keep order on the streets, or sometimes when an argument broke into violence on the Pnyx hill itself. That single space could hold twenty thou-sand, so when currents of anger or discussion became too rough, bloodshed was not uncommon.

Themistocles chuckled as Xanthippus joined him. They were both red-faced, but recovered quickly, though it nearly strangled them to give that impression.

'You are limping,' Themistocles noted. 'Though I give thanks for it. I was fading when you slowed down.'

'It's nothing,' Xanthippus said. He did not want to give anything like an excuse. Themistocles had won their race. He would not complain about it.

'I know the gymnasiarch by the Ilissus river – just a few stades from here. The new place. He'll make us welcome. He ought to, he is Leontis tribe – and he stood with me at Marathon.'

Xanthippus hesitated, rather than refuse. He needed to be rubbed down and oiled if he was to walk at all the next day. His knee felt like it was on fire and he could see the muscles fluttering around it. Yet his preferred gym was either the Academy, to the north, or one to the east of the city. More, he didn't want to feel indebted to Themistocles. Sweat dropped from the tip of his nose, making him rub his face with one hand. On impulse, Xanthippus nodded and Themistocles led the way, already breathing well.

'Age is a cruel thing,' Themistocles said. 'It takes all we have, little by little.'

Xanthippus felt his irritation grow.

'It is just an old wound,' he said tightly.

'It comes to us all,' Themistocles murmured, almost to himself.

Xanthippus raised his eyes to the heavens, asking for patience.

The gymnasiarch greeted Themistocles like a long-lost brother, crying out his name as he passed the gate and the cool outer cloisters to enter the main field. The river that ran alongside had been guided in a stream through sheltered groves, while the running track was new and clean. It was hard not to compare it with the peeling paint and weeds of the Academy. Xanthippus was impressed too by the care they received. He and Themistocles were laid down and mas-saged in oil, then rubbed clean with dulled blades of bronze or ivory. Dirty oil was flicked into a cauldron at the foot of the tables, where dark spirals mingled with gold as they separated. The smell was a little rank and Themistocles asked a slave to move it away, where the odour would not disturb him.

'You know, Aristides will not pay for new oil. Have you heard that?' Themistocles said. 'He uses the free drippings, no matter how foul they are.'

Xanthippus frowned as he lay on his back and watched his leg raised. The slave holding it was examining the knee with a critical eye. Xanthippus took a deep breath when the man began to work his thumbs into the surfaces of the joint, pressing fluid away where it had gathered. The pain was excruciating and it helped to talk rather than cry out. That he would not do, not in front of Themistocles.

'He does not like waste, then. Perhaps that is wise,' Xanthippus said through gritted teeth. His tone was strained enough to make Themistocles look up.

'Is your knee troubling you?' he asked.

Xanthippus waited a beat.

'It will be fine. Thank you for this, Themistocles.'

The big man waved a hand.

'I love this place. Whatever it costs me is worth it. Would you like wine? Half and half? Or one and three?'

Despite his reservations, Xanthippus agreed to the latter. He sat up to drink, so that the slaves working on his legs knelt before him. Further back, he watched pairs of wrestlers throw and hurt each other with fine ferocity. Themistocles observed them with a more expert eye, calling out congratulations when one move sent a man flying. The losing wrestler stood with his wrist held in the other hand, clearly broken. He beamed when he saw who praised him even so, before retiring to have it splinted and wrapped.

'I wonder if you appreciate this place as I do,' Themistocles said.

Xanthippus looked up as he finished his wine and lay on his stomach. Two men still worked on his legs while another huge fellow leaned onto the muscles of his back. With his

elbows, by the feel of it. Xanthippus grunted, prepared to
endure.

'I believe I do,' he replied.

'I don't know,' Themistocles said. 'You were born to the
Eupatridae. Your people had land, and land . . . well, it is
freedom, of a sort. With land, a man knows he will never
starve. He has a refuge when the world turns against him.
Gates he can shut, slaves to guard his walls. He has peace.
Your father was a wealthy man, was he not?'

'He was,' Xanthippus admitted warily.

'And your wife's family – by Athena, they have been rich
since the *Iliad*! You know Aristides worked with your wife's
uncle, Cleisthenes? Did you know that? He admired him
greatly, Xanthippus. Who can blame him? Cleisthenes –
the man who named the ten tribes, who set up the Assembly
and the council! What a mark he left, of greatness, on the
world.'

'And is that what you want?' Xanthippus said.

He wished Aristides were there to hear the arguments and
respond. He never seemed at a loss for words the way Xanthippus sometimes felt. Themistocles lay on the table with
his hair unbound and his limbs massive, like a lion enjoying
the sun. His skin was still reddened after the exertion of the
run. Yet he lolled, supremely at ease.

'I want the best for Athens,' Themistocles said after a time.

The truth lay somewhere beneath the words, Xanthippus
could sense, or perhaps it was simply that Themistocles saw
the best of the city in himself.

'I was born just outside the city, in the village of Phrear-
rhioi. Do you know it?'

Xanthippus nodded, though he kept his eyes closed. The
village was not wealthy, if that was the point. He recalled it
as clean enough, with fields of barley and wheat all around.

There were places in Athens so tightly packed the sun never reached the ground. It was strange to think of Themistocles as a man of open fields, when he seemed to fit city streets so well. Xanthippus wondered how such a beginning had produced the one who lay at ease alongside him. Perhaps, like the ridged muscles of his chest and stomach, Themistocles had taken what the gods had given and crafted something from it.

With a 'fwit' sound, old oil was flicked into a new wooden tub, leaving spatters of muck on the dusty ground. Fresh oil of clear gold was brought, with the massaging slaves dipping their hands into it. Out on the wrestling rings, dust stuck to the athletes as they panted. They would not strike true blows, even when their temper frayed. A boxing match would result and those were darker and more brutal than the wrestling ring. When he heard steps growing louder, Xanthippus considered sitting up once again to watch rival teams of runners lap the track. He decided against it. The day was too fine, the air too sweet. He raised his cup for more wine and leaned back against a leather and wood block placed to support his head. He murmured thanks to the man who worked on his knee. The pain was easing and he was grateful.

'My father was Neocles,' Themistocles went on, 'a man of no great estate or achievement. His parents disowned him and he never told me why, though I think it was probably for violence. My mother feared him, I remember that. He died when I was eleven years old, leaving my mother to raise me with little help. She brought me into Athens and we lived near the Ceramicus. Abrotonon was her name, a little blonde woman of Thrace, alone in this city without sisters or friends. Can you imagine? She worked every hour of the sun to keep us. I remember once I broke a pot – just a simple little thing, kiln-fired in blue. To me it was nothing, but she wept as she cleared up the shards. She could not replace it, though better pots than that are thrown out every day!'

He fell quiet for a time and Xanthippus wondered if the rumours were true that his mother had turned to work in the brothels to earn a wage. She had kept herself out of debt and so avoided slavery, which spoke well for her character. Xanthippus could not imagine a childhood of the sort Themistocles was describing and swallowed uncomfortably.

'We lived for a while in peace,' Themistocles said. His voice had gentled in memory. 'I loved to make her laugh. I might have ended my days as one of the boxers in a place like this. I trained in two of them for years, did you know that? In return for breaking my nose more times than I can remember, the tutors taught me a few things. I learned my letters, everything I could – anything I needed to raise myself up. From poverty, from . . . being commanded. I studied it all. When I had a little money, I hired tutors to teach me numbers and writing and argument and construction. Each step led to more and more. Do you see, Xanthippus? I listened to the orators in the Assembly. I watched and I learned – and I trained myself, body and mind. I became expert and I sold my advice and my crafts to others. I wrote speeches for strategoi and archons to give the Assembly – and we won our cases. We changed the laws. I think I hardly slept from the age of twelve to thirty, just about.'

'Does she still live, your mother?' Xanthippus asked. When there was no response, he opened his eyes to see Themistocles had his head raised on another shaped block, while a grizzled-looking fellow worked his legs back and forth, twisting the hips in their sockets until they moved as they should. It was as uncomfortable to watch as to have it done, Xanthippus knew.

'She died a few years ago now. The following year, the

Assembly made me eponymous archon. Can you believe that? She never saw it. She never knew there was a year named for her son, so that all Athens called it the year of Themistocles. There was no earthquake then, to steal the honour from me, no great flood or battle.' His voice changed subtly as his throat closed in sudden grief. 'I wish she had seen that.'

Tears showed in his eyes as he looked back. Xanthippus remained silent. He didn't know why Themistocles was sharing these intimacies with him. He found himself fascinated, but also stung somehow, as if he would have to defend his own easier youth and childhood. They had walked different paths, of course, but they were both there on that day in Athens, being rubbed down and drinking the same wine and water. Did it matter which path they had walked to reach that place?

'She would be very proud,' Xanthippus said.

'Yes. So when I hear Aristides saying being the named archon doesn't mean anything to him, that it is all a form of vanity, I think . . . I think perhaps he is a man who has known ease. I wonder how much he can truly understand of the lives of common men in Athens.'

'How much can any of us understand of other lives?' Xanthippus said. 'I see you – and I have listened to you. I know you are a man of influence and authority. I saw it at Marathon, in the way you spoke to the men.'

He noted the surprise in Themistocles to hear that. The man was convinced he and Xanthippus were too different to understand one another.

'Yet I see quiet dignity in Aristides,' Xanthippus went on.

'Arrogance,' Themistocles muttered, settling back.

Xanthippus hoped that was not aimed at him, though Themistocles was subtle enough to insult them both in a single word.

107

'Not at all. He makes a virtue of abstinence, of discipline. Men see that. He is a fine leader for this city.'

'More like a Spartan than an Athenian,' Themistocles said. Again, he had phrased it so that Xanthippus could not know whether he meant himself or Aristides.

'There are virtues in both!' Xanthippus snapped. He heard Themistocles sit up to respond, swinging his legs over once more.

'Oh, I know that,' Themistocles said. 'Though I have never enjoyed their . . . superiority, the way some men – of Sparta or Athens – believe they are a better breed, that better blood runs in their veins.' He shrugged. 'It brings me to anger sometimes. Aristides the Just, they call him, for his decency and his honour. Yet he has never known fear or starved. Can such a man truly lead this city?'

'He starves every day!' Xanthippus said. 'He wears a ragged robe and patched sandals and refuses all trappings of wealth. I have seen him make a meal from the scales and fish guts the fishermen leave on the docks. You said yourself he uses no clean oil at the gymnasia, only the leavings.'

'Yet he has estates and lands as great as your own. He disdains wealth, but he has more than any thousand of his fellows. To walk in rags? There is a colossal arrogance there. It grates on me.'

'Are you so different?' Xanthippus heard himself say. It was as close to an insult as he had ever come and he regretted it. Themistocles did not seem annoyed by it, but answered calmly.

'I know as well as Aristides what is valuable – and what is not. But I am of the people of Athens, Xanthippus. In all my labours, when I wrote legal arguments for others, I never refused my service to a man who had nothing. I demanded fortunes from archons of the Areopagus, when they wanted a will or to dispute a ruling of the Assembly or the courts. But if a man came to me in fear of his landlord, or because he would be made a slave by dawn for his debts, I worked through the night and I asked nothing for it. I have never forgotten what poverty feels like, Xanthippus. Aristides plays at my youth, yet sneers at my love of wine and food and good things in the same breath.'

He made a snorting sound, like a dog with water up its nose.

'I raised myself up from nothing!' he said. 'Which is a grand tale, is it not? They know it, the people of the city. When they see me, they see themselves. When the Assembly discusses building a new temple, they call for master builders and they listen to them speak – of costs, of the calculations and materials of their trade. Yet when they discuss how best to run the city, any man may speak. The same master builder might stand alongside the archons – and he will be heard. They listen to me then, Xanthippus, because they have learned to value the advice I give. Is that not wonderful? Without the right family, could I have risen so far in Sparta, in Thebes or Corinth? You know the answer. Yet here, I am known. It is why I was made eponymous archon over my peers, over men even like Aristides, who had to wait another three years for an honour I had *first*.'

There was bitterness in Themistocles. Xanthippus could see it, could hear it in his voice. Bitterness and pain and insecurity. Xanthippus wondered at the depth of it, even as he saw humour and amusement return to eclipse all the rest. The man knew himself and so he could laugh at his own weaknesses and never be surprised by them. It made him dangerous perhaps. Xanthippus was not sure.

'You see these men around us?' Themistocles said idly. 'Two metics from Thrace, foreigners brought to this gymnasium at great cost for their skill. Three more who are slaves, owned by the establishment. Two of them were born not a street from where I lived with my mother. Deneos here worked in the markets selling figs – and himself on occasion, before he came here. Now, I own a share of this place and I got him the job, so if I ask him to cut your throat, would you survive?'

Xanthippus froze. It seemed in that moment as if all those around him were watching him closely, waiting for him to respond. Themistocles laughed.

'You should see your face!' he said. 'These are your people too. They know you fought for them at Marathon. You are a hero, Xanthippus, just as I am. We are great men – achievers. Aristides does not stand over me in the esteem of this city, nor Miltiades.'

Xanthippus threw him a sharp glance at that, but Themistocles was once more watching the wrestling. After a while in silence, he spoke again, his voice less urgent and a smile ready on his lips.

'Now, I am for a dip in the pool, then a little food – perhaps a different kind of wrestling at the brothel inside the wall. There are new women there, I'm told, fresh off the boat from some strange place where they have never known the touch of men. It won't be true, of course, but it would be amusing to see them act the role, would it not? Every night, a virgin remade. Will you accompany me, Xanthippus? I find I have an appetite.'

It was all perfectly judged. Xanthippus felt overwhelmed, threatened and flattered by the trust and torrent of words, all while the evening sun shone warm on them both and white stone columns edged where they lay.

'That is enough now, thank you,' he said to the slaves around him.

Having felt the implied threat from them, Xanthippus

realised he could no longer lie down and let strong hands knead away swelling. Pain, after all, reminded him he was alive. He stood up from the benches and tested the knee. It was much improved. He took a silver drachm from his cheek and tossed it to the one who had worked the joint. It was half a day's wage and the man beamed and bowed as he left.

'You say we walked a different path to get here, to this place,' Xanthippus began. 'Though neither you nor I chose the steps we would follow. Perhaps Aristides is the most honest, as he has chosen poverty as a noble attribute – a life lived without waste or extravagance. I admire him for his certainty. You, though, Themistocles. What to make of you?'

He leaned against the bench once again, crossing his legs at the ankles, one hand across his chest and the other upright, supporting his chin on the palm. He regarded Themistocles as if he were a puzzle to be solved.

'Nothing at all,' Themistocles said. 'I have made myself all I am. Time, the favour of the gods and my own efforts. I need no other sculptors at this late stage.'

'Agreed. We'll make our free choices as men – as Aristides does, as we could not when we were young. I did not choose my tutors, nor the skills they taught me. Like you, I made the most of what I was given. I am what I have made of myself, with all the advantages my father could win for me – and all the influence that comes from wealth. Has my path brought me your way with people? Your golden touch? I do not believe it has. You and I are not the same. Yet I am a man of Athens and I see honour in you, just as I see it in Aristides. As I hope you see in me.'

'And Miltiades?' Themistocles asked suddenly.

Xanthippus felt himself freeze. By the gods, the man was as sharp as a razor! He needed to guard himself at all times with Themistocles. He inclined his head, speaking as one who knew there were other ears listening.

'He and I have settled our differences, Themistocles. The Assembly love him.'

'Yes,' Themistocles said, looking dissatisfied. 'Yes, they do. Will you come to watch the new ships blessed, when they are ready to sail?'

'Of course,' Xanthippus said. 'I will watch the sacrifices and drink water and wine and cheer with all the rest. Athens is my city. All that is good for her is good for me.'

'A fine thought,' Themistocles said softly. 'Come, then. Dine with me and take your ease. Perhaps I can persuade you to support me over Aristides when it matters. There is more to debate than just our styles and choice of oil. Come on. You are amongst friends here.'

Xanthippus thought that was not so. He could not say exactly why he didn't trust Themistocles, but there it was. Perhaps it was just that the man liked to win, and that to win, someone always had to lose. Still, he would learn all he could, even if that meant an evening guarding his tongue, in the company of whores and vipers.

Agariste woke as knocking sounded. She stared at the ceiling for a few blurry moments. Had one of the children cried out? The thumping sounded again and she saw light bloom as one of the slaves lit lamps from the fire's embers. The gleam came bobbing down the corridor towards her room. She sat up, letting the cover spill away from her breasts. No light where Xanthippus slept, so he had not returned.

One of the children began to cry, though she could not tell whether it was little Pericles or his sister. She firmed her mouth and rose from the bed. The staff would answer any call at the door and decide whether the mistress of the house should be woken. As if anyone could sleep through such knocking! Her mind filled with threats: Xanthippus dead, an invasion by the Persians, the city aflame with riots and insurrection. With a curse, she wrapped a robe around her and padded out into the main house.

The slave quarters had been dug into the foundations below the family rooms, so that she glimpsed frightened faces in the doorways. They had not dared to light their own lamps before the mistress allowed it. They waited as shadows, helpless to fate as their station demanded. Agariste clenched her jaw as she walked, wishing one of them had the sense to soothe the crying child. She had recognised the voice of Pericles by then. It was hard not to feel anger for whichever fool had chosen to wake the entire house, at Hera knew what hour of the night.

Of the fifty-four slaves in her household, just six had been trained with weapons to defend the women and children. Those men worked as cooks and masons and carpenters, but when the mistress was threatened, they took up swords and leather armour and stood before her. Others of the staff brought lamps to throw light upon the scene. They gathered between the main house and the wall by the road, falling in around Agariste as she came striding out. She showed no fear to them when the light washed across her. She was Athena, who wore a warrior's helmet. She drew herself up and hid the terror that made her tremble and her knees want to fold.

The most senior slave of her household was Manias, who had served her father and known her as a little girl. He had helped Xanthippus with his weapons and armour before going out to Marathon. With a blade in his hand, he stood by the iron gate and nodded to the mistress of the house, ready for her command. The road was hidden behind it, but a slot could be opened. There was a risk of a spear-thrust, of course, which was why he looked to her for orders.

'See who it is, Manias,' Agariste said, the breath catching cold in her throat.

He opened the slot and peered out. Standing behind him, Agariste saw the man's shoulders dip and the tension go from his grip on the sword.

'It is the master,' Manias said.

Agariste might have replied, but a voice bellowed outside.

'Door! What, are you all deaf? Open the door.'

Agariste did not release the others, though she signalled to Manias to pull back the bolts that ran from the iron door into the wall itself. It was unforgivable for Xanthippus to wake the family in this way.

The door opened and then shuddered as Xanthippus half-fell through it, held upright by two strangers. They seemed crudely amused rather than embarrassed. Agariste drew her robe more tightly around her as they tried to bow and not drop her husband at the same time. She could smell wine and vomit on them all and she raised a hand to her mouth.

'Where would you like him, mistress?' one of the men slurred at her, choosing to wink for some reason.

'I would like him left in the gutter,' she said. 'However, as you have woken my entire household to bring him in, leave him on that bench there and depart. Manias – give them a drachm apiece for their trouble, would you?'

Manias found two silver coins and passed them to the delighted men, who thanked him profusely. Xanthippus lolled on the bench with his head tilted back, already asleep. The other two stood in the doorway, looking blearily around themselves.

'Might there be something to eat as well?' one of them asked.

'No,' Agariste said. 'Are you slaves?'

Her manner to them would depend on their station, of course. In the half-light, it was hard to tell, as both young men were dressed simply, without rings. She was relieved when they nodded. She had been at a disadvantage before, but that vanished.

'You have my gratitude. And who is your master, to have brought my husband home in such a state?'

'Archon Themistocles, madam,' one of them said proudly. 'He has bought a brothel.'

'Wonderful,' Agariste said. 'This was in the nature of a celebration, then, was it?'

Both men nodded, though one of them was looking pale, as if he might be ill once more.

'Return to your master, with my thanks,' she said, as gently as she could.

She showed no further sign of her irritation at them, or her fury at her husband. They beamed at her and allowed Manias to push them back into the road. The gate was closed and locked and they could be heard singing as they wandered back towards the city.

12

The meeting of the Assembly was called with the low notes of conch shells reverberating over the city. Though the sun approached noon, the people of Athens barely paused in their labours. If anything, the bustling markets in the open Agora became a touch more frenzied as voting men tried to finish their purchases, pressing parcels of food into the arms of slaves. Those few women of the upper classes who were out on the streets stood back from crowds or turned for home, knowing from experience how they could be manhandled in a crush. Poorer women had no such restraints on their comings and goings. Some of them in the market stalls bawled even lower prices, trying to catch bargain hunters in the last moments before they had to leave.

Epikleos and Xanthippus were seated on the edge of the Pnyx hill, a few paces from the speaker's stone, the favoured spot already busy with clusters of men. Neither of them had contested a place on the flat rock that raised speakers the height of a man above the rest. They'd been summoned to a regular meeting, long scheduled. As if on a normal day, they'd greeted one another with the traditional 'What news?'. The truth was the news had already spread so far and fast that few making their way in had to be informed. The prospect of great wealth was exciting, like wine in the blood. It could be seen in the whites of the eyes, heard in nervous laughter.

Little by little, the Pnyx began to fill with young and old, drawn by curiosity and pride, by heralds and the conch notes, even a sense of civic duty.

'I wonder if they'll need the red ropes in the Agora today,' Epikleos said to his friend. He nodded as Xanthippus began to retort. 'Yes, of course they will. Our people do not like to be told what to do, even when it is for their benefit. The gods bless them for it.'

The Pnyx hill sat high above the valley that had the Agora at its heart, with stone steps wide enough for thousands to sit and listen to speakers. On normal days, it was not uncommon for just six or seven thousand to attend the meetings, barely enough to decide new laws or cases. On days like this, upwards of twenty thousand would pack themselves in.

With the news from Laurium, members were making their way in from demes outside the city as well as every part of it. Athenians being what they were, there were still stragglers, deep in conversation or bargaining for whatever goods or favours they had been trying to purchase.

The team of public slaves employed by the Assembly began the work they clearly enjoyed – dipping long looping ropes in red paint to herd the last voters up the hill. Depending on the public mood and the insults called to them, they could make it hard or easy to avoid. No one wanted to be touched by paint that would mark any item of cloth for ever – and skin for a week or more. Those red stripes were always cause for laughter and comment whenever they were seen, with men called 'laggard' or 'slowfoot', to the amusement of others with no voting rights at all.

Some slaves would always be caught in the red ropes. Neither they, nor women and children, nor the foreign metics had the right to vote, and so they were released, like smaller fish back into the ocean. Only voting males over eighteen remained. There were perhaps thirty thousand of those in Athens – three times the number that had stood at Marathon. From the ten tribes of the city, the Assembly appointed

117

a council, with officials and magistrates – and the epistates, chairman for the day, chosen by lot. It was said that any man over the age of thirty could rule Athens for a day, if he truly wanted. In constant flux, the system was designed to make a tyrant impossible. Depending on his mood and the quality of arguments, Xanthippus both detested and loved it, for all its chaos and its earnestness.

A ram was sacrificed by the speaker's stone, then carried, head down, by two sweating priests around the boundary, so that its blood trail marked a solemn line. Those within would make the laws that ruled them. Those without would obey those laws. They might allow no individual tyrants, but the judgments of the Assembly were cut into stone and displayed in the Agora. There, anyone could read them, metic, woman or slave, if they had knowledge of letters or a coin to have them read aloud.

'Who is epistates today?' Xanthippus murmured to his friend.

They both eyed the man climbing the steps to the speaker's stone. The title was the one they both knew from the phalanx – 'He who stands behind'. On the Pnyx, it was meant as a reminder that whoever led the city was also a servant of the people. This one was a stranger to them both and Epikleos shrugged.

'Pandionis tribe have the chair this month. I don't know them well. Leontis are due next, so I imagine we'll see Themistocles busy as a bee then. I see he is on the stone today. No surprise after this news. Aristides too.'

'There'll be a clash, then. Those two cannot agree on the days of the week.'

The man on the speaker's stone beamed out at the packed thousands of his people, gathered to hear the business of the day. Xanthippus raised his eyes for a moment.

'I wonder sometimes if there isn't a better way than this,' he said out of the side of his mouth.

Epikleos turned to him, smiling sardonically. It was a conversation they'd had before – one that all men of Athens had when they were in their cups.

'We've tried tyrants,' Epikleos said. 'Whenever a man of our class complains about the new rules, he always seems to imagine himself as the font of new laws. "Oh, the things I would do!" he says. It doesn't work, Xan. Bad tyrants always follow good ones. That much power over other men . . . it does not bring out the best in us. A lad can hardly sit on a throne without demanding a dozen young wives in his personal harem! Why should we endure another tyrant, no matter how well-meaning? The people would revolt against it now. I tell you, Xan. We sent the last one into exile and we could just as easily have killed him. Hippias was a man out of time, without even the sense to know it.'

'Who will speak?' the epistates bellowed over the heads of the assembled men.

There was a ripple of conversation, more serious than on some days. Any one of them could reply, if he found supporters in the crowd. Of course, if a brawl began, or a speaker offended the gods, the Scythian archers stood by to bear him off.

Xanthippus shook his head.

'There has to be a middle ground between tyrants and this – a new leader every day of the year.'

'"Every man can rule in Athens, at least for a day,"' Epikleos said softly. 'And of course the council of the Areopagus has power. The archons understand the people better than they do themselves.'

'Perhaps,' Xanthippus replied. 'There are some who would deny them a voice, as if no man's opinion is worth more than any other! If we ever go so far, Epikleos . . . Even now, listen to them!' He paused as arguments erupted and swelled across the Pnyx. Xanthippus shook his head. 'This is . . . messy.'

His friend sighed.

'There is nothing like this in the world, Xan. It may be messy, but it is wonderful.'

Xanthippus looked at him in surprise.

'You really have changed your mind? When, after Marathon?'

'Not then! Where were these when we marched out? Not half the voting males know one end of a spear from another. No, if I were harder than I am, I would say either fight for your city or be ruled by those who did! No, I was discussing the tyrannies with Aristides . . .'

Xanthippus tapped him on the arm. Themistocles had answered the call, climbing to the speaker's stone so that he would be heard. Raised above the crowd, with the Acropolis on his right hand to inspire him, his words would carry to everyone there. The epistates looked formally for supporters, concerned with his duties. Voices called out, hands held high to second Themistocles in his right to speak. His opponents raised no objection, seemingly content to let him begin. The sacrifices had all been made, the prayers to Athena and Apollo given. The leader for the day took his seat as Themistocles cleared his throat and opened the meeting.

'My friends, my brothers, Athenians. Every one of you will have heard the miners at Laurium have found a new seam – a thread of silver and lead ore as rich as anything we've seen before.' A ripple of astonishment went around the Assembly and Themistocles laughed out loud. 'Will you pretend to be surprised? Athenians, I know what you know. There are, what, ten thousand men working that mine?

More? This was never news that could be kept secret, not from the first moments. The whispers have gone round and the wealth belongs to us all. We of Athens are richer today than we have been before.'

They cheered him, or perhaps the idea. More, they went along with his assessment that they had all known the news. Xanthippus thought there would surely have been some who had not heard. Yet they would laugh along with the rest, delighted to be included. In that way, with just a few words, Themistocles made them all one. Epikleos grinned back at Xanthippus for his saturnine expression.

'If we were Spartans,' Themistocles went on, 'we would spend the silver on new barracks and . . . stones or pillars of iron. If men of Thessaly, we would surely buy horses. Men of Corinth, perhaps sheep or goats. Who knows? There are around thirty thousand men of voting age in Athens. I could have the demarchos of each of the hundred demes provide the exact tally. Perhaps we'll need to, when we've decided what to do with this gift of the gods. Twenty thousand foreign metics will not take a share, of course. All the women and children number some two hundred thousand, slaves around the same. Now, the wages for a working man are two drachms a day, just over seven hundred a year.'

He had the attention of the crowd, rapt as he plucked figures from the air. Xanthippus and Epikleos shared a wry glance. To qualify as Eupatridae, both men had to own or control lands that earned a fortune in grain – or silver, when it was sold. The new mine would not affect their lives in any great way. Yet they could see the gleam of avarice in the crowd, the sparkle of excitement. For many there it would mean a real change of fortune.

'What is his intention?' Epikleos murmured. 'He trusts you, Xan, or he would like to. Has he discussed this?'

Xanthippus shook his head as Themistocles went on, his voice strong and clear.

'The new mine could bring as much as a year's wage to every one of you, so I have been told. I have been to the site and seen the new trenches. Thousands more will find work cutting into the earth there. If you or your relatives have ever feared starvation, be assured of that – there will be work at Laurium. I tell you this because I know Aristides will be honest with you. He will tell you to take the silver from the earth, to refine it and stamp it in drachms and tetradrachms, to feed your families and build new homes. He will tell you to employ carpenters and tilers and buy meat and cheese and wooden toys for your children. He will say that such an amount of silver brought into the city will change hands many times, creating value and labour where there was none before. Aristides believes there is benefit to us all in such a find. In that, he and I are in perfect accord. Athenians will benefit, but in freedom, not in tiles and bricks and better roads.'

There was a rumble of discontent and Themistocles raised his hands, laughing along with them.

'Oh, I know, the roads are terrible. We should pave them. Perhaps Aristides will tell you to do just that when he speaks. After all, when the Persians march into Athens, they will be delighted to find good roads, with fine, flat stones to make the surface!'

He waited for a ripple of nervous laughter to end, then spoke more seriously.

'In Athens, we make our wealth in trade. We sell oil and figs and clay jars from our kilns. We import fish, barley and wheat for our bread. Our life's blood is in sea salt, dried on the sails of our ships, in the shine of old wood on the docks. The port of Piraeus is what separates us from men of Corinth, or soldiers of Sparta, or the horse-traders of Thessaly. We are seafarers, and we are a sovereign people, as Homer himself described us.'

He paused. His large head sank, as if in prayer, though his eyes stared into the distance.

Xanthippus blinked slowly, watching the man perform. The only sound was the susurration of the breeze and the flutter of robes. Xanthippus thought it was probably his imagination that he could smell the sea. When Themistocles raised his head again, it felt like a sacred moment had passed.

'What ships do we command now?' he asked. 'Miltiades took seventy triremes and the crews and hoplites to man them. Barely two dozen remain to patrol all our waters, to answer any threat that may arise. Yet those of us who marched to Marathon saw the fleets of Persia and their Phoenician allies. We saw sails and oars then, two, three hundred ships, more – all carrying horses and men. Creeping along our coasts unchallenged. Landing where they chose, threatening all we have, all we could ever have. If Aristides will stand and argue for roads and temples, ask him this: What good will they be when the Persians return? Unless you believe the Persians will not, of course – that a Great King who had never known defeat will take the blow we dealt him at Marathon and retire from our affairs! If you believe that, I have a pot to sell you, one Heracles himself used to own.'

He smiled with the crowd, but then became utterly serious, his brows lowering into a thunderous expression.

'The silver at Laurium is a gift from the earth – and from the gods. None of us expected it – nor have we done much to deserve such wealth. If we vote to split the silver between us, we will each have enough to buy a few baubles – a new roof, a new gate, stones for the road, or a slave. Such things are worth having. Such things will be valued by our enemies when they come! I ask instead that the new silver be added to a common fund, administered by officials of this Assembly to lay down new keels – a fleet the like of which this city has never known. One hundred, two hundred ships, whatever we can build and crew.'

He began to count points on his fingers, his right hand splayed before the left.

'Employment of craftsmen to build them – with stalls and markets springing up wherever they buy food and tools. Two hundred oarsmen and fifty hoplites to a craft – all young men earning enough to support a new family at home. Can you see it? The city growing in health and wealth and strength? Piece by piece, that wealth will come back into Athens – for food, for bricks, for tiles, for slaves. All I ask . . . is that we make it into ships *first*, before all the rest. You will have it back in time. Give it first to the wind and the sea – and it will save us all.'

Some of them cheered him, while others merely nodded, or stood in groups to discuss the idea. It took some time for the epistates to bring order and call for another speaker. A dozen hands rose, a few with friends willing to push them forward. Yet Aristides stood apart, surrounded by at least a hundred of his supporters. When he raised his hand and gathered in the folds of his cloak and robe, the others fell silent, allowing him to come forward. Themistocles descended to the ground as Aristides climbed the stone steps. Neither man looked at the other as they passed.

From the height of the stone, Aristides took a slow breath of warm, afternoon air, looking out over thousands of heads. The name 'Pnyx' meant 'packed in'. It was certainly true that day. All of Athens seemed to be there, watching.

After the broad shoulders and gestures of Themistocles, Xanthippus thought Aristides seemed a slight figure in comparison, more a scholar or a teacher than a fiery orator. The man's robe and cloak were worn, with the hem ragged and trailing threads that had darkened. His beard too was wild in places, though he looked healthy, both tanned and strong. As Aristides stood before the crowd, he raised one hand to his mouth and rubbed his second finger back and forth across his lips, his teeth showing. Whispers that had sprung up fell silent to hear him. Even those who agreed most strongly with Themistocles would not try to drown him out. It was a rare event for the epistates to have the Scythian archers step in to remove a speaker, for which Xanthippus was grateful. Beyond actual blasphemy, a man would always be heard.

'Themistocles speaks well – and he is a noble man,' Aristides began. 'On another day, I might have expected to hear his voice calling for this new silver to be spent on a feast for all Athens, or a shining force of cavalry, or shields and swords for another ten thousand of our young men. Of course, if the money owned in common is paid out, the choice will lie with those who receive it.'

He paused to let that idea sink in before going on.

'That is the only true freedom, I think. To spend what you have earned with the sweat of your brow, the ache of your back and the calluses of your hands. To spend your coins, or to bury them in a hole in the ground. To waste them on pleasure, gifts or alms for the poorest. Perhaps we would disagree which of those is foolish and which wise, it does not matter. If the money is in my hands, the choice of how to spend it is mine. If in your hands, the choice is yours – and you will have made a child of me.'

Aristides smiled gently, as if in reproof. He widened his stance and opened his arms to embrace all those who watched and listened.

125

'My friends, one thing is certain. If you are given a month's pay in silver — sixty drachms to hold, you will know the value of that sum. If you wish, you will purchase goods to that value, neither over nor under. If it is food, it will be sixty drachms' worth of food. If it is wood or the tiles Themistocles mentioned, it will be sixty drachms' worth of wood and tiles. If it is whores, it will be sixty drachms' worth of experience!'

He waited through the laughter and crude comments his words drew from them. He was like a fisherman in the responses he pulled out of the crowd, sending his hooks flying far. Xanthippus glanced across to where Themistocles stood pretending he was enjoying the reply. His smile was fixed and his eyes were slightly narrowed.

'I don't think Themistocles likes the way this is going,' Epikleos whispered at his side.

Xanthippus nodded, but Aristides was speaking again before he could say anything more.

'If you hand your sixty drachms to the Assembly to buy these new ships in a year or two, will you get sixty drachms' worth in return? Or will it go to the salaries of other men, administrators and officials perhaps? Will it go to feed the carpenters, or the teams cutting pine trees in the mountains? No doubt they will be well shod and have fine coats this winter, but what will *you* see for your coins? Will you come down to the docks to watch the ships built — and point to a single rib or beam and say with pride, "That piece there. That is mine." Perhaps. But I have never yet seen a great work spend its funds as efficiently as a man who values the coins he has earned.'

'What about the Persians?' a voice called from somewhere near the middle. Whoever had spoken was nowhere near Themistocles. Xanthippus wondered, though. It was not beyond the man to have salted the crowd with his own supporters.

Aristides flowed on as if he had planted the man himself, which was also possible. He and Themistocles opposed one another almost every time the Assembly met. The scores were roughly even and their struggle was the subject of betting and conversation across the city each month, with supporters on both sides coming to blows. Unfortunately, it did mean that Aristides would always speak in opposition, even when Xanthippus thought Themistocles was right, as he did that day. They needed a fleet. The idea was magnificent. Was this why Themistocles had courted his friendship after Marathon? For the first time, he considered speaking himself.

'What of the Persians?' Aristides replied. 'Should we fear them? The Persians have never fought a battle at sea. They are creatures of the land! What good could it possibly do to chase them at sea – at risk of drowning and shipwreck – rather than wait for them to step ashore and destroy them then, on the good earth? That is what we did at Marathon, as Themistocles would do well to remember. My nameless friend, we do not fear Persian ships, any more than we fear their men!'

He pitched it well, so that it felt like a crescendo. Xanthippus saw Themistocles dip his head to hide his fury as many in the crowd cheered. It was an easy point. The victory at Marathon still resounded with them, though a full year had passed. Yet there were many who did not cheer, who remained unmoved. He was not sure Aristides had done enough to sway them, though he had appealed to both hearts and heads.

In the lull, other men signalled they would like to add to the discussion.

'Will you give way?' the epistates asked.

Aristides bowed his head on the instant and stood back from the speaker's rostrum, though he remained on the stone rather than go down.

One by one, speakers were called forward. Some climbed to the steps to declaim breathlessly in support of a fleet, or money in their own pockets. Others called out questions from the floor and received scattered applause for their points, even as the debate moved on.

Aristides came forward once more to answer a specific question, but it was Themistocles who brought forth a cheer as he rose to explain his position. He took questions from the massed gathering and gave them time to judge his replies, so that he found himself deep in the details of his offer.

'Which way will it go?' Epikleos said at Xanthippus' shoulder. 'I could put a tetradrachm on Themistocles and make myself another, at least if I choose the right moment.'

Xanthippus frowned. His father had warned him against gambling from a young age. Having tried it anyway, he'd lost a small fortune and developed a lifelong dislike of those who seemed to have better luck.

'I would not have thought Themistocles had a chance,' he replied, aware of those around who would listen and take his lead. In such a way, a small speech from the floor could raise him to the stone dais. Xanthippus firmed his resolve and went on. 'Before Marathon he would not have swayed this crowd. What was Persia to most of us? Some distant empire. Yet half the men here saw that great fleet. You remember! As much as it galls me, I think Themistocles is right. We have funds no one expected. What better use can there be than this, for Athenians? Ships . . .' He tapped his forehead and raised his hand to be heard.

'Speaker here!' Epikleos said immediately, in support.

More of those who knew Xanthippus cried out his name.

On the speaker's rock, he could see Themistocles watching him, so Xanthippus dipped his head a fraction. Themistocles bent close to the epistates and directed his attention on the instant, pointing Xanthippus out. There was an advantage to being on the stone. When the epistates called his name, Xanthippus found a path opened before him, leading to the steps. He went quickly, ordering his thoughts.

Both Aristides and Themistocles stood back, rather than be seen to crowd him or show favour. Xanthippus had held a number of senior roles over the previous nine years. His wife's uncle had created the very laws that ordered their debates. More importantly, Xanthippus had commanded his tribe in battle. On that authority, he could sway a vote. Both Themistocles and Aristides knew it.

Xanthippus held up his hands and was honoured with silence falling. They gave respect grudgingly in Athens, but all the Marathonomachoi were favoured men.

'Athenians, I speak as Xanthippus of Acamantis tribe. My own experience prompts me to add my words today. You all know our laws: those who have been blessed with wealth support the city in public service. They pay for the construction of a ship, or they pay for a company and a playwright to produce a great work, as patron. Others provide food to those they employ, or sponsor feasts for all the city. I have done these things – and I have benefited from them. Two of the ships that went with Miltiades had my silver in their oars and sails. Yet I do not hold myself apart from you. On this day, we are all of the same class. It follows, then, that Athens can ask any one of us for our service. That is my first point.'

He paused, while a murmur of interest went around the Pnyx hill. Xanthippus clenched his jaw, ordering his thoughts. He had no idea how Themistocles livened them in quite the way he did. Xanthippus had the suspicion that any attempt at humour would be met with funereal silence. He felt himself flush at the thought. Better to press on with arguments.

'My second point is this. A ship lasts – longer than food, or tiles or . . .' He waved a hand, searching for another example.

'New robes,' Themistocles murmured.

Aristides raised an eyebrow at that, wondering if it had been aimed at him.

'New robes . . .' Xanthippus added. 'My triremes will row the Aegean long after I am in my tomb. That is a legacy – and it can belong to all of us. On this day, every man of Athens has the same choice. We must build this fleet.'

The crescendo was a little weak, but Themistocles led the applause, so Xanthippus was able to stand down with good grace. On impulse, he decided not to leave the rock and remained instead as Themistocles approached the speaker's stone once more.

'I give thanks to my friend, Xanthippus of Cholargos deme. His words brought to mind a last point, for those of us who have debated the meanings of the oracle at Delphi.'

Silence returned, so that Xanthippus could hear the breeze ruffle robes once more. He knew Themistocles was far too clever a man to risk being disrespectful, yet there was always the sense that he could bend anything to his will, if he saw a great enough need.

'The priestess of the oracle once told Cleisthenes that "Athens will rely on wooden walls". Do you remember that?'

The crowd murmured agreement – with more than a few pointing to the massive rock that rose above the city. Themistocles looked up at it.

'The Acropolis, yes. That is where the tyrant Hippias barricaded himself against the people – and the Spartan army that came to winkle him out. He thought wooden walls would save him. The oracle gave no details, but I do not think those were the walls the priestess of Apollo meant. They did not save Hippias!' He went on quickly as some in the crowd were already turning to speak to their friends, seeing it before the rest. 'I tell you, the wooden walls are the ships we will build. When Persia returns, we will "rely" on those wooden walls at sea! And the prophecy will be complete.'

Heads nodded in support and Themistocles smiled. He'd worried Xanthippus had stolen the heat out of them with his dry style. Yet the Assembly met four full days a month. They might appreciate grand gestures and crescendos, but they disliked being pushed. At times, dry argument was more persuasive than the most impressive flourishes of rhetoric. The moment was upon them.

'I call for a binding vote,' Themistocles said.

'I second it,' Xanthippus added, though hundreds more answered at the same time. Still, Themistocles acknowledged his contribution, leaning in close to speak.

'You are on the side of right today, Xanthippus. We truly need those ships. It is invigorating, is it not?'

The voting would not be the formal process of scribing a name onto a piece of pottery, but a simple movement to the edges of the Pnyx, the two sides counted and recorded. Xanthippus looked over the men of his city as they made their way to support or deny the motion. They had given up their entire day for this. Some of them would sit all the way through the afternoon and early evening to hear urgent cases in law. Others would bring points of complaint to be judged and settled by smaller groups of their peers. There was nothing like it in the world, and yet there were times when he wished simple deference played a greater part. The Assembly was like a powerful young bullock. It could be steered with a light touch, but it was young and confident and appallingly strong.

'It is . . . impressive,' Xanthippus said at last. 'You think the ships are truly the wooden walls of the prophecy?'

'Of course,' Themistocles said.

Xanthippus wished he had not asked as Themistocles clapped him on the shoulder and headed down to be counted.

The vote was in their favour, with the entire wealth of the new mine going to build more ships than Athens had ever known before. Aristides closed that part of the meeting with a formal acceptance of defeat on the motion. He gave way with gentle good grace, though a faint flush showed along his neck and jaw.

13

Ships were sighted at anchor along the eastern coast of Attica as darkness fell. If Miltiades had hoped to return to the port of Piraeus unnoticed, he would be disappointed. Night came slowly enough in late summer, but even in home waters, the captains would not risk grounding on unseen rocks, instead seeking safe anchorage until the sun rose once more. In half a dozen places along the Attic coast, that first glimpse sent runners away into the long purple twilight. For villages in that region east of Athens, noble houses like the Alcmaeonidae had always paid well for such information. Boys were employed, in their youth and stamina, to bring news of heavy-laden ships or the return of expeditions. Or word of a Persian invasion. Fortunes could be made and lost on that knowledge. While the moon rose and fell, lonely tracks through the mountains echoed to the slap of running feet as those lads earned their pay, racing to be first to the gates of Athens.

The Assembly was called at dawn, with news spreading from street-criers to the ears of those heading to work, or rising to attend trials at the Pnyx and the Areopagus. Though the work of the Assembly paid barely half a day's wage, most men saw it as a privilege. Yet on that morning in autumn, all such lesser tasks would be left undone. Miltiades had been gone from Athens since the beginning of spring – longer than anyone had expected. They had feared reports of a great summer storm smashing their triremes to pieces before they could reach shelter and be pulled clear of the sea's wrath.

Xanthippus came awake with a start when someone touched his arm. He lurched up and put his bare feet to the tiled floor, stifling a groan at the ache in his knee and twinges from his lower back, just above the hip. He had never known a wound there, but something had drawn tight over the previous year. It troubled his sleep.

'What is it?' he hissed.

The slave Manias had brought a clay oil lamp with him. The wick spat and crackled as it shed light. Manias placed it safely on the bedroom table before replying.

'The fleet, master. Miltiades has returned.'

Xanthippus was on his feet in an instant, his aches forgotten. There had been rumours of a disaster. Though Miltiades had gone hunting far from Athens, it was astonishing how news could travel, fishing crew to fishing crew, warship to merchant trader. The sea was wide, but with enough time, news travelled to every cove and inlet along the shores.

'Bring me . . .'

He stopped as he saw a clean chiton robe and sandals draped over the older man's arm. Xanthippus dressed quickly.

'Is Agariste awake?'

Something shifted in the man's expression and Xanthippus wondered if the slave of a previous household could ever be properly loyal to a new master. The law said Manias was his property, but Xanthippus didn't trust the man. A slave who had known Agariste as a little girl would never betray her confidence.

'I believe she did not sleep well, master,' Manias said.

Xanthippus paused in the act of putting a knife under his belt. Did Agariste have a lover? Perhaps Manias was there to distract him while some youth climbed out of a window. Stranger things happened every day in Athens, but he shook his head at the image.

Being disturbed in the night gave him the sense of preparing for war, but if it was just the return of the fleet, they had no more than rumours and gossip fit for the markets. For all he knew, Miltiades could have captured the Persian pay chests and won a great victory. Wild rumours describing plumes of smoke could just as easily be a Persian camp as any ships of Athens. He hoped so.

Xanthippus looked up when he heard one of the children call out nearby. They had their own nannies, of course, but it would not hurt to send Manias as well.

'Are you armed, Manias?' Xanthippus said.

The man's eyebrows rose sharply.

'I have a knife, but I can fetch my sword. Is there a threat to the family, master?'

'None that I know. I have a . . . feeling, a premonition. No more than foolishness, perhaps, but I would be happier to know you were with my children, ready to defend them.'

Manias didn't hesitate, as Xanthippus had known he would not. The older man bowed and rushed away, ready to give his life for the little ones. Xanthippus stared after him. There had been something odd about his reaction before. It was still dark outside – the light had barely begun to change. If Miltiades had truly returned, he would not be back in port until later that morning. He would not reach the Pnyx by the Agora for another hour after that! There was time.

In silence, Xanthippus made his way down the corridor that separated Agariste's bedroom from his own. His feet were light on the floor and he padded along, listening, knowing he made almost no sound.

He had never slept well with another in the bed alongside him. Agariste was the same, so she said. The heat of his body kept her awake. The very poorest men kept the same bed as their wives, but Xanthippus found he slept better alone, as befitted his class. He had the rooms, after all.

When he heard a groan, Xanthippus sprinted the last few steps. He forced himself to stop at her door, straining to hear. There was no honour in that, either, so he knocked and entered, dreading what he would see.

The window was open, with the night's breeze making the room cool. Agariste sat up in bed, a sheet crumpled and drawn up around her knees. She pulled it tighter as he came into the room, suspicion suddenly sour in him as if he had swallowed sulphur.

'What is it, Xan?' she said. 'Why do you look so terrible? Are the children all right? *Xan!* Are the children safe?'

Her concern for them broke through the madness that consumed him, so that he blinked. Only moonlight lit her, but she looked pale in it, like white marble. Shadows gathered around her thighs and one of her feet peeped from under the rumpled sheet.

'They are perfectly well,' he said, his voice grating. Was it warm enough to have the window stand so wide?

'What, then? Is it an invasion?'

It seemed Manias had not brought his news to the mistress of the house. Perhaps he would have gone to her if Xanthippus had not sent him to guard the children. To Xanthippus' eye, Agariste seemed genuinely confused and afraid – and something else, something wrong in her manner. He went to sit on the hard edge of the bed and she drew back a little.

'Why are you so angry?' she said.

Her eyes were dark and wide, her hair spilling in thick curls to her shoulders. She seemed to rock slightly back and forth as she watched him. He could feel her fear and yet he was not certain of the source. If it was guilt, he knew it would be the struggle of his life not to kill her.

'I thought there was an intruder in the gardens,' he said, watching her reaction, hardly trying to make it sound like truth. Nonetheless she gasped.

'I have seen no one. Is that why you are here with such a look?'

'That . . . and the news that Miltiades has returned. His fleet has been sighted.'

'Then we should give thanks to Poseidon for his delivery! That is only good news, Xanthippus. I will get up and see to the children.'

When he didn't move, she clutched her knees tighter.

'I certainly won't sleep now. Leave me to dress, please. I'll join you for a little porridge, or pancakes? Shall I have the cook make them? There is honey, or cheese if you prefer.'

As she babbled, he saw light moving outside the room. The house was waking all around them, with a dozen slaves already busy baking bread and rising to eat before the family. Even news of an invasion would not have prevented their day starting. Xanthippus went into the corridor and called out. The slave who came was a young boy from the stables, being trained to work in the kitchen. He carried an oil lamp with exaggerated care under the master's eye.

'I'll take that,' Xanthippus said. 'Return to your work now.'

The boy dipped right down in reply as Xanthippus took the lamp back to his wife's room. He lit two more from the wick of the first and deep golden light bloomed there.

Agariste had not moved from the bed. That was odd in itself. She sat with her knees outlined under the sheet and shadows pooling around her. Her eyes were huge and dark as she watched him, as a mother hen might watch a fox creeping through a sleeping barn, helpless and silent.

'What is it?' Xanthippus demanded. 'Something is wrong.'

He sat down more firmly on the edge of the bed and

leaned towards her. She did not pull away a second time, almost as if she knew it would reveal guilt. In that moment, he wished he could just reach inside and pluck the truth from her. If she had betrayed him, he needed proof. With nothing more than his own rage and suspicion, if he killed her, her family would destroy him. That was the truth of it.

He sat back.

'I will go out and search for that intruder, my love. I sent Manias to the children. Perhaps you should remain in your rooms until I am sure there is no threat.'

She did look pale, even in the lamplight. Sweat shone on her brow and, as he watched, a bead of it shone along her neck. The night had not been as warm as that, he realised. Suspicion hardened into a ball that swelled in his chest, choking him.

She stared, actually trembling. On impulse, he raised his hand to brush aside a curl of her hair that had fallen forward. His finger left a red smear on her forehead. He froze as he saw his palm was wet.

With a cry of horror, Xanthippus leapt back from the bed. The darkness that had seemed to pool around her was blood. Suddenly, he could smell it in the room, over the burning oil and his wife's perfume.

'What is this? What have you *done*?' he cried.

When she only gaped at him, he reached out and took hold of the sheet, then wrenched it away with all his strength. She tried to cling on to it, but the cloth slipped through her fingers, leaving her naked and bloody, curling into herself. A huge red pool shone wet on the mattress beneath. Her thighs were slimed with it, already dry in places, like red salt-rime.

'What?' he said, opening and closing his mouth. 'Are you hurt? Is it . . . your monthly blood? Tell me, Agariste! What is going on here?'

She was weeping, he saw. In moments, her beauty crumpled and became a sticky mass, tinged in red as she rubbed hard at her nose and eyes.

'I'm sorry, Xan,' she said between sobs. 'I'm so sorry. I just couldn't . . .'

Coldness touched him then, a chill that ran down his legs and made the hairs stand up. He knew women bled every month from an excess, that menstrual blood could make fields more fertile. Somehow, it was the source of life, stopping only when a woman was pregnant or too old to bear a child. He looked at his red-smeared hand and shuddered. He had seen blood before. More, he had seen menstrual rags before, as they were taken out to be buried. They had been spotted, like red coins. This was more like a battle wound, worse than anything he had imagined.

'Why are you *sorry*?' he snapped.

By the gods, should he comfort her? Was she dying? Thoughts of a lover fled from him, leaving him feeling useless in the face of a woman's mysteries.

'Why is there so much *blood*, Agariste? Is it . . . is it always this way?'

She shook her head and curled into a ball. Xanthippus stood over her for a moment, then began to roar for the midwife to be summoned.

A slave went pelting down the road to call the woman out from her own bed. Before she arrived, house slaves had wrapped Agariste in a clean sheet, while removing the others to be burned. Silence and calm greeted the midwife as she bustled in with a huge bag under one arm, clear-eyed and neat as if she had already been awake. Perhaps she had, Xanthippus thought, or perhaps she was used to being summoned by women who bled in the night.

Xanthippus found himself standing in the corridor, sent

away while the midwife examined Agariste. He heard his wife answering questions sleepily, like a child. He began to pace up and down. He could not lose her. She was the master column of his life, the one that held up all the rest. He began to pray to Athena, mother to Athens and all foolish men.

The sun had risen by the time the midwife came out and closed the door quietly behind her. Her face was pinched and serious.

Xanthippus had called for a bowl and cloths to clean his hands and face. The slaves of the house had brought everything he needed to where he stood in the corridor, so that he didn't have to leave that spot. He turned to her, desperate for news.

'Be at peace, Master Xanthippus. Your wife is safe. The bleeding has stopped.'

'Was it . . . a woman's problem? Part of her monthly bleeding?'

He hoped for a nod, but the midwife merely looked away into the distance, weighing how to respond. He considered grabbing her by the arm. His grip had been strengthened by spear and sword and he knew he could make the old bitch cry out. She began to speak before he moved, perhaps sensing his impatience.

'She took a draught. A mixture of herbs that interfere with the natural order of the body.'

Xanthippus felt like he'd been struck, the air rushing out of him.

'Like hemlock? A poison? Did she try to . . .'

'Nothing like that . . . She wanted to be sure she was not pregnant. I would not have recommended such a dose, nor the amount she claims to have drunk, which was surely too much. Pennyroyal and tansy, made into a tea, by her description. It brings on the monthly bleeding – even if . . . if there is a child growing. It ends the pregnancy, but it is dangerous. Sometimes the bleeding does not stop.'

'I see,' Xanthippus said. He nodded to the slave who still stood with towel and copper bowl. 'Find two silver drachms in payment. No, make it four. You have my thanks. Are you able to take payment yourself?'

It was a way of asking if she was a slave or a free woman. She bore no visible brand and her manner was of one used to authority, but it was not always easy to tell.

'I am a free woman, master. But I was not finished. Your wife will need . . .'

'You are dismissed,' Xanthippus said.

Something of his anger shone in his eyes, though he held himself very still. The midwife pursed her lips and nodded once before gripping her bag under her arm like a shield and walking stiffly away. Xanthippus was left in the corridor, staring at his wife's door. Somewhere in the distance, he could hear one of the children crying, either his daughter or Pericles. If he had not been woken with news of the fleet, he might never have known what Agariste was doing. He might even have found her cold and still in her bed, with weeping slaves all around. She had betrayed him, he realised, though not with a lover. With secrecy. Had she been pregnant? It was too much to take in. He thought he could hear sobbing through the door and he almost opened it. For an instant, he pressed his forehead against the wood and then turned and walked away, suddenly brisk. The sun had risen. He would be expected at the Pnyx, to welcome Miltiades home. He went faster and faster through the house, though the noise of sobbing seemed to follow him.

That there would be no great celebration was clear from first light. The remnant of the fleet they had cheered on its way came limping around the coast, seeking the shelter of the Piraeus port. Seventy ships had launched, but barely twenty returned – and they wallowed as their oars dipped and tugged at the waves, dragging them home. By the time they eased up against the docks and were tied safe, the crowd that had run down from the city had fallen silent. There would be no Persian coins tossed to children, no great display of wealth and triumph to tell in years to come. They watched as the crews disembarked along trembling wooden runners. Their demeanour told the tale. Many of them bore wounds wrapped in cloth, or the marks of some great buffet that had spread in green and gold and blue.

Miltiades had to be helped down. He leaned on a staff wedged under his armpit, sweating and pale. He might even have fallen if his son Cimon had not rushed forward and taken his arm to steady him. The archon's leg was wrapped from thigh to knee and it did not look clean. It was clear enough that Miltiades would not be striding along the road to the city, with the crowd throwing petals and cheering his name.

A cart was brought and his son lent his strength to help his father climb onto the back of it. Cimon walked alongside then, while Miltiades stared backwards as the sea dwindled from view. The crowd peeled away from the docks and gathered on the dusty road to the city. They had come for a celebration and instead found a funeral procession. Many of them dangled wine jugs stopped in wax. Others began to weep and hold children close as they counted ships and understood. Each lost vessel meant two hundred and thirty men would not return to Athens. Each would have been a husband and father. There were thousands of wives and children who had risked the open road to come to that place. When they understood their men would not be coming, it was like a blow. Some of them crumpled on the docks, or began to stagger. Children wailed at seeing their mothers cry so violently, tearing at their hair and pulling it in long strands as tears coursed from them. That was the sound that followed Miltiades as he was carried into Athens.

Over the noise of grief, Cimon looked at his father, seeing only glassy weariness. He was eighteen years old and already much fitter and stronger for the military training he endured every day. He had felt joy that morning when the news had reached him. His father was coming! Cimon had run out of the city in just a tunic and sandals, as if in a great race to be first to see the ships. Instead, he had witnessed terrible wounds and men drawn white as death by them. The ships were unmarked, but they were so few! The stench that came from them told of too many crammed in for too long a time, rowing, rowing home. Cimon shuddered, not at the thought of suffering, but at the thought of loss. He was ashamed for his father then. When Miltiades looked on him with eyes made sore by wind and salt, Cimon would not meet his gaze, choosing to remain silent.

14

High above the city, dawn on the Acropolis brought forth the priests of Apollo to greet the sun and give thanks for the god's patronage. The ancient temple faced east and they bowed to the source of light and life, chanting prayers and burning fragrant incense or bound branches.

From down on the Pnyx, Xanthippus saw thin trails of smoke rising from the temples on the cliff. Epikleos followed his gaze and nodded to himself.

'They will sacrifice a few fine lambs for the safe return of blessed Miltiades,' he said.

Xanthippus frowned. He did not like his friend's tone on such matters.

'Be careful, Epikleos,' he murmured.

His young friend knew him well enough to understand the warning. He shrugged.

'I make no judgement. The gods give and they take away. See poor Miltiades there, being helped to a seat! When last he stood in this place, he was a hero of Marathon. If the priests of Apollo wish to cook themselves a fine breakfast on the heights of the Acropolis, I do not think it will matter now.'

'Enough!' Xanthippus said, shocked.

It was well known that the priests took home the cooked meat of sacrifices. They burned the most sacred organs on the altars but, yes, fed their families with the rest. Somehow, Epikleos seemed to take that truth and demean it with his choice of words. Xanthippus shook his head when Epikleos made as if to speak again. His friend subsided, reluctantly.

Around them, the Pnyx hill filled with people. No Athenian could remain asleep or go to work on such a day. Xanthippus saw Themistocles was there, looking tousled as if he had been drawn from his bed just moments before. Aristides was on the other side, already surrounded by the senior archons of the Areopagus council and men of his tribe, all come to hear Miltiades' report. In that place, they were the same, with one vote and no more. Rich and poor: builders and fullers and landowners mingled, shoulder to shoulder, each with as much right as any other to argue matters of law and morality.

'There is excitement here this morning,' Epikleos said. 'Can you feel it? This is the beating heart of the city, Xan. I wonder if Hippias felt the same when he arose from his bed as tyrant. This morning, we are the tyrant of Athens.'

'The Assembly cannot be a tyrant. That is its purpose,' Xanthippus replied stiffly.

'Tell that to the mob when they start furiously scratching names on shards of pottery. We should at least allow a defence against being ostracised. Would you relish ten years away from the city, away from Agariste and your children?'

'There is no mob. To sway so many against a single man would take more than a whim or mere spite! He would have to deserve it.'

The thought prompted both men to look over to where Miltiades rested, his head bowed as if in exhaustion. He had not been given a chance to bathe or change before coming to the Pnyx. As they watched, his son accepted a package of cloth, unrolling it on the seat beside him to reveal a few olives, a piece of hard bread and a couple of silver fish no thicker than a finger. Cimon passed the collection to his father with a cup of cold water, concerned with filial duty. Xanthippus watched, sensing the mood of the crowd around him.

'He was untouchable before,' he muttered.

Epikleos smiled bitterly.

'Well, he isn't now,' he said. He looked closer at his friend, seeing anger there. 'Are you all right? You have been out of sorts since I met you.'

Xanthippus waved a hand impatiently.

'Agariste was . . . unwell. I had to leave her to come here. For this man.'

His gaze was fierce as he glared at Miltiades. Epikleos looked concerned, though it sprang in part from the fact that Xanthippus had mentioned his wife at all. In normal times, his friend shared nothing of his home life, considering it utterly apart in its privacy.

'I hope she is well soon, brother,' Epikleos said.

Xanthippus turned sharply, looking for any hint of levity. Epikleos seemed earnest. He nodded, falling silent once more.

The epistates that day was a man of Antiochis – the tribe of Aristides. Fresh in his post, he would have been appointed at the previous sunset. He climbed to the speaker's stone to address the gathering, a tall and overly thin man in his early thirties with a pinched and waspish expression, as if something he had eaten disagreed with him.

'Who will speak?' he asked.

Even in the silence, his voice was thin and reedy. It lacked the boom of a Themistocles or even the hard tone of Aristides that could send other men scurrying to do his bidding. There was no reply, as every head turned to see how Miltiades would respond. He sighed visibly, his massive shoulders rising and falling like a man giving up. He rose to his feet with a grunt of effort, leaning on a staff that ended with a crosspiece under his armpit. His son Cimon stood with him, ready to steady his father if he stumbled or fell.

'I would speak,' Miltiades said, raising his head. 'If you wish it.'

His beard had grown wild in the months apart, Xanthippus saw. It was still the man who had held back the wing at Marathon. The man who had almost sold his city into ruin.

'I know you,' Xanthippus said in a whisper.

Epikleos looked back at him, narrowing his eyes at the intensity in his old friend.

Two more men stepped forward to help Miltiades climb the last steps to the speaker's stone. The crowd murmured at the sight, while the wailing of women and children could be heard beyond the Pnyx, the wind carrying the sound. They had gathered to learn all they could, of course, as desperate for news as any of the voting men above. Young and old, they filled the streets all around. In the distance, some of them clambered, dark as ants, on the rocky hill of Ares, where the Areopagus council usually met. On this day, the archons were all in the Assembly. No one had the will to send men to punish those people clinging there. They had all lost something with Miltiades that year.

When he was in position, Miltiades raised his head and breathed deeply of the breeze.

'I am Miltiades of the Philaidae family, victor of Marathon. I am a descendant of Achilles, who was grandson to King Aeacus, who was son to Zeus. My father was the Cimon who raced chariots in the Olympics. I named my son after him, who has reached manhood and joined this Assembly of Athenians to stand at my side today. I give thanks for my return, as I grieve for those who have not returned.'

He took a breath and Xanthippus saw tears gleam in the man's eyes. He was suspicious enough already to wonder at the theatrical nature of the display. Those at the back would be unable to see. Would the general wipe tears away to be sure they noticed his sorrow?

'I left Piraeus with seventy triremes,' Miltiades went on. 'We headed east, intending to hunt for the Persian fleet along the coast of Ionia and the islands there. Yet from the first, whenever we berthed and interrogated fishermen, we heard of sightings. We were in their wake for a month at sea, I think. We ran short of fresh water and had to lay up on islands I did not know. There, I heard of colonies that had declared for Persia. Islands once loyal to Athens that had turned against us.'

He waited for a ripple of unease to end before going on. Perhaps without realising it, he raised his injured leg a fraction to ease his discomfort, so that he stood on the tip of one toe. It reminded them all of his wound. Xanthippus watched with his head raised and tilted to one side.

'I followed rumours and I paid silver to the captains of merchant galleys – to pirates and adventurers, all seeking their fortune in our waters. They said the island of Paros had turned to Persia and so I went there, widening our search, looking for the enemy. Our water casks ran dry once more and we starved. Yet I pushed on and my men trusted me.'

He paused to sip water from a cup his son held up. Xanthippus stood very still, his focus absolute as the man continued.

'We found them on Paros. The Persians had landed a hundred galleys there, two hundred, I do not know. They lay empty, abandoned, but there were horses on the beaches – huge herds, thousands of them. When we landed, they ran away. It seemed a paradise, empty of all signs of men. My captains began to land our hoplites, ready to march into the interior.'

He took another drink, his hands trembling.

'They came then, in greater numbers than I can describe. They were the slaves from the ships and the soldiers of their cavalry, all in a great rush from the trees and hills. They had hidden when they saw us coming and they caught us unawares. We fought – we made a great slaughter and spattered the white sand red as wine! Yet not all of us had landed and they were too many.'

He licked his lips where they had grown dry and cracked. His son rose once again with the cup, but Miltiades waved him away. He went on as if he could not hold back the words any longer.

'I do not know who fired the ships – whether it was one of mine or one of theirs. All the wood was dry and there was . . . screaming from those left within, unable to escape. The fire took hold on ours as well as theirs, spreading along the beach. Some of our crews got out to heave their hulls back into the water. Those who have returned with me to the Piraeus are the ones who were successful. The rest were cut down as they struggled to get afloat, or killed on the sand.'

He closed his eyes for an instant, honouring the dead.

'Our hoplites fought like heroes, every one. They were superb, but they were crushed and overwhelmed by men with clubs and knives, men who fought like they were possessed, with teeth and nails and savagery. We could not recover shields and helmets. I will make amends for that loss, to the families of the fallen. I can replace them, if they come to me, if there are sons to carry a shield and spear and helmet they would have inherited from their fathers. I can do that much.'

'You can do more,' Xanthippus said suddenly.

The gaze of thousands turned on him then and he found himself staring directly up at Miltiades. The man looked ill, too sick almost to stand. He swayed as he recognised

Xanthippus, and perhaps there was a sort of resignation there in the twist of his mouth.

'You will have your chance to question Strategos Miltiades, Xanthippus,' the epistates said.

His tone was one of reproof and Xanthippus felt Epikleos touch his hip in warning. He felt his anger surge, driving him on.

'I will, epistates. And I will have justice,' Xanthippus said. He ignored the intake of breath around the Pnyx. 'I accuse this man. He has failed Athens. I accuse him on behalf of the dead, for the blood and silver he has cost us. I call . . .'

'Please, k-kurios,' the epistates stammered, shocked into using a term of address for a superior. He had been made leader of Athens the night before and he was far out of his depth, unsure of both rules and precedents. The laws of Cleisthenes were barely twenty years old, but Xanthippus knew them well. 'Please reconsider! You are both Marathonomachoi!'

'Yes,' Xanthippus replied. 'Yes we are.' He held Miltiades' gaze for a long moment, until the other man was certain what would come. 'I speak because we are. I hold Miltiades to a high standard and I say he has failed. I call a trial.' He spoke only to Miltiades then, ill and stunned before him.

'How can this be fair?' Cimon shouted. 'My father is wounded, anyone can see it. How can he be brought to trial when he can hardly stand?'

'Nonetheless,' Xanthippus said softly. 'These are our laws. If you would speak in his defence, lad, you may. If not, I'm sure Miltiades can speak for himself. He is condemned by his own words, after all. I can say little he has not already admitted.'

Cimon looked in appeal to the epistates, who could only open his hands, almost in supplication.

'I will need to speak to the officials of the Assembly,' the epistates said, looking to them for support. 'We must select a jury. This is no ostracism. Miltiades is allowed to defend himself against such a charge. What *is* the charge?'

'Poor leadership, fraud, theft – all you have heard Miltiades admit,' Xanthippus said. He glanced aside to where Epikleos was rubbing a hand across his brow, his mouth slightly open.

'Then . . . then I should prorogue the Assembly, until this afternoon, or tomorrow. Until Miltiades has had a chance to make his defence, until . . . until I have had a chance to consult . . . Yes, yes, I think . . .'

Xanthippus shook his head. He could see Themistocles watching him with an expression not dissimilar to the one Epikleos wore. Let them stare! He had made his decision and he would not let some stammering fool of an epistates allow Miltiades to wriggle off the hook.

'There is no true written constitution in Athens,' Xanthippus announced. In theory, he addressed the epistates, who still floundered and wished the day had fallen to someone else.

'All our laws, all our trials, are decided by us, on the day. I have called a trial this morning. If there is business of greater importance, it can be delayed. If not, I would like to move to prosecution, defence and a vote.'

'But what punishment would suit these crimes you list?' the epistates asked plaintively.

Many in the crowd scowled at this breach of ritual.

Xanthippus shrugged.

'For the deaths of two thousand hoplites – Marathonomachoi all? For the loss of fifty galleys and all the free men who crewed them? For the fraud in asking for a command he was not fit to undertake? What else but death can be our answer?'

151

'Xanthippus,' Epikleos murmured over the sound of the crowd. 'Show mercy. He is much loved still, in some places.'

Xanthippus bit his lip. Themistocles may have been staring at him, but so was Aristides. It was important to him to show dignity in front of such men.

'Very well, epistates,' Xanthippus said. 'The day after tomorrow is already set aside as a trial day. I will accept a delay until then. It will give me time to examine witnesses.'

Miltiades looked down at him with red-rimmed eyes, like a sick dog that knew it was threatened but had no more strength to resist.

15

Xerxes walked on pale blue marble, polished to the point where he could look down and see a coloured shadow of himself looking up. It was as if he walked across the surface of a lake on a still day.

His father sat on his throne, fanned by slaves though the sun was sinking into the west. Dinner would follow, and at the thought, Xerxes looked for the little eunuch, Mishar, whose job it was to whisper about the Greeks each evening. He was there, dressed in a tunic of white silk, it looked like. New gold bands adorned his wrists and ankles, reflecting his rise in status.

Xerxes felt the eunuch's gaze on him as he approached his father and dropped to one knee. Only the crown prince and heir could adopt the pose. That was his right, judged by every one of the servants and slaves around his father. They understood such things to a perfect nicety. Even kings would prostrate themselves before Darius, full-length on the marble, so that their breath made it cloud. But not the crown prince, not the young man who would follow in his steps and rule the world. In that way, his father gave him honour – and helped secure his succession.

Xerxes waited until his father nodded and then rose to approach. He took his father's right hand in his and kissed him twice on each cheek, back and forth, before finally pressing his lips on those of Darius. There was a sweetness on his father's breath that troubled him, a scent of green datura.

'Are you in pain still, father?' he said.

The king's eyes were bloodshot, he saw, with a faint yellow tinge to the skin. Xerxes felt a pang of something like panic. He was not ready for this, not yet! He had ridden a thousand miles to Persepolis when his spies in court had reported the king ailing. In all the days of hard galloping, he had not considered the reality that lay behind his father growing ill. Men died. Xerxes knew that as well as anyone. He had witnessed executions by the thousand, seen men, women and children killed in battle, or simply for sport. There were always more, given the way they bred. Yet his father had been the rock on which the empire stood, unbreakable, eternal.

It shocked Xerxes to understand the man had lost weight beneath his robes and panelled coat, to see the way his throat had grown thin, so that lines of flesh stood out like wires. Darius was sixty-two years old. When Xerxes had left two years before to tour the kingdoms of the empire, he had not understood it was to prepare them for his rise to the throne.

'It is good to see you, my son,' Darius said. He smiled.

If kings and satraps might have flinched at that expression, Xerxes saw only affection. He kept his father's hand in his and pressed it. He felt the knuckles shift against one another, where once there had been muscle to draw the great bow or hold a sword. Xerxes found tears in his eyes and let them spill without shame. It was not so strange. Many men wept when they met the Great King.

'I have Physician Ganak to help me with pain,' the king said. 'He argues with Master Zhou and they take turns to dose me, or burn different woods so I can inhale the smoke.'

Xerxes glanced aside to where the foreigners stood, frowning at them. Both men dropped to the floor immediately.

The Indian doctor was white-bearded and ancient-looking, but moved well enough when the crown prince observed him.

A low rhythmic sound, like pieces of wood rubbed together, brought his attention back. Xerxes saw his father was chuckling.

'I trust them, Xerxes. Do not fear for me. They know what will happen if they let me die.'

'I wonder if they appreciate the full extent of it,' Xerxes said.

Both doctors lay on the marble, their hands up around their ears as if cradling their heads. The Chinese master was half the age of the other, but he lay perfectly still, showing good physical discipline. In comparison, the Indian was quivering, expecting death. Xerxes looked away from them.

'You will grow strong again, father. You must. I am not ready!'

To his surprise, he felt his father's hand tighten on his own, though it was like being held by a claw.

'You are. My life has been full and rich, with many blessings. No man lives for ever! Should I fear heaven? Why? It will not be so very different from life as it is now, though without the pain and discomforts of illness. I have prepared you, Xerxes. You are ready to sit this throne today. More, I have prepared my tomb, out in Naqsh-e-Rostam, in the mountains. The carvings are almost complete, yet I live – and I bless your patience. I have asked Our Lord Ahura Mazda for one last campaign. I have known sixty-two summers, Xerxes. With just a few more years, I will gather all our armies, all the host. I will bring a million men and more ships than the world has ever known. I will sail to Greece with them and I will witness the destruction of those who scorned poor Datis, who butchered our people in the surf.

The men who showed us only dishonour! The Greeks! The Greeks!'

His voice had risen and his colour deepened as his passion built. Xerxes felt a drop of spittle touch his face, but he did not move to wipe it away.

'Father . . .' he began.

King Darius sat up straighter, anger overriding his physical weakness with a huge effort.

'Mishar, come to me, complete your duty,' the king ordered.

The slave ran forward and threw himself down, his golden bracelets clinking on the marble.

'Master, as you command me.'

The eunuch rose to his feet and leaned in, his lips almost touching the king's ear. Xerxes felt his father's rage coming off him like waves of heat. The dark eyes were unblinking as Mishar spoke.

'Master, I obey. Remember the Greeks,' he whispered. He stepped away when the king nodded.

'I remember,' Darius said.

He gestured his son closer and Xerxes leaned in, as the slave had done before him. He saw no dishonour in that. All men were slaves to his father, even the heir. If Darius gave the order, Xerxes knew he would not leave that room alive. The Great King's authority was absolute and he shuddered at the thought of inheriting such power.

'The Greeks talk, my son. They have told the world of their victory at the fennel field, at the place they call Marathon. Every one of our kingdoms has heard how my army was broken there! It cannot go unanswered, Xerxes, do you understand? They were once the edge of empire. I would have left them in peace as satraps and vassals. Yet they chose to resist — and the world saw them resist. I have no choice now. If God is willing, I will live long enough to see the

Greek cities burn. I will see Athens burn, and Sparta and Thebes and Corinth and all the rest.' He paused to gasp for breath, staring off into the distance until the great heaves became less. 'They call their land the dance floor of Ares, have you heard that? The one they call the god of war. They have not *seen* the god of war, Xerxes. But they will . . .'

The king winced, his breathing growing tight. He pressed a hand into his side, under the ribs. Xerxes began to speak his concern, but Darius waved him away.

'It is nothing, just a passing pain. Tell those doctors to prepare more infusions and the smoke of poppy seeds. It all helps a little, but nothing works for long. I must endure dreams of terror and strangeness.'

He saw his son's worry and smiled once more, though the pain was growing in him and the yellow tinge to his skin seemed to have deepened.

'Go and rest, Xerxes. You rode far and fast to come to me. You are my heir, my beloved son. You will be at my side when I return to Greece, I give you my word.'

Lennox & Addington LIBRARIES

16

Every trial day started some time before dawn. Officials of the courts began a laborious process of choosing juries and magistrates by lot, then allocating individual court spaces around the centre of the city. Xanthippus was not surprised to be given the Areopagus. Three other courts were in use for the most serious crimes, but the great rock of Ares still had a sacred position in the laws of the city. Before the new democracy of Cleisthenes, the Areopagus had been the site of a council with almost unlimited power. Those noble archons existed still, as the reforms had not quite dared to cut them out completely. They hung on as a remnant, with all the authority of ancient tradition, but no clear role in the new order.

The rock itself was a massive outcropping that rose above the lower city. It could hold a jury of four or five hundred with ease, though the day would bake them all on the white stone. As the sun rose, Xanthippus paced from one edge of the Areopagus to the other, with Epikleos watching him. The magistrate who would preside over the trial had been chosen by lot and was a butcher by trade. He seemed delighted at the appointment and had warmly shaken Xanthippus by the hand at their first meeting. As seemed true of all butchers, the man was well fed and solid, with a crushing grip. Xanthippus did not have to ask to know he was Marathonomachos.

Epikleos watched the first jurors come up the steps, passing through the Scythian guards with solemn stares and then bounding to the top to find a good spot near the front.

'The loss of life has been admitted,' Epikleos said quietly. 'That is hardly a matter of dispute. Your only focus must be to prove he was reckless with those lives, that he should have scouted the island and discovered the ambush – and is therefore responsible, at least in part.'

Xanthippus nodded. He wished the point of accusation was how Miltiades had acted at Marathon. He was more certain of that, though proof was just as elusive. He eyed the jury, seeing serious expressions. They had called Miltiades a hero once, but that was before he had lost so many men and ships.

Xanthippus could feel sweat trickling down from his armpits, cold against his skin though the sun was barely above the eastern horizon. There was no sign yet of the accused. Miltiades had been under guard since his accusation, in preparation for the trial. He had not been allowed to return to his loyal crews or even his house in the city, not while such serious charges hung over him. Instead, he would have languished with his wound in the small prison close by the Scythian barracks. Xanthippus imagined the man was being dressed and bathed at that moment, ready to argue his fate.

'I have one of his captains as witness,' he murmured, looking through the written argument he intended to make. There were many words crossed through and he felt sweat prickle on his brow. He was no Themistocles to pour words like honey over a jury until they drowned in them! Nor could he express the truth that lay at the heart of his accusation. Miltiades was a traitor, bought by a Persian king. The rest was merely a chain to bind him.

Miltiades arrived in a bustle of supporters, all glaring at Xanthippus. The man himself struggled visibly with his crutch, his son Cimon at his side to help him. Men well versed in argument walked alongside, holding rolls of papers. They looked calm and well prepared, which of course was for the benefit of jurors still taking their seats. Volunteers over the age of thirty were not always easy to find on a trial day. The pay was less than a working wage, so in more normal times, it tended to be the elderly and the poorest who filled the seats. It was said to be their chief entertainment and the white-hairs were much mocked in plays about the law.

On this day, the interest around Miltiades had persuaded much younger men to volunteer for selection. Some of them were even those who had returned with the fleet, with as much right as anyone to put their names forward. Xanthippus saw a few with bound wounds and swallowed nervously.

'Do you see the sailors?' he whispered to Epikleos.

His friend peered at a group still coming up, noting how their gaits differed from men used to solid land.

'They think this great rock is a deck still,' he replied. 'What of it? They have a vote – and more reason than most to be here. Don't mind them, Xan. They have all seen friends drown because of Miltiades. It does not mean they will vote for him today.'

Xanthippus bit his lip. He watched sweating slaves bring the voting baskets to the top. No one was allowed to influence a jury as they gave their verdicts. There would be no holding up of hands, or standing on one side or the other, not in a trial. Instead, each man was given two bronze rods and a disc with a hole in the centre. The choice of rod was solid or hollow, representing guilty or innocent. No one could see which rod had been chosen when fingers were pressed over the ends. It meant votes could not be influenced or bought, at least with any certainty. In that way, the results of a trial were as clean and true as they could possibly be. Xanthippus eyed the men of the galleys and wondered how they would vote.

Four hundred was the number he and Miltiades had agreed for the jury. It could have been a thousand or as few as a hundred, but the number was a reasonable compromise. The last of them found a spot to sit or stand as the sun rose and the long shadows shrank. The day seemed peaceful at that height above the city, though a dozen trials would be taking place at the same time, with courts all over the heart of Athens. The law would be applied by juries and magistrates with no more expertise than the man accused. There were always some who argued for more expert judges, or juries trained for the task. Just a generation before, trials had been decided by the archons of the Areopagus council. Yet corruption had been rife and the judgments often tainted. Still, Xanthippus had been one of those who argued against putting the lives of men into the hands of the uneducated, the damaged, the spiteful, the poor. Themistocles had spoken in favour, which made a little more sense now that he knew more of his youth. Yet the truth was it worked as well as any other system – and it bound them together as Athenians. Xanthippus could not deny that. It was written in every face before him, in their keen interest and serious expressions. They would decide the fate of Miltiades that very day, in solemn dignity, passing judgement on one of their own.

Xanthippus breathed in relief when he saw the two galley officers arrive to take seats by him. It had been a scramble to find and interview both captain and hoplite, getting the story direct from their lips. It helped that they were both furious with Miltiades. Xanthippus met their gaze as they came and shook his hand, then sat down on wooden chairs facing the jury, ready to be called. Neither had looked away, Xanthippus noted in relief. Miltiades and his people took chairs on the other side of the magistrate, all facing the jury – seated or standing on the bare rock. Xanthippus and Epikleos, as his second, sat looking out across the jurors and the city beyond, lit gold in the morning sun.

The magistrate cleared his throat, then did it again and a third time, as if his nerves had overcome him and he could not begin. Just as Xanthippus considered rising in interruption, the man spoke.

'On this trial day in the month of Skirophorion, the year of Aristides, I convene this court under the laws of Athens and the wisdom of Athena. Xanthippus of Acamantis tribe and Cholargos deme is the plaintiff and chief accuser of Miltiades, hero of Marathon.'

Xanthippus kept his head down, though he heard Epikleos' intake of breath at such a cheap attempt to manipulate. It seemed the magistrate was not quite as uninvolved as he had seemed. Luck or the gods played a role in the selections, of course. That too was part of the process of judgment.

One of the Assembly scribes bent low to speak into the magistrate's ear. He flushed at whatever was said to him, but nodded. On matters of law, he would no doubt need to be coached through the process by more experienced scribes. He examined his notes once more, though they clearly swam before his eyes.

When the preamble finished, Xanthippus missed his own name being called, so that Epikleos had to nudge him. He rose and nodded to the official who stood by two large urns, one sitting on a block above the other. With formality, the man removed a peg from the base of the uppermost. A thin trickle of water began to pour into the lower, slowly raising its level towards a hole in its side. No trial could be won by exhausting the defence through days of accusation. Each speaker would have no longer than it took for water to spill from the second urn. The sound was pleasant on the Areopagus, like a stream.

'I stood with Miltiades at Marathon, in the left wing,' Xanthippus said, beginning to pace back and forth. Every eye was on him and a breeze blew across the rock, ruffling his hair. He had not intended to start in such a way, but the magistrate had put the idea into his head and perhaps that sting needed to be removed before he could go on.

'He was not rash then. He could have sent the left in with the centre and the right in one wild charge against the Persians. It might have won us victory, or seen us crushed. We cannot know. Instead, we held back and saw many of our friends killed.'

It was as far as he dared to go. Miltiades watched him with glittering eyes and the man's son was frowning in puzzlement as if he had not heard this version of the tale. Xanthippus knew he could not make the accusation. Miltiades had said he would counter with the truth that Xanthippus had disobeyed in the heat of battle. It would destroy them both.

He ordered his thoughts, wishing for fluency as he went on.

'We beat them, that day. We killed those who would have enslaved us, men who would have taken our women and children for their sport, who would have burned this city. We cut them down.'

He paused for a moment and bowed his head. In another man, it might have been artifice, but in that place, with the breeze in his hair, the memories were suddenly overwhelming.

'We were met on the road by the people of the city, come to greet us. They brought flowers and wine – red amaranth blossoms. We came to the Pnyx and we gave thanks for our deliverance. Miltiades was a hero that morning – and as one beloved of Athens, he asked us for ships and men. Seventy ships, with three banks of thirty rowers on each side. One hundred and eighty free men of the city to cut through the waves. With each ship, a dozen others made up the roll – two

163

cooks, three carpenters, sailmakers, a navigator and his boy. All from the demes and tribes of Athens. Alongside them were shield-men in bronze – hoplites with the equipment and weapons they had carried at Marathon, at my side, at the side of Miltiades. Some were from the left wing, others from the tribes of the centre, who were beaten back by Persians but did not break. Men who had re-formed in the face of a screaming, howling enemy bright with blood and sweat – and pushed back!'

Xanthippus had not appreciated how loud and stern his voice had become, so that the words lashed out across the face of the jury. He heard it then as the echoes returned to him. He took a moment to glance into the lower of the two urns, the one known as the clepsydra, or 'water-thief'. Water brimmed along a line. He had used almost half his time already! He mastered himself, though Miltiades looked troubled and his scribes had their heads lowered to their papers rather than meet the gaze of one who had been there.

'The heroes of Marathon went out with those seventy ships. Forty or fifty to a ship – volunteers all. Three and a half thousand of those who fought at my side while the sea hissed pink and red and bodies tumbled around my feet. They too were men of Athens, each one of them. All but twelve hundred were lost, a tragedy that leaves us immeasurably poorer, weaker. If the Persians come again tomorrow, we cannot send ten thousand out to meet them, not today. If their fleet comes, we cannot yet put ships in their path to defend Athens from a hostile landing. We are weak this year – and it is because of the arrogance of one man. Perhaps Miltiades thought he could not lose, in his pride. Perhaps he thought too little of the city that had raised him up, so that he did not mind her being stripped, left naked and afraid by his actions. Yet that is the result!'

Xanthippus found he was glaring at the jury, so that they too looked away. He tried to gentle his gaze, reminding himself he had to win them over, not harangue them! As he paced back and forth across the great rock, he saw others had come, standing outside the roped boundary. They risked falling off the sheer edge of the Areopagus to hear the trial. Yet they remained, and he understood that need to hear. It should not have been a surprise when his eye was drawn to Themistocles among them. Of *course* that man had come to watch the trial. He too had stood at Marathon. He had seen his lines thinned and the left wing held back, though the elite soldiers of Persia massed before him, the ones the king called Immortals. Xanthippus barely flickered an eye over Themistocles, but the connection was made even so. They knew one another – and Themistocles knew why he accused.

There was no sign of Aristides in the watching crowd. The man he actually wanted to impress had gone to some other trial. That hurt, but it reminded him of duty over passion, with Aristides as his example. Xanthippus glanced into the water urn once more, biting his lip. There was so much he wanted to say, but the restraint of time forced him to be concise. When he spoke again, his voice was quieter, so that those in the rear leaned forward to hear him over the breeze.

'We understand hubris, we Greeks. It is a danger for all men, but especially for us in our achievements. It tempts us and seduces us – to do more, to risk more, to try one more time. Do the gods not love us? Are we not glorious? Is one victory ever enough? That is the voice that tempted Miltiades. We cheered him – and he drank it in and still felt thirst.'

With relief, Xanthippus had brought himself back to the text he had prepared. He almost unrolled it, but the fluency of working without had been intoxicating and he was reluctant. The very thing he described in Miltiades was seducing him at that instant, he realised wryly. Instead, he took a breath and unrolled his scroll to the right spot.

'I will bring you Captain Arceus of the warship *Dolphin* and a hoplite from a ship well named *Justice*. You will hear an account of arrogance from Miltiades, of a landing made without proper scouting parties that turned into a slaughter. You will hear how one man's desire for glory tore the heart out of our fleet. I will ask you then for the harshest punishment, as befits the fortunes sent to the bottom of the sea – and the lives lost.'

He paused once more to bow his head. As if in answer, water spilled from a hole in the lower urn, ending his time to speak. Xanthippus nodded to the magistrate, who sat, stunned at what he had heard. The man wiped sweat from his forehead and his hand darkened the cloth of his robe when he wiped it down himself.

Xanthippus resumed his seat and Epikleos leaned in.

'Well done, Xan. That is a good start.'

'We'll see,' Xanthippus said, though he felt his heart beating so hard it made him dizzy. Pride was truly a danger, he realised. It was like strong wine in the blood to have other men look at him in awe. He glanced to where he had seen Themistocles and found the man staring back in his direction. Xanthippus dipped his head once and Themistocles copied the action, acknowledging one another.

Slaves refilled the water urns and topped up the levels as Miltiades rose to his feet. He looked very pale, his flesh more like dead marble than anything alive. Even in the morning cool, he was already sweating. The tunic he wore ended at his thighs, so that the thick cloth bandages were visible to all. Xanthippus had not seen the wound, but the entire leg looked swollen and there was a darker hue above and below, as if rot was spreading there. Xanthippus found himself wincing at the thought. He had seen such things before, when a wound failed to bleed clean and took on some foul vapour, becoming so corrupt it had to be cut out. The result was usually death. It was why they poured wine into wounds and packed them with wet bread as a poultice, draining the pus as it arose.

Miltiades leaned on his crutch as he stood before the jury that would decide his fate. There would be no striding back and forth for him, that much was obvious. Instead, he cleared his throat and began. Xanthippus sat forward, determined to hear every word. He noted the man's son glaring at him, trying to pin him with sheer hatred in his gaze. Xanthippus had no time for a stripling's spite.

'I stood at Marathon, yes, as you have heard. I stood with the same Xanthippus who makes this accusation . . .'

Miltiades paused and Xanthippus heard a faint sound from the hand that held the scroll as papyrus cracked under his tightening grip. If Miltiades claimed he had disobeyed an order in battle, he would rise and accuse the man of being a traitor. There would be chaos and tumult, but Miltiades would not survive it.

'He fought well on that day, against terrible odds. As did Themistocles and Aristides, who kept the centre. As did Callimachus, who held the right wing before his death. We stood as Athenians with men of Plataea. We stood against arrows and spears and swords — many more than I care to recall. I have sprung panting out of dreams a few times since then, remembering them! Did our victory evoke pride in me? Of course it did. Was it hubris for me to ask for a fleet to pursue our enemies? I do not think it was. Unless you would have left the Persians to settle and once again grow strong. Yes, I lost a battle on the island of Paros. I landed our men there, though I had been told the island had sworn loyalty to the Persians.

167

I do not claim to have been without flaw, only that in the moment, when decisions have to be made, mistakes are made too, amidst the victories. Men go before they have received orders, or hold back when they should go forward. If they are men of honour, they come to regret their failings, as I do.'

When he looked over to Xanthippus, his eyes were terrible, sore and red as if a fever raged in him.

'Yet as you sit here, on cool stone, to judge my decisions while the waves crashed and my officers looked to me for orders, you cannot know what it was like to be there. You think to punish me for my loss? I am punished every day by the thoughts of the men who drowned, by friends I saw cut down as I fought for my life. Yes, I was rash . . .'

He caught himself, aware that he had crossed a line in his own admission. A whisper went around the jury and those gathered to watch.

'. . . I went forward, with all the knowledge I had at that moment. And I lost. At Marathon, I won; at Paros, I lost. That is the life of a strategos and an archon – a leader. In the end, all you can ask is for more victories than defeats. That is all I can offer.'

He waved a hand as if to dismiss them all, his face twisting. It seemed their judgment was beneath his contempt. Xanthippus could hardly believe it when Miltiades returned to his seat, helped by his son. Had his illness so weakened him? His defence seemed to be at an end and he sat there, with his head slightly bowed, staring at nothing while the scribes he had hired fussed and tried to gain his attention.

The magistrate too seemed to have expected more. There was no sign yet of water spilling from the lower urn. The man spread his hands in silent question, looking around. When no one replied, he leaned over to one of the court scribes and exchanged furiously whispered questions.

'Strategos Miltiades?' he said after a time. 'Will you be bringing witnesses in your defence?'

There was no response from the man himself. Slowly his son stood. Cimon was a fine figure of a young man, though Xanthippus did not know him. He watched as the eighteen-year-old bent to kiss his father on both cheeks, then spoke to the jury. Xanthippus glanced at the water clock, willing time away.

'My father has served Athens – in time and blood and silver – his entire life. On land and sea. He campaigned in Ionia on our behalf, so that he did not see his family for years. In his absence, we tended estates and crops that fed the people, gave them bread and wine. All while my father Miltiades risked his life against armies of Persia. Marathon was his greatest achievement, unsullied, untainted. After that, the sea and the gods and a determined enemy brought him a defeat. See the wound he has taken for us, that could kill him yet! Do you even know the laws? If you must punish my family, after our long service, make it a fine we can pay, not death, not exile! My father is a hero of Athens. We owe him everything.'

The young man sat down, red-faced and furious. Xanthippus thought the lashing tone had not done his father many favours with the jurors, but it was hard to be certain. Miltiades looked so ill by then, he might fall from the seat. The man lolled there, barely conscious. Nonetheless, he would have to endure. The vote had to be carried out.

Water spilled and the magistrate breathed in relief.

'If the defence has nothing more to add, you may call your first witnesses, kurios,' he said, back on solid ground.

Xanthippus nodded. Noon would end the session and he thought he would have a judgment by then.

17

Before the sun reached its greatest height, the last of the witnesses finished their description of the slaughter on Paros. Miltiades had refused the right to question them, which meant the statements of the captain and the hoplite went unchallenged. The defence seemed to rest on a balance, that the jury should not punish a man for one great loss after a lifetime of selfless labour and successes. It was a simple message and there were nodding heads when one of his scribes summed up their position. Xanthippus did not know if he had done enough for the victory. For the first time since making his accusation, he faced the possibility of failure and what that might mean.

If Miltiades survived, he would surely be an enemy and a dangerous one. His son Cimon had marked his father's accuser with a stare that seemed to burn in its anger. Yet Xanthippus would not have taken it back, even if the chance to do so had been handed to him. Miltiades going free had been a stone in his sandal from the day of Marathon, a wound that would not heal. He knew what he had seen. The details were as clear as if they had been carved in relief.

The voting began as the first noon bells sounded across the city. Half of Athens would be making their way home for a light lunch, or strolling to one of the gymnasia for a rubdown and food from a street vendor. The jurors, too, would feel the first stirrings of hunger. Thin men all, they could not delay too long without something to feed them. Xanthippus watched as each one chose a bronze rod and worked it through the disc marked 'public vote', hiding whether it was solid or hollow by a grip between thumb and forefinger. Solid meant guilty, agreed beforehand.

One after another, they dropped the little things into a basket and discarded the other rod into a second, watched closely all the time. The tellers too were chosen by lot, as well as the men whose task it was to judge the count and confirm it. There was no room for corruption, not in a decision over a man's life.

Xanthippus felt tension leave him as he walked back to Epikleos.

'Not much longer,' he said.

Four hundred votes did not take long to count, even when each one had to be disassembled and held up to see if it was solid or hollow. A few jurors tried to catch Xanthippus' eye. He sensed their gaze as they turned towards him, but looked away. He did not want to guess the result until it was done, for good or ill. Epikleos watched them avidly, turning back and forth to get the first sense of victory and driving himself mad with the strain of it.

Xanthippus took a moment to thank the witnesses, still on their feet with tension. In theory, both ship's captain and hoplite officer had spoken only the truth, on oath to the gods. There could be no punishment for honesty. Yet the reality was grubbier and more human. Both were brave men. Perhaps it was relevant that they were also from families of means, who did not have to fear sudden poverty at the hands of Miltiades and his supporters.

Xanthippus frowned at that thought. It was well known that slaves had to be tortured before they could testify as witnesses. Only torture could be relied upon to bring an honest word from a man bound to serve a house and family. He had called no slaves for the trial of Miltiades. He wondered if he would have summoned some of the rowers if they had been truly beyond the reach of spite and malice. As free men, but without wealth or position, they had their reflections in the jurors. More, they had a voice and he had not asked for it. He grimaced at the thought, praying it would not be his own hubris that cost him the judgment.

Xanthippus breathed in and out, forcing calm and putting weak thoughts aside. The votes had been counted and the tally was being checked by solemn officials and the magistrate. There was no going back. As the philosophers said, each choice led to another and another, but no one could ever see what might have been. Or all men would have been as wise as Homer.

The magistrate bowed to the officials of the Assembly and returned to his seat. The jury too became still, waiting for their own verdict, as they did not yet know what it would be.

'By two hundred and sixty-four to one hundred and thirty-six, the judgment is against Miltiades. The accusation is proven. The verdict is guilty.'

There was noise then as four hundred jurors either swore under their breath or cheered and clapped one another on the back. There was no appeal against any sentence. Miltiades' life hung in the balance.

'You have him,' Epikleos said, his voice cutting through their clamour. 'So, will you show mercy?'

Xanthippus looked sharply at his friend. He shook his head.

'For losing a battle, I would. For taking Persian silver, no. My wife and children would have been sold with all the rest, Epikleos. There can be only one result.'

The last part of a trial was a delicate game of fine judgement. After a guilty verdict, both the prosecution and the defence would decree a punishment. With a show of hands, the jury could select only one of them. Xanthippus bit his lip as he thought. Too harsh a sentence and there was a chance the jurors would choose whatever Miltiades offered. Of course, the defence had the same problem. If Miltiades chose too light a punishment, the jury could easily go for the harder ending. Men liked to see blood; the advantage lay with Xanthippus.

When the magistrate had finished conferring once more and turned to him, Xanthippus did not hesitate.

'For hubris, for the death of thousands of men and the loss of a fleet for Athens, the punishment must be death. I would show mercy to this man in the manner of it, so I will ask that he be dispatched cleanly with a knife and his body returned to his family to be honoured.'

There was a murmur of appreciation in the jury and some of them nodded. Xanthippus had avoided the trap of asking for too violent an end – seeing Miltiades flogged to death, or pegged to a board on the city wall so that exposure and thirst drew out his agony over days.

Xanthippus took his seat as Miltiades struggled to rise. The man had grown paler, if anything, with dark patches on the ground where drops of sweat had fallen from his nose and chin. After a struggle, it seemed he would not make it to his feet. Miltiades pulled his son down and whispered furiously into his ear. Cimon hissed a question back, but then nodded, his mouth a thin line.

'In recognition of my father's service to this city, we ask for imprisonment for three months and a fine . . . a fine of fifty talents.'

Xanthippus felt his throat close in shock at the amount. A single talent of silver was worth six thousand drachms, the wage of a working man for almost ten years. Fifty talents was a sum to shock the jury and make them reconsider. It was said that there were ten thousand houses in Athens. Each household would receive two weeks' wages for such a fine! Xanthippus felt his heart sink. Or it would buy ships to replace some of those Miltiades had lost. Either way, it seemed the family still had wealth. With a short time in prison to satisfy the harshest critics, the offer was well judged. Xanthippus did not need Epikleos' glance back at him to know Miltiades would live.

The second vote was over quickly. The jurors accepted the fine and time in prison. The magistrate in particular seemed desperately relieved and beamed around at them. With little ceremony, the trial was over. Each jury member was handed a token to be redeemed against five obol coins for the day's service.

The events on the rock of Ares that day had been payment enough, Xanthippus thought. They would go home and tell their wives and friends every detail. He saw Epikleos look up sharply and turned to see Miltiades' son had come to stand by him. Xanthippus understood in the moment of stillness that he had made more than one enemy. Epikleos casually took a position where he could block an attack, but neither of them was afraid of a beardless young man, no matter how wide across the shoulders Cimon was.

'Fifty talents,' Xanthippus said. 'There are not many families in Athens that could pay such a sum.'

Cimon shrugged, his mouth turning up on one side. He held his hands almost as fists, low down on his hips, as he stood and confronted Xanthippus. More than a few watched the little scene, wondering whether there would be violence or further insult. Such things were not unknown. Epikleos raised a finger to summon one of the Scythian archers standing nearby.

'For my father's life?' Cimon said. 'It was part of my inheritance, but I would pay it again.'

'The trial is at an end,' Epikleos said to him. 'Your father will recover in his cell. By the time he is free, he will be well and strong. Good day to you now, Cimon. Tend to Miltiades.'

'Don't tell me my duty,' Cimon growled at him.

Xanthippus thought the young man might erupt and braced himself to straight-arm a rush. The Scythians were suddenly there in their armour, stepping between them, roughly ordering everyone off the rock and back to their lives. The moment of tension vanished in the noise and clatter. Xanthippus watched as Miltiades was helped down, step by step, his arm draped over his son.

'How touching, to see such devotion,' Epikleos said. 'Well, you won fifty talents for the city, Xan. If it's not what you wanted, it is justice of a sort.'

Xanthippus forced himself to smile at the archers growing red-faced around them, yet not quite daring to move Marathonomachoi on with a touch.

'I am for a little lunch – ripe figs, perhaps a few anchovies – something light: my stomach is churning still.'

Epikleos clapped him on the shoulder.

'You should go home. You should see Agariste, Xan.' He saw the sullen refusal in his friend, though Xanthippus would not explain what had happened. 'Xan, you won! She will want to know.'

There was a strange stubbornness in the set of Xanthippus' jaw as they walked. With a sigh, Epikleos gave up. He liked the young woman Xanthippus had married. It took some of the shine out of the day to see something had come between them.

'Did you see Themistocles leave?' Epikleos asked.

His friend shook his head as they left the Areopagus

175

behind. They walked the street to the Agora, where the market rush would be lessening. Juries from across the city would be heading there, to discuss their trials and find something to eat.

'He did not look too pleased, though some of that silver might go to crew the ships we're building. He should be delighted. After all, Miltiades is no longer the favourite son of the Assembly. His star has fallen – with his loss at Paros, his wound, the trial. He is no threat to Themistocles, not now.'

'You think that is why I did it?' Xanthippus said. 'I told you the reason. I owe Themistocles no favours.'

Epikleos shrugged rather than continue to argue, though he suspected it was subtler than that. The reasons for any action were rarely simple, any more than men and women were simple. Even so, his friend remained angry and halted at the edge of the Agora.

'Go on without me, would you?' Xanthippus said.

'Xan, I didn't mean to suggest you were one of his people . . .' Epikleos said.

'No. You are right. I haven't seen Agariste for some time. I should go to her – and my children.'

There was no arguing with him in this mood. Epikleos knew when he needed time away from the crowds, so he nodded. They shook hands with a brief grip, each man subtly reassured by the strength of the other. Epikleos watched him go before he headed into the market, to the smells of fried fish and olive paste.

18

Xanthippus walked the road to the estate outside the city, feeling his muscles and back loosen as he strode along. His knee felt strong, hardly hurting at all. No one turned to watch him, at least as far as he could see. He was able to vanish into the traders heading in and out of the city, looking to sell their goods or apply for citizenship. Athens took in the children of its citizens by right. As long as just one parent had been Athenian born, it did not matter where the sons and daughters had come into the world. Since the threat of a Persian attack in Ionia, there had been a steady stream of families arriving on merchant ships, all their possessions on their backs. They would find a new life in the city, or they would starve and be enslaved. Many would serve new masters before the year was out, but for those who worked hard and had skill, there was still nowhere else like it in the world.

He hammered on the iron gate of the house and waited while one of his wife's staff peered at him through a slot. Two slaves went up to the wall to stare up and down the street before it was opened, an excess of caution, though there was a mood in the city that disturbed him, a sort of anger or frustration – or fear, which looked much the same.

Agariste came out at a run when she heard her husband had returned. She appeared in a dress of white hemmed with a thick green band, as if a snake had wound itself around her. She was twenty-five years old and her skin was clear and unlined. Yet her expression was dark with fear of what he would say. They had not exchanged a word since he had found her bleeding three days before.

'Thank you for coming back, Xan,' she said, her voice trembling. 'Did the trial go well?'

'I imagine you have been told,' he said.

He saw a flash of anger come to her eyes then. She tilted her head, biting her lower lip for an instant as if to hold back words, then letting it go as she spoke them anyway.

'You are still furious with me? Is that it? Will you divorce me, then? Or force me to endure more days of absence while anger eats at you? I am sorry! I have said it! Did you read the letter I sent?' He shook his head and she flung up her arms in exasperation. 'I have tried to apologise, but I cannot undo it. I cannot go back.'

He took her by the arm, ignoring the soft gasp she made as he force-walked her into a study and kicked the door shut on the cloisters and green garden. There would be slaves within call, of course. No doubt Manias would contrive some excuse to knock on the door and check his mistress did not require his presence. Yet for the moment, they were as alone as they could ever be.

Xanthippus released her arm. Agariste rubbed it as she faced him and he saw the pale marks of his grip on her skin. She was afraid, he realised. She was shaking with it, like a boy before his first battle. He struggled to control the anger that flared in him.

'Were you pregnant, then?' he said. 'I assume that is why you took the drink.'

She nodded, wide-eyed and silent.

'You cost me a child,' he said, 'perhaps another son. And you almost died. Have you any idea how close I came to losing you? For what? Is it such a burden to be a mother to my children? To bear one more? I cannot *understand* you!'

'You don't know,' she said softly, 'what it is like. To be filled and swollen with a child. I endured it three times! I gave you two sons and a daughter – that is enough! Each one pulled and tore me. You have no idea. I spent months vomiting so hard my skin mottled with tiny spots of blood. Yet I did it! I bore them all, in my innocence. Is it so hard to understand I might want another year, or two or three, without going through all that again? That I wanted to raise the ones I had, not see my breasts swell with milk once more, my back aching, my skin stretching? I have done my duty. The tea was . . . for me.'

'And you are sure you were pregnant?' he whispered, eyeing the curve of her womb as she stood before him.

She nodded, fierce and afraid at the same time.

'If you had told me, I could have taken a mistress to bear children. Even Epikleos has . . .'

'They would not be your heirs,' she said. 'Or they would compete with Ariphron and Pericles for your inheritance. Or you would seek to put me aside and marry her! Why would I *ever* choose that?' She began to sob, tears streaming. 'I regret it, Xan. I do regret what I did. I only wanted a year or two without giving birth. I took the tea a dozen times with just a heavier bleed . . . Please don't *look* at me like that.'

'I am wondering how many of my children you have murdered,' he said. 'I'm going to go back to the city, Agariste. I think I will kill you if I stay here.'

'Please don't go. Just stay and talk with me. I am so sorry, Xan.'

She tried to embrace him and he pushed her back, more roughly than he had intended, so that she stumbled against the desk. A knock sounded instantly on the door at his back. Xanthippus mastered himself. He was no young man to be consumed by his passions. He turned to open the door and found Manias there, with a basket, looking past him in concern.

'The mistress asked me to bring her some fruit, kurios,' Manias said.

Xanthippus nodded at the lie. He took an orange and smelled it, breathing in deeply.

'Very well. I am finished here,' he said.

He did not look back, though he heard the soft choking sounds of Agariste weeping as he strode away.

Xanthippus came awake with a start, looking sleepily around at the narrow room of his town-house, in the shadow of the Acropolis. Knocking? The slaves would answer it. He felt fresh and alert, so it could not be too early. The house had served him well over the years when he didn't want to go home to his wife, when he and a few friends had stayed up all night to talk and laugh and drink, before collapsing and snoring through the mornings. The night before, he'd been uncharacteristically sober. The slaves had sensed it. Though he kept only six in that building, they had caught each other's eye in wonder as he'd requested a light meal and asked for his room to be aired and made ready.

He had decided to forgive Agariste. Her tears had moved him even in his anger. That was part of it. Her family could also make his life harder than it was, if they believed he had mistreated her. Even as one of the Marathonomachoi, he had not risen so far that they could not snag his hem and pull him back down, not if they set out to do it. Her father was a stern and pompous old man, who seemed to think Agariste could have made a better match.

Xanthippus sighed as the knocking was interrupted below. He could hear voices. Epikleos? Perhaps. He thought again of Agariste. The combination of tears and her beauty aroused pity in him, of course. More, it made lust rise, though that was mingled with pain. Could he trust her not to murder another of his children? In all the other times they'd argued, going to bed had helped, sometimes like a dam breaking after days of strain. Yet this time, he could not bear the idea of filling her with a child she might then go on to kill. The thought was an ugly one and he felt it twist his face into anger. He could *not* forgive her. He could not go home.

'Again and again, around and around . . .' he murmured wearily.

He could hear steps coming up the stairs from below and he rose, naked, taking a robe from where it had been laid out for him. Xanthippus yawned and scratched his chin, feeling the bristles there. He would have to go to the barber and gymnasium before he felt fresh and cool again.

Epikleos entered the room. His expression stole away any sense of welcome.

'Have you heard?' he said.

It was obvious Xanthippus knew nothing and Epikleos went on.

'Miltiades is dead. First night in the cell. They found him stiff and cold about an hour ago. His heart, the doctors say. His son has been told.'

'Was it his wound? The fever?'

'Perhaps. It played a part, of course. Perhaps being imprisoned and paying a fine to beggar even a wealthy family played its part as well. No one can say. Themistocles offered to speak at his funeral.'

'Of course he did,' Xanthippus replied. He rubbed his jaw, thinking. Epikleos watched him warily.

'How did you know I was here?' Xanthippus said suddenly.

'I didn't. I went first to the estate. Agariste was . . . upset. She said you would be here and so I came back. I take it you and she have not come to terms.'

'Not yet, my friend. It is too serious to discuss it with you, at least for now.'

Xanthippus had a horror of sharing the intimate details of his marriage with anyone. It gave another man power over him, somehow. At least Epikleos knew him well enough not to expect it.

'As for Miltiades, I think . . . I think I am delighted!' Xanthippus said. 'I asked for death – and here it is. He offered a vast fine to the city, which we will still claim. Can we still claim the fine?'

Epikleos nodded.

'If Cimon doesn't want to be exiled, he will pay it. Though I suppose fifty talents would make exile bearable enough. I imagine he will be bitter about it, but then he doesn't know what his father did – and Miltiades did cost the city hundreds of thousands of drachms. It is owed.'

Epikleos eyed his friend, seeing the amusement in him.

'Xanthippus, I think you should put on the most solemn face this morning, if you leave the house. Friends of Miltiades will be looking to see if you boast or laugh. Do not invite their anger, my friend.'

'Oh, I will be grave – and stern and dignified,' Xanthippus said, though his eyes gleamed with humour. 'The gods must truly be capricious. Today, they smile on me.'

He gave a great roar of delight, surprising Epikleos and making him grin. Xanthippus patted the air with one hand and pressed the other to his lips, laughing as he did so.

'That is all, I swear. No more. Will you come to the baths? I imagine there will be some sort of meeting of the Assembly this morning, once the news spreads. I'd like to be clean and to have eaten by then.'

'I've already had a little bread in wine,' Epikleos replied. 'Let me go out and judge the mood of the city. You'll find me on the Pnyx.'

19

Cimon swayed as he stood over his father's body, looking down on cold flesh. A half-full wineskin hung like a slaughtered lamb from his hand. The young man reeked of sour wine and vomit, the smell strong in that small place. He had remained there, just looking, for a long time. No one had dared interrupt him. Outside the room, the household waited in silence and whispers for the heir to say goodbye, unwilling to interrupt his vigil.

There was no mistaking death, not in its presence. He had heard of others who claimed it looked like sleep, as if their loved ones had breathed out and out and simply rested. Miltiades had not become a shade so easily. Separated from his family and friends, behind a locked door, Miltiades had gone from the world in delirium and pain.

Cimon reached out to touch a cold hand, a hand that had once embraced him, that had ruffled his hair. He would never again hear his father's voice, in praise or exasperation, not a single word. A priest of Hades had come to bless the body and send the soul safe to his master. That man waited in the doorway, his impatience showing. Perhaps he had seen so much of death he could no longer even understand loss. Fishermen care nothing for their catch, Cimon knew. The young man had brushed past the priest when he'd come through, or rather the priest had stepped out of his way rather than be flattened. There was something implacable about Cimon when he had been drinking hard.

The temple of Athena on the Acropolis had sent their

high priestess to honour Miltiades. She stood with her colleague just back from the threshold of the room, a motherly woman bearing a staff and a branch of green olives. When the priest of Hades bent close and murmured something, she shook her head sternly. Cimon's mother and her sisters were also present, there to wash and clean his father's body. Together, they stood as a group in careful, aware silence, like actors about to go on.

That was in part why Cimon had not moved for an age. His father had found his aunts irritating. That they should be the ones to wash his flesh, even just to look on him when he was vulnerable, when he could not *defend* himself from their judgement with his sharp eyes and sharper thoughts . . . it kept Cimon in the room, guarding Miltiades in death as he had not been able to in life.

Tugging at the leather tip, Cimon poured more wine down his throat, feeling it splash off his teeth and spill to run down his chest. He belched, feeling grief rise and fall as if he was the shore and loss was a great tide. There were times when he felt nothing at all, when he could look on the dark yellow wax of his father's face and see only death, not the one who had taught him the bow and the sword, who had instructed him in the duties of a man. Miltiades had triumphed at Marathon, saving the city from a Persian invasion. Every boy thought their father a hero. Yet Miltiades truly was one.

'They loved you then,' Cimon murmured, his voice breaking.

He had something he was meant to do, he recalled, some *duty* the priest had told him. He shook his head. He would not weep, not with them watching from under lowered brows. They would spread the word that the son of the great general had cried like a woman. He would not give them that. Through the day of laying out and the funeral procession the following night, even to the interment in the great cemetery outside the city wall, Cimon knew he would be watched. He was the head of the family and the heir to a great Athenian.

He drank again, filling his mouth with the thin stream and gulping. He was a fish swimming in wine, a thought that brought him close to choking, so that he had to steady himself against his father's marble bier until the coughing subsided. His stomach was full of bitter gall. The front of his tunic was stained with it. He realised he could smell vomit and had a vague sense that he was responsible. He waved the idea away and raised the wineskin again. He did not want to feel such grief, so he drank it to fragments, his teeth red with wine.

After a time, Cimon patted his father's hand, gripping it for a moment, though the touch made his own flesh creep. It was cold and stiff, and yet he trembled as he held it for the last time.

'I will honour you. I will see you safe, kurios,' he said.

The title fitted his father well enough. Cimon had thought the hero of Marathon could not fail. Yet even there, in that room, he could smell rot in the leg, still thick and inflamed, with lines like purple veins running into the good flesh. Beneath the wrappings the wound had soured, despite the healers letting it bleed free and dipping bandages in honey. Sometimes, the gods took even strong men. Hades welcomed deserving and undeserving alike for the underworld. In the end, they all crossed the river.

The thought jarred him and he fumbled in a pouch for a gold coin, with the image of a Persian archer on the soft metal. Cimon opened his father's mouth and slipped it into the cheek, wincing at the clink it made against the teeth. He felt tears come as he tried to close the mouth and saw it slowly ease open once more. It was unnerving to see movement, though he knew the dead could belch and twitch. His father had told him of men killed in battle who could suddenly sit up, hours later, terrifying those around them. Life held on, desperately.

Cimon pressed his hand over his father's mouth, holding it shut, for all the world as if he tried to smother him. He found himself sobbing silently as he did it, struggling to breathe as if he choked on a bone. When he took his hand away, the jaw had stiffened into place once more. He stood back then, breathing hard until he had mastered himself. The women would wail and shriek; that was their role. His was to be calm and stern, though the wine was strong in his blood and he knew he might vomit again. Still, his swimming senses were a comfort.

He thought of seeing pity in every face for the next days, until his father was in the family tomb. Surely his father's accuser would not be present. Xanthippus would not dare to join the procession. Cimon firmed his jaw at the thought. If he did, there would be blood. Honour would demand it of . . .

He heard the presence of Themistocles in the flurry of greetings and thanks from the outer rooms. His mother's voice, speaking in hushed tones of delighted awe. Cimon pushed out his lower lip as he stood there, his hand resting on his father's once again. He did not want another man to witness his private grief. He eyed the other door and considered just walking out into the gardens. He longed for it, but he would not abandon his father.

'I will not leave you alone, kurios,' he said. 'I will stand with you.'

For some reason, the words brought a surge of grief. He had to struggle not to break down and bawl like a child. He wiped his eyes as Themistocles entered the room, bringing with him a scent of summer and the warmer air outside.

'Thank you for honouring my father,' Cimon said as a

greeting. He knew he was slurring, while the room swam before him. Even so, Themistocles looked full of his own sorrow. He came forward and stood alongside as they looked down on Miltiades.

'He was a great man,' Themistocles said. 'He saved us all, every one of us.'

Cimon felt a rush of gratitude as he nodded. On impulse, he handed over the wineskin and watched as Themistocles directed the stream, swallowing over and over until Cimon found his eyebrows raising.

Themistocles gasped as he handed it back.

'Dark times call for a drink,' he said. 'Perhaps when the funeral is over, you will come to my gymnasium on the Ilissus, or a brothel I bought recently. I can promise you discretion – a private place to grieve.'

Cimon waved his hand, blearily.

'I have private places. I am my father's heir. All he owned is mine today, all of it.'

'And . . . will you still have it all when the fine is paid?' Themistocles asked.

Cimon eyed him suspiciously, but then deflated like his own wineskin, blowing air from his lips. The young man nodded and shrugged.

'We prepared the full amount. Fifty talents in silver. Have you ever seen so much? It will have to come in to the council building in a caravan of carts! Three hundred thousand drachms? And for what? A day of life? Perhaps I won't pay it.'

'You will,' Themistocles said softly. 'It bought your father an honourable death, instead of a knife, or worse. The gods gave him that much.' He thought for a moment before going on. 'If you wish, I will send men for it this evening – officials of the Assembly. We'll have it counted in the Agora and, yes . . . we'll bless your father's name aloud, so that every man and woman in Athens will know your family provided the silver.'

'That is . . . all right, that is a kind thing. That would please my father's shade, I think.'

'And you will not have to sell your properties? Miltiades was wealthier than I knew.'

'We have a new seam – and he dealt with some merchants. There are debts, but we will survive . . .'

Cimon broke off and looked up at Themistocles. Instead of going on, he took another draught and held out the wine-skin. As Themistocles drank, Cimon leaned in close and whispered to his ear.

'I am going to kill Xanthippus.'

Themistocles sighed. He made a show of replacing the leather tip over the spigot, sealing the wine and placing it to one side.

'No. You're not. If you did, you would be held in the same cell as your father. The next trial day is in a week. You would be dragged over to the Areopagus and your fate put to a vote. Xanthippus is a popular man. His wife's family are both wealthy and well loved. You would not be able to pay a fine great enough to survive that trial. That is the wine speaking, I understand. I heard nothing and if I had, the words are just anger and wind.'

'He is responsible,' Cimon said mulishly. 'My father's heart failed with the strain, with the shame of being taken up like a common criminal, of having to endure a trial, being p-put in a hole to rot! I swear . . .'

His voice had risen and Themistocles stepped in closer, blocking the doorway to the outer room with his broad back.

'Son, you must not make threats. There are other ears around, not just mine. Please. Don't say anything I will have to repeat in front of a jury. Xanthippus . . .' He waited while the young man hissed pain and fury at the name. 'Xanthippus brought a case for loss, for disaster. Your father's captains told the tale well enough. You have no cause for vengeance against him. He does not deserve death any more than your father did, can you understand that? Nor exile. We ostracise men who have grown too arrogant, who command too much power. That does not apply here, nor could you find the six thousand votes. Xanthippus is a name in Athens. More, he is a friend of mine and a good man, though I admit he seems to favour Aristides. Such men are beyond your reach, Cimon. You must see that.'

'I do not see that. I will find a way,' Cimon said. 'It does not concern you, kurios. It is for me and for my father, who was a good man. Who died in shame and pain, when he should have been tended by his slaves at home. I will find a way . . .'

'I will secure the silver for you,' Themistocles said. 'I can take that burden, at least, while you are in grief. I will have it taken to the council building in the Agora . . .'

'Where my father was held, in a cell. Where he died,' Cimon snapped.

Themistocles bowed his head as if in prayer.

'Yes. Though he did not weep or complain. He went like a man before his gods, Cimon. If you will permit it, may I speak at the funeral, to honour your father?'

The young man embraced him. Themistocles waited until the sobs subsided, the noise hidden in his robe.

'Your father was a great Athenian,' Themistocles said. 'He would want to see you grown to thirty, with a wife and children of your own. Don't make me bring you to trial. Do you understand? The laws bind us all. Your fate is your own.'

Cimon stood back, his eyes inflamed. Themistocles handed him a cloth and he rubbed his entire face with it, dabbing at sweat and tears. Cimon nodded to him and Themistocles patted him on the shoulder before going out.

The priest of Hades had begun a murmured conversation with his female counterpart. They stood stiffly in the presence of one of the names of Athens.

'Themistocles,' the priest of Hades said in greeting, bowing his head.

'Father,' Themistocles replied. He wondered how much they had heard.

Behind the representatives of the temples, Cimon's mother waited. Themistocles saw a rather dowdy, middle-aged woman with not much waist. He saw she wore a black dress with a gold necklace that could have adorned the throat of a queen. The family wore its wealth openly. Themistocles wondered what part of it had come from Persian coffers.

'Kuria,' he said, bowing and giving her honour in her own home. 'Your son asked me to secure the talents for the city treasury. I would like to make an accounting of every coin and arrange guards to have it all transported back.'

She waved a hand in the midst of her weeping, a cloth clutched to her face. There were no restrictions of dignity on the grieving of women. In fact, she had been unusually quiet, waiting for her son. Themistocles could not judge whether that meant true grief or something feigned.

'Take it,' she said, when he continued to wait for permission.

Such a sum could not be treated lightly, he knew. He really would need guards, perhaps a hundred hoplites in full armour. If he somehow lost fifty talents, he'd find the Assembly voting on his exile or death the following day, that was a certainty.

'Thank you,' he said. Athens needed every coin, after all. They had a fleet to build, a fleet that would crush the Persian ships when they came again.

He bowed to Cimon's mother and backed from the room, following a slave to a cloister stacked with wooden crates near the front gate. House guards stood watch, stepping forward with spears levelled until his right to stand there had been confirmed.

Themistocles broke a crate open while they all watched him. He ran a hand over the silver within, seeing how the guards stared. Perhaps they assumed any man would dream of stealing such a fortune. The truth was, he would not touch a single coin. He would emulate Aristides in that, rather than be brought down over petty accounting. No, he would show his honour by keeping the silver for Athens and the ships they would build.

'Bring clerks and slaves to keep tally,' Themistocles ordered. 'I want to count them here, before we leave.'

'Master, the coins have already been counted,' one of the guards protested.

'And if I get to the council building and find a dozen drachms missing, there are those who would believe the worst – of you, or me. No, better to make my own count, and be certain, than lose my life and yours for a few coins.'

The guard seemed to understand that quickly enough. He put his spear aside and cracked his knuckles, ready to help. Themistocles bowed his head solemnly.

'This silver is a sacred trust. Given by Miltiades to Athens, after the loss of ships and good men. We must account for every coin, in all honour. In peril of the loss of our souls.'

The gathered slaves seemed struck by his words. He hoped they were, though he'd still have everyone in that room warned, then stripped and searched at the end. So much silver brought greed to the fore, in slave and kurios, man and woman alike.

20

The hiss and flutter of torches was the only sound, thousands of them, enough to make the great cemetery outside the walls of Athens into a place of gold and black shadow, with too much light to see the stars above. Themistocles had not known so many would be present when he'd made his offer to speak. Nor that they would be so young. It seemed Cimon had his own following in the city, present that day to honour his father. Themistocles saw them lounging against tombs centuries old. Most had brought wine, unmixed and raw, too strong in his estimation. It seemed they had begun drinking during the procession out of the city, through the Thriasian gate and the road beyond. The cemetery crowded there, with tombs right up hard against the city wall and spreading always, year by year. Houses that had once been apart from the city's districts were encroached upon. It was not hard to imagine the graves spreading out beyond, until they ringed all Athens, or reached all the way to the sea.

Cimon had spoken to thank the crowd. His voice had been tight and choked, breaking as he talked of his father. It had been short and simple, unadorned, though all the more powerful for that. Themistocles considered it as he decided how to speak. The audience waited patiently as he stood, looking on the open tomb that would house the wrapped figure of Miltiades. He would join his parents and two of his sisters who had died in their youth. Their remains sat like dolls on stone shelves in the mausoleum, deep in the gloom. When the speeches were over, Miltiades would be raised on the shoulders of his son and his friends, to be carried in among the bones of his family. It was just flesh, of course. The shade was gone. There. That was where he could start.

'Miltiades has gone. Of that we are sure. He does not lie in the weary flesh that bore him. In his last breath, his soul escaped – and in that breath, he found peace. You may be sure he looked down on his son then, on his wife, on us all. I know that he was proud of Cimon, so proud it choked him. I know too that he could be moved to tears when he spoke of Marathon.'

There was a murmur of approval from beyond the crowd. Themistocles looked out, past the closest and the youngest standing in their white chiton robes, some with a shoulder bare, some covered. Further back, he saw a glimpse of golden armour in the torchlight. Hoplites had come dressed for war. He could see them now.

'Come closer if you stood with him on that day,' Themistocles said, as if he had summoned them with his words. It felt as if he had! They came in like the ghosts of battle and he had to smother his own awe to go on. Hundreds and hundreds of them had decided to wear their greaves and breastplates, to take up their spear, sword and shield as they walked out of the city on that night. To his surprise, Themistocles felt himself moved by their simple gesture. He had to rub at his eyes for a moment.

'I was there, in the centre that day,' he said. 'Miltiades sent us forward and I thought we would not survive. Not against so many. I knew I would die! I *knew* it was the end! But I stood with my brothers – my tribe, yes, but Athenians, Greeks! I could no more have left them to save my own life than I could fly. We stood as brothers and Miltiades knew we would not break.'

He paused, for a single beat.

'Though it was close . . .'

His smile brought a chuckle from all those who remembered. In its way, it was like a shout of memory. They had been there, with him.

'The Persian archers and slingers crept back like jackals to torment us. Miltiades held his wing ready, waiting for the right moment, the moment that would win the battle.' He paused again, staring into the darkness, ringed in bronze and fire. 'And then he came. We fought until they broke. I watched good men die around me and I knew each one was my brother, as Aristides is my brother, as Miltiades was, as Xanthippus . . .'

Themistocles broke off as a hissing began, looking confused, as if he had not played them like a set of pipes and drawn each note out.

'No, brothers, give him honour! The world has known winter and summer again since then. Perhaps some who were there have lost that sense of brotherhood,' he said. 'But on that day, at Marathon, we were all men of Athens. We fought for the children and the women. We fought for our fathers and our temples and our gods. One city, one language, one culture! One democracy! I know the sacrifice of those who fell, because I was willing to make it myself. The gods took the ones they wanted. They left the rest of us to mourn them, as I do, every day.'

He paused, and some of the younger men raised skins or amphorae to honour him. The hissing died away and, again, only the torches could be heard, while the city beyond the wall settled down to sleep.

'Good fortune turns like the seasons,' Themistocles went on, his voice so low they had to crane to hear him, as if he spoke a private thought only to himself. 'The gods allow greatness, and then for some the wheel moves on. For

Miltiades, it was not some failing of the sort that brings men down. It was not lust, or greed, or weakness of character. No ... he wanted to keep Athens safe by destroying an enemy.'

He was speaking slower than before, teasing the words out as he went.

'He landed ships on a shore where a fleet had been beached – and he knew he had them. He had tracked them on the trackless sea and he had brought them to ground. He had them. Those first ships landed hard in the surf, leaning over. The Persians watched them come, hidden in the tree-line, unseen in their thousands. If Miltiades could have brought all his crews and soldiers to land, he would have wrenched victory from them even so. Yet he could not. He had to watch in agony as his first crews were overwhelmed. He sent in the rest, but there were more and more of the enemy. The sand soaked in the blood of good men, of hoplites who had stood at Marathon, of oarsmen who didn't deserve to be slaughtered. Miltiades himself took a terrible wound in his thigh, a spear that gashed him and poisoned the wound. He was carried off that beach by those that loved him.'

Themistocles rubbed his eyes once more, seemed to emerge from a state almost of an oracle, where the truth and the words of the gods were drawn out, unstoppably. He gestured for a skin of wine from one of the young men. A chuckle went around the crowd again as he drank and smacked his lips.

'You lads should try a little water mixed in,' he said, to make them laugh. Even as they did, he went to end his oration.

'Miltiades was a great father, strategos and Athenian. When he won, it was because his character was noble. When he failed, it was because he was but a man. All of us fail. All of us rise again. If you have wine, raise it up to Miltiades, as he waits for the ferryman tonight. Let him hear you honour him. To Miltiades!'

Themistocles raised the skin and drank again before tossing it back to its owner and wiping his mouth. The crowd roared their approval and more than a few called the name of the speaker as well.

As silence came again, Cimon stepped forward, red-eyed, with five others, lifting the wrapped corpse onto their shoulders and carrying it into the echoing tomb. Themistocles waited for them to finish the duties and for the priests of Hades, Apollo and Athena to give prayers and sacrifices to ensure his welcome. Miltiades would not tarry long by the river. He would go on, to the Fields of Elysium, to be honoured by all those who had gone before.

21

Xanthippus walked to the council building, through streets busy with the trade that was the lifeblood of his city. Fifty men from each tribe formed the administration of Athens. They took charge of the cells and the treasury and acted quickly when the Assembly could not. More, they organised carpenters and smelters and labourers and shipwrights to build a fleet and dig silver from the earth. From just five hundred volunteers, all officials were chosen, including the epistates himself. Yet the life of the city was in the colourful glazes on pots held out to him as he passed by, in leather belts and fine-woven robes, in iron nails and clay bricks, in figs, wine and oil. There would always be shouts and debate and juries and war. The true heartbeat of Athens was the sound of coins dropped into a cupped hand. Xanthippus chewed his lower lip at that thought, hoping it was not a blasphemy.

He had been there to witness the entry of the Miltiades silver the week before. It had been hard to miss, Themistocles riding a cart with a pale blue cloak wrapped around him and an expression of solemnity on his noble brow. He had made such a show of bringing it in, Athenians had come to stand three-deep along the roads to watch the procession of carts and marching hoplite guards. They had begun to cheer and wave as word went round of the fortune, as if Themistocles had brought home the treasury of another city.

It had seemed almost the first act of the play that had been the Miltiades funeral. After the silver had been brought to the council coffers and counted again, a more solemn event had wound its way through the city districts that night, lit by thousands of torches. Men who had fought at Marathon had joined in, some of them in full armour to honour the man who had brought them that victory.

Xanthippus had stayed in his town-house and retired early. He'd heard from Epikleos how well Themistocles had spoken of Miltiades' honour and successes. There was no reason to speak ill of the dead, and by all accounts it had been a fine performance. It seemed there had been a sort of hiss when Xanthippus' name came up as part of the recitation of strategoi at Marathon.

He frowned as he walked along. In the days since, it had been hard not to sense a new hostility as he completed his business in Athens. Whether it was in the Assembly or the courts on trial mornings, in council meetings, at the port or simply overseeing the produce of his estate and holdings brought to market, hard stares and whispers seemed to follow him. Miltiades had been a popular man.

Xanthippus thought it would fade. It had to, with time passing. He had not killed Miltiades! Somehow, the story seemed to have taken hold that a great Athenian hero had been brought down by treachery and low accusation. Xanthippus stiffened as someone muttered a foul insult behind his back. A woman! He looked at her in fury. It had not been open enough for him to challenge, even if he could have found a way to do so without looking a fool. No, he had to ignore them in their pettiness and spite. It would settle down in time, or when the mob found some other target. In the meantime, he had to endure.

It might have been easier if he had been able to confide in his wife. Yet his relationship with Agariste had become a cold thing, a strain that smothered some part of him, so that he spent whole days clenched and miserable, as if he swam underwater and could not think. He did his duty by her when it came to the income of the estate, though the bills were settled by his servants and rarely needed his personal attention. He had taken the time to ride with each of his children, teaching them how to sit and grip with their knees. Agariste had come to watch the instruction and he'd been very aware of her there, leaning on a fence. There had even been a smile when Pericles came tumbling off and staggered bawling to his mother for comfort. Yet it had not stretched to her husband when he looked over. There was no warmth for him. He no longer knew how to close the distance between them.

The council building was an impressive construction, a statement of intent of a new administration, the edges still sharp. The old Areopagus council had their ancient stone, but this was for the people, built in limestone and brick, with polished columns. Each year, a new five hundred would enter the council building and run Athens. With all the checks and balances they had created, it worked; that was the wonder of it. Xanthippus felt mingled pride and exasperation as he was challenged and then recognised at the entrance. They were all so proud of what they had achieved! They took their responsibilities seriously and they gave part of each month to make it run. There was no written constitution. The laws depended on goodwill and tradition – and common sense. It meant the Assembly members felt part of the city, even the poorest, Xanthippus realised. Families like his own had given away part of their authority for a dream of something more. He had lost deference, in return for that common spirit.

He sighed. It did not seem such a fine bargain when market sellers hissed insults under their breath at him. Alongside the Agora, the Ceramicus was one of the poorest areas, where all the city's pots and urns were made. The roads themselves were made from tiny pottery shards, embedded in clay and

dust. The city wall was not far off and beyond that, the cemetery where Miltiades had been interred. Xanthippus stopped
suddenly before shaking his head. Someone else cursed him
for blocking the road, though he thought there was no special
malice in it. Xanthippus had not visited the tomb of Miltiades, to say his last words to the man's shade. It was owed, but
then it might cause a riot if he went, even a week later. It
would not hurt to wait for the blossoms to fade.

At the entrance to the council building, Xanthippus found
himself looking back, imagining the procession. How could
he have become the villain of the tale? He had won fifty talents for Athens by his accusation! Twenty-five galleys could
be built for such a sum, he reminded himself, or a man's
working wage paid for a thousand years! If that wasn't a form
of 'trierarchia' – the duty to pay for war galleys – he didn't
know what was. Would Miltiades have paid such a sum vol-
untarily? Of course not.

'Xan!' he heard, startling him out of his reverie. It was
Epikleos. Xanthippus raised an eyebrow to see his friend in
a simple tunic, his legs bare in the heat.

'Where are your armour and weapons? Are you not running today?'

'I handed them in at your house. I thought I'd get ready
with you, if that's all right.'

Xanthippus nodded, still glum.

'The er . . . the numbers are not . . . there are not many
with us,' Epikleos added, without looking directly at him.

In the months after Marathon, Xanthippus had organised
dozens of races through and around the city for any hoplite
willing to improve his fitness. They were run in full armour,
with shields, spears and weapons, exactly as they would need
in battle. At the height, over a thousand had joined them,
running in agonising sprint charges or a long lope around

the city walls to build lungs and stamina. It was gruelling and exhausting, but they had felt the benefit, with better wind and strength after just a short time.

The numbers had dropped off a cliff after the trial and death of Miltiades. In just a few days, the group had shrunk almost to nothing, as if word had spread that he was a leper, or cursed. Xanthippus wondered even so at the nervousness in Epikleos. Was he so stern, so terrible?

'How many today?' he asked.

'Perhaps a dozen from Acamantis, around as many again. No more than that, I'm told.'

'I hope the ones that have stopped coming never have to face another Persian line then, or charge their archers!'

Xanthippus could not hide his flush or his anger, though he felt guilty snapping at Epikleos, who bore none of the blame.

'Is it Cimon?' Xanthippus asked when he had mastered himself.

'He is . . . a charismatic young man,' Epikleos said, keeping his voice down. 'More like his father than I understood at first. He blames you openly for what happened, and he still has wealth, with all the influence that comes from that. The crumbs from his table are worth having, especially to poor young men. He has offered to train them himself, at new facilities at the Academy gymnasium.'

'That old place?' Xanthippus snorted.

Epikleos looked unhappy as he replied.

'They are rebuilding it – a new track, new gardens. Cimon's wealth pays for all, while they run together there, each morning now. He talks of a grand expedition to seek the tomb of Theseus, with himself as their leader. The manner of his father's death has won him many supporters, Xan. I'm sorry.'

Xanthippus cursed under his breath. He did not want to

be pitied as he ran practically alone, nor followed by groups of urchins throwing stones. Though it galled him, he decided to take a route right out of the city and down to the port. He would show them the ships being built there, with dwindling stacks of seasoned pine and oak, cut from forests hundreds of miles away and dried for years before it could be used. The new fleet was a vast enterprise that overwhelmed the port itself. Already, there was talk of building massive new quays and workshops, while every carpenter was asking twice the normal wage or threatening to walk away with his tools. Xanthippus waved a hand and spat on the marble, irritated with their greed, irritated with everything.

'I did not come to the council to hear Cimon's spite, unworthy as it is – undeserved as it is. Have the councillors put up the subjects for debate? I am waiting for some word on the new silver from Laurium. Some of the master shipwrights have not been paid in a week. They'll have to stop soon or starve, without funds.'

Epikleos nodded, though he looked unhappier than ever.

'The council has sent a delegation to Laurium to examine the works and assess the need for new labourers. I'm told they will report to the Assembly no earlier than a week from today,' he said. 'The word is they'll need to move to ten- or twelve-hour shifts to have a chance of producing enough ore. It all increases the cost – and, of course, the refiners and stampers are after more pay as well.'

'Which tribe has the spear-point?' Xanthippus said.

'Leontis is on for twelve more days – after that, our own dear Acamantis.'

'Another week to wait for the report, though! Why so long, if the problems are already clear to all?' Xanthippus rubbed his face with an open hand, over skin that looked red and rough. 'They've had months to organise shifts and construct new furnaces. This is . . . lazy, or the foremen are incompetent. Perhaps some idiot sons have been appointed where they should not have been.'

Once again he rubbed his jaw, scratching a strip with a fingernail.

'Themistocles commands Leontis, in all they do,' he said. 'Though he hides it. Why would *he* delay? Should I raise it with him?'

'Not if he is the one behind the delay,' Epikleos said. He could not help checking around to be sure they were not overheard.

'That can't be true,' Xanthippus snorted. 'If anything, he would bring *forward* the date of that report, or be urging them to spend more on workers. Themistocles was the one who wanted that silver for ships in the first place!'

'Perhaps. Yet he has not. He has been quiet over this. I think that will continue – unless there is some advantage for him.' Epikleos sighed, wearily. 'He is said to be close with Cimon after the way he spoke at the funeral. Cimon is spending silver like a Persian, I know that much.' They exchanged a glance at that, though it would not be said aloud. 'The council are just men, Xan. Just volunteers. They can be flattered and invited to dinners, given good seats in the theatre, made to feel important, who knows? Perhaps Themistocles seeks influence just to squeeze a better rate of pay for the miners and forge-men, with part of it paid back to the one who arranged it. All legal, as fees for the broker. A delayed report would benefit him then, as the silver dries up and people starve and riots begin in the Agora. Such things go on all the time.'

Xanthippus stared at his friend, unnerved by the possibility.

'The shipwrights are claiming double pay at the port,' he said.

'There you are. Can you blame them? When the need for their skill is so great? I'm surprised they are not asking for more.'

'But that will practically double the cost of the ships! What good will a pouch of silver do them when the Persian fleet returns? Are you saying Themistocles is behind such demands? I have never heard of such a thing!'

Epikleos spread his hands.

'You are not a deal-maker, Xan. Your wealth protects you. Men like Themistocles can raise a fleet or dig silver ore for Athens, but they are not above skimming cream from the deal or taking a cut to make themselves rich. He has no family fortune, I've heard. If he ever had, the way he spends would beggar anyone. Feasts and plays and new buildings, three triremes promised from his own funds? The people love him.'

'We will never allow another tyrant,' Xanthippus said sternly.

'Perhaps we'll raise one even so – one the Assembly choose. I'd say Themistocles wants to be first man in Athens, Xan, wouldn't you? Anyone can see. Miltiades might have stopped him, but you brought him down. Aristides still could – or you. Who else? Just be careful, would you? For all his laughter, Themistocles is ruthless, never doubt it.'

'You're wrong,' Xanthippus replied. He thought back to the day at the gymnasium, when Themistocles had talked of his childhood. 'I know him, better than you realise. He is . . . vulgar, loud, yes, all the things I find tiresome. He has little sense of the value of silver, I know that much. Yet I think he is a man of honour. He is a true Athenian.'

'I hope so,' Epikleos said. 'He is certainly the sort of man others follow. I saw it at the funeral. The trouble with that is where he will lead them.'

'He argued for the new silver from Laurium to be spent

on a fleet,' Xanthippus reminded his friend. 'Not his own enrichment, for slaves or roads and tiles. That was right – as I said at the time. I tell you, I would welcome two or three of him, if we had four hundred triremes as a result!'

Epikleos looked away into the distance rather than continue to argue with his friend, his doubts clear. Seeing it, Xanthippus felt his patience unravel. He was almost forty and the subtleties of politics and shifting alliances felt trivial, almost childish. In the natural pause, he patted Epikleos on the arm.

'Let me ask my questions inside. Give me just a short time and I'll come out. We'll run to the port today – and back.'

Epikleos groaned and smiled as he was expected to do, but his expression was worried as Xanthippus vanished into the council building. He had watched Themistocles speak at Miltiades' funeral. With an orator of such great skill, there were a dozen ways it could have gone. Yet the sense of Miltiades being a wronged man, a hero brought down by his accuser, had come from that eulogy. Perhaps not all the blame for it could be laid at the feet of Themistocles, but that was part of what made him dangerous. There was always another way of seeing. Men loved Themistocles – and they could see no evil in him. Epikleos knew Xanthippus admired the man, for his warmth and his extraordinary skill with a crowd – for all, perhaps, that Xanthippus was not.

While he waited, Epikleos scraped his foot across a shard of pot that crunched underfoot. For himself, in all honesty, he was in awe of both men, but they were made of very different clay. Few could move the Assembly like Themistocles.

Epikleos turned his hand so that he could bite a piece of nail on his thumb, something he only did when he was worried. Epikleos had tried to warn his friend, but Xanthippus would not hear him.

22

Cimon entered the gymnasium to the south of the city. He had not slept the night before and he could feel the scratchiness and sweat as weariness caught up with him. Yet at eighteen, he felt sharp even so. Sleep was just an interruption to life, an irritant that tugged at his sleeve when he wanted to go on and on.

None of the staff challenged him as he entered the gate and strode through the cloisters along the open field. That too was exhilarating. With his father barely in the grave, he had risen as a name in Athens. Part of it was from those who thought Miltiades had been poorly treated, killed unfairly after a lifetime of service. There were others who had been at Marathon who had pledged themselves to his son after the funeral procession. Cimon did not completely understand what drove those men, but he was willing to take their oaths. He did so without hesitation, though it made them clients of his family. That support would incur its own debts when they fell ill or were wounded. Yet he had not turned them down – and word had spread that he would not. He saw in them that Marathon had been a golden moment, when they had tested themselves and not been found wanting, when they had proved their courage in the forge-fire. Nothing would ever taste as sweet again, he thought. For them. He would find his own fruit – and make it run in thick juice down his chin and chest.

Themistocles had brought that support to the fore, with his speech at the funeral. Cimon still didn't know if the man had planned it, or whether he had simply reacted to seeing so many hoplites in armour, come to honour a name of Athens. From that moment, Cimon had been handed his father's mantle. Men who had commanded a phalanx had bowed to him – men with the influence no mere eighteen-year-old could match. Cimon had joined the Assembly, but he could not bring his own trials, nor put his name forward for any number of posts. He could not lead Athens until he was thirty. On that morning he knew two things: that he would, and that it seemed a long way off.

Themistocles was in the boxing ring, sparring lightly with another man. Both were naked except for the wrappings on their hands to protect the knuckles. Even then, too many of the trainers had hands that resembled meaty slabs.

Cimon felt a tremor as he approached. He knew there was a chance Themistocles would ask him to spar. Some men tested one another in this way. He wondered how well Themistocles had researched his habits. Cimon's robe concealed a frame of lean muscle – that was no secret. He ran or trained every day, building fitness until he and his friends were like young leopards in their speed and glowing health.

Themistocles glanced across at the figure approaching and then had to duck under a swing as his opponent tried to take advantage of his inattention.

'Enough, enough!' Themistocles said, chuckling. He kept one hand outstretched as he looked over, Cimon noted, to give him time to react to a rush.

The other man glared at the newcomer. He was red and veined, as if his skin had been scoured. He looked swollen in the face and body somehow, and sore, his mood close to anger.

'I paid for a full session,' the man said, tapping his fists together.

Themistocles turned back to him as if Cimon had vanished, his attention suddenly focused.

'What's that?' he said.

Cimon could hear the edge, though the man seemed not to.

'I said, I had paid for a full session!' the man snapped.

Themistocles stepped in fast then and Cimon saw he had been only playing or teaching before. He hit the man with a jab and then a hook, stunning him. When the other boxer raised his arms, Themistocles hammered blows into his ribs, first one side then the other. It made the fellow groan and try to protect himself. Themistocles danced a step and then hit him again with a flurry of hooks and an uppercut, stepping aside as the man collapsed onto the sand. He lay unmoving for a moment and Themistocles signalled one of his staff to roll him over before he inhaled sand and suffocated.

Cimon saw Themistocles smile, almost to himself, relishing the victory as he held out his hands to be unwrapped. Two slaves moved quickly for one of the co-owners of the gymnasium. It was just moments before Themistocles stepped out of the ring to greet Cimon, presenting a hand still compressed and pale from being held closed for so long.

Cimon accepted the grip, though sweat poured from the other man. There were different kinds of tests.

'I need to swim. You look tired, Cimon. I hope you took my advice to rest.'

'I sleep for a few hours in the afternoons,' Cimon replied as they began to walk. 'I can live without it – as long as I get to sleep a whole night and morning every few weeks.'

Themistocles groaned.

'By the gods, to be so young. I can barely remember it . . . when nothing hurt, when sleep could be banished with a word, when you could drink all night and run the next day!'

'You seem fit enough . . .' Cimon said.

Themistocles looked for mockery, but there was none. Neither was there understanding. Youth could not understand age and never had.

'I used to be paid to spar, Cimon. Six or eight bouts a morning. Believe me, you have not known exhaustion until you step into the sand ring with some young pup, fresh and hungry, while you have fought half a dozen before him. Yet it paid for my studies and it kept food on my table.'

He pressed a finger to his nose and moved it back and forth ruefully.

'This has been broken so many times, I have lost count, but it was worth it.'

'Surely, though, you don't need to be paid now?' Cimon asked.

'I need to train and be fit. If it pleases some householder to try his luck for a few drachms, I am willing. You were born to wealth, Cimon. I was not. Perhaps that's why I value the coins I earn.'

'I value the wealth of my family,' Cimon said, suddenly serious.

They had crossed the field and reached the banks of the stream that ran through the gymnasium, the source of cool water for them all. It was flowing well that year and Themistocles stepped onto a ledge of good marble and down into the waters.

Cimon watched the big man duck his head and come up blowing and spitting. For once, the eighteen-year-old seemed unsure how to go on. He looked around at the slaves waiting with clean robes and towels for Themistocles to finish. Cimon glanced over his shoulder and saw the boxer had regained his feet. He was standing, groggily, pointing angrily in Themistocles' direction, clearly unhappy about his treatment. Cimon grinned. The day was perfect, with blue skies and swallows wheeling high above the field. On impulse, he removed his robe and sandals and stepped down into the river pool.

'Ah! Very good,' Themistocles said. 'It cleans the blood, this cold. It is excellent for health. I spent most of a day once, seeing how long I could stand it. My legs went numb and my hands wrinkled like an old man, but afterwards, when the blood flowed thick and hard again? I performed wonders – and I was less stiff the day after, though you will not care about that, not yet.'

'I wanted to ask you ... something important,' Cimon said. He leaned back, so that the water reached his collar-bone. His feet stretched over marble onto silken mud, so that he could feel it between his toes. The sun was hot and yet his teeth began to chatter.

Themistocles gestured without looking away. The slaves packed up their equipment and vanished, so that they were alone.

'I am too old to mentor you,' Themistocles said. 'And I am attached to women as lovers. So if it is that . . .'

'It is not that,' Cimon said, his voice low.

Themistocles dropped the smile and rested one arm on the marble ledge, smoothing the surface of the water with his outstretched hand.

'What then? If you don't ask, I can hardly . . .'

'You said I should not kill the man who brought my father down,' Cimon said. He held up his hand as Themistocles began to speak. 'I have agreed. I have mastered myself, as you told me to.'

It seemed a grand claim for just a few days, but Themistocles did not object.

'I have hundreds pledged in support to me – more than you would believe, but not six thousand, not yet.'

Themistocles narrowed his eyes as he considered. He looked away for a moment and Cimon thought he was losing him.

'The laws are clear enough,' he went on. 'Any man may be ostracised, sent into exile for ten years. There does not have to be a formal reason, there is no appeal. It is just the will of the people, expressed in a single vote, like a summer storm. I am an Athenian, Themistocles. My father was Miltiades of Marathon.'

'I know it,' Themistocles said. 'But Xanthippus is a name. He will have support – and if I help you and fail, I think I would risk another vote on my fate.'

'Then you will not help me?' Cimon asked.

Themistocles grimaced, clearly caught. Then as Cimon watched, his expression settled.

'You have not asked, lad,' Themistocles said.

'Then I ask now! Will you help me? Will you add your supporters to mine? I will pay whatever you want.'

Themistocles stayed very still, though the cold was stealing into them both and they shivered even in the sun. Cimon saw a fish swim out of the river pool and across the lowest step, a flicker of brown trout.

'Very well,' Themistocles said at last.

'Name your price,' Cimon said, weak with relief. 'And I will match it, I swear.'

'I do have a price, it seems,' Themistocles said softly. 'Though in this case, it is not silver.'

23

It had rained the night before. Xanthippus could smell it in the dust, in the air, both thicker and sweeter somehow than when it was dry.

He had risen before the sun in his own room on the estate outside the city. Returning to visit Agariste had been for the children more than her. Perhaps for his own comfort as well, when he had the good humour to admit it. Xanthippus found the town-house rather cramped compared to the estate. Here, he was master – with all the facilities of a first-rate gymnasium if he chose to use them. He bit his lip, thinking of the brothel Themistocles had bought. Not all the facilities.

His son Ariphron had adopted a coldness with him that matched his mother, even in the set of the mouth and glowering expression. Xanthippus wondered how Agariste had explained his absence. He had not said a word to them about it himself. Such matters between husband and wife were not the concern of children.

He and Agariste maintained a coolly respectful distance whenever they met, even going so far as to speak of matters in the city and the family holdings. Yet he felt the strain of it, while the children seemed to as well, looking from father to mother with wide eyes.

Leaning against a column, Xanthippus stared over the paddocks, his eye caught by the moving figure on the far side. His daughter Eleni was growing up strong and lithe, her skin deeply tanned from so much time spent out of doors with the horses. She was in love with risk and would delight herself trying to ride two at once, with a foot on each broad back while she balanced and hallooed a hunting call. She had picked up bruises and scratches as well, though strangely it was little Pericles who matched her, more than Ariphron. Perhaps that was the burden of the oldest son, Xanthippus thought. First sons were often leaders; he knew that. The role came with a weight of responsibility they could not shed. Their younger brothers seemed not even to feel it. They tended to be wilder, to have more trouble bending their will to learning or discipline. Certainly it was Pericles who had developed a backwards dive into the river and then taught it to Eleni. The boy's tutors complained he missed half their lessons and yet he could rattle off verbs and declensions as if he'd heard them a thousand times. They beat him anyway, of course, Xanthippus thought with satisfaction. It would not do to let a boy think he had won, not at that age. If Pericles spent less time throwing himself into the air, he would be a prodigy. Xanthippus sighed. Ariphron disliked the river. His oldest son had been frightened by something in the deepest part, clambering out halfway between panic and rage. It did not matter. Men did not always learn to swim.

Xanthippus watched Pericles set up the blocks for a jump out on the field, always his daughter's willing helper. There was a part of him that wished for sons with half Pericles' nerve and half Ariphron's duty. Instead, they had too much of one or too little of the other.

The little boy struggled with a beam longer than he was tall, placing it on two baulks of sun-bleached pine just moments before Eleni came galloping at it. Xanthippus hissed in a sharp breath when he saw Pericles had placed himself behind the pole. If she struck it, it would hit him like a hammer.

They were too far off to hear a shout and it was too late

anyway. Xanthippus watched with a sick feeling of helplessness while his daughter cleared the pole without even a clatter of hooves. Pericles cheered her, jumping up and down and waving his hands. It made Xanthippus chuckle weakly, relief flooding him. He left the column of the house and walked across the dusty field towards his children.

Eleni was first to see him coming. She tapped Pericles on the shoulder to halt his chatter and laughter. He turned in confusion to where she pointed, then grew serious, standing straighter. Xanthippus felt his heart break a little. Somehow, their reaction forced him to be stern. He wanted to laugh and spin them round, but they stood almost to attention and he frowned and clasped his hands behind his back.

'Where is Ariphron?' he asked them.

Eleni answered, her voice low. The pony at her side pressed its muzzle into her armpit and she patted it without looking up.

'With his tutor, father,' she said. 'Is he in trouble?'

'What? Not at all . . . I just saw you two playing and I wondered where he was.'

'We weren't playing,' Pericles said, instantly defensive. 'Eleni is going to let me jump. I've been practising and I haven't fallen off for weeks now.'

The little boy was scuffed and bruised, giving him the lie. Without hesitation, Xanthippus pressed the point.

'Is that true?'

He caught the slight shake of the head from Eleni, but ignored it, wanting Pericles to speak. The boy said nothing for a moment, just staring at the dusty earth.

'No, I fell off this morning,' he said at last.

'Then why did you lie to me?'

'I thought you wouldn't let me try the jump . . . I don't know.'

Xanthippus found himself wanting to clip the boy's ear. He had strolled over, just wanting to enjoy a little of the laughter and life he saw between them. His mood had been golden, and yet in a few moments, there he was, forced to be a father and the judge of their actions. It was infuriating and he felt his own face growing red. He took a deep breath through his nose, determined to be calm as he studied his son. Boys could not raise themselves.

'Show me,' Xanthippus said.

Pericles looked up at him with wild hope, not quite daring to believe.

'A jump?'

'If you say you are ready,' Xanthippus said, grinning at his expression. 'Yes, a jump!'

His son gave a whoop and took the reins from Eleni as she tossed them to him. The little pony gave a surprised snort, mouthing the iron bit as it drew taut. Pericles would have been thrown from his feet if the animal hadn't gone along with him, but it did, whinnying in indignation.

'I'll set up the blocks,' Eleni said, squinting after him. She began to lift a lower one and her father waved her off.

'Leave it as it is, Eleni. Your pony can manage it. If he stays on, it will mean more to him.'

To his surprise, his daughter hesitated. In that moment, she reminded him of Agariste.

'This isn't . . . to punish him, is it?' she asked. 'You're not teaching him a lesson?'

Xanthippus sighed. He had feared his own father in his youth. The old bastard had been terrifying, somehow more of a man than he could ever hope to be. Yet time and experience had made them the same, it seemed. He shook his head. Some things were too much trouble to explain to children.

'Just leave the jump as it is,' he said.

She nodded curtly, clearly worried as Pericles made the turn at the far end of the field. As they watched, the boy yelled and dug in his heels, moving the pony to a canter, then a gallop. It was too fast. The boy perched like a flea on the beast's neck, gripping the mane and reins with his knees up around his ears. He would surely fall. Xanthippus suffered a pang of fear that he would see his son killed. Did age bring worry? Some weakening of the spirit that made it harder to shrug away risk? He couldn't . . . And Pericles was over, flying past in a thunder of hooves and wild yelling.

Xanthippus saw his daughter leap into the air with both hands stretched to the sky. He was smiling as she spun round and, for a moment, he was simply happy.

Her gaze slipped past him, a frown appearing. Xanthippus glanced over his shoulder as Pericles wheeled, lying flat on the pony's shoulders and talking in a rush of excitement, patting the skin hard enough to raise clouds of dust.

Two men approached them. One was Manias, there to escort another not of the household. Xanthippus felt his good mood vanish at the bustling manner of the stranger. The moment with his children had been private and precious. He had no desire for other eyes to intrude. The gaze Xanthippus turned on Manias was not kind, so that the house slave dipped his head and flushed.

'I'm sorry, kurios,' Manias said. 'This fellow is a messenger from the Assembly. He said it was urgent and could not be denied.'

'Epikleos sent me,' the young man said, giving a perfunctory bow.

He was breathing well but sweating, Xanthippus saw, with droplets running down his neck and making him shine. The sun was still rising. Xanthippus did not remember seeing him on the training runs.

'Well?' Xanthippus demanded, suddenly impatient. Dread filled him at the young man's hesitation.

'Epikleos sent me to say the Assembly is gathering to hear a vote of exile. They are breaking pots.'

'Who for?' Xanthippus said.

'You, kurios. I am sorry. You should come. Now, if it is not already too late.'

Xanthippus felt his mouth open and close. Pericles reached them and leapt down, the reins wrapped around his fists. He had not heard and he was still beaming, looking for the praise he had surely earned. Slowly, his smile faded into confusion.

Eleni looked shocked, disbelieving.

'Why would they do this?' Eleni said.

Xanthippus clenched his jaw before he spoke.

'For vengeance,' he said. 'But they will need six thousand votes to get rid of me. That is no small thing. It isn't over yet.'

Without another word, Xanthippus broke into a run in the direction of the gate. Manias would inform Agariste, or the children would. The messenger fell into place alongside him, serious-faced. In just moments, they were out on the road, heading back to Athens, where cooking smoke hung in the air and ten thousand households would decide his fate.

24

The Pnyx was still filling with citizens in white chiton robes when Xanthippus arrived. Epikleos waited for him near the speaker's stone, relief showing when he caught sight of his friend.

'What news?' Xanthippus said, with bitter humour. He tossed two silver drachms to the messenger and the man bowed and left.

'Cimon called it last night at the council, for dawn. I sent someone out to you as soon as I heard.'

'He still blames me for the death of his father,' Xanthippus cursed.

Epikleos nodded and blew air out in a long sigh. News of Xanthippus being present was spreading and faces were turning to see him. Xanthippus returned the stares with a steady gaze, refusing to let them think he was afraid or ashamed. No speeches were allowed, not for an ostracising vote. Designed to rob a tyrant of power, they took place almost in silence. After all, some great orator might have won the crowd to his side and denied his fate. Xanthippus saw the Scythian archers were watching him, ready to bear him away to the cells if he tried to interfere with the process in any way.

'I can't believe Miltiades' son has so many willing to support him!' Xanthippus hissed bitterly to his friend. 'Did that family find a gold mine as well?'

Epikleos didn't reply immediately. His expression twisted, as if he had bitten into an unripe fruit.

Ahead of them, on the Pnyx, a huge clay urn stood. Men Xanthippus had never met and would not have recognised in a crowd shuffled around it, each one bearing an ostracon, a piece of broken pottery. Each of those would have a single name scratched into the fired clay: *Xanthippus*. If a third of voting men put his name, if six thousand said he should be exiled, that was enough.

'Should I stand by the pot – look each of them in the eye?' Xanthippus whispered to his friend.

Epikleos considered and shook his head.

'That could drive some of them to anger. Stay back, Xan – and pray. They may not have enough.'

'There he is,' Xanthippus said, tapping his friend on the arm.

Epikleos looked over to where Cimon climbed the steps to the great flat of the speaker's stone. He approached the urn and dropped a piece of broken pot into it. He paused for a moment then to look down on Xanthippus. The expression was perfectly blank, the eyes hooded. Yet both Epikleos and Xanthippus felt his spite.

'No one can hate like a young man,' Epikleos murmured.

'*Too* young, surely,' Xanthippus replied under his breath. 'Can he win six thousand to his side just to condemn me? I am Marathonomachos! My family are Eupatridae landowners! We *feed* Athenians! By all the gods, Agariste's uncle *wrote* the law they are using!'

'Be calm, Xan. There – do you see Aristides?'

'What? He would not vote against me! He is a man of honour.'

Xanthippus felt his mouth hang open as Aristides climbed the steps and approached the urn. The man held out an empty palm, turning it back and forth until everyone understood there was no shard of clay in it. Then he shook his head and walked back to his seat. Xanthippus breathed out, his limbs feeling cold with relief. When Aristides looked across at him, he bowed, trembling.

'That was clever of him,' Epikleos whispered. 'And . . . brave.'

The Scythian guards were looking thunderous. Cimon was gesturing angrily with two of them. No one was allowed to disrupt a vote. Aristides had risked being taken up and thrown in a cell, just to show his distaste.

'He is a good man,' Xanthippus said. 'I have always known it.'

'I pray it is enough . . .'

A stir announced Themistocles as he rose from the crowd like a rock breaking the surface of the sea. He was suddenly there, climbing the steps. Xanthippus felt his heart beating faster, not daring to hope.

'If he does the same, I can still survive this. Bless Aristides. He has shown the way.'

He and Epikleos watched as Themistocles approached the urn and opened his hand. There was a piece of red pottery in it. He turned and met Xanthippus' gaze as he dropped it in with the rest. A murmur of awe went around the Pnyx.

Xanthippus felt blood drain from his face and hands.

'Oh no . . .' he whispered.

Epikleos was wide-eyed.

'Why would he do such a thing? I thought you and he were . . . friends, supporters! Damn him to hell for his betrayal, Xan!'

He had raised his voice and the Scythian archers were bustling closer to enforce silence. They bore clubs, Xanthippus noticed in a daze. The threat of violence was in the air and he dropped his hand to his waist, looking for the sword that should have been there. Instead, there was just the cloth of his chiton tunic and bare legs.

On the stone, Themistocles stepped out of the voting line and returned to the seats. He did not look at Xanthippus again. The sun reached noon and some of those who had voted went into the Agora to fetch food or a cup of wine and water. The life and trade of the city went on as the epistates called for the last votes and then sealed the urn with a strip of cloth dipped in wax. A bell rang out across the Pnyx. Xanthippus didn't move. Though his knee and lower back ached, he stood like a soldier and endured. His expression had grown stern and he did not speak again.

The wax seal had barely begun to stiffen before it was broken. The count would be immediate and final. In theory, Xanthippus could have stepped up to check and witness each piece, but he could not move from that spot. He was rooted in humiliation. When he did not respond, Epikleos put a hand on his shoulder.

'I'll keep them honest, Xan, don't worry.'

He went over and watched as tables were set up, with white cloth coverings. The tribe in control of the council that month were responsible, but Xanthippus' own Acamantis were there as observers, checking the count on behalf of one of their most senior sons. Epikleos moved among them as the pieces were poured out and the tally began, with each inscribed shard recorded and returned to the urn. The next day, they would be tipped into some hole for household waste, back to mere pottery and not the balance of a man's fate.

The count rose and rose, each mark like a wound as Xanthippus saw his life being undone, unwoven back to the original thread. The afternoon wore on as the officials checked the totals and compared their tally boards. When the vote passed six thousand, Xanthippus staggered a step, as if he had been struck. His knee was in pain from standing for so long, but after that, he tried to show nothing more to those who had brought him down. Cimon was staring, of course, desperate for Xanthippus to meet his eye and see the young man's triumph. Xanthippus did not know if Themistocles remained on the seats. He did not turn to face the one who had helped to destroy him. His life was in rags.

The final count was almost seven thousand votes. It was enough. The total was announced and repeated over the rise of angry noise in the crowds. Scuffles began between those who cheered it and more who were appalled at the result.

Xanthippus could hardly see as Epikleos came down and took him by the arm to steady him. There were no tears in his eyes, but he had stood in one spot since the morning and he could not make the world sharp. It seemed soft and blurred. He dipped his head to Epikleos.

'You have until dawn ten days from tomorrow to leave,' his friend said. 'I'm so sorry, Xan.'

'I know the law. Walk with me, would you?' Xanthippus said. He felt as he sometimes had after a battle, with exhaustion looming, but not quite able to overcome the pounding of his heart.

They did not stop to exchange words with anyone. The crowd parted. Some of them called out or tried to take his hand in sorrow. As he moved through them, there was a funereal air and many stood with heads bowed. It was as if he had already died. There was a brief scuffle as Cimon tried to get through to him, but the young man was held back by the press of others, placing themselves in between so that Xanthippus would not suffer some other humiliation. Aristides was one of those who stood in the way.

Xanthippus breathed long and slow as he reached the

Thriasian gate and walked alongside the cemetery. The tomb of Miltiades was visible across the paths, away from the main road. Xanthippus was tempted to pay his respects, to congratulate the man on his son.

'Why did Themistocles throw in his lot with Cimon?' Epikleos asked after a time.

'Because he does not fear him,' Xanthippus said. 'Themistocles wants to rule; you said so yourself. I should have listened to you. I should have . . . Ah, what does it matter now? Ten years! I cannot return home for ten years? What about my children? My wife?'

'Can they not visit? I don't know what properties you have, but if you must leave this part of Greece, there are others.'

'Nothing like the life I know *here*!' Xanthippus snapped. 'If I move to Delphi or Corinth, or Thebes, how often will I see Agariste and the children, with days or weeks on dangerous roads between us? What do you think?' He increased his pace, striding along the road out of the city. 'I am finished. Athens is my home and they have denied her to me.'

He reached the gate to the estate and raised his hand to thump on the iron, hesitating before the blow landed.

'I have given my life to Athens,' he said. 'This is my *home*.'

For the first time, his eyes glittered with tears and Epikleos embraced him.

'Would you like me to come in, to help explain?'

Xanthippus shook his head, his mind already on what he would say to the children. The day had begun with a moment of happiness. It already seemed another age, another life.

Cimon was still tight-faced, his jaw aching with the effort of trying not to gloat or show his victory. He and his closest friends had retired to a tavern to eat and drink. The noon meal was usually light, but they had all been thirsty after so long in the open air. With wine, a little food was only sensible. It meant that some forty of them were still celebrating as the sun set that evening.

When the door opened, Cimon looked up blearily, wine running in his veins along with his delight. He had raised a cup to his father more times than he could remember, so that his words slurred and the room swam. Ah, but it felt right – and no one would have denied him wine enough for three men after such a victory! There were times, when he drank, that he remembered the voice of his mother. It seemed one of her uncles had been a violent drunk. Whenever her son raised a cup of wine, she would wag her finger at him and remind him of the dangers. It was sometimes hard to drink enough to drown that little voice, he thought.

The crowd enjoying themselves on his silver had grown raucous over the previous few hours. The owners of the tavern were on the verge of tears as the group became louder and wilder with every passing moment. Yet when they saw Aristides had come, silence fell, the joy draining out of the room, so that they stared at him like bleary owls.

Cimon felt anger surge and he stood up, then almost fell as the room swayed. Gripping the back of a chair, he steadied himself.

'What do you want here, Aristides? Can I not drink in peace, with a few friends?'

Aristides began to answer, but another thought struck the young man and he went on.

'Or have you come to congratulate me? Well? You should.'

'I have not,' Aristides said, 'though I wonder if your father would be as pleased as you seem to be.'

'He would. Don't you worry about that,' Cimon replied. He looked pugnacious, his lower lip sticking out. Yet he had not lost all sense. He knew he was far too drunk to start a fight with anyone. Aristides was not a weak man.

'You and Themistocles have deprived Athens of a strategos, a leader in war. Perhaps you think such men can be found on any corner of the city.'

'Perhaps they can!' Cimon said. 'Perhaps I will be a strategos, like my father before me!'

'I'm sure you will, unless the wine destroys you. Yet on this day, you have weakened Athens. You, for your vengeance; Themistocles, for what? Ambition? To remove a threat?'

'My vengeance? My justice! Go on, old man, keep talking,' Cimon said, threateningly.

He was very obviously drunk and jabbed the air with a finger. One of his friends tried to grab his arm, but he shook them off as Aristides went on, infuriatingly calm and unafraid.

'If the Persians land again, next summer, we will not have Xanthippus – and that is a great loss. I wanted to be sure you understood what you have done.'

Cimon glared at him, arguments swirling, but not quite lending him the words he needed to answer. After a moment, Aristides nodded to himself and left. The young men in the tavern began to jeer, though they waited until he was out of the door. Cimon slumped into the chair and called for more wine.

'I think . . .' he said. 'I think my father Miltiades would be pleased we took . . . measures. I think we should drink this place dry in his memory. This. This is our time.'

A great cheer went up as he tossed a full pouch of silver to the owner. The man's eyes widened and he sent his wife into the cellar to bring up all she could carry.

25

Xanthippus stood by the cart and two horses he would take north and then west, across the land bridge into the Peloponnese. Corinth would be his home for the years of exile. It lay no more than three days of travel from the estate and his children. It was outside the region of Attica and so fulfilled the letter of the law. He had no particular feelings for Corinth beyond that. It was not Athens. It was not home. For a man in his position, all the rest of the world was much the same.

He was as ready as he could be. Ten days had been spent in feverish activity, passing on the work of a number of businesses to factotums and paid employees. It had been chaotic, but he'd left the family holdings in some sort of order.

Agariste had brought the children out to him. With both a chest of silver and his personal armour and weapons on the cart, he had hired four hoplites to accompany him to Corinth. They waited respectfully to one side as the strategos knelt and embraced his youngest son, Pericles. The little boy was shaking with grief, Xanthippus saw, unable to comprehend why his father was being sent away. Ten years was unimaginable to a child of his age, a lifetime, just when he had begun to really see his father. Just when he had begun to try and emulate him. The little boy started to sob and was shushed by his sister Eleni, who let him press his face against her shoulder to keep him quiet.

Xanthippus opened his arms to them both, crushing them to him, smelling grass and horses in their hair. He had spent more time with the children over the previous ten days than he had in the year before that. They'd followed him around like lost lambs and he'd found himself enjoying their laughter and talk. Even Ariphron, who had sided with his mother, seemed to have thawed. On that last morning, Ariphron was red-eyed, trying and failing to hold back tears.

'I will see you all when your mother brings you out to me,' Xanthippus said. 'Just a little while to let me get settled. It will go quickly, I promise.'

The truth was different. The roads were very dangerous between the cities. Each trip would have to be an armed expedition, moving slowly, interrupting all their lives. Xanthippus knew he would be lucky to see his children once or twice a year, and then only if Agariste willed it.

'We don't want you to go,' Pericles said.

Xanthippus nodded. The words were like a knife under his ribs. He didn't want to go either.

'The law is the law, son. I have my life – they have not harmed me. I can live anywhere but Athens and the region of Attica. It's not so hard, not really. Except that it takes me from you. That is . . .'

He could not continue. Xanthippus knew very well that there was no appeal. If he returned to Athens during the ten years, he would be executed. The law was iron and he could not stay a single day longer. He had told himself he would show only a quiet dignity in the face of that implacable truth. There was nothing to be gained by tears and wailing, so a man could only go well to his fate.

It was still hard to embrace his children one by one, to see their confusion and tears tug at something deep in him. He touched a finger to his eye, wiping weakness. Then he knelt and drew all three into an embrace, all arms and bowed heads and tears, wordless in his grief.

'You look after your mother and sister now,' he said to Ariphron and Pericles. 'Understand me? You are my representatives in the family. You will be grown men before I cross this gate again. You must be ready to take your place in the Assembly then.'

'I will destroy it,' Pericles muttered.

His father laughed.

'No. You'll know by then that there is nothing like it in the world. The rule of intelligent men, of lawful, decent men. Accepting no superiors, so that we are all equal before the law. It is not without flaw ... but in all my life, I've seen nothing better.'

Pericles nodded, though he could not accept it. The children stood back and Xanthippus turned towards Agariste. His young wife had twisted a fold of her dress to rope in her hands. She too was red-eyed, but it was different from simple loss. Her gaze accused.

They had argued until they were hoarse the night before. She was too used to power to meekly accept her husband being exiled. Even then, Xanthippus could see the stubborn set to her jaw. Her uncle would never have accepted such a result, she had told him. If he loved her at all, if he forgave her as he said he did, Xanthippus would not accept it either.

He had told her it would mean his life to stay one day more. The Assembly would not be denied, not once it had voted.

'Please stay,' she said.

He took the hands she held out to him.

'I cannot, Agariste,' he replied wearily.

'Stay and fight the decision.'

'It would mean civil war, my love.'

The last two words caught her, so that she froze. He had not used the term of affection since the night he had found her with blood staining the sheet.

'Well? What of that? It would be worth it for you,' she said.

'No, love, it would not. We would not win that war – not when it would be fought against Cimon, son of Miltiades, against Themistocles, perhaps even against Aristides. We would lose everything – and you and the children would never be safe again. It is just ten years.'

The words were hollow. Ten years away from Athens! From plays and markets and politics and arguments and trials. From the beating heart of Attica and all Greece. Ten years from the great port of Piraeus and trading all over the Aegean. Ten years from gymnasia and the men who took up armour and spear to defend her. There was nowhere like the city of Athena. His life ahead was ashes.

'I am sorry about the tea,' she whispered.

He nodded, bowing his head so he could touch his cheek to hers.

'I know. I am sorry too – and about the way I reacted. There is nothing like losing everything to remind a man what he values.'

He kissed her deeply, drawing her into his arms.

'Ask Epikleos for anything you need. He will help – and you can trust him. I will send word when I have a place in Corinth. Come out to me then, with the children.'

'I will count the days,' she said. She raised her head to be kissed again and he tasted tears on her lips.

'There, no more,' he said gruffly. 'I must be on my way.'

He broke free of his wife and patted the cheek of each of the three children, seeing how they were already growing taller. He climbed up to the seat on the cart and readied himself.

'Goodbye,' he called down to them.

Pericles and Eleni went to their mother's skirts and

Ariphron raised a childish hand in farewell as Xanthippus snapped the reins and forced the horses into a trot. The four hoplites mounted and took up formation around him, ready to fend off thieves or vagabonds. Xanthippus told himself he would not look back, but then did so anyway, watching the little group grow smaller until he could no longer see them against the glare of the sun.

In the spring, Aristides walked through the streets of the Ceramicus, on his way back from the port. He had gone down to the Piraeus to examine the accounts and the progress being made on the great fleet. They were used to him by then and had learned to answer his questions quickly and politely. It helped that he had replaced six of the port officials for corruption, appointing men he knew and trusted.

There was still waste; that was the nature of a great project. Wood they had purchased was found to be rotten or riddled with worm. Oil and tar was spilled with alarming regularity, while men lost tools at an extraordinary rate. Aristides suspected some of those were being taken home or sold in the local markets, but it was hard to prove. The city had to replace them, with the costs all written on good Egyptian papyrus and kept for the records.

Aristides smiled at the memory of so many new keels, so much industry and labour. It was true he had argued against spending the Laurium silver on ships, but in the main it was to act as a check on Themistocles rather than from any true disagreement. Arguments had to be tested and teased out. It was the only way to be sure they were sound. In his heart of hearts, Aristides thought Athens would always need ships. The threat of Persia had not ended at Marathon, he was certain. Nor at Paros, where Miltiades had failed to dig them out of their stronghold with the point of a knife.

There were rumours of garrisons marching in Ionia, drawn to the far west of the Persian empire, where the coast looked out over a dozen islands ruled by Greece. Merchant traders returned with tales of brash Persian warriors appearing in the markets there, of Persian officials selling licences for all sorts of activities – and woe betide anyone who could not produce his piece of slate or pottery when visited by the tax inspectors.

To Aristides, it felt like a fist slowly closing – the influence of an empire, where once the cities of that far coast had been either Greek or independent. It worried him, more than he could say. He was due to present the accounts of the port to the council that afternoon. He toyed with the idea of making a more general speech about the rise in Persian activity.

The thought was a sour one. If Themistocles was present, as he always seemed to be, he would challenge Aristides on each point, brash and funny if he chose, or patronising, as if lecturing a child. The man's arrogance was overwhelming, but perhaps even Themistocles would accept the empire was coming closer. In the past, King Darius had hardly acknowledged the far west, thousands of miles and hundreds of cities from his palaces and the heart. That had changed with the Ionian revolt and the burning of Sardis – then changed again with Marathon. King Darius had set his face against Greece then. He no longer drowsed and drank peach juice and forgot the distant reaches of the empire. His attention had shifted.

Aristides brushed the thought away, as if a fly had touched his face. Roads stretched across all Persia, with messengers carrying letters and jewels and tales of the interior. Trading caravans took slaves and scented oil to create perfumes as rich as any in the world. They returned with tales of monsters and men clad in gold, of striped cats as large as any lion, or huge animals with tusks tipped in silver. More than half would be fantasies and stories, told to entertain, but for a man who knew how to sift dust from good grain, there was always something to be heard at Piraeus.

Aristides had listened to a captain trying to sell his ship to the council, as the man discussed his last trade trip to the east. He had filled his ship with a cargo of ambergris, which could be burned as incense or made into perfumes. The man had been quite a character, a Roman, with peacock feathers cut short to fit his hat and a face so deeply seamed by sun and wind that it looked like stitched leather. Aristides had been drawn to the strange cargo of black lumps being heaved out of the hold. The captain had already found his purchaser and he was in a fine, ebullient mood when Aristides leaned on a rail next to him. From that man, he had heard rumours that the Persian king had grown too ill or too old to campaign. It was the second time Aristides had been told such a thing, but it was impossible to know for sure. Rumours fed on themselves, like a snake biting its own tail. Men who should have known better confirmed false reports simply by hearing them more than once, or in two cities along a coast. It was hard to know if a smear of truth lay at the centre of such things – or whether it was good or bad for Athens.

The crowds bustled in the Ceramicus, buying pots or hawking their wares to those who might. That part of the city was noisy and brash at the best of times. Each little workshop or house held pottery wheels, always squeaking, driven by pedals forcing them round and round. The potters there were always covered in dust and slip, on their skin and in their hair. They were said to pedal in their sleep, even. Those who did not make pots called out prices, competing for custom in constant chatter.

Aristides found the clamour wearing when he wanted to

just walk and think, but the Agora lay ahead and he knew he would be able to find a quiet spot there. He thought he might walk to the Areopagus and see what arguments were being presented to the juries. That day was a trial day and the city was busy as always, with jurors from demes miles around swelling the crowds.

Ahead of him, a man stood in the centre of the road, peering at something in his hand and swearing to himself. Aristides began to edge to the side rather than intrude on the ramblings and madness of another, but the fellow noticed him and put up a hand.

'Can you write, kurios? Can you help me with this?'

Aristides saw it was a piece of pottery in the man's palm, a triangle broken from some failed or unloved bowl. The road through the Ceramicus was made of shards much smaller than the one he held, the result of centuries of firing clay and discarding the broken pieces.

'What do you want to do?' Aristides said.

The fellow's change of expression was instant, like a child. The smile was reward enough and Aristides was glad he had stopped.

'I'd like to scratch a name on this ostracon, so I can vote today.' He held up a potter's nail, used to mark designs in the cheapest vessels before they went for firing.

'And you cannot write?' Aristides said. It was not a great surprise, though he saw the man was embarrassed as he nodded.

'I never learned, kurios. Can you do it for me? It won't take more than a moment.'

'Of course. Tell me the name and I will write it for you.'

Aristides took the piece and the long iron nail from him, holding it like a stylus. He looked up then as the man leaned close and touched his finger to the clay.

'Aris . . . tid . . . es,' the man said.

Aristides froze.

'There is to be a vote of ostracism, then?'

'Yes, kurios. If you could put the name . . .'

'Today? For Aristides?'

The man nodded, frowning at the delay. Aristides raised one eyebrow.

'Do you know this Aristides?' he asked.

The man shook his head, then leaned to one side and spat on the red earth at his feet.

'No, but I hear his name all the time. "Aristides the Just", "Aristides the Honourable" – what does he know of the lives we lead, eh? I am sick of all of them.'

'I see,' Aristides said faintly.

'Will you write it, then?' the man said, tapping the shard with his fingernail.

Slowly and carefully, Aristides scratched his own name into the clay.

'There. It is done,' he said, handing it back.

The man beamed at him, squinting at it.

'Thank you, kurios. You are a good man.'

Aristides went past him, to the end of the road and into the Agora. The Pnyx was not too far off and he could see crowds gathering there, looking clean after the dust of the Ceramicus. It had touched the hem of his robe, Aristides realised, darkening it further and staining the skin of his hands. Perhaps the potter had thought he was one of them, his robe patched and old, without oiled hair or gold rings or any sign of wealth.

With a heavy heart, Aristides walked towards the Pnyx and made his way to the heart of the vote. It did not surprise him to see Themistocles there, with Cimon not far off. The young man was visibly drunk again, Aristides noted. Cimon swayed as he stood on the great flat stone and his eyes were

235

glassy. Aristides shook his head at the sight. Grief was a corrosive force in a man's life. It had to be denied like any weakness, not drowned in wine. Still, Cimon was not his client, nor even a friend. His fate would be his own. It still rankled to see such a promising young man ruined, but that was the way of things. Some rose and some were destroyed. It seemed that, today, Aristides himself might fall.

He stood for a long time watching the voting. There was no clear pattern. Men of the outer city came up and deposited a piece with his name inscribed on it. Neither was there malice in their expressions, not for the most part. He was pleased at that. Yet as a rumour will feed on itself, so the process of voting brought more and more to the Pnyx. There was an excitement in the air and Aristides wondered how many would vote without even knowing who it was they would send into exile.

As the sun rose higher, he could not stand and merely observe any longer, not with Themistocles watching him. Aristides climbed the steps and saw how young men bristled around both Cimon and Themistocles. Their masters patted the air or murmured instructions to them so that they stood back and let Aristides approach. The voting went on as Aristides drew up and halted. Cimon was too drunk and too young to concern him, he decided. Instead, his gaze was on Themistocles.

'One by one . . .' Aristides said. 'You remove your competitors one by one.'

He waited, but Themistocles only gave the smallest of shrugs, while Cimon scowled in confusion.

'And what will you do now, Themistocles?' Aristides asked. 'Once I have been driven out?'

'I serve the city, Aristides. I am not responsible for the tides, nor individual votes.'

'Your answer demeans you. Can you not be honest? Here today, as they vote? Cimon has returned a favour, has he not? He has lent you his support today, with all those who look to him.' Aristides took a deep breath, calming himself. 'You have taken my position in the city from me. All I love. Will it be worth it, do you think?'

For the first time, Themistocles flushed, looking embarrassed.

Cimon sneered through his fog.

'You are the old . . . generation, Arilsid . . . Aritsid . . .'

Both Themistocles and Aristides ignored him.

'The people fear tyrants, Themistocles, with good reason. They will not let one man rise to rule, not without tearing him down. How long will you last, without me to stand on the other side of the scales? How long before they see you stand alone?'

'I do not seek power,' Themistocles said loudly. 'I don't interfere at the docks and report back to the council. I don't speak in every debate as if I am the only adult, as if my opinion is the only one worth hearing.'

'Your humility is refreshing,' Aristides said. 'I'd hoped for honesty from you, but I see there are too many ears around.'

He stepped away to look into the urn. The latest epistates was a stranger to him and didn't react as he peered in. Aristides nodded to himself.

'I see enough votes there. Ten days. Very well. I will prepare my estate.'

He was trembling with anger by then, so that he felt light-headed. He did not look at Themistocles again, though he felt the man's triumphant gaze follow him down and across the Agora.

Aristides unclenched his fists with an effort as he walked through the city he loved. He'd thought Themistocles had understood enough of the Assembly to put aside personal ambition. Athens needed the constant clash of wits to thrive, Aristides believed with a passion. His beloved city was more than just households and a city wall! She was an idea, of rule by the people, hammered on the forge every day, in trials, in debates, even in war. He accepted those laws, even though he knew Themistocles had made them work for his ends.

A thought struck him, making Aristides stumble. Had Themistocles been part of the downfall of Miltiades? Had he whispered in the ear of Xanthippus, perhaps? After that, a pact with Cimon? Aristides stopped walking for a moment, feeling suddenly cold. Had Themistocles put him forward as archon for the year? That honour had raised him up – and then his people had cut him down. Perhaps none of it was simple chance. Perhaps it was all a campaign. It left Themistocles almost alone in the city – and popular enough that he would not have to fear the broken pots himself. Still, the man had chosen to leap onto a wild horse. Sooner or later, he would be thrown.

The rejection by the people hurt deeply. Aristides did not weep or rage, however, not even when he was in his private rooms and there was no one to hear. He sat for a time in silence. There was no wine in his town-house, so he drank three cups of water and washed away the red dust that still clung to him. After that, he began to order his affairs, so that he could be ready. He was forty-eight years old. The thought of ten years away from Athens was like a hot forge-iron laid across his heart. Themistocles had taken almost everything from him. Yet his dignity and his honour were intact.

PART TWO
482 BC

26

Xerxes stood with his eyes closed after his climb, letting the sea breeze cool his skin. Abydos was a town built of ancient villages on the north-west coast, the very edge of empire. He wondered if it would ever amount to more unless they could build stone bridges across the deep water. His engineers said it was impossible to throw arches across so great a span, not with open sea running in between. Yet he had faith, in the ingenuity of his people, in the favour of angels. His father had once placed a bridge over the strait at Byzantium, only to see it smashed in storms. Xerxes had vowed to go further. To the west of Byzantium, he would span the Hellespont. His army would walk over the sea.

From the top of the hill, he could see another coast of brown and green across the water. Xerxes recalled his maps, produced for the eyes of kings and no one of lesser estate. Once the armies of his father . . .

He paused, caught up in old patterns. Xerxes breathed out, emptying himself. He had mourned. Forty kingdoms had grieved with him. It was four years since his father had died. There had been times since when all life had seemed unbearably petty, when the empire had gone so long without a shepherd that they had fallen into rioting and insurrection. Slowly, Xerxes had rebuilt his faith, both in life and himself. He had shaken off the vast perspective, the feeling that his entire life was merely marking time until he saw his father once again. No. Xerxes was now the Great King of the empire. He would live first.

Once *his* armies set foot on that far shore, that slender peninsula, they could march through Thrace and west into Macedonia, into lands they did not know, coming south at last to crash against the cities of Greece like a great wave. Xerxes had not forgotten his father's vow. King Darius had left only one thing unfinished, in all the richness and wonders of his life. Death had stopped him, but a man's sons could still act after his death! That was the very purpose of sons, to cheat the natural ending of ambition. Xerxes smiled at the thought. He had put his seed into the belly of his wife before leaving the heartlands. Amestris had promised him a son, a crown prince he could raise to greatness, as Darius had done. To make certain, she had buried seven boys alive, taking them from the families of small kings. It was a grand sacrifice, he thought, a gesture typical of her and touching in its faith. Perhaps, too, it was a reminder for him to be faithful. His father had once warned him to be wary of a woman who might watch while he slept. All the strength and authority in the world were as nothing while a man snored.

The breeze picked up, stirring dust around his feet as it passed by. Xerxes shaded his eyes and looked at the immense labour still continuing below. He had not failed to honour his father. That simple truth was written in the regiments moving like beetles on the land, in the great fleet that bobbed at anchor and grew every month. The labour and the costs and the training were sums unimaginable. Xerxes had sent his accountants away in the end, when they had grown worried and fearful. What was the purpose of wealth if not to make war on the enemies of his people? What good did it do to eat from plates of gold, to sip wine from jewelled cups, if Greeks still lived and laughed and scorned his father's memory? Xerxes had no need for a slave to whisper into his ear each evening. He could not forget the Greeks. In his dark times, he wondered if the defeat at Marathon had brought on the illness that had led to his father's death.

Xerxes found himself clenching his fists. He opened them slowly, seeing his palms had whitened with strain, like dead flesh. He had made one final attempt at emulating the greatness of his father. He had sent men in peace to every Greek city, offering vassalage, for dust and water. If Athens and Sparta had accepted his rule over them, he would have shown kindness, in his father's name. He told himself it was true. Darius had made him understand he had to be more than a king to rule an empire. He had to do everything he could to appear merciful. More, if they allied themselves to him, his new subjects had to be certain he would protect them, even against their own.

It was a hard path for him to walk, almost impossible. Many of the lesser Greek states and cities had accepted his offer, out of fear or love, it did not matter. Yet when Xerxes heard Athens had put his envoy on trial and executed him, it had been with a sort of joy. Sparta had thrown theirs into a well. He had actually laughed at the news, he remembered. The high path was too much for him and it was truly a relief to be able to put it aside. His offer had not been made from weakness after all, but from strength.

Xerxes was young and strong and certain, with an army and fleet without equal. He was pleased they had scorned him, without honour. It would make what followed all the sweeter. In putting down rebellions in Egypt after the death of his father, he had discovered he did not enjoy the destruction of the weak, not particularly. He had slaughtered the populations of entire cities to make sure they understood a Great King still ruled, but not because it gave him any pleasure. A warrior's pleasure came only from facing the strong – and destroying them so utterly they would never rise again. The moment when the cities of Athens and Sparta realised they would not be allowed to retreat, that they would be taken brick from brick and left as blood and dust, *that* would be his father's legacy.

It was a glorious thought, an intoxicating one, as if he drank wine in the cool air that filled him with every breath. He could see other hills around Abydos and right across the channel, the lands there that would lead to the west. Perhaps one day he *would* see stone bridges across it, joining a new western empire to the greatness of Persepolis and Babylon. He was in the prime of his youth. He had time. He would stroll through the ruins of Athens then, and tell his son about Darius.

Hearing the creak of armour drew his attention back from the infinite and the years ahead, so that Xerxes looked down the steep slope to where General Mardonius was making his way up. When he reached the crest of the hill, Mardonius threw himself to the ground. Xerxes signalled two of his watchful spearmen to let the man approach.

The general wore a panelled coat and a sword on his waist. Though the sun beat on them both, Xerxes was pleased to see Mardonius breathing only lightly. The general insisted on high levels of fitness in his men, unlike some of the lesser commanders. Xerxes too demanded it in those who served him, saying they owed the strength of their bodies to the throne. He could not abide softness of flesh, in himself or in those around him.

'Rise, Mardonius. See what a host I have brought to this place. Is it not magnificent?'

The two men stood side by side for a time before Mardonius replied. The view revealed an army like cities on the move, with a fleet of eight hundred ships in the strait and more coming in every day. This would be no tentative blow, as at Marathon. All the rebellions had been crushed. Xerxes was at last bringing the entire might of the empire to the western coast.

'It is a wonder, Majesty,' Mardonius said. His eyes darted back and forth as he drank in the scene. Xerxes nodded, pleased his general was using the perspective as he had intended.

'I have reports of the food caches in Thrace,' Mardonius added. 'They came under attack by some local king there, but our soldiers fought them off and burned their villages.'

Xerxes waved that away. The problem of feeding such a host was one he could solve with sufficient will, wealth and slaves. The empire spread like spilled honey, infinitely slow but unstoppable, covering the world in sweetness. His marching columns had supplies waiting for them at a dozen places on the other side of the Hellespont. His ships had been landing men and equipment for over a year, with local agreements enforced with gold or slaughter. It had not mattered to him how it was done. His order had been enough.

'Good. My father would be proud, I think.'

'He would, Majesty. He is,' Mardonius replied.

The man chose to drop to one knee and bow his head at the honour of speaking of the departed Great King. Xerxes smiled.

'He will be,' he corrected, after a time. 'I will command the fleet, general. I will close down the sea to the Athenians, like a fishing net drawn along the coast. At the same time, you will take the army across the Hellespont and march west with us. I will meet you in the ashes of Athens and we will shake hands then. Do you have any other questions for me?'

Mardonius thought for a second, rubbing a hand through the thick blackness of his beard, where his lips showed red and his teeth white as he smiled.

245

'When will the floating bridge be finished?' he said, after a time. The question made nothing of what would be one of the marvels of the age, if their engineers pulled it off. The Hellespont had never been spanned, not in ten thousand years.

'The first hulls will be in place today,' Xerxes said, pride showing. 'Persia is the light of the world, Mardonius. We have machines to draw wind from the air, water from the ground. This is merely the work of slaves – of ropes and wood and piles sunk into the mud beneath. Master Baloch tells me they will be stable enough to cross in a month, barring storms. If the crossings survive the winter, you will ride across that strait in spring, general, without the sea wetting the hem of your coat. I will set sail on the same day. With God's favour, we will achieve our victory before the end of the year.'

'The Greeks will surely know we are coming,' Mardonius said. He bit his lip at the thought, but he was the leader of all the armed forces of Persia and he worried about overconfidence.

'Of course they will,' Xerxes replied. 'They have had spies in Ionia since they burned Sardis, reporting back in whispers. Half the people on this coast claim ties of blood to the Hellenes. They talk and write and warn every day. It does not matter. No doubt, too, they will have noted our supplies in Thrace and marked the likely route we will take.'

'Such things do not concern you, Majesty?'

Xerxes looked down the hill to the port and the far coast disappearing into the haze.

'I have brought a million men to this place, general, as well as warships of Phoenicia and Egypt. I have not stinted in their training or their weapons, or food to keep them strong. I have done all this because the Greeks will know we are coming. On my order, our people have begun a canal across part of the route, so our fleet can avoid a treacherous piece of coast – and sail in safety where there was once only land! *Nothing* has been spared for this, not gold or men or blood. I have made preparations since my father's death – while he drove the empire to this great action before.'

Xerxes paused and bowed his head at the mention of his father, before going on.

'It is eight years since Marathon, general. My father's illness robbed him of the vengeance he deserved. I will put that right, in honour of his shade. After all, they've known we would come since then, if they had the sense of a child. No, there is no way to keep an army of this size a secret. Yet that is my greatest joy.' He showed his teeth then, like a wolf. 'They will know we are coming and they will try to resist – until they understand we are the wave that will break their walls, no matter what they do. We are the tide coming in, the end of all their dreams and ambitions. We are the fire that will burn them to ash!'

His voice had risen with each phrase, until it was almost a battle shout. On instinct, the general chose to prostrate himself once again, his hands touching his ears. Mardonius was a man of great personal and physical strength, who had served Xerxes' father with distinction. The sight of him lying in the dust cooled the ardour that surged in the young king.

He reached and took Mardonius by the arm, raising him up. It was an honour to be touched in such a way and Mardonius flushed like a bride, overcome.

'I shall not fail, Majesty. It will be as you say.'

The attention of the king was on the strait below, where ships and men swarmed.

'Look there, Mardonius, at the banks. Do you see?'

Far below, a ship had come down the strait and been lashed to the wooden quayside with great ropes of papyrus and white flax, thick as a man's arm. As both general and king watched, another approached, looking like a child's model at that distance. It came alongside the first, sculling closer until they touched. Both ships dropped anchor at prow and stern, then more ropes were flung over, rising like threads. Men scurried everywhere, busy in the heat as they joined the ships.

Sails came down and were removed and piled on the shore. Spars and ropes followed and then the great wooden beam of a balance crane was heaved over, with dozens of men working to unship the mast. A net of stones as counterweight helped them to lift out the great bole of pine, swinging it round.

'I see, Majesty,' Mardonius said.

'Yes. They pull masts like teeth to make my path across the waters.'

Onto the open hulls came more carpenters, carrying boards and pegs, drills and hammers. Xerxes smiled to see planking begin to fill the space, the first steps on a wide road that would reach right across the strait when it was done. His father had shown the way, at Byzantium. He had not made a bridge of stone, but of ships. His people would step from land to land.

'I could have had the fleet carry my soldiers, though it would have taken an age and lost me another campaign season. This is a grand gesture, a signal of my intent. Do you see, general? It shows we will not be stopped. Let the Greeks report I have tamed the sea, Mardonius. That I have no limits in all I devote to this.'

The general looked over at him, his eyes showing awe.

'It is true, then? Your Majesty went down to the coast and lashed the ocean?'

'With a stick, yes. Three hundred lashes – and then I branded it with heated irons. I did it where a Greek fishing crew could watch me. Oh, their faces! You should have seen it.' Xerxes laughed in happy memory. 'They were so afraid, general! Like children. I do not fear their Poseidon. Even his sea is my servant in this. I will not be turned back. "Remember the Greeks," Mardonius. That is what my father's slave used to say. I tell you this: when I am finished, they will remember *me*.'

Far below, Xerxes could see the movement of shoals of fish in the blue water, like shadows beneath the surface. Another ship made its way down the strait to be bound in place, a bridge from one empire to another. The masts would be cut down and hammered into the seabed to keep the bobbing vessels stable. His engineers had assured him they could make a platform able to withstand the storms that came racing down the strait in winter. Their lives rested on their word. Out on the waters, a dozen ships waited to come in, their crews busy with purpose. Xerxes smiled. It was a good day.

27

Themistocles struggled not to show his irritation. He had thought once that having a new epistates every morning had been a stroke of genius by the lawmaker Cleisthenes. No tyrant could ever arise, not in the time from sunset to sunset! He scratched his chin, feeling the bristles. Perhaps he should grow a beard, he thought, glancing at the latest Athenian to lead the city. He hadn't quite appreciated how often he would need to explain the realities of politics to a new man, pink and fresh from his ballot, determined to make a mark on Athens. It was . . . wearying.

'Themistocles?' the man said.

Hippothontis tribe, Themistocles recalled. To save his own life, he could not remember the man's name. With a new face every day for years, they all blurred in his memory, with few exceptions. Cleisthenes may have been a genius, but his determination to preserve democracy in Athens also averaged out the abilities of its officials. Worse than dealing with the fools, Themistocles hated losing the good ones. Just the day before, a young stone-carver had been epistates. Diophenas had been sharply intelligent. He'd pushed a jury to the right decision with just a few words and understood completely how to manage the council meeting. For once, Themistocles had found an ally. Yet the following sunset had come around just as quickly and Diophenas had gone back to his work carving posts and lintels. The new man seemed full of questions, but of the sort to frustrate rather than aid him.

'Are you unwell, Themistocles?' the epistates said.

What *was* his name? The tone was sneering and the man had taken on a faint flush, as if he knew he was being ignored.

'I am well enough,' Themistocles said.

The man raised his eyebrows.

'Then perhaps you have an answer, one I can take to the council. Where are the records for the mine workers? We have rumours of men being forced to pay a part of their income before they even receive it.'

Themistocles said nothing, though he glowered and lowered his head like a trapped bull. It was a historic arrangement, right back to the first dig on the new seam at Laurium. He had agreed a collective rate for the men, higher than it might have been, with a little taken for his labour. Such things were meant to be private, and they had been at first. If he had not been distracted in the city, he might have remembered to check the arrangement, to renew it with the overseers at the mine. Instead, faces and names had changed – and suddenly there were questions from the council about the little cart of silver ore that was collected each month without being tallied with the rest.

Instead of staying in command of the details, Themistocles had been forced to deal with a thousand other matters. Little by little, he had become aware of things left undone once Aristides had gone. Themistocles had never appreciated how many hours the dour little man had spent serving the city. It was not just the docks and the reports from the carpenters and shipwrights, not even the woodcutters and cartmen bringing in new stocks, or the lumber yards where wood was dried and seasoned. A month after Aristides had gone into exile, two men had brought a survey of the city sewers, with every private home and pit marked on a map that had cost a small fortune in labour. They'd needed paying, but they'd also wanted to discuss some scheme Aristides had been mulling to sink the main sewage runs beneath the surface of the city, so that they could not overflow as easily.

It was incredibly dull, but the work had gone on nonetheless, unseen, unrewarded. Without Aristides, or Xanthippus, or even Miltiades, much of the work fell to men of the council who had been elected for a single month. Men without particular skill, without vision. Of course, they came to Themistocles, more and more often.

'I will look into it, epistates, of course,' he said. 'I will bring a report to the council next week.'

'You said something similar last month, so I was told.'

Themistocles raised his eyes. He had relied on the constant change of officials to put them off, and it had worked for a long time. Unfortunately, they had begun to talk and discuss his reluctance. He saw it in the suspicious glances that followed him.

'It takes time to send men out to the mine, to question witnesses and examine the accounts there.'

'They should match the tallies in the council building, of course,' the man added.

Themistocles nodded. The epistates was probably right, but the two sets of accounts would never match. He cursed himself in silence for letting this get away from him.

Across the city, noon bells sounded. Themistocles swore aloud then, surprising the epistates.

'I must go, Diophenas.' He saw the hurt he had caused and realised his mistake. 'I'm sorry, that was yesterday's . . . Really, I must go. I am expected on the Areopagus.'

Themistocles hurried away, clutching scrolls under his arm and feeling rushed and worried. Where was the report on the fleet trials? He'd had it in his satchel, but then put it down on his seat while he'd gone to hear a discussion of leave and pay for the rowers. Left alone, they'd vote themselves six months of idleness and six drachms a day! He had to veto the wildest ideas put to a vote, using his authority as archon of the Areopagus. That won him no followers. In previous times, it was the sort of unpleasant job he'd have persuaded Xanthippus or Aristides to do. He'd never thought he would miss them, but he did. It turned out that leading a city, without that city being aware of it, was a little more complicated than Themistocles had imagined. If he'd actually become a tyrant, he could have passed off the work by order. Of course, they would have executed him.

Just a month before, Themistocles had attended plays in the public theatre by the Acropolis, comedies where his new political prominence was derided and mocked. He'd laughed along with the crowd to take the sting from it, but they were clearly wary of him. Athenians were many things, but not stupid. He would not have wanted to rule them if they had been. He'd seen off one attempt to ostracise him, though it had cost a fortune in silver and bargaining. He'd even had a hundred burly rowers ready to disrupt the process, but it had not come to that. When the bell rang out and the pot had been sealed, there had been just three thousand pieces of tile with his name on them. He grimaced at the memory. It had been a warning, but he had so much else he wanted to do.

He bustled to the Areopagus, the rock of Ares that rose from the ground alongside the Agora. That ancient seat had witnessed the rise and fall of many names. He had not expected to arrive harassed and sweating like any slave scribe!

All four of the city archons were present. Old men, long past their prime. They had not replaced Miltiades, Xanthippus or Aristides, as if their seats could not be filled by anyone else. Themistocles saw Aristides' spot was still deliberately empty, between two ancients. Was that a criticism? Death had taken one and the Assembly had ostracised the others. No one could gainsay those decisions, not once they had been made. He found his frustration growing. He had other calls on his time. The archons were a remnant of another age, of power lost. What authority they had lay in deference and tradition – a fragile state of affairs that could be withdrawn at any time.

'Gentlemen,' Themistocles said by way of greeting, taking his seat and arranging his scrolls. The satchel seemed to grow heavier every day. He would have to keep a slave with him to carry it. Should have summoned one this morning . . .

'You are late, Themistocles,' Archon Nicodemus said, his voice an old man's fluting tone. It was his name that had been chosen for the year past, though that was coming to an end. Themistocles assumed they would choose Hypsichides for the next. He looked to that old fellow, more ancient still, with his neck in sinewy wires and his bald head freckled and stretched thin. The honour was less when so many of them had been sent to exile. A younger, more active council of archons would surely have replaced those lost. It seemed a symptom of their fading star that they had not. Or perhaps they feared the rise of Cimon's people in the city. That young man was *very* much his father's son. Cimon had the quality of a leader, as hard to define as always. If the drink did not destroy him before the age of thirty, he would be a name in Athens.

'I have a report here, on the latest sea trials,' Themistocles began.

The fleet was his greatest achievement. In the years since he had argued with Aristides over spending city silver on oars and keels, Athenian ships had sailed as far as the new city of Rome in the west, patrolling the islands of the Aegean and establishing an Athenian peace. Even the Spartans gave way when they saw Athenian galleys easing into view. That fleet would be his legacy, Themistocles was certain. He never tired of reporting on its successes.

He realised he was holding the wrong scroll as he unrolled the papyrus. He put that down and rummaged in his satchel while the archons looked at one another.

'If you are not ready, it can probably wait,' Nicodemus said. His tone was sour.

Themistocles looked up and wondered how difficult it would be to snap him in two.

'No, I have it here,' Themistocles replied.

To his surprise Nicodemus held up a hand.

'We have more pressing news, Themistocles. From our friends.'

Themistocles stopped his search and closed the satchel flap, sitting back. He was tired and fed up, but they still watched him like hawks surrounding a rabbit. That was not an image he enjoyed, even as he saw it in their bright eyes.

'The Great King has gathered his army on the coast of Ionia, Themistocles. One of our people brought news only this morning, two weeks old. They are coming, it seems, after years of preparation.'

Themistocles felt his stomach contract and he sat forward. A headache began over one eye. Somehow, he knew it would remain with him for the whole day.

'There have been false alarms for years,' he said. 'How many ships? How many men? How close are they to marching?'

'We lost a couple of boys trying to find out,' Nicodemus said. 'We have a few guesses and estimates, but they move and they march and their ships infest the coast like sea lice. Two of our merchant galleys were boarded by their officials not a month back – in waters where Persians have no right to be. They took nothing, but their confidence is growing. They would not have dared such an act even a year ago.'

'When armies march, authority is whatever they can take and keep,' Themistocles said grimly. 'Or would you stand in front of an army holding a property deed, crying out that they have no permission?'

He made a growling sound of frustration, deep in his throat. There had not been a month in three years without some report of Persian ships, of Persian gold, of Persian soldiers like grains of sand.

'How many times have we listened to these reports now?' Themistocles said. 'Always, there is something to gossip over in the markets.'

'This . . . is not gossip, Themistocles,' Nicodemus said. 'The Great King himself has joined them. We have it from men who saw him on the coast. He is his father's son and he is looking across the seas to the west.'

Themistocles scowled. Fear seemed to grow with age. It was the strangest thing, like rot that ran through the heart of good wood. Young men felt too little fear, but then somehow it crept in and spread. He looked at Nicodemus and saw the old archon was afraid. With an effort, Themistocles gentled his tone.

'Tell me, are they just securing their western border or truly planning an invasion?'

'It is impossible to know for sure,' Nicodemus admitted. 'I suspect the Great King himself does not know. Yet the numbers, Themistocles! One of our people watched them mark out a field and count the number who could stand within the ropes. For a day, they filled that field over and over. Our friend was moved on and lashed for his curiosity, but he said he had never seen so many. He said . . . at least two hundred thousand, perhaps twice as many again.'

'That is impossible,' Themistocles said scornfully. 'If he said that, he was trying to make you fearful. Even counting slaves and women, you are describing all of Athens, just about. Who could even feed so many on the march? They would starve.'

'Some will come by ship, with holds full of salted meat and casks of water. They have the entire Persian empire to feed them.'

'How many ships?' Themistocles demanded.

'Hundreds. We do not know the number.'

'What *good* are you, then?' Themistocles snapped.

He closed his eyes for a moment as they recoiled, furious with himself. There was no honour in barking at old men.

'I apologise,' he said, bowing his head. 'You will understand the news is disturbing. We thought they would come after Marathon, but they did not. All word ceased out of Persia and there were some who argued that we would never hear from them again, that we had earned peace with a single battle. Do you remember those days, Nicodemus?'

'Their king died,' the old man said.

'Yes. And his son, this Xerxes, still remembers us. If we could only know his mind!'

Themistocles began to pace. The heads of the old men followed him back and forth, as if in a trance.

'We have had years of rumours and reports,' Themistocles said. 'Talk of armies drifting in and training and taking over the cities of Ionia. We live with the threat of invasion – though our great fleet patrols day and night. We will give thanks for the wisdom of that if they come!'

He saw Nicodemus roll his eyes and Themistocles let his mouth become a thin line. They owed him honour for creating the fleet.

'We live with the knowledge that they will come. Yet they

have not. I think sometimes the rise in unrest here is part of that. Two murders just yesterday! I do not remember such things in my youth, not when we had hunger and thirst to occupy us. No, these days, our people wait with the ground shaking beneath our feet, never knowing if the roof will fall in.' He began to pace once more, his hands clasped behind him. 'Now you say it is upon us? By Athena, we are not ready.'

'Even so, they will come,' the old man said. 'If the gods decree it, that will be the end.'

Themistocles stared at Nicodemus, wondering if it was age or a weakness of character.

'No. If they come . . . when they come, we will break them on foot as we did at Marathon. Our fleet will destroy them at sea. I swear it.'

'We are too few,' Archon Nicodemus replied, shaking his head.

Themistocles said nothing at first. He had seen the council of archons as an irritant for some time. He realised they were looking to him for answers. They had woken the Persian lion and the beast was coming. They were terrified.

'Send word to Sparta, then,' he said. 'They refused to give water and earth to the Persians, just as we did. Send word to Thebes, to Corinth – wherever there are men willing to take up the hoplon shield and long spear. They are Hellenes, as we are. Call on that kinship of blood. Tell them to train and build fitness, to sharpen their swords. Be sure they know the enemy is coming and threatens us all.'

'Even to the cities that welcomed the Persian envoys? Traitors will not fight,' Nicodemus said softly.

'Then they are fools. A flame does not spare one house over another, not when the whole city burns. Either way, if they come, we will meet them. Athens will lead Greece. At sea, on land.'

'I will pray for storms, or that the Persian king goes the way of his father,' Nicodemus said.

Themistocles shrugged.

'Why not? We thought they would march four years ago, but then Darius died and all the whispers stopped. We could be as blessed again.'

He chuckled, though there was not much humour in it.

'Either way, if they send a small force, as at Marathon, we will crush them. If they send a great host, they will starve before they ever reach Greece. Persian soldiers cannot grow wings and fly like harpies! Have you any idea how long it would take Persian ships and fishing boats just to row them across the Hellespont to Thrace? *Years*, gentlemen. I tell you, the first ones will starve or grow white-haired waiting for the rest! Really, how many can they even bring against us?'

28

Xerxes rode onto a wonder of the world, the hooves of his grey gelding making a hollow sound in the silence of a spring morning. Guards stood at attention on either side of him, so that they looked like statues lining the halls in the palace at Persepolis. Crowds had gathered all along the shore at Abydos. Readying his army for the great enterprise had drawn thousands of workers and their families to the area. Gold, silver and his imperial will had created a new city in that place. Now there were cobblers to make shoes and farmers bringing grain to sell in markets. New homes had sprung up on every hillside. The crowd filled the banks and hung in the trees like flapping pigeons, just to catch a glimpse of the king. They had cheered themselves hoarse when Xerxes had first appeared, praying with the priests on the shore as they dedicated the campaign to Ahura Mazda, god of gods, as well as Xerxes, king of kings.

Xerxes could feel the breeze increase in strength as he walked his horse across the wide causeway they had laid. The planks creaked in the sun and with the movement of water below. He had chosen the gelding for its placid temperament, over the stallion he preferred to ride. It would not do for his army and his people to see their king pitched into the sea by a nervous horse.

The causeway was perfect, though it had cost the lives of more than seventy men in its construction. The first attempt had been anchored to piles driven into the seabed from above, using huge frames and logs dropped and raised on pulleys. Yet it had been too rigid. Storms had come rushing down the Hellespont. Xerxes had read reports of how the section over the deepest part had risen and fallen well enough, but one of the anchored ends had torn free. The entire bridge had flailed like a whip then, smashing a hundred precious ship hulls to splinters. None of the guards stationed along its length had been found.

The broken vessels had been pillaged for firewood, of course. There was no sign of old failures as Xerxes reached the centre point and paused, taking in the view on both sides. He had beheaded the engineers responsible for the disaster, as a warning to the rest. The new teams had worked night and day to fling another chain across the strait in record time. A few more workmen had fallen in and been drowned, but the rest had laboured on.

Two priests waited for Xerxes at the centre of the road over the waters. They lay on sun-bleached wood, both men prostrating themselves as the Great King dismounted. The crowd's roar was a distant hiss out there, like the crashing of waves.

'Up, gentlemen. Be about your task. Bless me in my endeavours, and in my father's memory.'

Xerxes ignored them then as they set about chanting prayers of good fortune, sprinkling him with fresh water taken from the deepest wells in stone, where no light had ever shone. Xerxes looked out on a view that had not existed the year before. On one side, Persia vanished into the distance, the greatest empire the world had ever known.

On the other, Thrace, with its hills and mines, its farms and villages, its hunters and warriors. Xerxes smiled at the thought. To those primitives, his army must have seemed like statues of gold and iron, like angels walking the earth. The Thracian women were comely enough. A few had been taken up by his officers, though they tended to kill themselves, or occasionally the man who snored alongside.

Xerxes shook his head. It had looked for a time as if the tribes of Thrace would rise up and resist. He had sent imperial messengers to the towns and villages there, giving them a stark choice. Even then, he had been forced to make an example of one gathering of kings determined to refuse his authority. They had not stood a chance against his Immortals. It was all so unnecessary! He had no quarrel with them. Like the boats that groaned under his feet, they were just a bridge to lands beyond. Xerxes smiled at that thought.

Beyond Thrace, the mountains of Macedonia rose like blades on the maps. Persian merchants had visited the towns along his route for years, learning all they could. Xerxes himself had never seen those lands. The kings there were said to be warlike and to field armies of spearmen, clad in bronze like the men of Athens. Xerxes wondered if they would stand in the path of General Mardonius when he marched half a million men through their heartland. They too were the bridge. He cared nothing for Macedon, not that season. Greece was his prize – the Athenians and the Spartans who had scorned him, like a wound that would not heal.

Xerxes listened as the priests invoked his father's support in heaven. He closed his eyes for a moment, joining the chant in rhythms he knew from childhood. The repetition calmed him, bringing him peace. In the breeze that touched his skin, he thought he could feel his father. More, he thought he could hear the voices of children, laughing and calling to one another.

Xerxes breathed in sharply, filling his lungs with cold air. If the Great King had come to see his son's creation, Xerxes would carry his spirit as a noble breath – right to the cities of

Greece. It was a glorious concept and he felt certainty take hold. Not even the priests would understand, he realised. Other men dreamed, only to see their dreams made dust. Xerxes was not of their kind. His hopes became bridges. His dreams became vengeance, an arrow sent from his father's bow that had been in flight for a long time. It would land in the heart of Athens.

When the priests had finished and lay quivering on the causeway, Xerxes let them both take his hand, granting them honour. The younger one held on for a beat too long, whispering prayers and benefactions, his mouth wet as he kissed the royal knuckles.

Xerxes reached for the knife on his belt, but the priest had the sense to let go and fall flat. For a long moment, the king looked down on him, considering whether he should bless the bridge in blood. Xerxes could feel spit drying on his hand and it would have been a fitting sacrifice. God stood with him. His wife Amestris had borne him a son and crown prince, named Darius, of course, after his father. That final piece of the plan allowed Xerxes to leave on the campaign at last, his succession secured.

He had health and strength, and perhaps, the voice of his private thoughts whispered, perhaps his father's reign had been mere preparation for this. Xerxes had lashed the sea and bound it with a ribbon across its surface. Oh, it was true the fishermen and merchants had complained. It had not been possible to leave a gate in his floating bridge of ships, so that those on the west had no way through to the eastern part of the Hellespont strait. Some of the richest traders had ridden as a group into the new city, full of pompous indignation as they made demands of his governor.

Xerxes glanced back to where they swung in the breeze. They looked like little brown birds from where he stood, hanging on strings. The imperial governor of Byzantium had chosen to remind all the rest that they served, they lived, only at the whim of the Great King. There had been no more complaints after that.

Xerxes felt calm and purpose flood through him, the mark of his father's spirit, he was certain. He left the priests to their trances and whispers and mounted again. Almost in answer, the causeway shifted, rising with some great surge of the waters below. It was . . . oddly discomforting. His engineers had said it was three thousand paces from one side to the other, a wonder and a marvel that had allowed his army to cross over the previous weeks. He could almost imagine the sight as if he flew above, or stood again on the high crag. It would have been like watching sand or a wineskin draining, one side to another. Hundreds of thousands of men, carts and horses had made the crossing. They waited at that moment, on another continent.

Xerxes rode slowly on. He kept his horse on a tight rein as the animal began to step high and snort at this strange road that lifted and fell with the sea. In reply, Xerxes dug in his knees and trotted the last part, slowing only to let his mount step gingerly down onto steady ground. For an instant, that too seemed to rise and fall, then settled.

Ahead of him, imperial regiments stood in perfect array, long banners flapping in the breeze. They had remained in place as the sun appeared on the horizon and the Great King had begun his crossing. Even as he watched, one of the men fainted in the heat and stillness, left where he lay with Xerxes looking on.

Mardonius and more than ninety senior officers formed their own square by the ramp to the bridge. The administration of such a host required clerks and written orders, a second army almost, just to administer the first. The simple task of feeding so many, or replacing worn kit and weapons, required another town to follow, with cooks and trades and slaves of its own.

Each one of his generals had been trained by his father, proving both their competence and their ability to survive. Many were also the sons of his father's most trusted friends. In the presence of Xerxes, they dismounted and stood with bowed heads, the reins in their hands. They could not lie flat without letting the horses go loose. Xerxes noted that fact with a shiver of anticipation. This was life on the march, already beginning. Rough and simple, it excited him.

Xerxes trotted his mount towards them. Mardonius did come forward and knelt in the dust, his haunches in the air. Xerxes rewarded the man with a smile, gesturing for him to rise. Mardonius would not speak first, of course. It meant that silence stretched between them. Xerxes turned his horse in place while a breeze blew from over the waters.

His father had always found it easy to converse with such men, from the lowliest soldier in the ranks to a veteran general of thirty years' experience, warriors of flint and dust and iron. If the old man's spirit resided in him that morning, it was quiet. Xerxes felt he lacked the same ease of manner, retreating instead to formality and stern orders. Still, as long as they obeyed, it did not matter.

'I am pleased, Mardonius,' Xerxes said at last.

He waved a hand at the standing squares stretching into the far distance, but his gesture took in the bridge itself. He felt his breath catch as he saw both its importance and its fragility. What if another storm came while he was away? His army would be stranded. There were far too many for the mere land to feed. They were a capital city on the march, without half the chains of food and water that allowed such a city to survive.

It was a horrible image, of regiments slowly starving. He had used every old ship in the fleet for the first road and its replacement. The hulls he had employed all needed to be baled as it was, with slave boys living beneath the main causeway, working all day just to keep the seawater from rising. He thought he had heard their voices as he'd stood with the priests. If a storm battered them apart, or if the waters rose too fast and some of them sank, the great floating road might break again. He would . . .

'Your Majesty? It will be all right,' Mardonius said.

He had seen the sudden change of mood in the young king, as he had a thousand times before in the previous months. Xerxes worried about everything, where his father had been content simply to trust his wishes would be fulfilled. Perhaps it was the lot of a son trying to follow in his father's greatness; Mardonius did not know. His own four sons were competent soldiers, rising in the ranks of the Immortals with very little supervision from their old man.

For a moment, Xerxes closed his eyes, overcome by the simple words from his general. He felt tears sting him and blinked them away.

'What if the bridge sinks or breaks again, Mardonius? How will you come home then?'

'When victory is ours? We'll have the fleet, Majesty. If you wish, you could order those captains to form a bridge. If there was no longer any danger, no need for them at sea, you could have all our ships lashed together and planked over in days, weeks at the most. We could leave the masts in, perhaps, or cut down the cross-yards to use as . . .'

'Yes, I understand,' Xerxes said.

He felt peace run cool in his veins once again. His father's spirit. He had forgotten for a moment that he carried the old

266

man. There were no problems that could not be overcome, not in that perfect union.

'From this moment, Mardonius,' Xerxes went on, 'as I set foot once more on the land across the bridge, you are in command here, with my blessing. You will come from the north; I will come by ship. We will meet in Athens, as God wills.'

Mardonius lowered himself again to kiss the young man's royal sandal. The general's heart filled with pride, for his people, for Xerxes and for the army he loved. They had been formed for this, as a potter shapes clay. In the years since Marathon and the disaster of that fool General Datis, Mardonius had trained them and hardened them and armoured them. The gold of the Achaemenids had flowed in a torrent and if any softness, any weakness, yet remained in his men, it would be burned out in the mountains and hundreds of miles ahead.

'I swear it, Majesty. We are your sword. We will not let you down.'

Xerxes allowed his general to cup hands to help him remount, then rode back across the bridge. On the other side, his fleet waited at sea, already raising anchor as they watched his progress. Sails were filling out in the bay, while thousands of oars dipped and swung.

Only his flagship still waited on the docks, Immortals in white cloaks on deck to salute his arrival. Xerxes breathed deeply as he watched his horse taken up in a sling, whinnying piteously as it was swung on board. He had planned the campaign for years, every detail. He had lived and breathed the destruction of the Greeks. For his father, for the insult of Marathon, for how they had scorned his offer of earth and water – but also for himself, for his own need to burn their cities to ash.

'I will make an ending,' he whispered in a personal vow.

The coolness he felt could only be his father's spirit in his veins. He had known that creeping cold many times before, when he had drunk an infusion of poppy to help him sleep. Yet this time he was invigorated.

'Thank you, father. I will be the glad shout, the battle roar. I will be your answer to them – and my own.'

Xerxes walked over planking to join the crew, accepting the ceremonial sword of fleet admiral as his feet touched the deck. He would command at sea, as Mardonius commanded on land. They would strike Athens from both sides and his enemies would understand at last what they had done.

29

Themistocles wondered if there would be blood spilled that evening. When the arguments grew heated, it was an easy thing to imagine. Yet they had come, at his formal request. Though nine-tenths of the delegates he'd sent had returned with a refusal, thirty separate cities and regions had answered Athens. Perhaps hundreds of small fish had not, but those who had travelled to the neutral ground of Thessaly, to the city of Larissa, were among the most powerful of the Hellene states. Sparta had come, the linchpin, along with representatives of Megara, Chalcis, Sicyon, Arcadia, Corinth and two dozen others. It confirmed Themistocles in his belief that Athens could be the leader of all Greece, with the right men to guide her. With himself to guide her.

Unfortunately, whatever spirit of cooperation had brought them to that place was fraying even as he watched. Perhaps the wine was part of it, or arguments that seemed nothing more than idle discussion. He'd heard better on any single day listening to the Assembly in Athens. Only the Spartans kept their eyes down, Themistocles noted, placing their hands over wine cups whenever the tavern slaves approached to refill them. They looked about as sour as he might have expected. At home, he'd heard each Spartiate warrior had seven helot slaves to tend him at all times, to treat him like a god. Themistocles wondered if arrogance was the result. They could not *all* be masters.

He watched as the Spartan Cleombrotus clapped another Greek on the shoulder, approving whatever he had muttered.

There was something coiled in the Spartan group, though there were just four of them. They were powerful figures, but so were many of the men there, at least those who had known a life of hard physical labour. Themistocles had noted the Spartans all bore a lattice of pale scars on their arms, testament to thousands of hours on the training field or perhaps in earnest, in full battle against other men. Cleombrotus was in his forties or fifties at a guess, lean and powerful across the shoulders, younger brother to the battle king of Sparta. Themistocles had never met King Leonidas, a name that meant 'son of the lion'. He thought it was a sign of trust that the man had sent one of his own family, or at least he hoped it was. The Spartans had two kings, each to act as a balance for the other. It was not quite the tyranny of so many states, but neither was it the free votes of the Assembly. Themistocles knew the Spartans saw Athens as ruled by the mob, a city of constant argument and chaos. That was fair enough. He thought of Sparta as a backward place, a joyless military camp where they let their women run with the men.

Cleombrotus sensed his scrutiny and looked up. The man raised his eyebrows in silent question, calm and unworried. Themistocles inclined his head, giving the man honour. Presumably, Cleombrotus could speak for his brother. He too bore scars on his bare arms, pale against the deep tan of a life spent outdoors. The Spartans were survivors, Themistocles could see, veterans who had faced enemies and survived. He needed them.

The plates were taken away and the tavern servants retired. Themistocles had ordered it so and brought his own house servants to tend anyone who needed more wine, grapes or figs. He rose from his place and silence came quickly enough. They had spent the day discussing what they would do, but he sensed he had not carried them all. Crucially, the Spartans had not yet committed to the work ahead. It was one thing to attend a meeting of Greek states called by Athens under truce, quite another to agree to follow them into war.

Themistocles cleared his throat.

'I have spoken to you, in groups and as individuals. I have shared the intelligence that found its way to Athens, on fishing boats, in messages from trusted merchants, from spies and friends on the Ionian coast. I think you know by now that the Assembly of Athens would never have sent this call unless we understood the threat to be grave and real . . . and immediate.'

Not even the chairs creaked as they listened, hanging on every word.

'The fate of Greece will be decided in this room,' Themistocles went on. 'I wish it were an exaggeration, but we know the Persians are coming. The only reason they have not marched before was the time it took putting down the revolts. You know how King Xerxes responded to those. Thousands were butchered: in Egypt, in Libya, in the Ionian cities. The rebellion spread far and, for a moment, some of us thought Persia might even break apart.' Themistocles shook his head. 'It was not to be. He has bound them together, even more strongly than before. Xerxes is young – and as ruthless as his line. The examples he has made . . . are deliberately savage. Every report that reaches us says the same thing. Persia is at peace once again, while blood and tears dry.'

Someone leaned over to a friend and whispered a few words, resulting in a chuckle. Themistocles nodded and smiled.

'Athenians, eh? Always talking. It is our way, though I fought at Marathon.'

He watched the Corinthian flush at being singled out, but nodded to him. At least he had come.

'I have faced these same Persians on the field of war,' Themistocles said. 'For months afterwards, we kept finding jewels, or pieces of gold and silver. Even their dead carried fortunes. When we made a great fire to burn the bodies, we had boys sifting the ashes for droplets of gold for a month, bringing back their finds to the city.'

'Were they brave?' one of the Arcadian contingent called out.

There was a longing in that room for humour. Men needed it when the news was bad. Themistocles considered his response for a moment, then decided to tell the simple truth.

'Brave enough.' He watched the Arcadian's smile fade. 'They stood in good formation and they did not break — though the sea was at their backs and their king watched, or one of his lords. We never saw him. Perhaps they could not run. In the end, we had to kill them all.'

He saw the Spartans look up at that, watching him. Cleombrotus knew very well his people had not made it to Marathon in time. Themistocles and Aristides had gone out to meet them the following day, when they finally arrived, having force-marched for two days and nights without rest. The dust and sweat on the Spartans had stilled the quick humour in his throat that day, for which Themistocles was grateful. More, there had been a kind of madness in their eyes. They *hated* to fail. No barb he might have fashioned could have hurt them more than their own shame – but they would have remembered it even so. Themistocles shuddered to recall their expressions. The men who sat with Cleombrotus were the same breed, like mad dogs with the will and discipline of men. They were terrifying. He was pleased to have them under the same roof, with a common enemy.

'The shield drills protected us against sling-shot and arrow. Not all of you use spears as long as the Athenian style, but they were effective. When it came to the shield wall, the Persians were brave enough, but they carried no hoplons of their own and they were vulnerable. If they bring the same armour and arms to another battle, I would bet every drachm I can earn or borrow on us beating them.'

There were nodding heads and smiles enough at that. More than a few bent close to others and a dozen conversations began. Themistocles found himself clearing his throat once more, interrupting. His people! He loved them, but given time, they would talk a man to death, Athenian or not.

'I have two reasons to doubt my own judgement,' he said. 'Between us, we can put . . . how many? Athens will offer two hundred ships, eight hundred archers . . . eight thousand hoplites. Can Sparta match that last?'

He waited for the Spartans to dip their heads reluctantly. They were famously reticent on the strengths of their army, but he had to know. Themistocles hid his relief.

'The rest of you can field thirty or forty thousand between you – at most. Not all will be fully armed hoplites, not all will be experienced. When we stand together, we will have no more than sixty, perhaps seventy, thousand Hellenes.'

He paused for a moment. What he was about to say was not news to them, but the comparison was still stark.

'The Persians can put at least five times as many in the field. Some reports are of half a million.' He waited through the murmur of disbelief and dismay. 'Not all will be fully armed warriors, not all will be experienced, but there are so many, we will be hard pressed.'

He saw by their expressions that he did not need to elaborate further. They knew the stakes, just as he did.

The Megaran stood up at the back, a short warrior with a black beard close-cropped. He looked around thirty, in his prime.

'How can we stand against such a host?'

'I don't know that we can,' Themistocles replied. 'I know that Athens will. We will meet them at sea and I pledge our one hundred and eighty ships in service of all Greece. Forty thousand rowers and hoplites, gentlemen. We have trained every son – and we will hold nothing back, nothing at all. Understand that. We will ram their ships and drown anyone attempting to make landfall. Gentlemen!'

He had to call again to interrupt the nervous conversations breaking out across the room. With bad grace, Themistocles gave way to one of the Corinthians. He did not know him, except by the reputation of his city.

'Corinth can add forty galleys to this alliance.'

Themistocles blinked in surprise as the man sat down. He had not intended to request ship numbers, but he rode the moment and gestured calmly to another as he rose, a man of surpassing ugliness and a broken nose that suggested a youth spent fighting.

'The island of Cythnos has but one trireme to pledge,' the man said. 'But our entire navy stands with you.'

There was laughter at that, though it died away as one of the Spartans stood.

'I am Eurybiades, of the Spartan fleet. We have only sixteen galleys to patrol our coasts. It is all we need. Our rowers are helots, but each ship carries forty Spartiate warriors. If there is to be fighting at sea, we will play a part.'

Themistocles nodded. He expected the Spartan to take his seat once more. When Eurybiades did not, Themistocles had to pause in the act of acknowledging one of the Arcadian officers.

'I can pledge our sixteen,' Eurybiades went on, 'but I cannot give up its command, nor accept the command of others in war. That is our code, gentlemen. If I went back to tell the ephors and kings of Sparta that I had given our fleet to the orders of Themistocles of Athens, I would be given a knife and a quiet room to make my ending.'

Themistocles hesitated, thinking fast. He missed Aristides then! That man could spin an argument from spiderweb and Themistocles was coming up short.

'Our ships ...' Themistocles began, 'have trained in manoeuvres you will not have seen, could not attempt with just sixteen. We have tactics and formations, commands you will not have heard . . . a thousand things.'

To his dismay, Eurybiades sat down. With anyone else, Themistocles would have counted the point won. With the Spartan, he had the suspicion that the man had laid out his offer and saw no reason to discuss it further. Themistocles might have gone on speaking for an hour and made no impression at all. He wondered if Aristides could have done any better.

Themistocles bit his lip. He was on his own in the room, with vital decisions that would affect the lives of every man there. It was also true that whatever he agreed with the Spartans could be revoked when they were at sea, or when battle was joined. He closed his eyes for a long blink, knowing this was exactly the sort of Athenian low cunning that the Spartans detested. Too many beats of time had passed already, with fresh conversations breaking out.

'Athens accepts your offer to lead the fleet, Eurybiades. We are grateful. Are there any dissenting voices? Good.'

The Spartan dipped his head in acknowledgement, though there was no triumph in it. It was truly as if Eurybiades knew there was no alternative.

Themistocles took a deep breath, settling his nerves. He dabbed at his forehead, where sweat shone.

'The second reason victory will be hard is the numbers

here tonight. Where are our brothers this evening? I sent delegates all over Greece, west and east and north, right to Macedonia. You answered, but the influence of Persia spreads further every season. I know some will have been bought off by coins and promises, made slaves by gold archers.'

'None of that matters,' Cleombrotus said.

The senior Spartan spoke softly, but the whispers died away as the others realised who it was. His voice was warm and low, like a growl. He tapped Eurybiades on the arm and rose to his feet, as if they had agreed it was his turn. The Spartan's mouth twitched as he found the rest of them literally looking up to him.

'Themistocles has spoken much of ships, though wars are never won at sea. We will face the invaders on land – and we will prevail.'

To Themistocles' astonishment, the brother of the king of Sparta sat down as abruptly as he had risen, as if he had finished and said all he wanted to say. They were infuriating, almost as if they understood exactly what would annoy an Athenian and then plucked that note, over and over. Themistocles rose again, this time with half a dozen others wanting to speak. To his pleasure, they gave way when they saw he was on his feet. In truth, they were less hostile than the Assembly.

'Athens stands – with our wooden walls at sea, with all our hoplites committed to war. When they come, we will accept Spartan command on the field. Shall I put it to the vote?'

Cleombrotus rose once again. To Themistocles' irritation, he shrugged.

'If you wish. You know we will command. We do not accept orders from other Greeks, Themistocles, even those of Athens.'

The gathered men groaned or grumbled at that. Cleombrotus waited for the sound to die down, his gaze turning back and forth as he looked for opposition. He would not let them blow air and roll their eyes to keep their dignity. There were two great powers in that room and two alone. Cleombrotus challenged them with his flat stare, forcing them to accept what they knew to be true. One by one, Themistocles saw them look away or dip their heads. They were like dogs with a lead wolf, accepting him. It was astonishing. He wondered if it would work on the Pnyx.

'You have my oath,' Cleombrotus said, looking across the room to Themistocles. 'That is what you wanted, isn't it? I speak for my brother, King Leonidas. If the Persians come, we will march to meet them on the field. Five thousand Spartiate warriors, five thousand lesser men . . . and our helots. It will be a good day.'

Themistocles opened his mouth to speak, but the Spartan rose and left, his three companions trooping out behind him. The brother of King Leonidas glanced only once at Themistocles, a quirk of his lips indicating at least some humour.

When they had gone, a subtle tension left the room. Themistocles wiped sweat from his forehead. His return to Athens was already days overdue. The Assembly would be demanding his report with increasing urgency, and the fleet was hardly ready to fight a mock battle, never mind a real one. He had wanted this, he reminded himself. He had wanted to lead. He had just not expected it to be quite so much work.

'Will you accompany the Athenian hoplites?' his friend the Megaran asked.

Themistocles scratched his chin. He had built the fleet himself, from the silver of Laurium, to training captains and rowers to their labours. The thought of leaving it to another was like a physical pain. He needed good men. He needed strategoi. His heart sank as he understood what he had to do. It was against the law, but in his heart of hearts, he knew laws were for lesser men. He would make them anew, if he had to persuade the entire Assembly to do it.

30

Themistocles stood on the Pnyx, facing Athens. In response to news of his return from Larissa, the centre of the city was packed. There had to be twenty thousand on the Pnyx hill alone, with at least as many around that rock, in every street. Most could not hear a word, but with talk of war on the wind, they had come even so, to be there.

The archons of the Areopagus had taken positions close to the speaker's stone, with the epistates of the day. For once, it was a man Themistocles knew, from his own tribe. There was no sign of fellow feeling, however. Themistocles was losing the crowd, he could feel it.

'If I had not given command of the fleet to Sparta, we would have lost their ships – and perhaps their army as well. Can you deny it?'

'The motion under discussion is whether you should have returned here first to seek the approval of the Assembly,' the epistates said.

Themistocles glared at him.

'No man here has supported this Assembly with more energy than I. I sought the support of all Hellas as your representative.'

'As a tyrant, then!' someone shouted from the back.

Themistocles forced a smile, raising his voice to carry as far as he could, though it strained his throat and stole subtlety.

'Never! I have honoured Athens and this Assembly with my every breath. Yet in war – and war is what we face – we appoint strategoi, do we not? In that moment, faced with losing Sparta from our alliance, I chose to accept on behalf of us all.'

He gave way to Cimon, as Cimon expected all men to do. The Assembly member did not yet have his father's powerful presence, but it was coming, Themistocles thought. As a shepherd can feel the first heat of summer, he could sense it. Though all the senior roles of the city were denied to Cimon until his thirtieth birthday, he had established himself as a name. He would certainly be an archon and a strategos like Miltiades. Yet he had been raised without his father's hand on his shoulder. There was a roughness, a simmering violence in Cimon. He had learned to harness other men to his service, though with little subtlety. Cimon wrenched savagely at whatever reins fell to his hand. With war coming, Themistocles thought there was a chance the young man would break free of all restraint.

Themistocles kept a smile plastered across his face, but he had been accused and jostled and irritated since the sun rose. He had seen himself once as a master of those around him, capable of employing the currents of public feeling to take him anywhere he wanted to go. He shook his head as if in sorrow, feeling his thoughts moving sluggishly. Had he lost that sense, that delicacy? Age stole many things from a man. Had the scythe of time taken his ability to read a crowd? How many greybeards had he known who no longer seemed to understand the conversations of the young?

'. . . of walls built across the isthmus,' Cimon was saying, haranguing the crowd.

Themistocles dragged his attention back, realising he had missed the main point. By Athena, he was tired! He rubbed his face, wanting nothing more than a little wine, a few hours of sleep. He had to struggle to listen to whatever Cimon was saying, though it seemed to support him.

'If the cities of the Peloponnese believe they can live behind those walls while Persia rapes Greece, they are certainly mistaken! Sparta has but sixteen warships. The Persians could land armies anywhere on their coast. Yet that does not matter. If the Spartans and the Corinthians believe they are safe behind their barricade, they might not engage. Remember, we are their allies only by necessity. Themistocles made them understand we had a better chance together than in two parts. That is a victory, regardless of how it came about.'

Cimon stepped abruptly away from the speaker's stone, as if he disdained their support. Some of his people cheered him even so. Yet there were not enough of them, even though he had offered his fields and harvest to any man of Athens who needed food.

Themistocles saw dozens more wanting to speak. He felt his eyelids droop at the thought of listening to them all. Though he loved them, by Apollo, they burned the hours.

He knew he could not leave the Pnyx, not without securing what he had come for. Themistocles sighed to himself. One hand hid the other as he tugged one of his fingers and then twisted. The joint popped and dislocated, as it had a dozen times before in his life. It was an old wrestling injury, but the effect was immediate. Pain snapped him back to sharpness and his thoughts flew. He approached the stone again and the epistates gestured for others to take their seats. They had summoned Themistocles, after all. He had the right to speak.

'Thank you, Cimon,' he said, formally, before raising his great head and voice. Themistocles felt his jaw jut as he looked across his people.

'You have all heard the reports!' he said. 'One by one, we have had witnesses traipse their way up here to tell their

281

stories over the previous months and years. Will you deny all of those? Persian soldiers spotted in Macedonia, building camps and forts and cutting roads. A bridge of ships across the Hellespont! An army of such numbers no two men can agree. A fleet of empire, commanded by Xerxes himself, with his brothers as his officers. They come! At last! And they will be *met*!'

They cheered that, some of them, though it was no full-throated roar. They were afraid, he realised. The angry accusations of him having overstepped his authority were all because they were afraid.

'We have people watching in the north,' Themistocles continued, 'ready to gallop in with the news. When their army appears, we will march to meet them. Athens and Sparta and Corinth and all the rest of our alliance. An alliance you sent me to secure for the Assembly. If the price of that is Sparta in command, I am willing to pay it – and a thousand times more. I stood as the representative of this Assembly and I gave over the command.'

'What of the fleet?' someone called in anger.

Themistocles felt his finger throbbing as the first pain died away, leaving him drained. He knew the fleet better than any man. It was the source of his authority in Athens, with over thirty thousand employed and paid as rowers. The entire city seemed to work on his ships in some role or other – certainly the bulk of the Assembly. They thanked Themistocles for that wage and took pride in the labour. On that day, it seemed they felt he had given their service to Sparta, that he had thrown them aside like an old lover. Of course, the one thing he could not say was that he had no intention of following a bad Spartan order. No, he realised. He had to say something or he would lose them.

'We will have over three hundred ships in our alliance.

A fleet of Hellenes, of rowers and hoplites and archers and bronze rams. I will be there, among you. Cimon, too, will have command of a dozen ships.'

He looked to the younger man as if in question, though it was all agreed. Only his youth had limited Cimon to so few. Cimon nodded, accepting.

'With me will be Eurybiades of Sparta,' Themistocles went on. 'No, gentlemen! Are you geese? You demean yourselves with your hissing, no other! You will treat that name with honour. Eurybiades stands with us, as all Sparta stands with us. There is no place for petty rivalries, not this year. We stand together or we die alone. Understand that! There is no retreat, no place where we can retire to lick our wounds. This Persian king comes for *us*. He comes to burn, rape and murder. He comes to *own*, to make all Greeks slaves. I tell you, there is no hiding place.'

He paused a beat.

'The senior officers will put our fleet where it can bring oars and rams and force of arms to bear. Like a spear thrown to kill a running man, we will send them to the bottom of the sea. Yet in the end, it will come down to the crews. You know it better than I do. When battle is joined, your ships will be on your own, hunting like hawks and leopards. You will hole one enemy and pull back, faster and more cleanly than any of their poor slave rowers. Or you will board and make their decks red, then burn their hulls and go on! Will it matter then whether a Spartan or an Athenian brought you to the battle? You will know I am watching, regardless!'

He got a better response from that. He tugged his finger, the pain increasing until it popped back into place, relief washing through him. It would be sore for days, but he had needed the edge. There was still so much to do. After years of reports, the Persians were truly marching. They no longer

283

attempted to hide their presence in Thrace and Macedonia, with huge food stores guarded by encamped regiments. More, the imperial fleet was out under sail and oar. There were new reports every day, and suddenly, after so long, time was short.

'I call for an extraordinary vote,' Themistocles said. 'As befits a time of war. I cannot do this alone, gentlemen. I need seasoned leaders, experienced strategoi. I need Aristides . . .'

The noise of the crowd trebled in an instant. Over that tumult, he saw Cimon glance sharply in his direction. Themistocles held his gaze, refusing to look away though the young man stood as if he had been struck, visibly stunned. Themistocles bellowed over the crowd.

'And I need Xanthippus. I call an extraordinary vote – to overturn their exile. To bring them home.'

He watched Cimon approach him and did not pull away as the younger man took his arm. He could smell wine on Cimon's breath, but he did not sway or blink. In fact, Themistocles had the sense he was controlling great emotion. It spoke rather well for the son of Miltiades.

'You truly need them?' Cimon said.

'I do. In peace, I would go on without both men. Can you imagine what calling them home will cost me in pride? Yet to save Athens? In war? Both men fought at Marathon, Cimon, with your father. Against that, my pride is just a rag. My city matters more.'

Cimon nodded, moved enough by his words to clap him on the shoulder. It was a symbol of casual dominance, but Themistocles made no attempt to avoid it. The young man had surprised him yet again.

The noise of the crowd was a clamour around them, with violence in the air. Scythian guards were shifting at the edges, reminding all the young firebrands of their presence.

'Aristides and Xanthippus,' Cimon said softly. 'They might not come. If they believe you were behind their exile.'

Themistocles smiled bitterly. He had wrestled with the idea for some time, but the same truth applied to them as to him.

'If I know Aristides, he will have teased apart every whisper of memory until he is certain, at least to his own satisfaction. Still, they are Athenians, Cimon – and Athens is under threat. Nothing else matters. Not the law, not my pride, certainly not theirs. They *will* come. They have to – we need them. Now, help me win this vote.'

31

The sun was brutal in the valley. Months of hard labour had turned the men such a dark brown they looked like polished wood, especially when they shone with sweat. Many of them still had sections of flaking skin across their bare shoulders that came off in sheets. They had learned not to peel it away, revealing paler skin that would then blister. Instead, they worked and ate and slept, wearing just a cloth around their waists, or perhaps an old chiton tunic, black with dirt. They endured like soldiers, heaving posts upright and hammering them into the ground, drinking water and then sweating it out, stopping under a spreading plane tree to eat lunch when it was brought. It was a simple life and Xanthippus had thought it might have a sort of nobility to it. Felling an oak, sawing it into posts and then sinking those posts all the way around a huge cattle enclosure had seemed honourable work. He had watched the foreman, Pelias, as he explained the task to another, then joined the work crew for just two drachms a day.

Pelias had been wary of him at first, seeing the scarred arms and manner of a soldier. Yet Xanthippus worked as hard as any of them, earning blisters and splinters, then calluses as the long summer days wore on. He had settled into the task, staying almost silent with the other men. He did not need companions or friends. They seemed to sense that in him and left him alone for the most part. One fool who had tried to take his bowl of stew had frozen when a hoplite knife appeared from nowhere, held against the warm flesh of his groin. The man had put the bowl down with more care than he had taken it up, though Xanthippus had not said a word, nor risen from his seat.

There was a certain pride in feeding himself through his own labour. The coins he earned were not many. They could be held in a palm that was scratched and split and battered, but they were completely his. He could have had Agariste send funds each month from the family estates, but he preferred not to be a supplicant. Some things were more valuable than mere silver – his pride was one. As far as he had fallen, he was no man's slave, to be fed and kept warm like a hound.

Xanthippus had been burned lean by his exile. He had written letters in the first couple of years, almost constantly. For the longest time, he'd tried to continue his life as it had been. How does a man spend ten years away from home? From his family, his city and everything he loves? He would be fifty by the time he was allowed to return to Athens, a period too long to just wait out. Xanthippus had understood at last that he needed to work, to train and remain fit, but also to occupy his hours. Time hung heavy on a man with no purpose. He had never understood before what a punishment too much time could be.

Agariste had brought the children out to see him just once, a few months after he'd left. It had been a huge undertaking, or at least she'd made it seem as if it was. Her complaints about the days on the road had been a clear warning to him. He'd vowed not to ask again, until she offered. Of course, she had not. He had not seen his children for six years. Ariphron would be almost ready to join the Assembly. Eleni would be fifteen and Pericles would be thirteen, almost fourteen. It was impossible to imagine.

'Hold it steady,' Xanthippus said.

The man gripping the post had a tendency to flinch as the

287

hammer came down. He would have been better wielding the hammer, but Xanthippus didn't trust his aim, not when it was his hands underneath. The man was not a mute, but like Xanthippus, he spoke only rarely.

Over and over, Xanthippus brought the iron head down, pounding the post into the ground. They had covered an extraordinary amount of land with the fencing, so that it stretched right back to the farmhouse in the distance. Not that Xanthippus had seen the family. He was just a labourer, there to think and lose himself in heat and repetition.

He sighed. He thought too much, he always had. There were times when he realised whole days had passed unnoticed, somehow sliding by. Yet they were mere instants, moments, not the great oceans he had imagined. He had taken up a dozen different jobs in his exile, from breaking horses to constructing a roof, to writing speeches for clerics in Corinth, men hardly able to believe one who looked like a carpenter could form letters as well as any temple scribe.

'That's it for today,' Pelias called.

The men didn't argue. They gathered up the spades and hammers and tossed them onto the work cart, then formed a weary queue for the silver coins. Xanthippus took his with the rest, almost out on his feet with tiredness. He wondered if he could ever feel at peace.

It was an hour's walk to his home, on the edge of Corinth. By the time he reached it, his feet were like lead and he was walking almost in a daze. He needed food and perhaps a cup or two of wine.

A cart and pair of horses stood in the road, with four armed men waiting. The scene brought him back to sharpness. His door was open! He could hear his dog whining at his approach. Xanthippus felt his hand drop to his waist, but there was only a pruning knife there, with a wooden handle.

Even so, he took it up and held it ready to slash as he entered his home.

Agariste was out of place in his little kitchen. He recognised her but still stood with a stunned expression. He heard the metallic sound as the knife fell from his grasp, but didn't stoop to pick it up.

'Agariste?' he said, filled with dread. 'You didn't write, to say you were coming.'

Her face was pinched and taut. She nodded as he went on, fearing the news.

'Is it the children? Is Ariphron all right? Pericles? Eleni?'

'They are all well, Xanthippus. I have come to bring you home,' she said. 'The Assembly voted.'

'It has only been seven years,' he said, trying to take it in.

His eyes slid to the second person in the kitchen, watching him in silence with her hand over her mouth. His mistress, Alia, was of Corinth, a woman with two children and a dead husband who had passed away while she was still coming into her beauty. It was she who held his dog, though the big brown mastiff struggled in her grasp, unable to understand why he was not allowed to go to the master. Xanthippus held up a hand to quiet the dog's whining. From the tension in that room, he guessed Agariste had understood her role in his household.

'The Persians are coming, Xan. I thought . . .'

To his horror, Xanthippus saw his wife's eyes fill with tears. Agariste rose from her seat and pushed past him into the open air. He was left in the room with his mistress, standing like stone. As if her strength failed her, Alia opened her hand and the big dog bounded towards him, fussing and wriggling. Xanthippus had named the animal 'Conis' as he was the colour of dust. To any Greek, though, the name carried a shadow of death with it, of men returned to dust. It

289

suited an animal as ferocious-looking as any monster Heracles had ever defeated.

'So that's it?' Alia said. 'I thought you said we had more time.'

She was being brave, he realised. Just that morning, they had lain in bed together, as they had for the best part of four years.

'I never lied to you,' he said softly, patting and rubbing the dog. 'You knew I would go back to Athens, to my family.' He made himself say it. 'To my wife.'

He could hear the creak of harness and cart outside and was suddenly fretting. Seven years! Had Agariste expected him to live like a hermit? It was too long for a man to spend alone. He could only thank Athena there were no children to bring back. That thought chilled him. He held out his palm to Conis and made him sit.

'Alia, if it turns out you are pregnant, bring the child to me. It would be a citizen of Athens and I can . . .'

'I am not pregnant,' she said.

She spoke with such certainty, he guessed she too took the herbs and tea that bled children away. His women all seemed to shrink from bearing his children. For a moment, just a heartbeat, he wanted to strangle her. He was not a weak man, however. He mastered himself.

'The house is yours, to sell as you wish. Conis too. There is a little gold and silver in my cloak, upstairs. I must go, Alia.'

'Because your wife calls you back to her skirts,' she said, a note of acid creeping in.

'Because my city calls me,' he said. It sounded like an excuse and he would not allow it. 'And because my wife has come, yes. I never lied, Alia.'

'You did, Xan. You lied with every touch.'

He stared at her for a long time and then went out, stepping up beside his wife without a word. As the cart moved away from the home he had known for seven years, he heard Conis whine. Xanthippus shook his head, too tired to think. He gave a low whistle. If someone tried to hold that dog then, he knew they would have been dragged across the room. He looked back to see the big beast barrelling down the road after him, leaving a wake of rising dust. Though he was weary, though Agariste sat with a face like thunder, the sight of his dog's massive head and wide grin lightened his heart. Conis howled as he ran, until Xanthippus put out his arm and the dog leaped up to him and was heaved on board, trying to lick his face with all its might.

Neither Xanthippus nor Agariste spoke again as the road took them east, to the narrow border that separated the Peloponnese from the rest of Greece. Soldiers of Sparta had built a huge barrier there, with just a narrow gate and a resulting queue of carts and people that stretched back half a day. After they had waited for a time, Xanthippus reached across and took his wife's hand. She yanked it away from him, so he spoke instead to the dog.

'Conis? This is Agariste. She is my wife and you will protect her and keep her safe. Do you understand?' The dog made a sound partway between a whine and a cough. 'Good boy.'

Xanthippus lay back and closed his eyes, lolling and dozing. Agariste said nothing, staring coldly ahead until they passed the barricades and staring Spartan guards, then turned the cart towards Athens.

Aristides sipped a tisane of jasmine and mint, satisfied with his morning's work. The batch of pots coming out of his kiln were exactly as he had imagined, a blue glaze that reminded him of the sea on a summer's day. He had proved the colour would remain true and he had a dozen packed in, with charcoal banked underneath and the bricks hissing and chinking under an intense heat. There was peace in their creation and it pleased him to sell them in the markets of Ithaca.

The population of the island was small and he had more simple glazed plates stacked in his workshop than would ever be bought, but he caught his own fish and had restored a little one-roomed place that suited him. It looked as if Odysseus himself might have walked past it when he returned from his adventures. Aristides had taken work in a dozen places to learn the crafts to restore his home. His kiln had come from first attempts to make tiles. He'd volunteered in a potter's for the best part of a year until he had the skill and knew how to find the right clays and make the charcoal.

He smiled as he sipped the drink, breathing in scented steam. He had built the roof first, to get him out of the cold and rain. After that, he'd shaped a door and hung it on leather folds, then later, working in a forge in town, he'd bartered his labour in exchange for iron hinges and a handle. That first door had warped and he'd had to sell a few plates for seasoned wood to replace it. Each piece of the house had come from his own mind and hands. Though it was tiny, it was perfect, close by the shore, where fishing boats came in and unloaded their catch. In exchange for a hot drink or some loaves from his kiln, they would leave a fish or two. Greeks understood hermits, after all. Aristides had let his beard grow long, though there was no wild look to his eyes, nor visions to disturb his sleep. When he sat still in the evenings, watching the sea, he was at peace. Most days, the same red cat came to sit with him. Aristides had not given her a name, as he thought he was not her master. Still, he fed her scraps and had taught her to give him one paw and then the other.

Out on the sea, he saw two triremes race. He watched idly, noting the eyes painted on the prows rise and fall in the swell. The trierarchs were competent enough, though he had little expertise in the tactics of the sea. Beyond accounting for the costs involved, anyway. Those he did know. For a time, Aristides amused himself estimating the cost of creating the ships, then crewing them with rowers. Assuming a full complement of men, it was a staggering total. Only Athens could have kept so many at sea.

When the ships came closer to the shore, he saw they both bore banners of an owl, symbol of Athena. That brought a pang, almost a nervousness. He had not thought of the terms of his exile for a long time. Yet some part of him had counted the years. They had not come for him.

One of the ships dropped anchor further out. The other dipped her oars with superb precision, surging for the beach. It seemed they were intent on making a landing. Aristides glanced back at the kiln he had built against the wall of his little house. If the glaze was to develop, he knew he would have to pump more air in, working leather bellows to drive up the heat. Temperature seemed to affect the final colour, though he had not yet understood how.

The galley drove up and up the beach, seemingly unstoppable, like a knife blade cutting through the sand. It slowed at last and only the twin rudders still rested in the surf. Aristides watched as hoplites threw rope ladders and walkways down to the sand, clambering out. Some local lads had been mending their nets and stood with mouths open, not yet sure if they should run or cheer.

Aristides shot another glance at his forge. He could hear the plinking sound of stone growing cool. He needed to get back there and build it up. A forge had to be tended, everyone knew that. Yet he stood rooted, unable to turn away from Athenians after so long.

The trierarch himself, the captain of the galley, climbed down and called something to the fishermen. They pointed to the dirt track that led up the hill, though the town was visible from the coast. A sacred place to Greeks, with red roofs, white walls and a wide shore. Aristides wondered . . . His thoughts were interrupted by the trierarch himself.

'You, sir, we seek the Athenian, Aristides. He is said to reside on this island. Do you know him?'

'I am Aristides,' he replied.

The captain blinked, but recovered quickly, as befitted a military man.

'It is an honour to meet you, kurios. It is my duty to tell you that your exile has been ended by order of the Assembly.'

Aristides put down his cup and took a long breath. Without another word, he walked past the captain and his men. After a moment of confusion, the captain shrugged and followed him. In a short time, the ship was towed out into deep water. Behind, on the shore, the kiln Aristides had built was left to grow cold, his pretty blue pots forgotten.

32

The council building had been built around a meeting chamber. Open to the Agora along one edge, it held the five hundred Athenians chosen by lot each year from the ten tribes. For a few days each month, they sat on white stone benches to discuss the administration of the city, from the fleet and mines to murder cases. The most pressing matters would then be presented to the Assembly for a public discussion and vote.

It was a light and airy place, with sun streaming in and the noise of the market nearby. Themistocles had intended to lounge on one of the benches as Aristides and Xanthippus were shown in, a figure clearly and magnificently unworried. Yet when the doors were opened, he found himself rising to his feet as if pulled on a rope.

The two men who entered looked fit, he thought. In comparison, Themistocles was paler than either of them. He said nothing as the councillors backed from the room and closed the doors. He had asked for a private meeting, though he thought there would still be ears somewhere. The only true privacy lay under the sun, in the open air.

Aristides wore a new robe of white linen. It seemed to have irritated the skin at his neck, where a raw red stripe showed. Themistocles watched as the man caught sight of him and approached, taking a seat a few spaces further along. From that side, they could look out onto the Agora, with its busy crowds and street sellers.

'I give you greeting, Aristides,' Themistocles said formally.

Before Aristides could reply, Xanthippus was striding up to where they sat, using the benches as steps. He carried no weapon except his anger, but Themistocles felt the stone behind his knees even so. He could not retreat, would not.

'I called you both from exile,' Themistocles said quickly. 'I demanded an emergency vote and won it, with Cimon's help.'

'You cost me seven years,' Xanthippus said.

His voice was hoarse, but in speaking the words, the anger faded. Themistocles had lost some of the cocky arrogance he remembered. There were new lines on the man's face and in the stoop of his shoulders. Xanthippus scowled in confusion. Where was the laughing kurios he had known before?

'You would have remained for three more had I not called you back,' Themistocles said. 'Let there be only honesty between us. Strike me if you want, but then sit down and listen. Don't stand and glare. We don't have time for that.'

'Why would I strike you?' Xanthippus said in sharp triumph. 'Are you behind it all, then?'

'Come and sit, Xanthippus,' Aristides said. 'Let us hear what he has to say.'

Xanthippus clenched his fists, though Themistocles was so broad across the shoulders, it was hard to imagine knocking him down. It would certainly take more than one blow. He hoped the same was true of himself.

'I am glad we found you,' Themistocles said.

He could not quite bring himself to sit down while Xanthippus stood breathing hard and still looking as if he might run mad. Instead, the two men stood facing one another awkwardly.

'I sent men to fetch you, but somehow your wife already had word. She must have been on the road before the Assembly had even finished voting.'

'Do not speak of my wife,' Xanthippus said.

Themistocles nodded, staying silent and wary. Time stretched as neither man gave way.

'I was not called back for this!' Aristides snapped. 'Both of you! Sit *down.*'

It was nothing to do with obedience, they told themselves, only that the words gave them an excuse and broke the tension. Whatever salve they used on their dignity at being scolded like children, both Xanthippus and Themistocles took seats on the same side.

'Thank you,' Themistocles said to Xanthippus. He felt sweat break out and wondered how he would have reacted if the situation had been reversed. Not too well, he suspected.

'In a moment, I will bring in Cimon,' Themistocles went on, his voice quiet and certain. He saw Xanthippus look troubled. 'As you forgive me, he can forgive you – for Athens.'

'I have not said I forgive you,' Xanthippus replied, though there was less heat in it than his first madness. 'There will yet be a reckoning, Themistocles.'

'There always is,' Themistocles said, sighing.

He went to another door and rapped his knuckles on it. Cimon entered immediately, as if he had been standing with his ear against the wood.

Both Xanthippus and Aristides rose to their feet. Cimon walked like a leopard, or a warrior in his prime. Still in his twenties, there was a spring in his step that spoke of muscle and strength and training to kill. Cimon was intimidating, but there was only a cold sternness in his face.

Xanthippus saw the young man was armed and breathed out. He understood the point, or hoped he did. If he was safe, if any of them were safe, only when the others were unarmed, there could be no peace. If Cimon could stand with a sword on his belt and then leave it in the scabbard, perhaps there could be an accord between them. It was subtle, but Themistocles was a good judge of character.

Xanthippus hoped that was still true. If Themistocles was wrong and the son of Miltiades decided to avenge his father, Xanthippus was dead.

'Aristides . . . Xanthippus,' Cimon said.

He stopped before them, on a lower step. It was hard to remember the lad who had stood with his father at trial. Cimon's hair was cropped short and his face had changed, losing any boyish planes. He radiated strength and will.

'Cimon,' they replied almost together, their voices overlapping.

The young man dipped his head, though he did not take his eyes from Xanthippus.

'Themistocles has convinced me he needs you both. I accept his judgement. However . . .' He held up an index finger as if interrupting, or listing points one by one. 'Xanthippus. You were wrong to bring my father to trial. If you will admit that, I will put aside any enmity I feel. Can you do it?'

Xanthippus stared at him, his thoughts whirling. Themistocles cleared his throat as he began to speak. The young man changed his gesture sharply to a flat palm, warning him to be still.

'Oh, sit down, boy,' Aristides said. 'He was not wrong.'

'I have no quarrel with you,' Cimon snapped, stung.

Aristides shrugged.

'Nor I with you. It does not change the truth, or the past. Themistocles called us back early from our exile. I imagine the world is about to end, which is why I am here, waiting for him to tell me what he wants. You? Who are you?'

'I am the son of Miltiades!' Cimon retorted.

'Were you at Marathon, with us?' Aristides asked. 'We were, we three. We fought alongside your father. Either way,

Miltiades died of his wounds – almost ten years ago. So be wary, boy. You have lost much. So have I. So has Xanthippus.'

Cimon stared at him. He had imagined great drama, with Xanthippus forced to repent, to admit he had been wrong. Instead, a man he respected had rattled his plan, throwing him off as he built to a climax. He turned back to Xanthippus, but the moment had lost much of its power.

'I cannot change the past,' Xanthippus said.

It sounded weak to him, so he forced himself to speak again. If Cimon drew his sword, perhaps they could grapple with him before he killed anyone. He took a deep breath.

'I was not wrong, Cimon. I did my duty – a duty that exists because Athens is worth more than us. Our freedom is worth more than our lives, certainly our labours! Can you understand? It has never been clearer to me than today, setting foot in the Agora once again. There is nothing like our Assembly in the world, Cimon. Outside our bounds, there is just men telling others what to do – tyranny. I spent my years of exile in Corinth, on the Peloponnese. It took me a while to see what was different there, but when I understood, it was a hammer's blow. Nothing changed! In Athens, we talk, we trade, we innovate. There is change every day, but always with the consent of the people. Always. I saw a man hanged when he criticised a nobleman of Corinth. There was no outcry from the people, as there would be here. Beyond blasphemy, we can say anything. We are free to praise Sparta, but the Spartans are not free to praise us! That is the difference between Athens and the world. Our law comes from the people, not at the whim of judges or kings. By Athena, I swear I loved them for it, even in exile, even cast out.'

There was awe in Cimon's eyes as he realised he understood

a man he had hated. Aristides too looked moved, as if he could weep at what he heard.

Xanthippus breathed out slowly.

'That is why Themistocles called me here today, though he knows I would strangle him in a heartbeat. What freedom we have won is worth my life — sweeter today than in seven years.'

Both Cimon and Xanthippus glanced at Themistocles. Under that twin gaze, he nodded confirmation. Xanthippus chuckled, though there was bitterness in it.

'I'll work to preserve all that is good. That is all any of us can ask. No matter what it costs. So in the end, we can say, "We did the best we could, with what we knew."'

'Would you do it again?' Cimon said softly, almost in wonder. He too seemed to have been drained of his rage, the reality an intense disappointment compared with the scene he had imagined. Xanthippus was not a monster, but an ordinary Athenian, lean and thoughtful, tanned and strong.

'It doesn't *matter*,' Xanthippus said. 'We can't go back. I have more regrets than you can imagine, Cimon. But I cannot undo a single stitch, do you understand? The great moments of your life are still ahead. Yet if you only take a step when you are certain you are right, you will never move at all. I will say this . . . I am sorry your father died.'

'Thank you,' Cimon said.

Themistocles looked from one to the other.

'I can see I was right . . .' he began.

Xanthippus swung from where he stood, in a surge of anger so complete he saw only white light and felt no pain, even when he spun the big man round and sent him crashing and sliding across the benches.

Themistocles groaned and Xanthippus felt a twinge of fear as his anger vanished and he remembered how Themistocles had liked to box and wrestle. His fists closed, though one ached from the blow. He would not retreat, not that day. With a calm expression, Xanthippus watched Themistocles lever himself upright. A red mark showed where he had been hit as he came back to stand by the other three. His gaze, however, was all for Xanthippus.

'That was not an honourable blow,' Themistocles said. Xanthippus waited as the man considered. 'But we have more important work before us. If we are all finished with old grudges? Yes?' One by one, they nodded. 'Good. The past *is* past, gentlemen. The future, however, is all to play for. Persia is coming, by sea, by land. And I can't stop them, not alone.'

Despite the pain in his jaw, Themistocles realised he felt lighter than he had before. Aristides was a fine strategos on the battlefield. Just the thought of being able to pass the Athenian hoplites into his command was a huge weight that lifted away. Xanthippus demanded respect and won it with sheer will and ability. He could be trusted, no matter what the stakes were. Cimon was a firebrand, yes, aggressive, brash and disrespectful of authority, but he had become a charismatic leader. Such men strained the seams and bonds of peacetime, but in war, they came into their own. Themistocles had not been wrong, he thought with relief. He needed them all.

33

Xanthippus walked out of the city. It had been a long day and he was weary, but also filled with a satisfaction he had not known for too long. It was not that Aristides had been given command of the city's hoplites. Any tyrant could have given the command with a wave of a jewelled hand. No, it was that the council had called an emergency meeting of the Assembly – and the voters of Athens had formally confirmed Aristides in the role, setting aside his exile. The record of that decision had been cut in stone and mounted in the Agora for any man or woman of the city to read.

Xanthippus smiled as he walked, lengthening his stride. Aristides had called every hoplite in the city to a training run the following dawn. The route would be to Marathon, there to camp and return the next day. Aristides would assess their readiness and if Xanthippus knew him at all, he would sharpen that knife until it could draw blood just by looking at it.

Xanthippus had been disappointed at first not to be given command of a thousand, as a strategos. He had assumed his role at Marathon was the reason Themistocles had called him back. Yet the man he had punched had other plans. Until he was thirty, Cimon was too young for a senior position in the fleet. Themistocles needed a second in command and it seemed he trusted Xanthippus.

That was the strangest part of coming home, perhaps. Xanthippus had spent years imagining his revenge on Themistocles, but he had never doubted the man's skill, nor his love for Athens. It seemed Themistocles had understood that about Xanthippus as well. Whatever their personal history, they shared enough. It was a revelation. The following morning, while Aristides took his hoplites on the first training run, Xanthippus was expected at the docks, to take ship out to the fleet. He would have to learn a vast amount in a very short time, but he found himself excited by it. There were far too many triremes for Themistocles to command alone, especially with the factions coming in every day, and a Spartan trierarch who was already making a nuisance of himself.

Xanthippus shook his head in amusement, chuckling. There was no one else on the road and he could hardly contain the thrill of being dropped back into the politics of home. His exile had been a grim existence in comparison, he realised. He thought Alia would be interested to hear – and then he stopped in the road, suddenly, staring into the distance. He was missing her, though he did not think he would be sharing that thought with Agariste. If his exile had come to a natural end, Xanthippus knew he might easily be considering ways to bring Alia back to Athens and establish her in a quiet street. It was not so uncommon.

He began to run, stretching out his hips and tired muscles. His lower back ached and his knee started to complain after just a few steps, reminding him of his age. He would not bring Alia into the path of Persian soldiers, not that year. She would be far safer on the outskirts of Corinth than in Athens. The decision brought a pang of disappointment and he shelved the subject, to consider later on. The heart was a complex thing.

His mood lifted again as he reached the door to the estate and hammered on it. A slave he did not know climbed to the top of the steps to peer at him with a frown. It brought a flush of anger, just to be considered a stranger in that place.

'Tell your mistress, the kurios is home,' Xanthippus snapped.

The man vanished and the door was pulled open just moments later.

He had come back with Agariste in the small hours of the morning, drowsing together on the cart. The children had come out by lamplight to greet their father, standing in a row like any other group of strangers, until Conis bounded over, wagging his entire body and slobbering over them. Xanthippus had not known then how much their faces would have changed. His daughter Eleni had grown. Her brown eyes were watchful and wary of him, where before there had been smiles and easy laughter. His two sons had patted the dog with more enthusiasm than when they took their father's hand. They had allowed him to embrace them, but it had felt like duty. Xanthippus had never felt less comfortable than in those moments.

The sun was setting as he entered his home, at once so familiar and so subtly strange. The door to the road was closed behind him, securing the estate for the night. Conis came skittering out, skidding on the tiles and making little sounds of happiness as he wove in and out of Xanthippus' feet in clumsy adoration. A dog was good for a man, Xanthippus thought.

Lamps had been lit in the house and the gleam beckoned him, warm and secure, everything he had dreamed a thousand times in his years away. He had hardly noticed it in the dark the previous night. Now, he stood and gazed on his past. Agariste would be waiting for him to enter. In that moment, he could not. He heard the soft sound of hooves on turf and turned to make his way around the house to the field, Conis trotting at his side.

In the soft grey twilight, he saw Pericles put a horse to a

jump as high as any Xanthippus had ever seen. The beast he rode was powerful and lunged at it, tucking in its front legs as it flew over. They seemed to hang for a time in the air, then landed, front feet and back, his son patting the horse's neck and turning him in place.

Eleni was there – and Ariphron too, watching. They were oblivious as he and Conis walked out of the shadows. Xanthippus had not been part of their lives for so long, he wondered if he ever could be again. Themistocles had taken that from him, but it was an old pain, long scarred and gone cold. He was home, with war coming. He loved them, but not in a way that clutched at his heart, not in that moment. He loved them as he loved Athens. He would give his life for them even so.

They turned without alarm as he approached them, though he saw a stillness return to their manner. Ariphron and Eleni took a step alongside one another, as if they thought to line up once again. Pericles watched him from horseback without dismounting, a certain hostility in the clear gaze. Xanthippus' smile tightened. He had felt a simple joy as he approached them. It seemed to curdle as it met the reality. They did not know him.

'I remember watching you learn to ride, Eleni,' Xanthippus said, 'over a much smaller jump, with a little pony. Yes! Pericles stood behind the pole, just there. I was worried that if you missed the jump, it would take him off his feet.'

Neither of the two boys replied. They watched him as they might have watched any of their mother's friends. Eleni beamed in memory.

'I remember!' she said. 'I was on Shadow. He was wonderful.'

'Not Shadow,' Pericles muttered.

His sister glanced at him, but went on, caught up in the memory.

305

'We sold him when Peri outgrew him – and I bought Soldier here. He's Peri's horse, really, but he likes me more.'

She grinned and Xanthippus thought how beautiful she was, how full of life. Conis wagged his tail at just the sound of her voice.

'The pony's name wasn't Shadow,' Pericles said again. 'It didn't have a name. Nor is this one Soldier. They don't have names.'

'They do when I ride them,' Eleni said, keeping her smile in place.

Looking from one to the other, Xanthippus could see it was an old argument.

'I don't see that it does any harm to name them,' Xanthippus said gently. 'I called my dog "Conis", you know. "Dust", after his colour.'

Pericles glared at him and Xanthippus could see him struggling between a desire to reply and sensible caution.

'And your mother and I named you, all three of you,' Xanthippus went on. '"Ari-phron" means "great mind". You are my firstborn, the great-nephew of Cleisthenes, who gave us our democracy in Athens.'

His oldest son lost some of his glower at that.

'And "Eleni"?' his daughter said.

Xanthippus smiled.

'It means "light" – a torch in the darkness. Because of how my heart lifted when I heard your mother had given birth to a girl. I chose that one.'

She was delighted at that. Silence fell. Pericles said nothing, while Eleni looked from her brother to her father, then lost patience with their quiet clash of wills.

'And what about Peri? What does his name mean?'

'It means "famous",' Pericles said under his breath. He seemed annoyed by it. His father nodded.

306

'It does. Your mother had a dream of a lion on the night before Pericles was born. Such a vision does not come often, or to many. She gave you the name as an ambition, that one day all men would know it.'

'And you, father?' Eleni said. 'How did you get yours?'

'My mother dreamed of a pale horse,' Xanthippus said with a shrug. 'I do not know what that dream meant.'

To his surprise, he found he was enjoying the conversation, that something tight had eased in him. Perhaps it had been the laughter of his daughter, he thought. Men needed women for such things, or life would have been a dark and pitiless place. Even with a dog.

That thought made him look past Conis to the house. He took a deep breath.

'Why don't you see to this fine horse – Soldier, was it?'

He was pleased when Pericles just rolled his eyes, without the saturnine darkness he had shown before. Xanthippus patted him on the back, realising how much he had missed embracing his children. He opened his arms and all three came naturally in without another word, crushed to him in the evening light. Conis pushed in amongst them then, making them smile.

When he came into the house, Xanthippus' eyes were still red. Agariste was there and he saw the anger in every line of her, the stiffness and resentment. As he approached, she raised her arms to fend him off, but he smothered them and hugged her tightly. He felt her sob against his chest.

'I have been a fool,' he said. 'I'm so sorry.'

34

The sun glittered on the water in a million flecks of light. The Acropolis of Athens could be seen from the port and Xanthippus bowed his head to Athena, murmuring her prayer. On impulse, he added prayers to Poseidon, whose realm he had entered, then Ares for the war to come. Apollo had been his childhood hero, so Xanthippus added lines to honour the sun and source of life, then called to mind Theseus and Heracles. There were many gods and guardians of Athens. He felt them all around him, thick as bees, while the little boat rocked. It was hardly more than an open shell, twice the length of a man. Two benches sat across the width, thick pine, sun-bleached and worn. Xanthippus eyed the pair of rowers, seeing strength and easy endurance. They were dark, with white hair on their forearms. Like the boat, they had known years of hard use. Xanthippus wondered if they would keep their favoured spot when the war came. He doubted it. The fleet would need every rower, especially men as competent as these.

He sat in the stern and they faced him, side by side, while the trireme grew to fill his vision. The massive port of Piraeus dwindled behind, built stronger and dredged deeper by Themistocles, so he had been told. Themistocles was a hero in that place, Xanthippus had discovered. So many men owed their livings to him, he was beyond any fear of exile, at least that year. Xanthippus did not know how he felt about that.

He put such thoughts aside. He was out over water deep

enough to drown a man. It was not calming to imagine a darker, colder world beneath his feet, with grey sand and unseen fish flapping slowly through the gloom.

Ahead, the trireme wallowed; there was no other word to describe it. Xanthippus had known merchant vessels that almost seemed to fly, with sails taut and creaking. In comparison, the broad-beamed warships seemed horribly unstable on the deep water. Neither sails nor mast were visible. He understood they had been taken down for the sea trials, as was normal practice. With the oars drawn in, the great ship seemed almost helpless, like a piece of stick bobbing on the ocean. Even as he watched, the approach of his little craft brought the long oars out, with shouted orders carrying to his ears. Three levels of sweeps splashed down, fully ninety men to a side, all sitting so close their sweat dripped onto those below.

Like the legs of some strange insect, the oars reached the waves and the rocking motion eased. Xanthippus swallowed his nervousness, relieved he would not have to try and climb on board a ship rising and rolling as it had been before, smashing white spray into the air.

Above the oars, he could see men walking on the bare twin deck. A trench ran from one end to another, right down the centre, giving light and air to those labouring below. It was a machine, Xanthippus thought, like the wooden cranes on the docks or the children's toys sold in the Agora. A wonderful, intricate machine made by men. Made to hunt. Made to drown.

His own pair of rowers worked tirelessly to bring him alongside the stern. They kept station then, as if they thought he knew exactly what to do. Xanthippus looked blankly at them until he saw the closest oars were being held almost flat, so that a man might step onto them. The ship still rolled back and forth as some ripple of great waters passed beneath them.

Before his fear could overwhelm him, Xanthippus swallowed and grabbed one oar while heaving himself onto another. With his heart in his mouth, he stepped onto the one above, feeling like a spider crawling from twig to twig. It was with huge relief that he reached a wooden ridge he could wrap a hand around. As he clambered onto the open deck, Themistocles leaned in and offered him a hand.

'Did you not see the ladder?' Themistocles said.

Xanthippus looked where he pointed and saw rope steps flapping about in the swell. While he stared, the bottom five or six plunged beneath the surface. It seemed, if anything, more perilous than the oars. It was tempting to claim he had chosen the oars out of some caprice, but he refused to lie to a man who thrived on weakness.

'No. You have a great deal to teach me,' he said.

He leaned over to see what had become of the two rowers. They were still there. One of them stood ready with a net bag of Xanthippus' kit. Themistocles had warned him not to bring more than a cloak, a razor, a flask of oil and a waterskin. He had added only a cheese wrapped in cloth and a small statue of Athena in limestone, given to him by Agariste.

Xanthippus watched anxiously as one of the crew tossed down a rope, barely longer than himself. The trireme was so low on the water, it looked as if the sea would come in through the oar-holes at any moment. His two ferrymen knew their trade, however. They tied the bag on and then it was pulled on board and placed at his feet. Sailors moved quickly in all their tasks, he realised. There was life to the ship, a bustle on all sides. It was exhilarating, though he felt exposed on that wide deck, without even mast or spars.

For luck, Xanthippus tossed a single silver tetradrachm to

the two men: four drachms and wages for a full day. It was only when the coin was in the air that he saw how hard a catch it was – a glint of silver, all while the boat rocked underfoot. Somehow, the closest oarsman snatched the silver piece, though he almost went over backwards to do it. He and his mate beamed then, raising a hand in salute and triumph, then rowing away at an even faster pace than before.

Themistocles patted him on the shoulder as Xanthippus picked up his sea bag.

'I chose you for how you lead men, Xanthippus. Not your seamanship.' Themistocles thought for a moment. 'Though, yes, you have a great deal to learn and little time to do it. You will need to know the limits and the strengths of these ships – and their crews. We have developed tactics, but it is hard to know what will work until we meet the Persian fleet at sea. Here, let me introduce you to my esteemed colleague, Eurybiades of Sparta.'

Xanthippus watched as Themistocles leapt the open part of the deck to cross to the other side. He did it as easily as walking across, though it must have been as wide as a man was tall. In truth, it was not hard to make that long step, though Xanthippus had an uncomfortable sense of faces below turning up to see him. Someone was hammering down there, Xanthippus thought, and swearing while he did it. The ship's carpenter and his lads, presumably. Xanthippus followed Themistocles across, wondering if he would ever make the leap so casually.

On the other side stood a Spartan, resplendent in red cloak and white tunic, moving subtly with the motion of the ship as it rose and fell beneath their feet. The man's legs were bare, but his cloak reached down past his knees, far enough to protect him from the chill of the sea wind. Xanthippus felt himself shiver at the prospect of weeks or months at sea.

Just the thought brought a sense of loss. His reunion with Agariste had stolen almost all the night and any chance of sleep. He still smelled her perfume and could only pray the wind would whip the scent away as he grasped the hand Eurybiades offered and felt an iron grip come to bear.

On all sides, ships began to pick up the pace. Xanthippus could hear waves smacking against their hull as the trireme somehow came alive. He wanted to rush to the side and drink it all in. Instead, he did his duty, bowing to the Spartan.

'Ah, the exile, returned!' Eurybiades said. His voice was softly hoarse, reminding Xanthippus of a cat, purring.

'My name has gone before me, then,' Xanthippus said lightly.

Though the man gave him back the hand he had tried and failed to crush, he was still testing. In truth, Xanthippus did not resent it. They needed to know and trust one another, in just a short time. It could be no other way. The words followed the thought.

'I am Xanthippus of Cholargos deme, Athens. Acamantis tribe, if you wish, though that is a new thing in our city, barely a generation past. I am Eupatridae – a landowner, you might say.'

'A farmer,' Eurybiades said, still prodding him.

Xanthippus smiled and clapped the man on the shoulder, watching to see how he reacted. To one who considered himself superior, it would be an insult. The Spartan seemed unmoved by the blow. Xanthippus wondered if Eurybiades was so used to physical violence that it had been beneath his notice. He had met wrestlers who hardly noticed any knock, at least until it drew blood. That was a troubling thought.

'Other men oversee my land,' Xanthippus said. 'But, yes, I feed families in Athens. I am myself a strategos and soldier. I stood at Marathon. What are your memories of that battle?'

There was a long silence. Xanthippus could sense Themistocles readying himself to say something conciliatory, but the Spartan smiled and nodded, satisfied.

'I was in the column that reached you a day late,' he said. 'I have regretted it for many years. We were . . . forbidden from leaving earlier. The ephors of Sparta . . .'

He stopped and shook his head. Such things were not for outsiders, though Xanthippus could have groaned in frustration. Neither he nor Themistocles moved to interrupt, and after a time, Eurybiades went on, awake to their interest.

'Your runner came rather late, as I recall,' he said sourly. 'I remember I intended to take a whip to him later on, until I heard he had burst his heart.' He folded in his lips so that they protruded in two ridges. 'Still, it was my one chance to face the Persian Immortals! I would like to hear all you remember of that day, perhaps this evening? I would be honoured to entertain you on my flagship.'

It was a surprising offer, but Xanthippus agreed immediately. A Spartan warship was a rare thing in those waters. It might be his only chance to see one.

'It would be my honour, trierarch.'

He used the title innocently enough, to a man who was captain of a Spartan ship. Yet it brought about a sudden stop to the growing goodwill between them.

'Address me as "navarch" while I command the fleet,' Eurybiades said.

Xanthippus dipped his head.

'Yes, navarch. I apologise.'

The Spartan waved it away.

'The first time is forgotten. Make no mistake twice and there will be nothing but honour and respect between us. Is that clear?'

Xanthippus did not need Themistocles to be staring at

him with wide eyes. They would face a Persian fleet. He had put aside his vengeance for lost years because of that. Merely accepting the authority of a pompous Spartan was nothing in comparison.

'It is, navarch,' he said calmly.

Eurybiades nodded.

'I should think so. Now, call my boat, if you would. I will expect you at sunset. The invitation includes you, of course, Themistocles.'

'Duty keeps me here, navarch, though I wish it were not so.'

Xanthippus had no idea how to call the man's personal boat, but Themistocles signalled to one of his officers and a banner was raised on a dory spear. They stood in respectful silence until it arrived and Eurybiades climbed down. He moved well enough, disdaining any help.

Xanthippus wondered who else would be listening on board. It was an odd sensation. He was used to speaking his mind and caring not at all who heard. Yet the fleet surging through the waters around him was not just Athenian, for all they had provided over half the ships and crews. It was Greek, a grand confederation. He felt his heart fill with excitement and he went to the side to watch.

Dozens of ships skimmed the sea together, like a flock of birds flying down the coast. The rows of oars swept a little like wings and white wakes sizzled and hissed behind them. Some of the ships were grey, but many more gleamed gold in new pine and oak, with rams shining wet as they rose out of the waves and then crashed down. It was simply beautiful.

'You will not enjoy the food tonight,' Themistocles said.

'What food?'

'Whatever slop they serve on the Spartan ship. I thought they were playing a joke on me when I went over, but they weren't. They live like Aristides, all of them. You would think with all that training that they'd enjoy a little wine and spiced lamb. But it is always some dark brown muck, and bread you could use as a weapon. That's what you get in a society without money! No one can buy anything better than the rest. What's the point of that? Still, I would not like to be the Persian who tries to board one of his ships. That much I am sure of.'

Themistocles saw something strange come into Xanthippus' expression and followed his gaze out across the sea. The land was not far off and the ships moved like pond-skaters past the route both men had marched to Marathon, an age before. Themistocles looked over his shoulder.

'Give me our best speed!' he bellowed.

The trierarch at the stern rose from his seat and grinned at the challenge. He gave the command for 'ram speed sixty' to the keleustes, the order-giver who stood with only his head and shoulders sticking out of the hold. That man vanished to roar at the oarsmen and the pace picked up immediately, faster and faster. Unseen in the hold, a drum began to sound to keep both wings working together and the ship heading straight.

'Doesn't she fly!' Themistocles said. 'As fast as a man can run, for sixty beats. Ramming speed, with all our weight behind the spear.' His pride was evident, joy rising like sap to flush his face in the wind.

'What is my post in all this?' Xanthippus said, raising his voice to be heard over the shouts and drumbeats from below. Their ship had surged forward, running down those ahead and leaving the fleet behind for a brief period. He could feel flecks of spray touch his skin. It was hard to resist the pounding of his heart.

'I need a second in command I can trust,' Themistocles

said. 'You are that man, if you want it – so your role is as much as I can place on your shoulders, whatever weight you can bear. I need you to command a part of our fleet. You'll meet your captains and work with them, learning all they know, all they can do.'

'How many?' Xanthippus said.

Themistocles looked sideways at him.

'How many do you want? If you say thirty, it will be a help to me. If you say ninety ships, I'll give them over to your command, in groups of six. Don't look so shocked. Cimon is not yet thirty and there are few senior captains who'll take orders from a youth – even a son of Miltiades. There is no template for a fleet of this size, Xanthippus! If you command ninety, that would take a weight off me, in battle. Think of it as a strategos. No, I need you to! I will decide when and whether to engage, but the sea is wider than any battlefield, far too wide for signals or shouted orders. When the masts come down for battle, we are too low, too close to the water, to see far. I need officers in a tight structure, in command of smaller groups. I need men I can trust completely to take the fight to the enemy.'

With a lurch, their speed slackened almost to nothing. The motion of the sea could be felt once again and right down in the thalamos, the deep hold, Xanthippus could hear men breathing so hard it was like a cry of pain with every exhalation.

'Speed has a cost, then,' he said more quietly.

'It does. The fitness of our men is our greatest resource,' Themistocles said. He lowered his voice. 'Though the Persian rowers will have been at sea for months by the time they reach us. They are said to be slaves. Who knows how well they are fed and watered? I expect to be faster and more nimble when the oars are out. I pray to Poseidon and Athena

316

that we are. Those two fought over Athens once. Let them both bless us now, their favourite children!'

He smoothed his hair back with one hand, lighter streaks made gold after so many days at sea.

'We cannot expect them to collapse before us, Xanthippus. It will be hardest of all on those who labour below. All they know is the work of the oars. We give the orders and set the speed. They have to match it, though their muscles burn and sweat pours. Believe me, the amount of water they drink shows their labour.' He nodded to the trierarch. 'Half speed there. Have the rudder men make ready for turns.'

Xanthippus saw how Themistocles was careful to speak directly to the ship's trierarch, preserving his authority over the crew. It was a delicate balance, with the fellow repeating the same order to the keleustes without a delay.

'What part, then, does our Spartan navarch play?' Xanthippus asked.

Themistocles snorted.

'Eurybiades? He has sixteen Spartan warships, that is his part! I had to agree to let him lead the fleet, or we would have lost the strength of Sparta, not only at sea, but also on land. I will accept his orders if they are right, Xan. Not if they are wrong.'

He saw the other man frown and shrugged.

'It is not ideal, but we need them. Even I would not like to face the Persian army without Sparta. It would be like sending in Aristides without his sour disapproval.'

Xanthippus smiled at that, but Themistocles breathed out and shook his head.

'The truth is, they are coming. We have reports and sightings along the coast of Thrace. Thank Poseidon they are no great sailors! They are afraid of the deep rollers, of hidden rocks and summer storms – with some justification in waters they do not know. Instead, they creep along the coast in fits and starts – and keep their armies always in sight on the shore, like children too afraid to strike out on their own.'

He rubbed his face and Xanthippus realised how terribly weary Themistocles was. He wondered when the man had last slept.

'We don't know when they will come, only that it will be this summer . . . or if not then, next year, next spring. They have to come now they have launched. They are too many to hold the ground or wait for the perfect moment. Their food supplies have to be limited, no matter how long they planned this. If the rumours are true about their army, perhaps half of them will starve to death and spare us the trouble of killing them! Or a storm will send their ships to the cold sands beneath us. We can pray for such things, but in the end, they have begun the invasion and they cannot stop, not now. They are falling – and they will strike us. Our fleet will meet theirs and we will decide the future: of Athens, and of Greece. After all, what is Greece without us? That's why I called you back.' Themistocles chuckled. 'That is why you have left your wife and children once more to stand with me, on this deck. Some things are worth more than our lives. You know it.'

'I do,' Xanthippus said softly. The fleet had caught them up once again, but he no longer felt the wild exhilaration from before.

35

The meal on board the Spartan ship that evening was every bit as bad as Themistocles had promised it would be. Xanthippus and a dozen officers ate in silence and he was still hungry when he rose from the table.

With the moon high overhead and the fleet at anchor, it was a peaceful scene, in waters he knew well. There was little sense of the great Persian war fleet on its way to wreak destruction, closer every day. No doubt they too were at rest that night. He hoped so.

Xanthippus walked the long deck with the Spartan navarch, noting every detail, while the rowers slept wrapped in their cloaks, like the pupae of moths in the darkness. There had been no wine to accompany the meal, so he was surprised when Eurybiades produced a skin, pulling the stopper with his teeth and passing it over. It was raw stuff and strong, so that Xanthippus had to wince as he turned away and passed it back.

'I wanted to ask why you were exiled,' Eurybiades said. He looked out over the sea as he spoke, then drank deeply from the skin.

'Did Themistocles not tell you?' Xanthippus asked.

'He said you have some foolish system in Athens, where any man can be sent away for no good reason at all. He swore it was true, though I thought it would be . . . more than that.'

'It is a guard against tyrants,' Xanthippus murmured. 'Though I was not one. Still, I must trust the people – and the gods. There is no other authority in the world.'

'There is violence,' Eurybiades said. He drew a knife from his belt, a curved and wicked thing that caught the moonlight. 'If I hold this knife to your throat now, will you not say whatever I tell you to say? There is authority in that.'

Xanthippus stood still, judging the man.

'There is some truth in what you say . . . but even a Spartan sleeps. You cannot keep an entire people in bondage. If it takes a lifetime, or a dozen of them, they will rise up.'

Eurybiades chuckled.

'The helots in Sparta have been slaves for hundreds of years. Their children are born slaves, their grandchildren serve Sparta in the same way. Believe me when I say authority can be absolute.'

Xanthippus kept his eye on the man as Eurybiades put away his knife and drank from the wineskin once more. Themistocles had been certain they needed the Spartan, with his ships, his crews – and the army on land. Xanthippus felt a desperate need to argue for the Athenian constitution with every part of his strength. Yet he could not. On a Spartan warship, with war coming, he could not.

'I am a man of Athens, navarch,' he said. 'I was sent into exile and I went. I was called home – and I came home. I give my life for Athens – and I will obey.'

'There. You see to the heart of it. That is all I wished to ask!' Eurybiades said.

He passed back the skin and Xanthippus drank again, though it seemed more bitter than it had before.

When he was returned to his own ship, he felt exhaustion lying heavily on him. Xanthippus climbed the rope ladder and gave the word of the day to the guard who challenged him.

He wrapped himself in a thick cloak and lay down with dozens of sleeping shapes on the open deck. Xanthippus found himself encouraged as he stared up at the stars. The fleet had spent the day in manoeuvres, practising formations and techniques, from simple mass turns to charges in a wide line, protecting one another's flanks. Xanthippus understood that one well enough. In the phalanx, a hoplite held his shield to protect the man next to him – and trusted his life to another doing just the same.

Sleep beckoned and then withdrew from him, drifting further away. He fretted that his ignorance would get men killed. When his stomach began to gripe, he silently cursed Spartan food – and Themistocles for assuming he would know how to fight a war at sea. Even simple things were new. He had seen men emptying their bowels at the stern that day, hanging bare over the rushing water. Rowers used their left hands and a bucket of seawater to clean themselves. Xanthippus had seen a few using small, rough stones, while one or two had old rags they'd wash out and dry, kept as precious luxuries. There was no privacy at sea; he'd learned that much already.

The ship rocked at anchor on still waters and he felt peace. He would transfer to his own command the following day – Themistocles had not wanted him to look a fool on his first ship. That had been the purpose of his initiation. Beneath him, the ship creaked, as if it had a voice. He felt his spirits rise, almost inexplicably. Athens was threatened by the might of all Persia, but he was back! Once more he was in the heart of life!

He felt Themistocles' trust in him, as a weight pressing on his pride. He would not let him down, Xanthippus promised himself, yawning. He would learn everything and he would be useful. It was not as if he had a choice.

After all, his people had been seafarers for thousands of years. Xanthippus saw competence on all sides. They would face the lion coming for them. They would be the shield . . .

*

321

The stars were a blaze overhead, littering and speckling the night sky in such dazzling splendour, it was hard to see the patterns some said were there, the shapes of gods and heroes from the past, watching over them.

One Greek trireme rested on the sand, the crew sitting around a fire of driftwood on the beach. Another had been drawn up a little further down the coast, its crew choosing a spot they knew and liked, well sheltered from a sudden squall. The last of the three bobbed and swung at anchor, with just a few men aboard in case the wind rose and it dragged. The ships were so shallow in the draught that they brought even experienced sailors to vomit over the stern, at least when the swell grew restless. When the oars bit, the ships were steadier, like stones skipping across the waves.

They had been on that stretch of coast for weeks, waiting for a Persian fleet that might never appear. It was restful work and what sense of nervousness or dread they had known in the first few days had slowly faded. Though the trierarch captains were disciplined enough, they were not averse to letting the men fish for squid and mullet as the stores ran low. The weather had been kind and they stayed close enough to shore to run onto it whenever dark clouds threatened. It was the great weakness of oared ships, that they could not survive even a mild storm at sea. Merchant vessels sometimes weathered great tempests with just a scrap of sail and deep keels to keep them upright. In comparison, the triremes were death traps. The moment the swell grew strong and they began to lean, water would come gushing in through the rowing benches.

For men who lived with a chance of drowning each day, it was always a relief to send their ship easing up onto good, clean sand and then clamber out, bows and knives ready to catch anything they could add to the ship's stores. At that time of the year, it was not hard to find turtle and bird eggs of a dozen different colours and sizes, all ready to be gathered up and cooked.

Those around the fire were blind to the night beyond. They did not see the Persian ship that came out of the north. No lights showed as it glided unseen on the still waters, using the shelter of the land that had led them to that place. If the lookout on the ship at anchor had been alert, he might have seen white patches of oars kissing the waters. Instead, Androcles was whittling something for his love in the local town, all his attention on the piece he was carving under starlight. She would appreciate it. They always did. He'd left dozens of the things in ports on all the coasts of Greece and as far as Rome. Reminders of his touch, for his little doves to sigh and pat as they went past to piss in the mornings.

Androcles looked up in confusion as something bumped against the hull. He rose from his seat on the open deck, walking carefully to the edge. There was no railing there and men who had been drinking all had stories of going over the side in the darkness. It was one reason they learned to swim and wore no armour while they were on board. Men who wore armour never came back up.

The young man had his whittling knife in one hand and a crude statue of a turtle in the other. Originally from the island of Aegina, the turtle was his home symbol and graced silver coins all over the Aegean. This would be a particularly fine one when it was finished. He padded across the deck, feeling with his bare feet and wary of the edge.

'Polias? Tyros? Who's there?' he hissed.

Some of the crew could have made the swim from shore. They had lost two men the month before in some sort of race that had started on a beach and with a full skin of strong wine. The trierarch had forbidden any more contests of that sort, but then he was asleep at the stern, snoring under his awning. Androcles had the suspicion that the captain was a fool, but he didn't want to be the one responsible for waking him for nothing.

He leaned over and made a confused sound as two shadows leaped up, rushing at him. Androcles drew in a breath to shout and wake the captain, but they grappled him, pinning his arms and pressing a hand against his mouth.

The crews on shore were half-asleep when one of their number gave a shrill whistle, then shouted to rouse them. Despite the drink and rich food, they tumbled out of their cloaks and grabbed shields and swords. The closest ship's hull gleamed like a great fish in the moonlight, but there was no sign of any attack. Cries of pain and anger sounded somewhere out on the waters, thin at a distance. They turned in confusion to the watchman. He pointed furiously further out, jabbing the air.

'Look!' he shouted. 'The other ship. Its anchor has gone.'

Beyond the first, the other trireme was drifting on the tide, turning almost prow on, so that it seemed a narrow shape. They muttered in dismay at the thought of the trierarch waking to find himself aground. There would be floggings in the morning without a doubt.

In shock, they saw oars rattle out all along its length, then plunge into the water and pull. The ship seemed to leap at the beach as they gaped. Questions from panicking men filled the air until the long hull slid hissing onto the sand and came to rest. A light showed on the high prow and they fell silent, as if they were experiencing a vision of the gods.

Dark figures began to throw dead men from the deck, splashing down into the surf, or thumping onto black sand like dead birds. In the light of a swinging lamp, some of his own crew recognised Androcles as he was brought forward, his arms bound by the two who held him. The light there revealed Persian beards, their ringlet hair oiled and shining, wet as dolphins. They smiled as they cut the young sailor's throat. As Androcles heaved against his bonds, his eyes dark with death, they cupped the wound with their fingers, flicking red spatters and chanting in a language none of the Greeks knew, as sacrifice to their god. While the sailors watched in horror, more ships came sweeping in, packed with their enemies, armed and ready for slaughter.

The third crew exchanged grim glances, the decision forced upon them. Whatever loyalty they owed the others, they had a duty that came before all – to bring warning back to the fleet and Themistocles. As one, they hared away along the beach, heading into the darkness to where they had left their galley tied and safe. Cries of anger and betrayal sounded from the others, but there was no help for that.

Their ship seemed much further away than it had earlier that evening, when there had been light to see. If they could reach it, if they could float her, they could bring word that the Persians were further south than anyone knew. Behind them, they heard the first clash of arms, with strange chanting and terrible cries of pain.

36

Before dawn, Xanthippus had brought up his kit from the hold. He unwrapped a cloth and cut a curl of cheese rind. When it resisted being chewed, he left a bit tucked inside his cheek, like a coin. The cook had brewed some sort of stew from grains and vegetables. The men ate without obvious relish, as if it was just another duty. It was already clear that fresh food and meat would be a rare pleasure at sea, if they appeared at all.

Themistocles was awake and busy before anyone, of course, proving he needed less sleep than his fellow Athenians. Yawning, Xanthippus wondered what it cost him to seem so . . . unyielding. While he waited for a boat, Xanthippus oiled and sharpened his weapons, including the iron leaf head of the long spear. The lion on his shield had been touched up, of course, after Marathon. Agariste had employed some great artist to remove the scratches and battering of war. It gleamed gold in the morning sun and he smiled to think of her. She was still young enough to have another child. More importantly, he was not too old. He had proved that.

When the boat arrived and hailed the ship, Xanthippus prepared to step down onto the ladder. He had not expected a formal farewell, but Themistocles was there, suddenly, taking his right hand. They exchanged a nod.

'Learn all you can,' Themistocles said, 'then join me back in the city tonight, with the other captains. You'll need to get to know them.'

Xanthippus nodded sharply, determined not to fall in as

he clambered into a boat at the apparent mercy of the slightest wave.

With the sun of Apollo sitting on the sea like a golden fruit, he was rowed to another trireme. It was far older than the one he had left, with timbers grey or bleached white by decades. To Xanthippus' eye, his new ship sat lower in the water and looked weary, somehow. The mast stood tall and a sail had been gathered at its foot, ready to be raised to catch the wind. That would be a new experience.

The boatmen put him close and he knew to grip the ladder let down for him, holding on for dear life as he struggled up. He had no doubt he made it look hard, but he was just pleased not to fall in, especially when a roll submerged his ankles. He climbed fast as the ship swung the other way and sprang onto the deck. His legs were strong and he felt like a boarder in that moment.

A captain of Athens was there to greet him, wearing a plumed helmet and the armour of a hoplite. Xanthippus smiled as they shook hands, then waited for his bag to be attached to a rope and drawn up to land on the open deck next to him. Trierarch Ereius had to have been sixty years of age, his beard and chest hair completely white, though the former at least was neatly trimmed.

'You are welcome on my ship, strategos,' Ereius said. 'Your friend has told me all about you.'

'My friend?' Xanthippus said, immediately wary.

'Epikleos? He said he fought beside you at Marathon.'

Xanthippus looked up in delight at that. The preparations for war had kept him busy, almost frantic. He'd known Epikleos was on one of the ships but had seen neither hide nor hair of him, lost among forty thousand sailors.

It was with real joy that he saw his oldest friend climb out from the hold.

'Xanthippus! Don't believe a word of what old Ereius tells you. He is a tyrant with thirty years at sea, though the men adore him.'

To his credit, Ereius chuckled, standing back while Xanthippus and Epikleos embraced.

'How are Agariste and the children?' Epikleos asked.

'Well. Better. Pericles and Ariphron have grown up straight and strong. I've heard you visited many times while I was away. Thank you.'

'It was nothing, Xan. I just . . .'

'No. My sons needed someone to be there, when I could not be. I will not forget.'

Epikleos flushed and looked embarrassed, his usual calm humour lost. He nodded.

'I'll let our noble captain show you the pride of the fleet. I'll make sure the cook has something good for lunch, Xan. We'll catch up then.'

They gripped hands again and Epikleos swung down into the nether regions of the ship, whistling as he went. Xanthippus felt the trierarch watching him.

'You truly do not mind that he visited your wife for years? You must be very good friends.'

Xanthippus gave a snort.

'His interests do not lie in the same direction as mine, trierarch. I have no fears on that score.'

'Ah,' Ereius said. 'I did wonder. From the way he speaks . . . He loves you, you know.'

'Yes. But I cannot give him what he wants.'

The trierarch looked to where Epikleos had climbed down to the hold.

'If he prefers older men, I wonder . . .'

Xanthippus waved a hand.

'You do not need my permission. He is his own man. He

is, however, my greatest friend and a Marathonomachos. He should be treated with the utmost courtesy.'

'Of course!' Ereius said.

Xanthippus glanced at him and thought it was no accident Themistocles had placed him in the hands of such an experienced trierarch. Before the sun had moved on the horizon, he had seen every part of the ship and even hung off the prow to look down on the green ram cresting through foam below. The officers were then lined up to greet him, Epikleos grinning at one end. It seemed he was in charge of the hoplites on board, a small group of veterans, some of whom greeted Xanthippus almost in awe. They all knew Themistocles. If that man felt he needed Xanthippus so much he had to break an exile to bring him home, Xanthippus had to be extraordinary. As he was introduced to officers and hoplites, Xanthippus glanced back the way he had come. The ship of Themistocles was already lost to view in all the rest. He was alone, to learn.

The rowing crews were brought up one by one onto the narrow deck: the thranitai, who rowed on the highest level, the zygioi of the middle seats and the thalamioi, who rowed in the deepest part of the hold and were said to suffer most in rough seas. Xanthippus took their hands with a quick grin and a dry grip. They were all free men of Athens. Many would have stood on the Pnyx to hear discussions. Perhaps some had even voted for his return, he told himself. He tried not to think that some of the older ones could just as easily have voted for him to be ostracised. They were a burly-looking group, with powerful shoulders and grips of iron, so that even his soldier's hand felt mangled and sore before the last of them had gone past. Still, their strength pleased him. His life depended on their endurance.

When the formal greetings were over, the crew resumed

their duties. Ereius was chuckling as he took Xanthippus by the hand and crushed it once more, a clasp hardly less strong than the Spartan the day before. Though his fingers were pale and bruised, Xanthippus took an odd pride in that. Epikleos had lingered and the trierarch had not sent him away to his duties.

'I understand this is all new to you, strategos,' Ereius said. 'Don't worry about the ship. My little bird will go wherever we want her to – and these lads are the best afloat. Some of the new Athenian crews have slaves rowing them now. Mine are first pick, well trained. They know their orders. You'll see.'

Xanthippus wished he felt the same confidence. For that matter, he wished he knew the first thing about war at sea.

He glanced at Epikleos. At least there was one he could trust completely.

'On the orders of Themistocles, I am to select ninety ships, trierarch. My intention is to gather them in groups of no more than six, to work together.'

The captain's sudden frown cleared at that part.

'Six, even twelve would be hard enough, strategos. Ninety is . . . I do not want to say "impossible" to a man I have been told to teach as fast as anything I've ever done. Do you understand? I've fought sea actions against Aegina in the past, with dozens of ships on the water at the same time. As soon as battle begins, it's every crew for themselves. The best ones win, or the luckiest, or the most blessed by the favour of the gods. The rest are rammed and sunk – or boarded, which some say is a worse fate.'

Xanthippus nodded to show he understood, hiding his frustration. Without the chance to speak to Epikleos in private – if there was even such a place on a trireme – he had no idea if Ereius was one of those who took pleasure in being an obstruction, or whether maintaining command in a fleet

330

action of hundreds of ships was truly impossible. Without knowing the man a little better, it was hard to tell.

Themistocles had brought him back from exile, as a strategos he could trust. Xanthippus could understand that. At Marathon, Miltiades had needed Aristides, Themistocles, Xanthippus himself and half a dozen others. Some had died in the years since. Others had been ostracised by the Assembly and never come home. Xanthippus clenched his jaw at the thought. They were sorely missed. Good strategoi were rare. Their presence meant an archon could shore up a weakening line, or resist a sudden flanking attack. He could move ranks in his imagination and see the grand scheme carried out.

Xanthippus did not know if the same rules applied at sea. He understood he would have to learn as fast as a bright boy, just to be of use. He prayed to Athena he would never have to choose between orders from this captain, the Spartan who thought he led the fleet – and Themistocles, who clearly did.

'Trierarch Ereius,' Xanthippus said formally. 'Back in Athens, I've seen codes and messages sent by torch pattern, right across the city, using shields where holes have been punched in the skin.'

'That might be all right from the Acropolis or the Pnyx, strategos. Wouldn't work in the daylight, though, not at sea. And we don't sail at night, not ever.'

There was definitely a hint of pleasure in the man's obstinacy, Xanthippus could see it now. Perhaps Themistocles had sent him to Ereius to instruct as well as to learn.

'Have a look at the other galleys, strategos,' the captain went on.

He took Xanthippus by the arm and Xanthippus let himself be guided to the bare edge, though the hissing sea rushed by and seemed appallingly close. Not for the first time, Xanthippus wondered if a railing wouldn't be a fine idea.

'See how low they are on the waves, strategos,' Ereius said, 'how they rise and fall. We can approach the enemy abreast, in a line, or in files if the width of sea is too constricted. That works well to protect our flanks. But when the fighting starts, it becomes chaos, strategos. I've seen it.'

The implication was that Xanthippus had not. It was all the more irritating for being true.

'Just yesterday, Trierarch Ereius,' he said, 'I saw a boat summoned with a banner held high on a spear. Such things are possible, if you have the will.'

'That boat must have been waiting nearby, strategos . . .' the man began.

Xanthippus spoke over him, his voice growing hard. He had no time to be gentle, though it lost him the man's friendship.

'If you do *not* have the will, I will relieve you immediately from your post, Ereius. I will call a boat for you and send you to the rear, to wait out the day's manoeuvres. At sunset, when we return to the port of Piraeus, I will have you dropped on shore to walk into the city, alone. Do you have family there? Then you will explain to them why you were left behind, while the fleet sails against a terrible enemy.'

'I don't . . . Themistocles . . .' Ereius tried to begin.

Xanthippus raised his voice another notch and went on.

'Themistocles appointed me. That is the end of his involvement. Now, if I have no faith in your ability to follow my orders, I have no choice but to return you to Athens in disgrace. I will lose your experience and not look back. Do you understand me?'

The trierarch's face had lost its jolly expression and become flushed as Xanthippus spoke. The captain nodded sharply, though he was already opening his mouth to continue his objections. Xanthippus raised a finger and watched the man's mouth close with a snap. Epikleos was staring at nothing, his face blank as he waited in intense discomfort for the clash of wills to end.

Xanthippus smothered his own dismay at the turn the conversation had taken. Regardless of his lack of sea knowledge, he had no time to be liked, nor to persuade a trierarch who honestly thought he was master on his own ship.

'We serve, Ereius, you and I, at the order of the Assembly,' he said coldly. 'An Assembly which is here, all around us, rowing these galleys! I know my people, Ereius. I know they are ingenious. So indulge me, as a hoplite, as a soldier, would you? Without scorn, without ridicule. Is that clear? Or shall I take command?'

Xanthippus was not completely sure what that would entail, or even whether he could enforce that order with a crew that were presumably loyal to the red-faced and trembling man standing before him. Yet he showed no sign of weakness as he waited for his answer.

After an age, the trierarch dipped his head again.

'Please don't take my ship from me,' Ereius said. 'This little bird is all I have.'

Xanthippus turned him with a hand on his shoulder, putting the ill-feeling behind them. He would not fight a battle more than once, not if he had fought it well. Instead, he looked up to the sail that billowed overhead, held by ropes so taut they seemed like iron.

'I want to try signals on the masts . . .' He paused as Ereius began to turn towards him. 'Yes, I know — masts are unstepped in battle and laid down in the hold, or even abandoned on shore to save the weight. Even so. I want to establish the principle — a few simple signals with banners flying at our greatest height. I was returned early from exile

333

to serve my city. Let us find out if there is any advantage in my being here!'

He allowed the trierarch to retreat, heading off to give the orders. Epikleos chuckled when Xanthippus turned to him. He expected criticism, but Epikleos only shrugged.

'He knows now that you will not bend. Fine, he needed to understand that. Trierarch Ereius is a good man, Xan, however. The crew work hard to please him and he runs a tight ship. You'll see.'

Xanthippus nodded, though he felt colour come to his cheeks. He wondered if he would find the right balance in his manner, or whether he would just continue to humiliate and break honourable men.

37

The fleet that returned to the Piraeus at sunset was exhausted. It showed in the rounded shoulders of rowers as their triremes reached a berth and were tied on. In shadowy groups, they trudged across walkways to the stone quays, heads down, looking for food, wine and blessed sleep. Thousands began the walk into Athens, murmuring and laughing, meeting friends and comparing experiences. Without orders, unconsciously, those who had spent the day in formations under Xanthippus drifted alongside one another. They had watched for his flag signals all day, raised on masts or long Athenian spears. At that point, there were still only two — cobbled together from the main colours they had been able to find while at sea. 'Attack' was red, with a piece of cloth formed from an old Spartan cloak. At least one white robe had been torn into a hundred strips to signal 'form the line'. All the men knew Xanthippus had sent boats to Themistocles looking for a blue cloak, but either there was no such thing to be had or, more likely, the owner preferred to keep it whole and himself warm.

No doubt the city would provide other colours to signal 'retreat', or perhaps 'slow approach', or any one of a dozen other possibilities. Half the conversations in that slowly moving group of weary men were about the orders it was even possible to give at sea, over great distances. On land, Xanthippus may have been a battle veteran — hoplite and strategos. At sea, he'd had to discover from first principles what could be done. He had driven them hard all day as he learned. They spoke his name with pride despite their exhaustion, the Athenian who had come back from exile, who cried 'Again!' over and over until he was satisfied. Those crews had followed his orders from dawn till dusk, without complaint.

As darkness came, light and laughter bloomed in the taverns in the port and across the city. Forty or fifty thousand men all looking for wine and a meal made Athens raucous for a few hours. Little by little, peace returned as they fell into snoring sleep, in chairs, on benches, sometimes on the street itself, with street dogs curling alongside them for warmth.

Xanthippus could see some of the captains yawning as they took their seats, setting off others around them, so that the hands raised to open mouths spread in ripples. The council building was busy that night, but there was also impatience in the air. Themistocles and Eurybiades had summoned them there, while their men had the luxury of simple sleep and comfort, their labours forgotten for a night.

Xanthippus took a seat facing the benches, alongside the Spartan navarch and Themistocles. He felt the Spartan's gaze crawl over him, whether in challenge or simple interest he could not be certain. Either way, Xanthippus had earned his right to be present in that room. His formations had worked themselves to complete collapse all day, but the results were being discussed in every tavern in Athens.

Cimon entered in a noisier group of captains at the back of the council hall, wearing his youth like a brand in comparison to all the older men hardly able to remain awake. Xanthippus watched as the young Athenian strolled down the central aisle and took one of the seats reserved for senior officers. Cimon seemed oblivious to the stir it caused, so that Xanthippus readied himself to speak in his defence. The young man had worked as hard as anyone that day. His authority had showed in the sharp responses of his twelve, darting across the waters like fierce predators. More than once, Cimon's ships had caught and pinned those Xanthippus had made 'enemy' for an action. His dozen triremes were as fast and disciplined as any other group in the fleet.

The Spartan Eurybiades shifted in his seat and made a sour expression, but he chose to chew his own lip rather than speak in complaint. He had seen his Spartan ships 'killed' more than once, forced to turn onto rams they could not avoid. His own flagship had been hemmed in twice, unable to get free. It did not matter that he had not formally yielded; they knew. He had not enjoyed the experience of cheering Athenians. Still, he made no objection to Cimon's presence alongside, though the young man had yet to see thirty summers. It did not hurt that Cimon was broad-shouldered and dark with black hair down his arms and chest. He was every inch his father's son.

When they were all present, over three hundred trierarchs had been crammed into that meeting hall. Almost two hundred were from Athens, but for the rest, the Agora that ran alongside and the Acropolis that loomed above were places of legend, almost, like the sanctuary to Apollo at Delphi or the flanks of Mount Olympus. A full moon sailed above the city, bathing her in pale grey. Some of the men looked in awe through stone columns across a city they knew only by reputation – Athena's own.

Themistocles had found time to bathe and change into a white robe that left his right shoulder bare. His hair was still wet. Most of the other men still wore ship tunics, cloaks and sandals, though the air was thicker and warmer in the city. In comparison, Eurybiades and his sixteen Spartans still wore breastplates over long tunics and the famous red cloaks, bare

337

thighs revealed as they sat together. Facing them, Xanthippus wrapped and unwrapped his hand in a fold of the robe Agariste had found for him, dyed a pale blue. It would be torn up and distributed the following day. He had not intended her to come herself, but his runner had brought her to the council building. They had stolen a kiss there, while some of the other men whistled and made her blush. She still waited outside, with Epikleos to guarantee her safety. Xanthippus knew his friend would defend her honour with his life. There would be no trouble for a woman out after dark, not that night.

'Navarch, archons, trierarchs . . .' Themistocles began, looking around until he was sure he had their complete attention. 'It is my honour to play host tonight in Athens. Would you address them, Eurybiades?'

The Spartan had obviously expected the invitation. He stood and nodded to the fleet captains as Themistocles sat down. Xanthippus looked over in surprise, but it seemed Themistocles was determined to treat the man with honour.

'The Persians have not sprung our crews waiting for their advance, not yet,' Eurybiades began. 'When word does come, we will have three or four days – at most – to sail north and hit them. Each dawn before then is a gift of the gods, to train, to grow fit.'

He half-turned to Xanthippus, considering his words. Xanthippus stared back as if carved from stone and Themistocles moved uncomfortably.

'I have seen new flag signals of red and white being used today. These are to cease. They are a distraction in battle – and I will not allow my captains to be distracted.'

Xanthippus stood up quickly.

'Navarch, the results have been . . .'

The Spartan talked over him as if he had remained silent.

'There is only one order in battle, at least for us. When the Persian fleet is sighted, we must approach and engage. Our task is to sink, board or burn. I will not play the battlefield at sea. In fact . . .'

'In fact, Eurybiades, you command the fleet,' Themistocles said, the richness of his best Assembly voice filling that place. He patted the air near Xanthippus, who sat down reluctantly, fuming. 'Though I think this is an internal matter for the ships of Athens. I witnessed a dozen small group actions today – one ship caught by three, a clear "kill" as they worked together. I believe you were involved in one or two yourself.'

He bit his lip for a moment as the Spartan glared at him. Xanthippus knew Themistocles would choose his words carefully. In that, he was the veteran and the Spartan was just a newborn. Even so, Eurybiades was as stubborn as all the men of his city.

'If the order is always simply "attack",' Themistocles went on, 'why have leaders and officers at all?' Themistocles spread his hands in simple appeal. 'Navarch, you command the fleet, but this is a matter for Athenian captains, I think. Forbid the tactic to your Spartan crews, of course, but from what I witnessed today, Athens sees the value in smaller formations – and the signals between them. I hope we can depend on your wisdom in this.'

Themistocles sat down as if the point had been settled. He looked over the group and appeared to be selecting another trierarch to speak. Eurybiades stood still and Xanthippus shook his head in irritation. The Spartan was wreathed in his own fury, growing redder by the moment.

'If that is your final word . . .' Eurybiades began.

To his surprise, the archon of the Corinthian ships called out over him.

'Corinth stands with Athens, Eurybiades. They pinned

my crews today six times, just by calling in, or scattering – some flag signals they had devised themselves. It worked, which is what matters. I would know more of those.'

Eurybiades closed his mouth as Xanthippus looked from one to the other. Not only did Corinth have forty galleys, but they were one of the cities of the Peloponnese peninsula and either an ancient ally or ancient competitor to Sparta, depending on your view. The sudden involvement of Corinth had stolen the wind from Eurybiades' sails and he floundered.

Xanthippus rose again to stand alongside the Spartan.

'May I speak, navarch?' he said.

Eurybiades frowned but inclined his head and took his seat. Xanthippus chose to calm them, to give the Spartan time to reconsider.

'My captains have named two tactics that worked best today – "periplous", or "sailing around", and "diekplous", the spear-thrust.'

He cut the air with his hands as he spoke, warming to the subject. All eyes were on him as experienced men evaluated what he had to say.

'With the first, the aim is to flank an enemy, to bring our rams to bear on his stern quarter, where he is weakest. Like this, you see? Two ships on one can achieve it, while three on one can force the kill. Where one ship alone faces another, an alert trierarch and helmsman can always turn to present the prow. It is a chaotic, exhausting business then. Numbers matter – and flag signals can be vital to bring them to the right spot. What we have today is very crude, though I saw some successes. When this blue robe of mine is torn up, we'll have another signal tomorrow.'

There was a chuckle in the room at that and he acknowledged it. A glance aside showed him Eurybiades was still looking like thunder as he went on.

'Diekplous – sailing through,' Xanthippus said, with a flat palm held outstretched. 'Our broad line becomes a point. It is dangerous, as our first ships break through their line in column, then fan out to use the rams against their side planking. Both of these work better when the captains can see individual archons and act on group orders. The final tactic is one we have called "kyklos", or the circle. It is the last throw of the dice, if we encounter numbers so great as to overwhelm us. In that case, we pull the line back in a hollow cup formation. Each trireme forms on the next as the withdrawal . . .'

'Thank you, strategos,' Eurybiades snapped.

It was a clear dismissal and Xanthippus sat. He had spent a day in fascinated experiment, just seeing what worked. He had come away with his blood seething in him, filled with excitement. Yet he knew Themistocles needed the Spartan, not just for his ships, but for the army his city could put in the field. Accordingly, Xanthippus bit his tongue and listened.

'I have made my position clear – and you have spoken to counter it,' Eurybiades said. 'This is, no doubt, how the Assembly of Athens makes its decisions, yes?'

There was a bitter note in that, almost a sneer. Xanthippus waited, wondering where he was going. Eurybiades suddenly shook his head, as if he had weighed what he had heard and still could hardly believe it. To Xanthippus' surprise, the Spartan began to pace back and forth. Even Themistocles settled back to hear.

'On the field of battle,' Eurybiades said, 'Sparta has no need of counsel. Ours is a craft honed over centuries of study and labour. We have no equals. And yet . . .'

The Spartan took two quick short breaths, as if he was about to leap off something high.

'And yet . . .' he repeated, 'at sea, our Spartan crews depend on the simplest of tactics. We draw close and board, over-whelming any enemy. The ship is a mere transport. The ram is for the rare occasion when an enemy hull has to be sunk, perhaps, or if they present their flank in an attempt to escape.'

He paused again and rubbed his chin. Not a man moved. It felt as if they were present at a birth, or some titanic struggle.

'What I saw today seemed chaotic at times – a madness of ships, all rushing here and there without pattern. Yet what you describe has an obvious advantage. Three trained men will always beat one; two with less certainty. One against one, equally matched, goes on until both are exhausted. If the same can be said of our ships, bringing rams to bear, it should be . . . explored. I withdraw my objection, on all counts but one.'

Xanthippus felt his slowly spreading grin freeze on his face. Eurybiades turned to him.

'What is the signal for withdrawal, this kyklos formation?'

'Navarch, I thought it might be a black banner, but I have not practised it with the crews.'

'And you will not. There will be no withdrawal, no retreat while I command the fleet. That is the limit of my authority.' He glanced at Themistocles, who nodded, giving him the point. 'That is what I *say* the limit is. Is that understood?'

Xanthippus felt Themistocles turn to stare at him, but he was not a fool. He bowed his head.

'Of course, navarch.'

'Very well. I will join your ship for tomorrow, to observe the signals and formations.'

Xanthippus smiled rather tightly as he agreed. The Spar-tan was trying, at least. Trying to overcome the stubbornness of his home city, the centuries of certainty that meant noth-ing at all at sea. Unfortunately, it seemed Eurybiades would

342

be watching his every move from then on. Xanthippus shrugged off the worries that threatened to undermine him. He was an Athenian. He would just out-think the bastard.

The moon was yellow and huge on the horizon. The small ship crashed onto the beach in the twilight, hissing up shingle and tilting so far over it came close to rolling. The crew inside had rowed to the point of death to escape their pursuers. It had not been enough. Some eighty of them had floated her, then rattled out the oars while Persian sailors beat the water and chanted in time. That had been two nights before, with all their friends and colleagues murdered on the beach.

The second night had been spent at anchor, lost in darkness on an unknown shore without a single lamp lit. Even then, they'd barely slept, waiting for shadows to come out of the night. In that part of the sea, there were just too many shoals and sandbanks, ready to trap the unwary and leave them helpless. If the Persians had come close, hunting, they never saw them. Yet at the first grey light, three black galleys were there, far off on the cold waves, already turning to begin the chase once more.

That day had driven the crews to madness. They had rowed with their eyes closed, concentrating on just going on and going on, stroke after stroke, while the Persians drew closer. It was easier to pursue, always. Men were born hunters and it sapped the will to be chased down like a deer in the forest or fish in a net.

However long it had been, they had exhausted themselves, reached a limit. Four of them had burst their hearts and fallen still and tinged with blue into the hold, untended even by their friends. There were greater stakes.

They had discussed the best place to reach the mainland, with a dozen different choices. The only moment of joy that day had come when one of the Persian ships ran aground on a sandbank they all knew as The Nail. They had cheered then, hoping the others would break off to rescue or attach ropes to the unfortunate ones. They had not. Two ships had swept the sea behind them, relentlessly.

In the end, the choice had been made by their own weakness. A better cove lay further down the coast, but none of them thought they could reach it. Even the beaching speed they tried to bring about was feeble, so that the ship still rocked in the waves.

They tumbled out, collapsing onto the sand on hands and knees, while friends roared at them to get up and begin running. They helped each other, the strong dragging the weakest, while the Persians aimed at the shore and surged forward.

By the time the soldiers landed, they found only tracks heading over the dunes, inland. The officer walked to the top to stare out into the mainland of Greece, the first time he had set foot in the realm of his king's enemies. He turned to his second in command, a friend, but also a man he suspected reported to the king's spymaster. The officer looked into darkness, but there was no sign of the Greeks.

'We'll pursue them, of course. It should not be so hard to run them down.'

His companion made a snorting sound. He hated to run. It was one of the reasons he served the Great King on board ship.

'They're on foot,' he said with a shrug. 'By the time they reach anyone, we'll be raising a cup of wine in the ashes of this "Athens". You and I will have a dozen new women to serve us fruit and wine, with little boys for pleasure. We'll need every ship for all the slaves and gold, the way I heard it.'

The officer eyed his companion, wondering if it was deliberate temptation. There were listeners everywhere in the fleet, so it was said. He could not allow a whisper of uncertainty, or he'd find himself questioned with fire and iron, deep in the hold of the king's flagship.

'I'll send men after them in the morning,' he said. 'With a couple of trackers to read their steps. When the king asks me if I did all I could, I will not be found wanting, my friend. Not this year, not if there are such riches to be had.'

He looked back over the sea then, to the single galley that dropped anchor even as he watched. He and his fellows were the scouts, the clearers of paths. The main fleet was behind, coming closer every day, like a mountain slowly falling. He closed his eyes for a moment, enjoying the silence and the breeze. There was a certain peace just in being away from the eyes and endless rules of the king's court, with a thousand men struggling for position and taking insult at the slightest provocation. It felt like drowning, sometimes. He shook his head, sensing the gaze of his ever-watchful companion. Some things would never be said aloud.

38

As dawn broke, the people of Athens were already filling the streets. They had gathered in darkness and silence, following priests of Athena and Poseidon and Apollo, as well as Ares and Hades, heading to the foot of the Acropolis. There had been no call to assemble, no horns blown. Word had flown around the city on dark wings the night before. Just two ragged sailors had made it back, bearing news of Persian galleys and the slaughter of their crews. On stolen mounts, they had reached the city walls and collapsed, trembling with hunger and exhaustion. The city had roused around them in the night.

It was time. The first wire of gold on the horizon revealed dense crowds, walking with heads bowed up to the temples on the highest point of the city, to make offerings there, to make sacrifice. A dawn bell tolled across Athens then and some of them clutched amulets and murmured prayers as they went.

Xanthippus walked hand in hand with Agariste, their three children at their heels. Epikleos had found them the night before, bringing the news they all dreaded. He climbed the sloping path alongside his oldest friends, making their way up the great rock of Athens, the most sacred part that sat above all. It had been the site of palaces and kings, long gone to dust. It was where all eyes turned when they were threatened, offering refuge. For those who laboured upwards, the Areopagus and the Pnyx were far below, made small by height and shadows. Under threat of war, this was the heart of Athens, in the silent faith of those who gathered there.

Epikleos suddenly had tears in his eyes, though he said nothing and only shook his head when Xanthippus looked over in concern. It would have betrayed the moment to explain, but to be there, on that morning, with his people all around, was something Epikleos thought he would never forget. It reminded him of dawn before Marathon, ten years and a lifetime before.

Even the slopes of the Acropolis could be filled. The people perched or stood, crammed together like bees come to rest in one great swarm, tens of thousands of his people, lit gold in the morning sun. Xanthippus heard his name whispered as he was recognised, with blessings called that became a multitude of voices. They had voted for him to be summoned home from exile and they felt responsible for him. He had sensed it in the weeks since his return, that he was known in Athens as he had never been known before. Perhaps it was just that they didn't want to be wrong, but he felt the weight of their hopes on his shoulders. He had confided as much to Themistocles and, for once, the big man had only nodded and gripped his shoulder. Themistocles understood.

A narrow path remained open and Xanthippus walked through the crowds to the very top, where the ancient temple to Athena Pallas stood, goddess of the city. Alongside it, a new temple was rising, still unfinished – dedicated to Athena Parthenos, the virgin. Fine new columns and reliefs had been carved into the walls there, with precious gold gleaming. Statues of tyrant-slayers had been raised on that high rock, even a marble figure named for Callimachus, who had fallen at Marathon. The whole history of the city was remembered there. The gods watched.

Lamps had been lit in the darkness, spilling light down to

347

the city below. As Xanthippus brought his family to stand with the rest, they were extinguished, one by one, replaced by the sun.

Themistocles was there, with a group of young men and women Xanthippus realised were his daughters and sons. The man's second wife stood with him and, more than anything else, her presence made the hairs on Xanthippus' neck rise. In all the years he had known Themistocles, he had kept his political and home lives apart.

Xanthippus felt his grip tighten on Agariste's hand as he looked across the Acropolis and saw everyone he knew, all gathered in one place, to burn incense and pray to Athena, with war ahead. Aristides was there in breastplate and greaves, oddly warlike and strange without his ragged robe. His solemn authority showed in the hoplites who gathered around him. Cimon too had come, with his friends in a crowd by the temple wall. The archons of the Areopagus council were present, all the Eupatridae landowners come to stand together. Everywhere Xanthippus looked, he saw faces from his past, though some had aged and grown white-haired in his years away.

He understood then why Epikleos had suddenly become red-eyed and stumbling on the path. It was all they were, all they had made from rocks and cloth and laws, as fragile as a child's life or a gilded bowl thrown into the air.

The priests and priestesses of Athena came out to stand before the packed crowd. Others of the different temples bowed to them, giving Athena the honour of the day. The priest of Hades knelt in the dust. Even death would give way to her.

Her acolytes wore robes of white and bore daggers and sickles, as befitted the goddess of defence and the home. Xanthippus closed his eyes as they began to chant together, raising branches of amaranthus blossom. He felt his son Ariphron at his side, as tall as his father. Xanthippus put his free arm around him. Pericles and Eleni gathered in close and they stood, as one family, in simple awe and prayer as the appeal went on. Around them were his people, in hope and desperation, in faith.

A ram was sacrificed, its blood spilling onto gold plates. The service ended with Athena's own words to them, her promise to protect the people of her city. She had vowed to arm them and teach them war. Her shield was in their will and strength. Xanthippus felt his breath come sharply at the power of it, until silence fell again and the people began to drift down to their lives and the city below.

When the service was over, he felt a weight lift and he found himself smiling at his children. He had tried not to look at the sea as he stood there. Pericles was already pointing to the dark line. Yet at such a distance, even the boy's sharp eyes could not make out the shapes of Greek galleys waiting. Those ships were there at anchor, in the strait between Piraeus and the island of Salamis, waiting for their crews to return, waiting to be brought to life.

On the way down, Xanthippus pressed his wife's hand, making her look at him.

'Do you remember what I said to you on the morning before Marathon?' he murmured. He saw Epikleos look up and then away rather than intrude on a private moment.

Agariste bit her lip as she considered her reply. He had asked her to kill the children, to save them from capture and slavery.

'I do,' she said. 'They are no longer so young.'

'I know,' he replied, leaning close, so that their heads touched like two lovers walking together. 'But if we fail, you must run.'

349

Her face hardened as she understood. Xanthippus felt his anger return as she shook her head.

'You said nowhere would be safe if they come,' she replied.

'Go west, with the house slaves to protect you. I have left a list in my study of Greek cities that refused our call. The Persians will favour them, I think. You and the children could begin again, far from here.'

She stopped suddenly, so that he stumbled on the dusty slope.

'Do you think this place is yours alone, Xan? These people are mine as well. I love them, in all their talk and prayers and chaos. I love Athens, in my bones, in my *womb*. I cannot just . . . go somewhere else. Whatever happens, we'll return here, to rebuild.'

'Agariste,' he said more firmly, 'if the fleet fails, if the army cannot stop the Persians on the land, Athens is *gone*. They are coming to make an example of us, do you understand? There will be nothing left. If you see Persian soldiers marching from the north, or their ships in the port, you must gather the boys and Eleni and just go. Promise me you will. I cannot leave otherwise.'

'*That* is a lie,' she said, smiling through tears. She raised herself on her toes and kissed him. He smiled, flushing. Agariste gestured at the crowds around them. 'You will go out with the ships,' she said, 'because the people ask you to. Because you love them.'

He might have argued, but she kissed him again, stopping up whatever he was trying to say.

At the base of the hill, the fleet crews were embracing their own families and setting off to the port in a great stream. They walked with heads high and Xanthippus saw Epikleos shifting from foot to foot, impatient to join them. Xanthippus wiped a tear from his wife's cheek and kissed her once more. She held him with her head buried in his shoulder, as the children came around, seeking the reassurance of closeness.

Xanthippus found himself chuckling, though tears stung him. One by one, he embraced his sons and daughter.

'How proud you make me!' he told them. His daughter blinked her own tears away and hugged him so hard it stole his breath. 'How beautiful you are, how perfect! You must be good for your mother now. Keep her safe, so that I don't have to worry about you.'

'You will worry anyway,' Agariste said. 'But I will keep them safe.'

'Thank you,' he said, breathing deeply. 'I'll come back, Aggie, if I can.'

Epikleos put an arm around his shoulders and guided him away down the road to the port.

'There is a fleet waiting for you, old friend,' Epikleos said. He still seemed moved. 'They are a fine family. You must truly be very proud of them.'

Xanthippus looked at the younger man, seeing the pain in him.

'They are your family as well. You know that, of course?'

Epikleos could not reply as they broke into a jog with thousands of others, heading towards the fleet. After a time, he patted Xanthippus on the back, a gesture that said all that was needed.

When they reached the port, every fishing boat and merchant had been pressed into service to take crews out to the triremes. Xanthippus caught sight of Themistocles on another one, heading to his flagship. For once, Themistocles looked stern with all that lay ahead. He seemed to sense Xanthippus watching and grinned when he recognised him. Both men acknowledged one another before they were out of sight.

'There is a part of me that relishes this,' Epikleos said.

Xanthippus shook his head.

'Please. *Please* don't anger the gods today.'

Epikleos chuckled, acquiescing. The trireme that would carry them to battle lay ahead, long and grey in the morning light.

'I just meant that there is no more complication, do you see? No politics. Aristides is gathering the army. You and I go to meet the enemy, because we have the courage and will to do it. All else falls away. I find the simplicity . . . comforting.'

'You are a madman,' Xanthippus said. 'But I am pleased you are here with me.'

'Well, it's not as if you have any other friends,' Epikleos said, smiling when Xanthippus looked at him in surprise.

39

Xerxes lay back on a long couch, closing his eyes in relief to find solid ground beneath him. He had not appreciated what a luxury it would be not to have his cabin rocking back and forth at all hours of the day and night, never ceasing, never still. He could not recall the last time he had slept for more than a few hours. He actually felt himself drifting into a doze and sat up.

His pavilion was a place of peace and calm, the world beyond shut out. Slaves burned incense and waited with platters of fruit, gathered from where he did not know. Perhaps Mardonius had brought them with him, as a gift.

He opened his eyes, looking on the general of his armies. Mardonius wore his beard in black ringlets, bound together with a single gold cuff. It reminded the king of an otter pelt. Once more, Xerxes experienced a delicious shudder at the trials of a campaign. He had wanted such things, safe in his palaces. He had not known then how the rocking sea would make days pass in a misery of sickness and loose bowels, or how hard it was to be clean without pools and slaves dedicated to the task. He sighed. He had not known a thousand things he knew then. How often the entire fleet had to stop for water, so that they crawled from stream to stream along the coast. It was not the wild charge he had imagined, but the alternative was watching men die, or so he had been told. It seemed the rowing slaves could survive on just a little food, but they needed water every day, to fill every cask they possessed. Even so, some of them expired and were thrown overboard. Each morning began with corpses committed to the deep. They bobbed in the wake of the fleet and the first ones drifted past the ships behind, so they were seen. Little sharks bumped and tore at them then, so he had been told, like dogs feeding on deer.

He felt his thoughts drifting and cleared his throat, making Mardonius look up from his respectfully downcast gaze.

'I am ready to hear your report, general.'

'Majesty, there is nothing of great note,' Mardonius began. 'We lost men in fighting in Macedonia, as you know. Some of our injured have succumbed to their wounds since then – three in the last few days. I hanged a few dozen for rape or theft – not enough to affect our strength.'

He hesitated, wondering if the king should be told of desertions. It was impossible to move hundreds of thousands of men through a foreign land without having a few wander off, drawn to some lonely farmhouse, or following a pretty face glimpsed in a market. Outside of the Immortals and senior officers, his men were often simple types, Mardonius knew. He could have told a thousand tales of regiments marching for days in the wrong direction, or losing the only map to a food store, or watching vital supplies ridden over a ravine by one drunken fool. Armies wore out on the march, that was just the truth of it. He did not think the young king wished to hear of that, however.

'Majesty, your army is lean and strong, made into wood and leather over hundreds of miles. They are devoted to you, as am I. We will be there, alongside the fleet.'

Mardonius bowed his head again, wondering how long he would have to endure the king's drowsing mood. His back hurt and one of his fingers had filled with pus from a simple splinter of iron that had gone deep. The damned thing had to be drained again. He could feel it throbbing. Of course it was his right hand, so that it hurt doing almost anything. He could feel the prickle of sweat on his brow as he sat there, wasting a morning with a son of Darius. The old king would never have drunk the milk of the poppy on campaign, no matter how stiff or sore he had become. Mardonius hid any distaste he felt as the young man seemed to drift off once more. Xerxes was no sailor; they'd all learned that much. He'd insisted the fleet and the army should advance in sight of one another, regardless of terrain or the conditions at sea. Mardonius thought the young king was responsible for the loss of over a hundred ships when he'd refused to let his captains seek safe harbour, all while a gale rose around them. All because the army had not come into view! Mardonius repressed a shudder. He still remembered that march, with his scouts riding themselves ragged and killing precious horses to pass back news of the fleet. He'd lost men too that day, men who had fallen and refused to return to their place in line. He'd stained the earth in his wake with their blood – and in truth, he had no time for weakness. Their lives – his life – were to be spent in service of the Great King. Mardonius might pray not to be thrown away, not to be wasted, but it was the whim of Xerxes and the elements that would decide his fate, long before he met the Greeks.

'Would it raise the morale of the men to have me inspect them?' Xerxes said, his eyes snapping open.

Mardonius struggled to hide his dismay, but the king was not watching him, instead lying back and looking to the billowing cloth above his head, suddenly fascinated by it. Even so, Mardonius did not think he could ignore the question.

'Majesty, they are a ragged crew, after so long on the march. I think, with your permission, that they should show you greatness by shedding the blood of your enemies. God smiles on us, Majesty! To be here, in the land of the Greeks, with their cities open-legged before us, ready for the plough. We stand in the shadow of your light, Majesty, and it is glorious.'

The king did not respond for a time and Mardonius subsided. An inspection would delay them for a week or more. It would take that long just to parade the men and wash the worst dust and grime from them. He prayed in silence that the king would not follow through on his threat.

'I am . . . overjoyed, Mardonius, as you say,' the king said dreamily. 'To be here, after so long. How far is it to Athens now?'

Mardonius cleared his throat. His finger was throbbing along with his heartbeat, quite extraordinarily painful. He wanted to mop the sweat from his brow, but he did not wish to seem nervous.

'The scouts report a range of mountains four days' march from here. We will find the passes through, of course. I'm told Athens is three or four days of hard marching beyond.'

Xerxes sat up, his gaze sharpening.

'So close? Truly? Have you seen sign of their armies?'

'Only Spartan scouts, Majesty. They appear sometimes, to watch us on the march. I send out archers, but we have not yet brought one down.'

'It does not matter,' Xerxes said, with a wave of his hand. 'Let them see and fear me. They scorned my messenger, my offer to accept them as vassals. Perhaps they regret that now that I have come!'

He rose to his feet and stood swaying, so that Mardonius felt a cold horror. If the king's excesses brought him to fainting, his general could not lay hands on him, not even to catch Xerxes as he fell. Yet if he stood by and did nothing, his life would surely be forfeit. He decided to prostrate himself on the canvas floor.

356

There was no crash. The king chuckled, lost in imaginings.

'Don't hurt their scouts, Mardonius. Let them carry what news they wish of me. I want them to know, to fear. I want them to feel the earth tremble! Now, I will go back to my ship and you will go back to your men. Keep my ships in sight! We will sweep them . . .' He waved in frustration, unable to find the words. Instead, he clapped both hands together, his expression suddenly vengeful, so that small white teeth showed. 'No . . . we will *crush* them between us.'

King Leonidas stretched out as he increased the pace, feeling his limbs loosen and his old hip injury ease. At fifty, he was proud of his strength and fitness, though he was not the sort of fool who denied the effect of time on him. It still felt right to swing along the road, his red cloak fluttering. His helots bore his shield, sword and spear. They were smaller men than the Spartan king, less powerful of frame – born to a race who had been slaves as long as the histories of man. Hundreds of them trotted like hounds in his wake, carrying the battle kit of all his guard.

At the head of the column, three hundred Spartiate warriors swung along, lost in contemplation. Some of them had talked quietly that morning, but as the day waned, the grim mood of battle was settling on them, stifling laughter and light talk. They could all see the mountains ahead, rising slowly green and brown, with the sea dark on their right flank. They had reached the city of Plataea the night before, having marched two days from Sparta and through the barricades on the isthmus. Men of Plataea had joined them then, running for their weapons and armour as the Spartans came loping through. Others had joined the column as soon as they saw the red cloaks. Leonidas looked back to

Demophilus of Thespiae, with seven hundred warriors alongside. Those carried their own spears, never having earned the labour of helots. The man seemed in awe of the Spartan king, as he should have been. Leonidas had not told him all that lay ahead, nor that there would be no greater army of Sparta coming to join them. He found one fist clenching as he strode along, putting the stades behind on the road. With an effort, Leonidas relaxed.

The priests had come close to making him break his word, given by his brother to the Athenians. When they'd said he could not march against the Persians, not until the festival was over, Leonidas had been caught between obedience and outrage. Just the thought of it made his fist clench once more, this time unnoticed. War was forbidden during the festival of Apollo Carneios. In all his life Leonidas had never disobeyed the ephors, nor scorned the gods. Sparta was a dry place, a precarious place, without the natural gifts of other regions. They survived only with the blessings of Apollo and Ares. No man could pit himself against the gods of the sun and of war, not without destruction.

Even so, he had stood stunned for a time, with torches spitting and hissing at his back. Leonidas was a man used to making decisions. He had given his word to his brother to swear an oath. They would fight alongside Athens, though he despised those Greeks for the effete whores they were. Even so, he would not see their vanity exposed by Persians, their blood spilt. Yet he was not allowed to complete that oath and take the ten thousand and their helots out to the field of battle. He had to wait three more days, while the Persian flood approached a range of mountains where they could be stopped!

In that moment, when he had stood like stone and despaired, the priest had reached out and touched him on

358

the shoulder. He'd felt the coldness of an old man's bony hand and he had remembered what had been forgotten.

Years before, when he'd been made king on the death of his older brother, Leonidas had visited the oracle at Delphi. He'd crossed the gulf of Corinth in a small boat and walked alone to see what his reign would hold. He remembered the priestess sitting above the crack in the stone, where Apollo's sleeping breath wreathed her in smoke. She had been beautiful, he recalled, though her eyes were terrible, as one who had seen and known too many things.

She had promised him a terrible choice, on a day then far ahead, between the destruction of Sparta, and his own death.

He smiled as he walked along, remembering her surprise when he'd laughed. He'd been so young! So certain of his strength and youth. He'd feared the revelation of some greater catastrophe, some twisted riddle of the gods that would lead to betrayal or dishonour. Instead, she had offered him a choice he would always have made, a thousand times over. His death, to save Sparta? Leonidas knew he could throw it away with a shrug. He would fling his life from him.

As the priest had touched his bare shoulder, he understood the time had come upon him. In quiet dignity, he had thanked the old man and knelt to him for his blessing. When he rose, Leonidas had summoned his personal guard of three hundred. After that, he had called the perioikoi – the warriors who lived around Sparta but were not of the elite. They had not been bound by the laws of the ephors, any more than his personal guard. Leonidas frowned as he considered the thousand men who had answered that call. They owed him loyalty unto death. Had he skirted his oath? No, he was certain. The men who marched with him that day were of the Peloponnese, but not of Sparta. With his helots, with those who had joined him from Plataea and Thespiae, he had six thousand, marching towards the mountains.

As the land rose near the coast, Leonidas could see galleys out on the waters, with the red sails of Spartan ships leading them. More ships than he could believe. He knew Eurybiades for a good man. Leonidas turned his head and whistled to the helots trotting in his wake, calling the name of the one he wanted. Dromeas was one who seemed born to run, who loved the freedom of it. The young man was in his twenties, with a black beard marked by the jagged scar that had brought him to Leonidas' personal group of helots. Dromeas had outrun a group of three young Spartiates in training and, of course, they had beaten him savagely in response, leaving him with a great scar from his forehead to his chin. Leonidas had offered the man a place in his retinue – *if* he managed to beat them again. Though blood had run down his chest and spattered his thighs, Dromeas had summoned his will and left them in his dust for a second time that day. Two of them had left the training – one to join the perioikoi, another to family in Corinth. Dromeas had run a thousand days since then for the Spartan king who had seen his value and his will.

Leonidas clapped Dromeas on the shoulder as the bearded young man came alongside.

'I have a task for you, Runner,' he said.

Perhaps another would have taken the nickname as an insult. Dromeas wore it with pride. Leonidas was a man to follow.

'Go down to the coast and find a fishing boat, anything that will take you out to the fleet. Find the ships with red sails and seek Eurybiades. My message is for him.'

'Red sails. Eurybiades,' Dromeas replied. He began to breathe long and slow, readying himself for the run. He was far leaner than the warriors in that column, bones showing beneath tiny fluttering muscles around his chest.

'Tell him, "Leonidas will hold the coastal pass." That is all.'

Dromeas did not wait to be dismissed, but set off, his bare feet raising little swirls of dust. Leonidas nodded. Every one of his helots was extraordinary in some way. He had chosen them all carefully, as befitted men who would stand at his back in the midst of battle.

The ones who marched with him that day had come because he was the battle king and he had called, in a time of crisis and war. They did not know Leonidas marched to his death. He accepted it, as he had always known he would. He would give the priests the time they asked of him, to honour the god Apollo – and gather the army.

Leonidas felt a pang at the thought that he would not lead them then, when they came out, ten thousand strong – the army of Sparta, without equal in the world. They would be his answer then, to the Persians. They would be his vengeance. He smiled as he marched. The air was sweet and clear. The sun shone and the sky was a perfect blue. It was a good day.

40

The sea was calm as the fleet raised sail to clear the headland. Over the previous weeks, Xanthippus had taken charge of fleet training. Under his watchful eye, they had worked themselves to exhaustion, over and over, building fitness in the rowers and hoplites alike. At times, he had put hoplite crews into the rowing benches, so that they had some idea of the limits of that labour. They would never again complain as a trireme fell behind, not after an experience that had left them panting and stiff for days of pain. Nor had it hurt the free rowers to drill with sword and shield. If they were boarded, they would have to fight.

Whenever they'd returned to Athens, Xanthippus had organised runs against the hoplites training with Aristides, right round the city. Little by little, the contests had become more serious. The army had led for a time, but the fleet had slowly reeled them in, keeping a close tally. The honours had still been roughly equal until the week before, when Cimon had led forty sailors to cross the line first. It was not a small thing. Xanthippus had accepted the victor's wreath from the hand of Aristides, then passed it to Cimon, to a roar of acclaim from his crews.

Under sail, the fleet seemed a vast enterprise as it hissed and cut through the sea, each crew turning a single yard beam back and forth to catch the wind and swell the cloth. They were not as fast as when the oars rattled out, but the rowers did not complain as they rested like hunting dogs, lean and strong, fed better than they had known before

Xanthippus returned from exile. He had insisted on eggs and meat and wine for them, over and above the slop of beans and pulses they usually consumed. Even in a few short weeks, the results showed in their muscle and health.

They were free men of Athens, but they accepted the authority of the Assembly for the highest stakes. No one let his neighbours take the burden, not with parents, wives and children left behind and depending on them. Xanthippus could see it in each of them – and found himself inspired by it. They strove together, against a common enemy.

In the late afternoon, Themistocles ordered the fleet to put oars out. To a drumbeat, the sails were dropped and tied into packs, taken down to the holds. With the decks clear, the masts were unstepped, great wedges hammered out so the lengths of pine could be lowered after them, into the arms of oarsmen. Some ships secured the mast with iron hoops and rope, so that it formed one edge of the deck, like a stub rail.

The transformation never failed to make Xanthippus' heart pound. The oars were stored lengthways in the hold, like old bones. The three banks of men below were expert in their labours and could ease them up, across and out in moments, the result of endless hours of training. Each ship briefly became a clumsy thing without its sails, then suddenly soared back to life, as sun-bleached wings struck the waters. The first strokes made light of skills they had won over months or years. Oarsmen worked in perfect unison and if one fouled another through drunkenness or lack of care, he risked a beating that night, or even being cast overboard on a late watch, when all else was silent. Their task was to row at whatever speed was asked; to work one bank while the other reversed, so that a ship could turn inside its own length. They could not see more than the waves rushing past on either side and they had to trust the officers standing on the deck and roaring orders to the keleustes of each ship. Only that man, standing with his head and shoulders out on the deck, could see the action all around. Those below laboured on in trust and pain and perspiration flung from wet hair.

The flagship carried Themistocles, the city banner of an owl streaming from his ship's high stern like a long tongue. Xanthippus saw his own captain keeping an eye on it. He too watched for a steer and orders as the sun began to ease down to the horizon.

When Themistocles swung off the main course, Xanthippus felt the trierarch's gaze on him and nodded. The man had given him no trouble at all since their first clash of wills on that very deck. As one, the fleet slowed to half pace and used the tillers at the stern to begin long gentle turns closer to the coast.

They had passed the great headland, into waters where the motion of the deep sea was different, rolling the whole ship. The next great landing place was one Xanthippus had thought Themistocles would leave in their wake: Marathon, where the beach was sheltered by the great spit of land that had included Eretria. Themistocles was heading to a spring a little further along that part of the coast, a place the fleet knew well from a dozen previous landings. The casks were full that day, so Xanthippus thought they would just stop for the night, safe from a sudden squall.

It did not hurt to remind the men of a victory, hard won, nor that their officers had all been part of it. It mattered, too, that they were safe from storms. The danger was always there. Any crew of their number could tell tales of some close brush with drowning, as their ship dipped and took on water. The threat was constant, with only skill, balance and officers who could read the sea keeping them alive.

The counterpoint was their extraordinary speed, enough to smash another ship, with three rows of oars heaving them on, sending them like a racehorse across the waves. No mere sails could match their pace, not even for a moment. They were a fine breed, but too fragile for rough sea.

The Spartan ships responded with the quick neatness Xanthippus had come to expect from them. From the deck of the flagship with Themistocles, he knew Eurybiades would be watching, holding his people to a higher standard than the rest. The navarch had spent a day observing the new flag signals as Xanthippus and his trierarchs practised. Xanthippus was still not certain Eurybiades would respect them in the heat of battle. He hoped so – the Spartans were his vanguard, his breakers of walls. Behind them in formation came the Athenian triremes, with those of Corinth bringing up the rear and all the others of their alliance. In all, they had three hundred ships of Greece – Xanthippus could still shake his head in awe when he considered the sheer number of rowers and hoplites in them, never mind the labour and fortunes that had gone into their construction. They were the wealth of Greece, her wooden walls.

With the plain of Marathon in sight, the fleet anchored as soon as they were close to shore, safe from the waves pulling them further onto the beaches. It was strange to think that they chose that place for the same reasons the Persians had years before. Perhaps they could have gone further in a day, Xanthippus thought, but it would be good for the men.

'Are we going ashore?' Epikleos said.

He had climbed up from his tiny berth in the hold, in response to the sound of anchor ropes whirring out. Xanthippus shook his head. It was not something he wanted to discuss, with so many in earshot. The truth was that Themistocles had given the order in private the night before. Men

lost their nerve, sometimes, no matter how well they had prepared or how firmly they swore loyalty. The crews had said
their farewells to those they loved. The enterprise had begun.
If they were allowed to spend a long first night in reach of
the city, Xanthippus agreed with Themistocles that some of
them would surely vanish by the morning.

'Not tonight,' Xanthippus said. 'Themistocles . . . wants
us to get used to being on board. No shore leave from
now on.'

He looked sharply at his friend, and if Epikleos suspected
there was more, he did not press it.

'Will there be more training drills?' he asked.

Xanthippus shook his head.

'I don't think so. Perhaps Themistocles or Eurybiades . . .
no. Any ships manoeuvring now would fall behind.'

He became aware of faces turned to hear. The men were
desperate for any scrap of information. Little boats rowed
between the triremes, carrying officers and stores while they
sat at anchor. Whatever he said there would spread from ship
to ship with extraordinary speed.

'Unless the plan changes, we'll go north until we cross the
Persian fleet. We'll stop them in our waters. Our trierarchs
know their ships and crews. They know the flag signals and
the formations. We have honed them to a fearsome sharpness. The enemy have no idea we have so many ships out to
send them to the bottom. Take heart from that, Epikleos.
May the gods keep them blind a little longer!'

Epikleos looked a little pale around the mouth as he nodded. The reality was rushing down upon them and somehow
clashed with the normal routines of their lives. Around
them, three hundred ships prepared a cold and glutinous
stew. Some seventy thousand men rested there, scattered
along the coast of Attica. Xanthippus and Epikleos felt their

ship tug on her lines and settle, like a horse brought to a halt on a long rein.

They were close enough to see crews and ships they knew on all sides. There were few strangers in that fleet, not after their close association. Men raised arms in salute or greeting, but there was none of the usual laughter or cheerful insults that marked their lives. They knew what lay ahead and yet they did not feel ready for it, not then. They had trained together, sweated and sworn together. The reality was still unfolding before them. They would bleed, they would die together as well. They would drown and kill and win, or lose everything that mattered, when the time came. It was a strange brotherhood. As he stood there, Xanthippus wished once again for a railing, so he could have gripped it and stopped his hands trembling.

41

The flagship was by far the largest vessel in all the forces Xerxes had brought to Greek waters. He had not appreciated how slow it would be, so that each day's end found him towards the rear, though some oar-slaves had died in their labours to keep up with the main group.

Even so, there were comforts. He walked the deck with Immortals standing as sentinels, facing the sea. The flagship sat higher on the waves than most of the Phoenician triremes. It rolled as a result, but took on less water and seemed so heavy that it was hard to imagine being thrown over by a wave. He set his jaw at that thought. He still struggled to sleep on board. Wooden ships seemed alive in the noises they made, never mind the constant motion. There were horses in the hold, as well as the live animals kept for food. They all whinnied and shrieked in the night, dragging him awake in cold sweat. He had sprung up from nightmares dozens of times, so that dawn found him on deck, sipping a hot tisane with a cloak wrapped around him. Only opium worked, though of late it had brought nightmares that left him ill and retching. He had taken to sleeping on shore whenever there was no threat. He still remembered one perfectly sheltered cove in Macedonia, with no route down to it from the land. He had slept a full night then, like a child in his slumbers.

He shook his head. This was the reality of a campaign: salt spray drying on the skin; the scented oils that failed to hide the smell of sweat and bowels; the beard he had grown, then shaved off when it drove him mad with itching. There was little luxury on board ship, which forced him to focus on more serious matters. Half a dozen small boats were winging out to him. They spent their days empty, on ropes behind the main triremes, hissing along until they were needed to carry men or messages.

He watched ropes flung and the passengers clamber up the side of his flagship, choosing the best moment of the roll to climb. In normal times, he knew he would not have greeted them himself. A king had servants whose role it was to protect him, to act as his shield. It gave Xerxes a little satisfaction to see the aghast expression on the face of his seneschal as the king waved him back. He had left ceremony behind. This was a war fleet and he would not stand on his dignity.

The first to reach the deck was Mardonius, with others close on his heels. The flagship rail was lined with shields in the Phoenician war style, giving a safe place to duck behind in a battle. Only two breaches allowed them on board. They converged on the young king, prostrating themselves.

The only one who hesitated was the one who most intrigued him. Artemisia of Halicarnassus was Greek, though her little region had been a satrapy of Persia since at least his father's time. Still, her mother was from Crete and she had known Greece in her childhood travels. She was one of the guides Mardonius most relied upon, but the only woman. She had brought five ships to his fleet, with crews of free men. Yet even a queen would bend.

Xerxes made a downward gesture with his right hand. She knelt rather than lay flat. He frowned at that, but let it pass rather than look petty in front of all the rest. Would his father have done the same? He did not know. He thought he saw a glimmer of amusement in her eyes as she rose with all the others. Xerxes stared at her until she looked aside. He was less at ease with women, especially those who claimed royal blood and the loyalty of trireme crews. There was no one else quite like Artemisia in his fleet and he wondered what would happen if he took her to his bed that evening. It would surely cost him five ships, but he had lost many more than that in squalls and on unseen rocks.

He watched her in silence and, of course, none of the others dared speak. She looked up at him again after a time, raising one eyebrow. A handsome woman, he thought. But too much trouble. He preferred a more pliant sort, who would be less likely to stab him in the eye, as she had reportedly done to an unfaithful lover. He blinked hard at the thought, as if a piece of dust had become trapped. Amusement appeared once more in her expression and Xerxes looked away. It was a trivial irritation. Perhaps because of her titles, she misjudged the relationship between them, of master and slave. If she continued to concern him, he knew he could give her to his guards to be chastised.

Xerxes led the way to the main chamber below. Its existence gave his flagship a broader beam than all the others and separated his banks of rowers. The partitions of his cabin had been knocked down and cleared for the meeting of captains, but the long room retained a faint scent of damp as well as rose, musk and narcissus.

The table had been bolted to the floor so as not to shift in rough seas. The captains and senior officers had to edge along the sides to take their places and then sit at his order on the chairs made ready for them. Forty of them had come at his command. They smelled of salt and sweat and seaweed, Xerxes realised, though Artemisia bore some floral scent in addition that he could not recognise. She watched him closely, he noticed, judging him. It might have been infuriating in his court, but there, he felt his jaw jut and his determination grow.

'Gentlemen . . . Your Majesty,' he said. The words felt odd in his mouth. At least Artemisia spoke the language of his fathers. Some of the Greeks who had come to offer dust and water needed translators to stand by them and whisper. They were always a step behind, which irritated Xerxes. No one else would dare speak over him.

'You may examine my maps before you leave, those of you who do not know this coast. We have anchored within the shelter of the island of Sciathos. To the west, there is a strait of calm water that leads inland, then turns all the way south, past Marathon, around the headland and there, to Athens. Mardonius? Report on the progress of our army.'

The general rose to his feet, so that all the rest turned to him, Greek and Persian alike.

'Gentlemen . . . my lady. There is a range of mountains ahead of us that we should reach by tomorrow afternoon. One more march will put us there – as you come west along the strait. By the time you turn south, we should be through. We are looking for local scouts now, who know the area.'

'May we see the map?' one of the other captains asked.

To Xerxes' irritation, the man spoke in Greek, but his cabin servants still moved, accepting his authority. The king forced himself to remember his father. Whatever hatred he felt towards the Greeks had to be smothered when it came to those who had asked to be allies. Most of them still hid from him, quaking in their cities and just hoping to survive the great invasion. At least these men – and one queen – had come to serve alongside! Xerxes had accepted dust and water from the hand of Artemisia herself, though her ships were better proof of her oath. He glanced at her again, wondering if she was younger than him. Her skin was as delicately flushed as any young woman, but she painted her eyes in kohl, so that it was hard to tell. Xerxes found himself

371

looking away as the group leaned over the map, in awe of something that had cost more gold than they would see in a lifetime. It was the labour of years by expert cartographers and sailors, roaming that coast and taking note of every island and fresh spring. Only the land was blank, or marked with a few vague lines. His father had commissioned the thing at huge expense, before Marathon.

'There is the strait – and the route we will take,' Xerxes confirmed. He ran his finger along the map as far as he could reach. The papyrus stretched the length of the table, held at the corners with lead weights taken from a box by his servants. For a time, it was as if they stood above the world as gods. He enjoyed the sensation, as well as the murmurs of fascination in the assembled captains.

He nodded to Mardonius.

'As soon as you are through the mountains, we will turn south and keep pace with you. You'll reach Athens while I take the fleet around the southern tip.'

'What of their fleet?' Artemisia asked. 'Athens will not let us pass without challenge. They will have warships, Majesty. No man knows how many.'

Xerxes smiled in turn.

'We have more, Artemisia. I do not fear their ships.'

The answer did not seem to reassure her, he noticed. Instead, she pointed at the range of hills Mardonius would have to cross to keep up with the fleet.

'And these,' she said. 'They do not look as high as they are, not on this map. I have seen these, in my childhood, travelling with my father.'

'You know them, truly?' Mardonius replied before Xerxes could.

Artemisia shrugged as all the men at that table turned to her.

'Only once, when I was a little girl. I remember them as crags . . . too high to climb.' She frowned in memory. 'I saw steam issuing from the ground in places. My father told me the name of a pass along the coast . . .'

'There is a pass, then?' Mardonius pressed. 'One an army can go through?' He looked pleased, even relieved.

'Yes,' she said. 'The mountains are sheer, but they end just before the sea. There is a narrow beach there . . . rockfall and sand . . .' She looked up as a word flashed into her mind. 'Thermopylae. That was its name.'

'I will walk it,' Xerxes said, suddenly. 'I will stand on Greek soil, in honour of my father.'

He saw Mardonius blink in surprise, the older man silent as he considered his response. Before any objection could be voiced, Xerxes went on.

'The fleet has good officers in command. I have no vital role here. Mardonius tells me these mountains are the last great obstacle before the plain that leads to Plataea and Athens – the two cities that sent men to Marathon. I would rather watch them burned than remain with the fleet.'

He did not add that the thought of sleeping once more on firm ground filled him with a sort of longing that was almost pain.

Mardonius bowed his head, constrained by the cramped quarters from doing more.

'It would be a great honour, Majesty,' he said.

Xerxes glanced at the queen of Halicarnassus once more. Artemisia was chewing her lip as she stared at the map, lost in memory rather than her usual acid humour.

Xerxes dipped his head, pleased with a decision made.

'Pass the word,' he said to his most senior captains and officers. 'Be ready. We are on a war footing from this moment.'

42

Xanthippus leaned out from the prow, looking left and right as his trireme hissed through the waves. He had asked Themistocles for permission to scout ahead with two other ships, the three of them skimming over dark blue waters. Epikleos stood with him on the other side, his arm wrapped around the high carved beam. A figurehead of Athena stared out with them, arms back, as if she too had to hold on. Below, a bronze ram crashed through waves, dripping white froth. Though neither man spoke a word, their faces showed exhilaration.

Land reared as low brown hills on either side, that part of the strait no wider than fifty or sixty stades – a morning's march if it had been solid ground. The Greek fleet had come through the pinch-point of Chalcis barely six abreast, then spread out to fill every part of the great channel, wider than the Hellespont. There had been the glorious sense then of a hunting wolf pack, out seeking prey.

The great dog-leg course they had chosen was slower than risking open sea, but neither would they see half the fleet smashed in gales or heavy waves. Beyond the spit of land that sheltered them, the open ocean was too perilous for warships. Even under sail in calm waters, Xanthippus saw galleys dip and bob like driftwood on the wash from the rest, always at risk.

Persian warships would be just as fragile, so Xanthippus hoped – or even more so in waters they did not know, far from their home cities, far from solid land. His Athenians were sailors born, he had discovered, men in love with the sea and all the crafts that went with mastering her. Perhaps it would make the difference.

Three hundred ships and over seventy thousand oarsmen and hoplites surged in his wake. When Xanthippus looked back, it was to see sails of red or blue or the yellow of the sun, as far as the eye could see. Spartan ships were still the first rank, with Eurybiades back acting the navarch there. Themistocles commanded the Athenian group, with Xanthippus as his formal second and Cimon's dozen young captains in the centre. For those who had stood at Marathon, there were odd echoes of the past. If Miltiades had lived, if Aristides had not already marched from the city with the army, it might have seemed like the great battle was to be played out once again on water. Xanthippus hoped for the same result! Behind the main body of the fleet came the forty warships of Corinth and the rest of the Greek alliance. They looked to Sparta to strike first, fast and hard, with the fleet of Athens behind, as the hammer of deep waters.

Xanthippus and the two scout ships had eased ahead of them at dawn, with the dog-leg part of the strait still to navigate. The currents were unique there, with experienced tillermen saying a steady hand was needed if they were to come through without at least one ship dipping too low and being swamped. In those waters, Xanthippus and Trierarch Ereius made no attempt to intercept orders between the lookout, two sailors on the tiller and the keleustes in the centre bellowing quick adjustments down to rowers in the hold. It did not count as a war-turn while the spit of land eased by on their right shoulders. Xanthippus could still feel odd rhythms underneath the keel as the trireme hit cross-currents.

He looked down as something moved beneath the surface, then gasped at the sight of dolphins. The creatures raced along with them, sleek and grey, like shaped sky moving through the water. The messengers of Poseidon had come, a wondrous good omen for all that lay ahead. It was a moment of absolute perfection that somehow went on and on. Why they chose to shadow the ship, Xanthippus did not know. It could only be the god's blessing.

He did not look up even to call a warning as Epikleos leaned out beside him in awed silence, holding on to the prow with just one arm. There had to be a dozen of them, with two much smaller than the rest. As Xanthippus turned to say something, one of the largest leapt right out of the water, leaving him speechless.

Epikleos was yelling something over the noise of the crashing prow. Xanthippus dragged his attention back and looked up, shaking his head at having witnessed something divine, a message of the god's protection. For those who faced war, it was . . . His stomach dropped away as the trireme cleared the headland.

Xanthippus leaned back, holding tightly to the high prow. At his feet, dolphins still played and swam, but he no longer had eyes for them. Ahead, the sea filled with a fleet, wider and wider, in such profusion they seemed to sweep across the great strait like a wooden wall. He put a foot on the lookout's step and raised himself up on the prow, his mouth too dry to call warning. The strait had to be thirty stades across there, but it sparkled white with oars beating time, stretching from one coast to another. Even as he gaped, horns began to sound on both sides, warning of an enemy in sight. Xanthippus heard Epikleos roar new orders, sending the crew to their battle posts and to ready weapons. The sound of running feet was loud as everything loose was cleared away in short order.

Xanthippus swallowed, still overwhelmed as a slow fury began to build in him. These were despoilers, come to steal and burn everything he valued, come to take the freedoms of Athens, the temples of the gods, the children who trusted them for safety and peace.

As he jumped down to the deck, the dolphins vanished, going deep. It did not matter then. The warning had been given.

'Trierarch Ereius!' Xanthippus called.

The captain was coming up from the hold, looking pale at the sound of horns. He bustled to the prow. Xanthippus waited only a moment for the older man to take stock and understand.

'Prepare for battle, trierarch. Signal "form line" and "engage" to all ships, if you would.'

The captain blinked nervously as he understood.

Above them, the sail yard came crashing down, allowed to drop harder than it ever had in drills. Ropes skipped and whirred across the deck, making a helmsman jump aside. Xanthippus frowned. He had trained the crews and practised with them a thousand times. Yet the reality of battle, with drowning and death rushing down upon them, was always something different. Half the training had been to just keep them moving in an emergency rather than freeze. They had not imagined facing such a vast enemy in the confines of the strait, except perhaps in nightmares. He prayed to Poseidon to bring them safely through, thanking him for his messengers.

The sail coming down was a signal to the ships behind. When Xanthippus went to the stern, he saw the action repeated from one end of the fleet to another, with oars rattling out and beginning to sweep together. The pace of the fleet increased as they approached the tip of land on their right side.

From the high stern between the steering oars, Xanthippus saw a streamer of blue and red unfurl, moving as a living snake in the wind. Form line; attack. He heard the slow drumbeat begin below, settling the rowers, warming their muscles for hours of toil ahead. The ship's boys filled water-skins from casks in the hold, ready to take them to whoever cried out in thirst. The men in the holds would row until they yelled in pain, until muscles failed and quivered and spit was iron in their mouths. Some of them tied their hands onto the oars, ready to keep stroke, no matter what it cost. The spirit was stronger than the flesh. It did not matter how many ships the Persians had brought. They would be met; there was no turning back.

Themistocles knew there was no point trying to call the sixteen Spartan ships into formation. Eurybiades had made that clear enough, in his disdain for what he still called Athenian cunning. It had not taken a great mind to suspect the Spartan ships would go straight at the enemy the moment they were sighted.

Those ships surged ahead, even as he watched. Themistocles saluted them ironically, knowing there would be no one looking behind as they went at the Persians. In some respects, it was the right tactic for a limited sea lane. Neither he nor Xanthippus had expected to find the Persians driving so far into Greek territory. The conditions were cramped and all the more dangerous for it. When the fighting began, it would be bloody chaos. Themistocles smiled to himself, though there was no humour in it. He knew the men who sailed with him. If there was not enough clear sea to manoeuvre, they would just have to make some by sinking enemy ships. All they had to do was hold the strait and prevent the Persians coming any further south.

As the fleet dropped sail and set out banks of oars, Themistocles felt the speed increase as a sudden surge. The

Spartans had eased ahead, coming abreast of the three with Xanthippus. It made sense to have an unbroken line to meet the enemy. Themistocles raised his eyes when he saw the Spartans ignore the three scout galleys, pushing past as if they were too slow.

'Greeks and their games,' Themistocles muttered. 'Go swiftly then, my Spartan leopards. Tear them apart.'

He saw Xanthippus raise blue and red and felt his breath come faster. Themistocles lifted a hand to the signal boy waiting for his order. The child nodded fast as he spoke, giving the impression he was simple, or just nervous at speaking to the first man of Athens. The boy raced to the stern and, in moments, the same banner caught the wind, snapping and darting. The entire fleet eased into ranks, back and back, forcing order. It made Themistocles think of an advancing phalanx and he muttered prayers to Ares and Poseidon, asking for their aid that day.

The fleet training showed as they came round the headland, rank by rank, those on the inside slowing a dozen strokes to make the turn. Themistocles blessed Xanthippus for that, knowing that they would have lost ships if he hadn't come home from exile. He thanked himself too for his wisdom in returning Xanthippus and Aristides to Athens. Perhaps there would be a reckoning for that, in time, but he knew he truly needed them that day.

Themistocles found himself swallowing hard as the line of warships formed around him and the headland fell away, so that every ship of Sparta, Athens, Corinth and the rest were heading straight for an enemy fleet that seemed to fill the sea from edge to edge.

'Ready, boarding crews!' he roared over his shoulder.

The trierarch repeated it, followed by the keleustes. He heard the jingle of kit and weapons being clashed together as

379

the hoplites came on deck, though it was all for show – they had been ready since the first warning horns sounded. Those still droned on from some of the ships in line, though Themistocles wished they would stop. The sound was mournful. They all knew where the enemy were by then. They all knew what they had to do.

'Ready, oarsmen!' Themistocles said. 'Ready, keleustes!'

The wind seemed to steal his breath, though he knew it was just nerves. Every order had to be clear and strong, beyond any misinterpretation. This was where the training would reveal itself, he hoped, thanking Athena once more for Xanthippus. To smash the hull of another ship then manoeuvre away safely took the finest judgement. Orders had to be passed to a hundred and eighty oarsmen down in the hold – and there, amidst the sweat and flying spray, obeyed. If just one bank missed a beat or fouled their oars, the ship would be as vulnerable as a child's wooden toy.

Forty galleys formed the Athenian line that had Themistocles in the centre. It was as many as they could fit abreast without danger of running aground or fouling the oars alongside. Even then, he saw half a dozen fall back into the next line, having overestimated the sea room. Such a manoeuvre was impossible under sail, but with sweeps out and good men on the tiller, they could indeed make a line almost as tight as a shield phalanx.

Ahead, Themistocles watched the Spartan sixteen approach the enemy with no sign of hesitation. Nineteen, he realised with a sudden fierce grin. Xanthippus had forced his three to a higher speed, matching the pace of Eurybiades so that the Spartans would not take first honour alone. Themistocles began to chuckle at that. Athens too would meet the Persians in first blood and cracking timbers. The sound died in him and he shivered, telling himself it was the sea wind.

Further back along the strait, Themistocles thought he could see some of the Persians turning. His eyes were sharp enough over distance, but he still summoned the signal boy and had him describe everything he saw. The Athenian lad was wide-eyed with the honour of it, but he spoke clearly enough, rattling out a hundred details and answering questions as best he could, with little understanding.

The first test of a fleet engagement was in the courage of its captains, Themistocles knew. He and Xanthippus had trained the men as best they could, though the Spartans had scorned it, saying they knew full well how to approach an enemy and would take no lessons from Athenians. Xanthippus had talked the other captains through those first moments even so. Some of the Spartans had set aside their pride, at least when Eurybiades was not present.

War galleys approached prow to prow and ram to ram. It was an impossible blow. Even a perfect line would see both rams grinding away down the sides and the ships passing one another at boarding range. The danger then was all for the oarsmen. Themistocles gripped one fist in another behind his back. He thought of those massive wooden bars wrenched out of hands, crushing men.

There had been one accident in training, with two ships shearing against one another and cripples made of good Athenians. The example had not been lost on the rest, with a dozen dead and broken men taken off at the port, unable to walk again. The lesson – and the warning – was clear enough. A single glancing blow could ruin a galley's ability to move, leaving them helpless for a strike below the waterline.

The answer was to have keleustes and oar crews ready to pull in the oars on one side, just as soon as they knew which way it would go. Boarding crews stood ready then, with shields and swords or spears on deck, waiting for the grinding note and screams from those too slow to move on either side.

Themistocles felt his throat had gone dry. He wondered if Xanthippus was experiencing the same sense of sand and dust in his mouth. The man had recalled it being the main thing he remembered from standing at Marathon, years before. Themistocles felt a tap on his leg and looked down at the signal boy, holding up a waterskin.

'Thank you,' he said, pulling off the cap and directing a flow of blood-warm liquid into his mouth. It helped and he smiled, making the boy beam.

Beat by beat, the fleets soared together, their speed seeming to increase as they came within a dozen ship-lengths. The waves were calm, but thousands of oars chopped hard at them, battering them to foam. Themistocles called for his boarders to be ready once again. He wore a pale blue cloak over a breastplate, with a helmet ready at his feet. Few of the boarding crews wore armour of any kind, to give them a chance to survive falling in.

Themistocles felt suddenly helpless, a passenger whose heart thumped fast and hard in his chest. He had a silver coin around his neck that his mother had given him. It had a stamped image of Athena's owl in the silver, polished by decades against his skin and hers. He kissed it, pressing it long against his lips as Xanthippus and the Spartans crashed into the Persian fleet ahead.

Themistocles was close enough to hear screaming. He found he had dipped his chin as if he was about to enter a boxing ring. It felt the same and yet different. His life and terrible injury were still the stakes, but for once, he was *not* alone. His people stood with him. They would stand or fall together.

43

Xanthippus glared forward, watching a Persian ship close to within a few lengths and grow, faster and faster. Arrows began to fly from the enemy, one of them thudding into the deck at Xanthippus' feet. He called for his shield then, painfully aware of how vulnerable he was. One of the boarding crew brought it to him and the sight of the snarling lion on the golden surface was a comfort. He saw another arrow arcing in and raised the shield to send it skidding away.

The ships seemed to leap at one another. The chance to turn aside had been and gone – neither captain could present his flank and escape, not then. A failure of nerve would mean death for everyone aboard. As close as they were, they could only hold the line and commit to striking the enemy head-on. Xanthippus watched, his mouth like leather, so that he champed and tried to wet his lips. The Spartans surged on both sides of him, though he doubted Eurybiades had meant to allow him the centre of the line, as if Xanthippus led the Spartans into battle. He could actually see the man himself in full bronze armour, waiting for the killing to begin like the vicious old hound he was. Xanthippus nodded to himself at the thought. He needed that savagery, that cruelty. His fleet crews needed to delight in killing if they were to survive. All the things that gentled a man had been left behind. Humour, decency, a sense of fairness – all those made him weak when another tried to cut his head from his shoulders.

Xanthippus watched the enemy officer borne close and

closer still, until he stood as if on a racing horse, just the width of a room away. The final moment vanished and rams cracked hard against the bow timbers beneath the surface, the strongest part of the war galleys. Both ships shuddered and slid aside in the same instant, with a terrible grinding and cries of fear from those in the hold. The sound was a long groan, almost thunder as the sliding prows began to crush oars.

Both crews had been sweeping fast and hard to keep the pace and smash the enemy. Until the ships met, they could not have known which side would need to pull oars in or be broken.

Xanthippus had no eyes for the desperate work going on below. He and the Persian officer were passing one another. He saw the man dip his head in greeting, as if they were not in bitter conflict at that moment. Xanthippus was out of range for a sword-thrust, but he snatched a spear from one of the hoplites standing close and threw it across the gap, taking the fellow in the stomach, so that he fell to his knees. A hornets' nest of arrows came in answer and the Greeks raised their shields and dipped down as shafts rattled off the bronze or stuck in the wooden deck.

The Persian ship had arranged shields all along its length, Xanthippus saw. A simple railing allowed their men to rest ovals and circles on it, then crouch behind them. He could see Persians in full armour there, itching to risk the leap as the ships ground past one another. Oars still splintered beneath his feet, though whether they were his own or Persian, Xanthippus did not know. He found himself breathing fast, ready to be attacked. Some of the old soldiers said they missed it, that wild alertness and emotion that was being alive in the very face of death. Xanthippus felt only a dark rage. This was the empire, come to burn and kill. They had to be met with anger so complete it would overwhelm them like a storm at sea.

He turned his shield as the two galleys overlapped, then made his decision.

'Boarders with me!' he called.

It looked to be just a step, but he found himself leaping hard, straining every muscle rather than risk falling into the dark line below, where oars were still snapping like bones as the ships slowed.

He landed on a foreign deck and raised his shield to take the blow of a sword. He struck back while he still held the other man's sword high, a solid blow to the man's shoulder that ruined it. A second cut sent blood spattering across sun-whitened wood. This was battle as he knew it, Xanthippus thought. The hoplites formed up around him and growled as they went forward, a sound to chill the hearts of the enemy.

The Persian rowers were all slaves. Xanthippus could see them, naked and filthy, looking up at him from the hold, revealed in the bar of light from a central trench, not too different from the Greek design. He could smell them, a scent so thick as to coat the back of his throat. He hoped they would have the sense to stay down.

Persian warriors came running to attack the hoplites massing on the deck, with more climbing up from the hold. They rushed the Greeks with wild cries and Xanthippus found himself battered back a step. Yet his boarders had the numbers and they knew the discipline of the shield line. On a solid deck underfoot, they cut Persians down and tossed bodies into the sea in quick jerks. In just moments, the deck was clear again, though two men still clutched the grips of steering oars at the stern and gaped at strangers facing them with bloody weapons.

Xanthippus opened his mouth to give an order and snapped it shut as the hold erupted. Filthy, long-haired men heaved themselves up all along the trench. He thought for a moment that they were crying out for freedom, until one of them cut the throat of a hoplite and was stabbed through the chest by another. They came on like madmen, with grey teeth and screeching cries. The hoplites were forced back by sheer weight of numbers, unable to do more than punch swords through the scabrous mass of human flesh pushing at them.

Xanthippus found himself glancing back at the trireme still alongside. He saw his men hacking slaves down and reminded himself of his vow. There would be no retreat. Whatever those oar-slaves thought they were doing, he would not give them back their ship.

'Kill them all,' he ordered, his voice a weapon, so that some of them flinched from it.

His hoplites steadied their retreat and bent to the work, making the ship run red. It was brutal labour and when it was done and the ship was littered with the dead rowers, they were all panting hard. Xanthippus struggled for breath. He was no longer a young man.

'Steady now,' he told his men. 'Rest your arms. Come back with me to ours, so we can sink this bitch.'

He saw Epikleos gesturing as he turned back. How long had it been? An hour? The sun seemed to be in the same place in the sky, which was impossible. Yet the battle lines were still plunging through, with only the Spartans on to their next attack. Ships had been upended in their wake, he saw, or drifted, manned by the dead. Line by line, the fleets would fold into one another, with every ship's length forward bringing more danger on all sides.

'Xanthippus! Come back!' he heard Epikleos bellowing.

386

He looked up to see a Persian warship already turning, drawn to them in their helplessness.

'Back! All of you!' Xanthippus shouted.

He made the leap with forty hoplites, though two of them had taken wounds to their legs and missed the jump with shouts of terror. One went into the water and vanished in a stream of hissing bubbles. The other clung to the deck he had almost reached. When the two ships swung together, he was caught between them. Hands reached for him, but the pressure broke his ribs and his eyes glazed as they heaved. He fell away then.

'Right oars! Back for your lives!' Epikleos was yelling.

The prow began to swing out. He and a dozen men were heaving the first Persian ship away with spear butts, allowing the oarsmen of the left bank to take their seats below and rattle out the sweeps once more. The movement revealed Persian oars made stubs, all along its length. The sea moved with a slick of splinters and broken oar blades.

Xanthippus felt the ship tremble as the rowers heaved below. The Persians had seen an easy target in the Greek warship. He hoped the enemy captain could feel his stomach clench as that trireme began to turn to face him.

'Oarsmen, ready!' Xanthippus said, clapping Epikleos on the shoulder to signal he was back in command. 'Give me half speed forward. Be ready to draw in!'

He waited for the keleustes to pass on the order before speaking again. Their drills had beaten the first clash of oarsmen. They had to keep winning that race, until the initial clash was over.

He looked back only once to the crippled ship they had to leave behind. Someone else would pick it off and send it to the bottom, though the labour had all been his.

'Ready, boarders!' he shouted again.

The hoplites roared in response and Xanthippus found himself grinning, though there was a taste of metal in his mouth. He had a memory of his own shield knocked back against his face and paused to spit blood over the side. His teeth would be showing red, he realised. His crew had won a victory. Like a fire lit, they wanted more.

He looked left and right. Two Greek ships listed, the men within drowning as he watched. The sight was like a splash of cold water on his face. Yet on all sides, the Spartans had crashed through the enemy lines. He could see overturned Persian hulls, wider in the draught than the Greeks, as he judged it. Another Persian galley burned, giving off a great pillar of black smoke, while desperate figures leapt for the sea. Those crews weakened by the fighting would be picked off, one by one. Numbers would tell in the end.

One of the enemy captains had come in close to ram a damaged Greek trireme. His target looked adrift, the crew busy repairing damage. When that ship came back to life and turned sharply to face him, he tried to sheer off and go after a weaker target.

Xanthippus saw the move begin at the tiller, with the Persian officer jabbing orders and two men heaving at the great oars there.

'He's trying to turn!' Xanthippus roared. 'Give me ram speed, right now! Ram speed! Twenty beats!'

The keleustes echoed the answer and the ship sprang forward. The right banks of rowers were a touch stronger than the battered left, so that they drifted. Xanthippus did not call a correction as it helped them match the path of the fleeing Persian. He tried to continue the turn and head for safety, but there was neither room nor speed enough to save him.

The ram struck and holed the enemy ship, exactly as the Persian had intended to do to one of theirs. The hoplites cheered even as arrows rained down. Yet it was the sting of a dying wasp as water poured in below and terrified screams began to sound. Some of the Persian soldiers even tried to leap aboard the Greek ship rather than remain on a sinking vessel. They were cut down and the keleustes ordered all rowers to back oars and pull them clear. They heaved in a frenzy then. A sinking ship was a terrible danger, capable of taking them down with it.

They might have watched that galley sink, but the sea had filled with dozens of actions going on all around. Xanthippus swallowed blood in his mouth rather than spit once more and nodded. Themistocles and the second line had gone through. The third rank of Greek ships was approaching them, ready for battle. He raised an arm as they passed and the men cheered to see him.

A Persian ship steered closer, somehow unmarked and untouched. Xanthippus signalled the turn.

'Mark that ship!' he said, pointing. 'She's ours.'

His helmsmen heaved their charges over and the oars bit as the orders were passed on. The hoplites on deck hunkered down, ready with their shields and spears to go again.

44

Xerxes felt his heart beat slow and strong, as mountains grew before him. He was a warrior king, setting his face and his strength against his father's final enemy. When the wind whipped around him and stirred the dust, he breathed in, hoping the spirit of Darius could see his progress, or join him.

Xerxes had chosen to ride that day, wearing a cloak of imperial purple over a white tunic that left his legs bare. After so long at sea, he found his muscles had grown weak and he frowned as he rode along, unaware of how it put fear into the regiments marching south. The soldiers of his hazarabam thousands, even the officers of his Immortals, exchanged worried glances. The arrival of the Great King had changed the mood of the entire army under Mardonius, from the very instant Xerxes had set foot on land and stood amongst them.

His presence meant that a living god walked with them – and served as a reminder that they marched to war and faced a terrible enemy. To do so in the presence of the Great King stiffened spines and raised heads. If there was fear in them, at the thought of being reprimanded or punished, there was also pride, and love. They were far from home, but Xerxes was with them.

When his horse shied at something, Xerxes leaned over and cuffed the animal across its ears, then rubbed the same spot. The mount was skittish, but tall and very strong, a prince among horses. Xerxes looked around him, aware that he had been riding in a reverie, letting the land pass as if he drifted. He shook his head. He had eaten better in the previous two days than the month before. His stomach had awoken on land, so that even the simple bean slop his regiments endured made his mouth fill with saliva. He burped into a hand at the thought, but still felt hungry.

It took an effort of will to look up, knowing that his gaze would be met by men desperate to be able to say the king had seen them, that he had noticed them or spoken a single word they would treasure and repeat to their children. He had not appreciated before how many eyes would follow him in the camps, without walls and private rooms. Wherever he went, his men watched every step and exchange, as if they drank his image. He found it surprisingly wearisome, so that when he retired at last to the pavilion raised for him each evening, it was with a great sense of relief simply to be private. The evenings were drawing in, at least. The days were shorter than the height of summer, though the sun was still hot overhead and the skies as blue as a Persian lake.

Greece was a dry land, he had come to realise, though he had known deserts where each breath was a contest between life and death. Even so, his regiments had been found gasping before Mardonius refilled the water casks whenever they passed a spring or stream. They had not been able to leave food stores so far south and so they were already on half-rations, with supplies running low. Yet they were almost there. Xerxes and Mardonius and all the senior men had pulled off an extraordinary migration. Over three hundred thousand had marched all the way from Thrace to Greece, around the great arc of the coast. Mardonius had lost no more than eight hundred in that time, to accident, weakness, disease or execution. It was an incredible achievement, brought about by an empire's wealth and organisation. Xerxes felt the pride of it swell in him.

The young king glanced over his shoulder and saw regiments of ten thousand stretching back and back, with the camp followers and carts bringing up the rear in a great cloud of dust that rose to the horizon. It made him realise the ground was sloping up towards the hills. He rode with the sea on his left-hand side, the great fleet accompanying him, with horses and soldiers ready to snap shut on Athens. They would be the anvil; he the hammer brought down. It was a fine thought.

He saw the mounted scouts raise a hand in warning, pointing to the sea. Xerxes swallowed against a knot of anxiety and kicked his mount to a trot. The path through the mountains took him close to the shore, which pleased him. He had grown used to watching the slow creep of his army while he sat on board the flagship. It was satisfying to mirror the same action on horseback, watching the fleet. That morning, they had kept station with him, heading for the great turn that his Greek allies said would take them south.

He did not trust the men of Thebes, for all they had offered him dust and water and sworn their lives to his care. Despite his father's wisdom, Xerxes found it hard to accept a people willing to betray their own. He had viewed the queen of Halicarnassus, Artemisia, with similar suspicion – and she had some Persian blood and a closeness of culture that explained some of what she was. Still, the woman disturbed him, with her dark eyes and lingering gaze, so that he was happier for her to remain with the fleet, well away. Power was a dangerous thing for a woman, Xerxes suspected. It corrupted, made her less submissive. There was a reason men imposed obedience on them, from the palaces of kings to the homes of simple labourers. Women were happier with a master. As were men, he considered. A flock needed only one shepherd, after all. With an effort, he put Artemisia from his thoughts.

Xerxes did not know if the Thebans had heard of his maps or knew the extent of the campaign that ended at Marathon. He did not need their knowledge of the land to guide this particular arrow, but it helped to test their loyalty, even so. They had confirmed the existence of the pass that Artemisia said would take his army around the great crags. He would be able to watch the fleet as he marched along the bare shore of Thermopylae, with the great hammer of Persia at his back.

When he reached a low hill and reined in, his horse began to crop at the wild grasses there. Xerxes took a slow breath and peered into the distance. He brought one hand up and joined thumb to the other fingers, an old scout's trick that focused his sight further.

Though the distance was great, he could make out the fleets heading to meet one another. The Greeks had brought more ships than he'd known they had. He found himself holding his breath as the fronts met and drove through, as if his hammer had shattered the anvil it struck. The edges of the fleets blurred into one another and he saw ships overturn and plumes of black smoke rise. The battle went on and on until he could not be sure who had the best of it. There was no sound capable of reaching his ears, so that all he heard was the order to halt behind him, with the command rippling back on hundreds of voices until the entire army crashed to a stop. That noise of tramping feet and horses had filled his ears for days. The comparative silence was eerie, especially when he imagined fear and shouts of rage and pain going on, with choking, drowning men slipping slowly down away from the light. He shuddered at the thought.

Xerxes turned when Mardonius rode up with a dozen senior men. The older general would have dismounted to prostrate himself, but Xerxes held up a hand, turning back to the clash of fleets.

'I cannot tell . . . whether we are winning,' Xerxes said.

Mardonius gave a quick grimace, as if he had cracked a tooth on something he ate.

'The numbers tell the tale, Majesty. Look further back and see how few of our fleet have even reached the battle. The grindstone turns at the front and we have . . . two or three times as many ships, more. With captains who know you watch them, who know they must drive through the Greeks to join you, to feel your imperial light fall on them once again.'

Xerxes dipped his head, though he was not a fool. He had endured flattery his entire life, from men who wanted favours, or who hoped to influence him or turn away his wrath. He was not immune to it, especially from those of his father's generation, as Mardonius was. Yet he knew not to trust words alone. He glanced at his general and saw a stiff back and relaxed hands on the pommel of his horse. The man did look confident, Xerxes saw with relief. He realised it was in his gift to inspire others, not least his own general. The young king raised his head and tried to relax his own hands.

'Lead us then to this pass, Mardonius, this Thermopylae. If it is as narrow as our Thebans claim, we'll need to push on at speed to keep the fleet on our flank.'

'As you wish, Majesty.'

Mardonius glanced at the sun, low down on the western hills. 'It isn't far now. We will make camp close to where it opens and go through in one push at dawn tomorrow. The fleet will have gone on by then, I have no doubt.'

45

The month of Boedromion brought shortening days. The sun still felt like summer, especially when a man had to fight under its lash. Xanthippus blessed Apollo for his clear light and fortune in war, then blessed Athena when the Persian fleet pulled back before true darkness. Xanthippus had not known if they would continue to fight all night in their frenzy, though it would have been utter madness. Without light, both fleets would have been in danger of ramming their own ships. Just as important, the crews were all exhausted. Some of the rowers snored where they sat, leaning back with eyes closed in the creaking blackness below.

Without formal agreement, both fleets pulled apart in the twilight, seeking safe harbours for the hours of night. Xanthippus had watched for the half-moon to show, waiting for some scheme or trap to spring under its light. He hoped the Persian captains were just as nervous. It wasn't until midnight was upon them that Xanthippus allowed Trierarch Ereius and his crew to seek shallow water and drop anchor. Even then, they risked running aground or tearing the bottom out on some unseen rock. Ships had settled on all sides and the little boats they towed had been drawn in. Xanthippus had been about ready for sleep when one of the small craft bumped alongside. The summons was for him, from the Spartan navarch.

Two sailors rowed him back across dark waters, saying nothing. When they found their own ship, Xanthippus heard the slap of rope against wood and reached blindly for it, lurching up the ladder to the deck above. A figure challenged him with a drawn blade and he gave his name, then waited for Eurybiades to be told he had come.

Clouds revealed the moon overhead while he stood there, making the sea glitter in a long line. The Spartan ship eased up and down at the prow, the motion almost restful. Xanthippus yawned suddenly and scrubbed a hand over his face, wishing the endurance of his youth hadn't vanished like a dream. There had been a time when he'd thought nothing of staying up all night and fighting the next day if he had to! In his fifties, he preferred enemies to come at him only in the mornings.

He heard Themistocles come aboard when the man's voice sounded a few feet away, making some dry comment that had the boatmen chuckling. Xanthippus turned to him in the darkness and murmured his name.

'Is that you, Xan?' Themistocles said, too loud.

'Are you trying to signal the Persians or something?' Xanthippus hissed at him. 'Keep your voice down, would you?'

'Oh, they'll all be snoring by now, I'm sure, ready for tomorrow. As I should be, instead of here, summoned by . . . Ah, Eurybiades! What an honour!'

Though no lamps had been lit, moonlight had revealed the navarch rising from the hold. Without a word, the Spartan gestured for them to approach. Xanthippus and Themistocles might have exchanged a glance, but it was too dark.

Xanthippus heard another boat bump against the side. He hesitated as Themistocles went forward, leaning out to see who it was, then lending an arm. He held it steady as Cimon grasped his hand and sprang up, so lithe and fit Xanthippus felt like an old man in his presence.

Half a dozen senior officers had been called to the Spartan flagship. Xanthippus followed Themistocles down to a cabin in the bowels of the trireme. Two benches lay alongside a narrow table and a small lamp had been lit, swinging from the timbers above and casting the dimmest of golden glows on their faces. Xanthippus stifled a yawn as he took a seat. He had fought for hours that day and truly lost count of the number of ship actions. He thought if he tried to remember them one by one, he would drift into sleep.

He bit his lip hard enough to cause him pain, needing to be alert, caught between the desire to check on his crew and his duty there. The truth was, Epikleos and his ship's captains could see to binding wounds and repairing broken timbers. His role was more than a fighting ship officer. Even so, he felt torn. He had formed bonds with his crew that day and he had felt their confusion as the boat came to take him away.

'Gentlemen, I congratulate you,' Eurybiades said. He stood before them, wide-shouldered and stern as any tutor.

'Is there wine, Eurybiades?' Themistocles asked suddenly, perhaps just to be difficult.

'We used the last of it to wash wounds,' Eurybiades said with a shrug. He opened his mouth to continue, but Themistocles went on immediately.

'*What?* My dear boy, you should have let me know! I would have brought you some, if only for me to enjoy now. The thought of going in again without a skin or two tomorrow . . . I won't be able to enjoy it if I think of you Spartans without even a drop of wine, I tell you.'

Eurybiades blinked slowly as Themistocles rattled on. The Spartan had never understood his Athenian counterpart. On that night, it was no more than a token effort. Themistocles was almost too weary to argue. Xanthippus saw him smother a yawn when he stopped talking. The Spartan navarch only stared, considering.

'If you have an excess . . . I would welcome a few skins,' Eurybiades said slowly. 'Perhaps you can send your boat back before morning. That is not why I called you here, however.'

Xanthippus saw Cimon lean forward like a hunting hound as the Spartan went on. He sat straighter himself, while sleep washed along the shore of him, threatening to pull him under. The little cabin was too warm, that was the trouble . . . He came awake when Themistocles reached across and tapped him hard on the forearm without looking round. The Spartan went on.

'I have had word from my own people. King Leonidas has taken position in the only pass through the mountains. He will hold it against the Persians as they come.'

'Can he block it?' Themistocles said sharply. 'The only pass there is the path along the coast. I know it well. It is a little wider than I would have liked, but if the Spartan army has chosen to hold there, perhaps it will serve. Have they sent word to Aristides and the hoplites marching out of Athens?'

To their surprise, the Spartan did not reply immediately. Eurybiades looked irritated and chewed one side of his lip in a manner less certain than Xanthippus had seen in him before.

'According to the messenger, King Leonidas does not have the full army with him. He has only his personal guard and some thousands of . . . others, allies and helots.'

There was a beat of silence before Themistocles asked the question.

'Why?'

'The army cannot march during the feast of Apollo.'

'We celebrated that feast a week ago, in Athens,' Themistocles said, his voice higher than usual. 'But your king has taken just a few thousand against the entire Persian army?'

'He gave his word,' Eurybiades said. 'If Leonidas had to stand there alone, he would. I wish I could be there with him, if my duty didn't hold me here! My king!'

He rubbed a hand roughly over his face, so hard he left pale marks.

'The army will come out when the festival ends in three days. It is the will of the gods.'

Eurybiades glared round as if expecting them to argue. No one said a word and he subsided.

'We did well today. I think we sank or boarded as many as eighty ships. We have lost around forty of our own, with all their crews. I kept my triremes in the heart of the fighting and I saw four of them rammed and sunk as a result. Men I called friends and brothers. A quarter of Sparta's fleet.'

'And we will do as well again tomorrow,' Cimon said suddenly.

The young man seemed to be frowning at the Spartan. Xanthippus looked from one to the other, unsure what was going on.

'No,' Eurybiades said firmly. 'The numbers – the losses are too great. If we hold them here, if we do just as well as we did today, we will be worn down to nothing – and they will still have hundreds of ships. Have you ever seen so many?'

'I never thought I would see the day when a Spartan coun-selled turning his back on an enemy,' Cimon said softly.

Themistocles was close enough at the table to lay a hand on the younger man's arm, stilling any further words from him. Eurybiades froze. His fist clenched on the table before him so that the muscles of his right arm swelled.

'If you knew a little more of war,' Eurybiades said, 'you would know a leader may withdraw when the odds are against him – without stain on his honour. He may pull back in good order, to fight again where the odds favour him rather more. Where the land is better or his reinforcements have come. You are a young man and too wet behind the ears to know how to address me. I suggest you note well how Themistocles tapped you on the arm then. Rein yourself *in*, boy.'

Cimon had already made his decision before the Spartan had finished speaking. He dipped his head and Themistocles pulled back his hand. Eurybiades went on, his words slow and precise, as if he crafted each one from stone.

'We have seen the size of the Persian army marching south – towards Athens, towards the Peloponnese. King Leonidas stands in their way, though he has only his guard and a few thousand. He cannot hold that pass of Thermopylae, not for long. How many days then before Sparta too has them in sight? If we pull the fleet back tonight, before dawn, we can still protect the peninsula of Sparta – and of Corinth. King Leonidas will not have given his life in vain. I know that coast as well as my own home. We can block them there and prevent them landing.'

'Prevent the fleet landing where they can assault Sparta and Corinth, yes, I see,' Themistocles said coldly. 'But what of Athens?'

'We cannot save Athens,' Eurybiades said. 'You've seen their fleet, you've seen the vast stain of them on the land. I have never known as many on the field of war. Athens . . . is gone. You must realise that by now.'

Themistocles lost all the lightness of manner from before. He rested his own fists on the table and for a time it seemed they were the only two men in that small room.

'We cannot save Athens because the Spartan army will not march during a festival,' he said softly. 'Your King Leonidas swore Sparta would join Athens and Corinth and all

400

the rest of our allies on land – if we held the Persians at sea. That was our arrangement.'

'Never doubt the oath of my king,' Eurybiades growled. 'He has given his life rather than break that vow, risking his own honour and worship of the gods! Speak not one word more of Leonidas! The world could fall and he would still be in that pass, waiting for the enemy!'

Eurybiades had half risen from his seat, but he mastered himself and sat down, smoothing his tunic and cloak. After a moment, he spoke again, his voice once more calm.

'My sole concern is for this fleet – facing more ships than I knew existed in the whole world. When they have broken the last of us, where will Athens be then? What of Sparta then, without my ships to keep that coast? I lost a quarter of my fleet today. If tomorrow is the same . . .'

He seemed to realise the Athenian had drawn him into an argument and snapped his mouth shut.

'As navarch of the allied fleet, I have given you your orders. I will withdraw the fleet at first light and refuse engagement. Send word to Athens overland if you wish. Tell them to run for the Peloponnese. We'll make our stand behind the barricades there, on land and at sea.'

'No,' Themistocles said. His voice was utterly confident and he even smiled as both Cimon and the Spartan looked at him in amazement.

'If you take the ships of Sparta and Corinth with you,' Themistocles said, 'it will not be with those of Athens. Not on those terms. Every day we win here is one more the Persians are delayed in whatever plans they have made. That is beyond dispute. I must refuse your order, navarch. I believe you are in error. So – the ships of Athens will remain to block the Persian fleet. We'll last as long as your King Leonidas, at least.'

401

'And those of Corinth,' another voice sounded.

All eyes turned to the Corinthian. The man only shrugged when Eurybiades glared at him.

'My captains saw no action today,' the Corinthian said. 'I won't go home until we have taken the measure of these Persian crews. Put us in the vanguard tomorrow and set us free to attack. We'll send these bastards to the deep.'

There was a growl from the other captains and Eurybiades matched it in frustration, silencing them.

'Either I am in command of this fleet or am I not. Which is it, Athenian?'

Themistocles said nothing and only waited until the Spartan was certain no one else would speak in that room. Eurybiades gathered himself in cold dignity then, his anger vanishing as he twitched his red cloak into place, ready to rise.

'You command then, tomorrow,' he said. 'As you seem to have done today. In time of war, I will make no threats, Athenian. But if we survive this, you and I will find a quiet place and I will make my objections clear to you.'

'Very well,' Themistocles said.

He rose as the Spartan stood, out of respect and also in case the man lunged at him. The Spartan's anger could be read in every quivering line, for all his self-control. Eurybiades left the cabin and the tension seeped away as all eyes turned to Themistocles.

'Eurybiades is a good man . . . though I think his judgement has been shaken, perhaps by worry for his king. We cannot aid Leonidas by pulling back, only by completing his task. While he holds the pass, we remain. We will give the army time to form.'

He shook himself, as if moved. Xanthippus could see the effort it took for Themistocles to smile and adopt a more reasonable tone.

'Now, someone whistle up my boat, would you? Look to me for signals tomorrow. We have them bottled up. Win another day. Check your water and make sure the men eat. And get some sleep if you can,' he said to the captains. 'We'll take the fight to them tomorrow. Corinth – you have first rank. Be sure – Sparta and Athens will be watching.'

They trooped out past Spartan soldiers on deck watch. Xanthippus saw Themistocles lean in to Cimon and paused with the pair of them, waiting for the boats.

'Do you know, Cimon,' Themistocles said, 'why good men are thirty years of age before they can be an epistates or a magistrate, or hold any of the council posts?'

'I am sorry. I . . .' Cimon began.

Themistocles spoke over him.

'It is because the twenties are the most perilous years of a man's life. He is no longer a boy. He feels he is fully grown, that he can be a father and a husband, that he can argue with wit and wisdom and clarity. And he is both right and wrong. If he works hard and well, he will have all the qualities he wins for himself, all coming into glorious season. Yet he lacks the wisdom and experience to temper them. He drinks too much, perhaps. He acts . . . rashly, perhaps even to the point of arguing with a Spartan navarch on his own ship.'

'*You* argued with him,' Cimon said, a note of anger in his tone.

Themistocles nodded.

'I did, yes.' He waited until the young man understood that was not his point and deflated.

'I'm sorry,' Cimon said.

'Your father would be proud of the man you are becoming, Cimon. I look forward to seeing you speak in the Assembly, in a free Athens. I pray that you will have the chance.'

Themistocles heard the bump of boats against the side and leaned over, nodding to men he knew.

'Look for my signals tomorrow,' he said. 'It will be a long day – and your father will watch every beat and stroke of it. We cannot let them go through. Leonidas holds the army in the pass. Every day we block them at sea is one more they cannot join up and crush our people. Aristides is already out in the field, gentlemen, with all our hoplites, all our hopes. The Spartans and the men of Corinth will march to join him, when they are ready. We just need to give them time.'

46

At dawn, Xerxes watched his scouts come back through the lines. They ran well enough, but their faces showed confusion and fear as they reached the king and prostrated themselves on the sandy ground. The day was cold and the king shivered as he stood with the sea breeze rushing through his standing ranks.

'Report to me,' Xerxes said.

Mardonius too had reined in and dismounted, desperate for news. For an entire day, they had sent a number of messages to the Greeks waiting in the pass, offering them a chance to surrender. There was no need to throw away their lives for nothing. The Spartans were renowned for their skill and Xerxes had hoped for a peaceful settlement, perhaps even to meet the king who stood in their centre, with spear and shield, his helmet topped by a high crest of horsehair.

One of the messengers rose faster than the other two. Xerxes gestured for him to speak.

'Majesty, they have not withdrawn as you commanded. They remain still, across the narrowest part of the coastal path.'

Xerxes pursed his mouth, biting the soft skin on the inside of his lip. He'd thought it would seem a grand gesture worthy of his father, to agree to spare the small force arrayed against him. By all accounts there were barely enough of them to block the pass. They stood with sheer cliffs on their left shoulders and the sea on the other.

'What are they doing? Just . . . standing there?'

'They are braiding one another's hair, Majesty.'

The words brought a moment of silence as the Persians listened and decided not to look up for the king's reaction. After a pause, Xerxes spoke again.

'You told them we would blot out the sun with our arrows?' he said softly.

The messenger trembled, he saw, as if he had caught an ague in the morning cold.

'Majesty, their king replied that it was good news, as they preferred to fight in the shade.'

Xerxes nodded.

'I am my father's son,' he said, raising his voice. 'I make war to have the world shake to my steps. Not out of spite or anger, but only because God himself has decreed my right to rule. In my father's memory, I have sought to show mercy. No more, now. No more.'

He turned to Mardonius, smiling in a brittle fashion that made him seem made of wax.

'General. Darken the sun as I promised. Then, if any of them still live, send my hazarabam thousands, then another and another. Fill the pass with our soldiers and cut them down. They are just men. Allow no surrender, no grand gestures. The Spartans have refused my mercy. Grind them down, these who dare to stand against me, until there is nothing left.'

Mardonius grinned as he bowed. He had marched for months to reach this place. At last, he had an enemy and a purpose.

'Thank you, Majesty. It will be done.'

Within moments, regiments of archers were jogging forward, their steps a clatter on the broken grey stones of the coast. Xerxes only wished he could see the faces of the Spartan warriors when they understood he had not been making an idle threat. He had thousands of archers and each one carried thirty arrows in a hard quiver. Between them, they could cover the sun.

Xerxes glanced up at the cliffs. He would have liked to look down as the Greeks were slaughtered, but there was no path visible. The dark crags rose like shadowed blades, impossible to climb, all while the sea crashed against that part of the coast. There was but one way through. He just had to sweep the defenders away.

Out on the sea, he could see the fleets manoeuvring. In the grey dawn, they readied themselves once more for the day's labour, for the plunge and spite and savagery of war. Xerxes had brought them to that cold coast, but it was his father's oath and promise they would enact. The royal house of Persia had remembered the Greeks well enough. Xerxes felt his eyes sting with pride.

The ships of Corinth fared badly against the first ranks of Persian galleys, losing a third of their number before Themistocles furiously ordered them back. He let the gasping crews rest then, sending in fresh galleys of Athens, though his heart pounded at a greater stake than anyone else endured. The allied cities had sent smaller numbers in their fleets, but with almost two hundred triremes fully crewed, the Athenian ships were literally the Assembly at sea – the free men of Athens. Behind them, they had left women and children, the old, the slaves, the foreign metics. Every man who could hold a sword and shield was either in that fleet or marching with Aristides away from Athens. There was no place of refuge, no safe harbour. They either won or they gave up all they were, all they would ever be.

Themistocles was a hard man, he knew it. He had seen death in many forms; he did not think it could ever make him weep. Even so, he felt his breath catch as he witnessed a ship of his own city rammed and sunk with horrible speed, barely an arrow-shot off his prow. Some galleys rolled right over when they were rammed, showing grey hulls. Others just went under, slipping away.

The small drama was over quickly enough. The Persian pulled back and rowed clear, while the cries and prayers of Greeks were silenced in a hissing sea. Only a few figures bobbed to the surface as Themistocles passed by. His people, face down and still.

He felt himself trembling in rage and grief on their behalf. It was not enough to be better than the Persians. The awful tragic truth was that no matter how well the Athenian crews fought, they were still only men. They grew weary and the pace slowed. As the day wore on, crews who had boarded three ships and rammed two more, who had avoided being sent down half a dozen times, would find themselves faced with a fresh Persian galley, rowed hard and recklessly. Heroes were brought down by their own exhaustion.

Themistocles blessed the name of Xanthippus then. The only response was to call back entire groups of ships, to replace them in the battle line with fresher crews of their own. In open sea, the Persians might have overwhelmed them. In the strait, the captains under Xerxes had the same problem. Too little space to manoeuvre, with so many pressing behind that it meant every galley fought until it was overwhelmed and sunk. It was made worse as sea lanes slowly choked up with broken or burning vessels, with bodies like flotsam, rising and falling with the waves.

In the late afternoon, Themistocles called back Xanthippus with a group colour flown from the prow. Each captain of that group raised his own until they were all ready to ease clear in good order rather than turn and risk being rammed amidships. They came back as veterans, with blood on the decks, panting and weary, but still proud. They cheered and raised spears to Themistocles as they came to rest.

The ships under Cimon moved through them and took the brunt of fresh Persian crews. The truth was, Athens was such a key part of the fleet, they had to be called on more than any of the others. They would bring more destruction, but their losses would be much greater.

Themistocles found his stomach was painful to the touch, the muscles aching from standing tense for so long. The Persians seemed to know their king watched them, that their army fought on the coast to reach the plain beyond. They were terrible in their fierceness. Some of them broke men and oars recklessly to engage, fighting even as their ships sank, with freezing waters rushing in below their feet. A few of those vessels rested almost on the surface of the sea, submerged and yet sitting there like ghosts. Persian warriors waded across wet decks then, until Greek archers picked them off or just rowed past, leaving them behind.

Cimon was directing his crews well, Themistocles saw. Even as his own trireme moved to ram a lone Persian, he watched Cimon's ship halt and reverse at good speed, the rowers working blind and praying the lookout was sharp. The triremes were fantastically fast in calm waters, darting like dagger blows. Themistocles showed his teeth as Cimon let the enemy slide on through and then called for ram speed, taking that ship in the middle. It was a death strike, the ram holing it deep and then pulling back.

Themistocles braced as his own ship thumped into an enemy galley. The blow was not hard or fast enough to shatter the timbers, though he thought he saw cracks in the hull. Instead, enemy soldiers readied themselves to leap. Before his trierarch could order the rowers to back oars, half a dozen men landed on the deck. They were all young soldiers and they rushed at Themistocles, ignoring the threat of hoplites reacting at their backs. He shoved his helmet on and picked up a long spear at his feet. His shield was too far and so he drew his sword and waited for them.

The man who reached him first was grinning in delight. He did not expect a spear to flicker out between his legs, making him stumble. The Persian's first blow turned into a flail for balance. His eyes widened as Themistocles chopped the short blade into his neck, then eased back a step to let him fall. The spear was wrenched from his hand by the action, making Themistocles curse. Three more rushed him, but they were cut down from behind with quick, savage blows. Themistocles nodded thanks to his panting hoplites.

Some of the Persians were still dying as they were heaved over the side. One tried to hold the man who kicked at him and had his throat cut in reply. The rest of their crew watching on the enemy ship howled and jabbed the air in frustration, but the gap was too great — further every instant as the galleys slipped apart. A few of them raised bows and Themistocles ducked for his shield, holding it up. He heard the clatter of shafts on metal as his men did the same, but there was still a cry cut short. He set his mouth in anger. Forty paces separated them by then. He could see where the sea hissed and frothed around a broken point in the enemy hull. The plunge and rise of the sea had lifted the ram, he could see. The broken timbers lay right on the waterline rather than below. Left alone, the Persians could patch it with a piece of sail and a bucket of tar.

'Ram speed!' he called at the top of his lungs. 'Ready shields and spears. Hit them again.'

47

Leonidas looked out on a landscape where arrows grew thick as hog bristles or stems of lavender. He tossed his shield to one of his helots, waiting to wrestle the shafts out that had pierced the metal skin, leaving it puckered.

The battle king flexed his hands and looked left and right, at those men in thick red cloaks who made his personal guard. Every one of them was over forty and had fathered at least one son for Sparta, safe and well at home while they defended the king. As importantly, every one of them had earned their place at his side. He had known most of them his entire life, from rituals to drunken brawls, like sons or brothers to him, every one. They were his family. He knew every ailment, scar, strength and weakness in them.

They were in good spirits, he was pleased to see. The storm of arrows had not troubled them unduly. Each Greek soldier carried some form of wide, round shield, large enough to crouch and shelter beneath. On a broader battlefield, they might have looked for a moment to rush and scatter the force of archers, but on that coast such a move would have taken them away from the narrowest point.

Leonidas had given and repeated his orders. There would be no counter-attacks, no wild rushes forward, not even if the enemy seemed to break and run for their lives. Under his command, they would hold the pass. The task was simple, with a beginning and an end.

Leonidas knew there was dismay in the ranks, at least beyond his own Spartiate guard and the perioikoi. He saw it in the faces of the others, as they understood and came to terms with it. The men of Corinth and Thespiae had expected to join the armies of Sparta and Athens, not a tiny force holding a pass against numbers so vast they could not even guess how many stood against them.

The battle king felt a touch of guilt at that. They did not know he had come to that place to die. He was the sword master of Sparta, descendant of a demigod. He had chosen his own fate, without regrets. Yet the path along the coast was wider than he had known. He needed them to hold it, even at the narrowest point.

Ahead, the archers of a foreign king had pulled back. The strange weeds of their shafts littered every part of the ground, in fragments and shifting pieces where they had struck rock. Steam rose in wisps in some places, hissing as it touched pools of seawater. The land actually was warm underfoot there.

The archers had indeed blotted out the sun for a few moments. The Spartans and their allies remained even so, defiant as the storm fell away. Their helots had cheered then, to show they were alive. It had been a good feeling.

Leonidas watched as the pass ahead filled with marching soldiers. They came with banners and drummer boys, he saw. They wore panelled coats and carried long shields of their own. He noted swords too, ready to stab and lunge. Leonidas nodded. Well disciplined, well equipped. He had faced the same sort a dozen times in his life. He was still standing.

He had a long spear in his right hand, with a sword and kopis knife on his belt. His helmet was a weapon when he lunged with it, as was the shield his helot brought forward and settled on his left arm. He rolled his neck, feeling bones click and crunch. He was no longer a young man.

'Give thanks to Apollo and Ares for this opportunity,' Leonidas called over his shoulder. 'There is no retreat from here. This is where we die.'

The Persians broke into a run, coming at him in a line sixty or eighty wide, crammed in tight in dozens of ranks behind. It seemed they meant to smash the force of Spartans and perioikoi, to fling them away with a single charge. Leonidas set his feet on the land. *His* land, under him. He felt his blood thrill as the Spartan front rank locked shields and raised spears. The wall of thorns. Every man of his guard was a master of his weapons, hardened by battle and training. They held that pass like an iron bar laid across it.

Sunset came early for those who stood in the shadow of the mountains by Thermopylae. Xerxes could see great bands of gold still lighting the sea beyond, illuminating ships as they struggled wearily, like fighters clinging to one another rather than fall. It was the end of another day and an unnatural gloom fell across his army as they waited to go through the pass.

He could not understand why no great cheer was going up, why his regiments weren't surging forward. Mardonius had sent in Assyrians, then a hazarabam of Medes. Xerxes had heard the sounds of battle begin, the cries of pain and anguish over the clash of metal on metal. The hills on his right hand echoed them back at him. It was a clamour he had known from the cradle and he found it restful. Yet there had been no trumpet pealing victory, no chanting Persian voices raised in his honour.

He saw bodies floating in the sea. At first, he thought it was some carpet of waterweed or broken oars from the fleet. Then he saw the tinge of blood in the waters like a cloud around them. He rode his horse closer to the edge and saw hundreds of the dead lying like cordwood, head to head, head to feet, face down and face up. There were no red cloaks amongst them, not that he could make out. He shivered as he sat his mount, wondering how many had drifted down and down, lost to sight, to be plucked and bitten by strange creatures on the seabed.

He called his messenger, trying not to show how desperate he was for news.

'Pass word to Mardonius. Tell him I would hear his report.'

The young man raced away and Mardonius appeared in short order. The older man looked exhausted, the bags under his eyes seeming to have grown. Xerxes let him dismount and prostrate himself, not yet sure if the man deserved praise or censure.

'Why are we not yet through, general?' Xerxes asked, his voice carefully gentle.

Mardonius knew he was in danger and kept his head bowed.

'Majesty, they are like devils. They have killed a great number of our men.'

'I see. And how many of these Spartans have fallen?' Xerxes replied.

Mardonius was not a weak man. Though he knew it might cost him his life, he answered firmly, praying the son had at least some part of his father's strength of will.

'Very few, Majesty, as far as I can tell. They are . . . unusually skilled. Our men could not break through.'

Mardonius had gone deep into the pass to watch the Spartans fight. He had come away ashen at what he had seen. Yet they were men, he told himself, not demons, not truly. They would grow weary, they had to.

'The arrows had no effect on them?' Xerxes was saying.

'What are they, men of bronze?' He laughed, but it was a brittle sound and it had fear in it.

'They are disciplined, Majesty. They use shields and spears well. I truly cannot say if they lost men today.'

'Pull the rest back – and interrogate them. Speak to those who faced these Spartans and learn all they know. Tomorrow, we will send in my Immortals. Have the entire baivarabam come to the front and make ready. At dawn, I will send all ten thousand in.'

Mardonius prostrated himself once more. He was not sure if his own command was in danger, or even his life, but it was the right decision and he did not hesitate. He had never seen anyone fight as well as the Spartan shield line. Mardonius had a vision of the Persian army slowly ground against them, a knife ruined on a spinning stone. The Immortals were the best soldiers of the empire, taken from every regiment and trained together as an elite. Only they could stand against the Spartans.

Xerxes dismissed his general without praise or comfort. It was already growing dark and at sea the fleets were pulling apart in grumbling truce, seeking safe harbours for the night. As he mounted up and trotted his horse to where the Immortals pitched their tents, Xerxes was not sure if he felt dismay or not. He had brought a vast army to give him the edge in a land he did not know. He had gathered a huge fleet to steal away any advantage they might have had on the deep waters. The losses to that point had not changed those truths. His army would crush the Spartans in the pass, if he had to spend a hundred thousand men to do it. His fleet would break through, if they had to lose two ships for every Greek trireme. An empire had resources enough to smother the Greeks, like crops drowned in a great flood. If Xerxes stood

415

in the end in Athens, he would not care how many had died to put him there.

The Immortal officers wore white, panelled armour. Mardonius stood with a group of twelve of them, gesturing to the pass. They became aware of the king's presence and scrutiny in the same moment, dropping to the ground and waiting for his command to rise.

'Up, all of you,' Xerxes said. He watched how they leapt to their feet, strong and fit and healthy. It raised his spirits to see them so eager for the fight.

'You are called,' Xerxes said. 'First in, at dawn.'

'Our lives are yours, Majesty,' the Immortal general replied.

Mardonius gave a sharp nod – a promise – as Xerxes rode on. These were not Medes or Egyptians, or any one of the subject nations. They were pure-blooded Persian warriors. Their presence on the field of war would send a ripple of fear through their enemies. The white coats stood out against the darker earth. They would not fail.

48

Leonidas roared defiance at the men coming at him. He could feel blood seeping down his side and he had taken any number of blows. His arms felt so heavy he could barely lift them. He had rotated the lines, saving his guard and letting the perioikoi take their turn, until they too began to fail. He'd called the rest forward then, though they lacked the years of Spartan training that made flesh like bone and bones like bronze. He had lost count of how many times he'd rotated the Spartan guard back in to let the others rest, over and over, asking more of them than any of the others.

The Persians had given them no respite. They had sent in their white-clad Immortals, rank after rank, as if there would never be an end to them. The Spartans had slaughtered them by the hundred, by the thousand. They'd heaved bodies into the sea just to keep the ground clear underfoot. All while their spears broke or were wrenched from their hands.

They'd drawn swords then and found new strength. The perioikoi had surged forward at Leonidas' command, men who had lived and trained around Sparta since boyhood, yet never been considered true Spartiates, true men. For the first time in their lives, they had been called to war by the battle king of Sparta himself. When Leonidas congratulated them, some of them had tears in their eyes.

By noon, there were no spears left whole. The golden shields were cut and cracked, while even the Spartan guard stood panting, with many of them bleeding freely from cuts they could not stop to tend. The Immortals still came on, though the ground was littered with the dead, and gold buckles and brooches lay scattered like stones. Whenever there was a break in the slaughter, Leonidas ordered the helots to drag more bodies out of the way. He had noted how many seemed to have festooned themselves with the wealth of kingdoms.

Leonidas did not reprimand them, though not one of his Spartiates had stooped for such treasure. They had no gold coins in Sparta, no silver. There were different kinds of wealth. That had never been clearer to him than in that pass.

Twenty-eight of his guard had been killed, dragged down by cloak and stabbing blades. Every one of their killers had been hacked from life by enraged men, but Leonidas felt their loss, both in the line and as king to them. It brought home the reality he had learned at Delphi. He would not walk away from this place, not if Sparta was the cost. His life would end between the sea and the cliffs.

He knew too that he had won time for the army to take the field, behind him. Leonidas had tried to grant them three days, long enough for the festival of Apollo to come to an end. There was a symmetry to it, he thought, battering one shield aside and killing a yelling man half his age, gashing a throat under a beard as black as night. His own beard came through in patches of white, Leonidas thought ruefully. Age crept up on a man, on a king. It was a strange thought, given that he stood on his last day. His arms seemed to lighten at the thought, so that he moved well, almost in memory of his youth. They could not stand against him then. Those who came within his range fell dead, their blood spooling and curling in seawater.

It was a good finish, he thought. He would go in the flower

of his strength and be spared the weakness of the very old. That was its own blessing in a way. Leonidas thanked Apollo for the honour of dying as he had lived, without compromise or weakness forced on him. Old men grew mellow in their weakness. He had not been made to change and he was grateful.

As the sun began to dip and vanish behind the crags, Leonidas looked up and felt his stomach sink, recalling the rocks he had jumped from into the sea as a young boy, the sense of space and falling that brought something like nausea. High on the cliffs, he could see men in white, panelled armour trotting like a line of Persian wolves behind a single figure. They had found some goat trail or shepherd's path to take them around the pass.

It was the end, he knew with sudden certainty. As soon as they had enough men behind him, they would come from both sides and catch his little force between.

His only regret was for those of Plataea and Corinth and Thespiae who had come with him on this last great task, even for the perioikoi and the helots. They had all fought with endurance and courage and not one had run or been driven from the field. He had lost both friends and strangers that day, but he was proud of them all.

Perhaps because the Persians had sent men around the pass, a lull came. The lines tramping towards them died away and all those with Leonidas were suddenly wilting, leaning on their thighs and gasping hard, sweat pouring from them despite the sea wind. Leonidas called for fresh water, but there was none. He did not know how long it would be before another Persian regiment took up the task and he thought quickly.

'We have held this place,' he called to them all, 'against unrelenting attacks. Your honour is proven, all of you. You have my thanks. You see those above, on the high paths? It will not be long before they are marching in behind – and there will be no escape then. Even so, our work is complete. Know that. We gave the armies of Sparta and Athens – and yes, Megara and Sicyon and all the rest – time to form up. We won that for them.'

He glanced ahead and his heart sank when he saw a new line of soldiers making ready, coming in. He looked left and right and caught the nods of his personal guard. They would not leave, not while the battle king remained. He had known that from the start.

'Go now, quickly!' Leonidas called to the rest. 'I will stay to give you time to get clear. Go home – and carry the news of what we did here. Go!'

Some of those at the rear turned and trotted into the gathering gloom, hundreds of them. A few wept as they went, though whether it was in relief or at his sacrifice, they could not have said themselves.

'Well?' Leonidas asked those who had stayed.

His personal guard raised their swords and shields as if he had not spoken. He'd known they would not show their backs to anyone, not even the army of Xerxes. Yet the perioikoi remained as well, another seven hundred or so.

'You do not need to stand with me,' Leonidas said. He heard his voice choke and break and thought it was surely weariness.

The men of the perioikoi saluted him with raised swords. Ahead, the marching lines of Persians exchanged worried glances, unsure what this meant.

'Yes, we do,' one of the perioikoi said.

Leonidas saw his helots too were still there. They would not, *could* not, leave until he released them.

'By my word as king of Sparta, I free all helots who stood

in this place with me today. Let no man call you slave from this moment. Now, go.'

'If we are not slaves, you cannot order us away,' one of them pointed out.

It was Dromeas, the runner. The young man carried a Spartan shield, taken from one of the fallen perioikoi. As Leonidas watched, the man picked up a sword and jammed a kopis dagger into his belt. The battle king smiled, though his heart broke to see it.

Around half the men he had brought to that place left as he had asked them to do. Almost two thousand stayed at his side. Xerxes sent men against them and when darkness came, he allowed no respite. His men lit torches in the pass. Those with Leonidas fought on in mindless weariness, cut down one by one. Helots – free men all – were killed when they became too slow to stand against fresh soldiers. The perioikoi went hard, slashing and growling, wounding with every blow. Yet they did fall.

Dawn brought Immortals rushing in from behind, determined after a night crossing the cliffs, without sleep, to make an end to the dishonour. They felt the sting of shame at the Great King being forced to wait, mocked and derided by delay, scorned by red-cloaked Spartans.

Attacked on both sides, the Spartans formed square and locked shields, still blocking the way. Xerxes himself came deep into the pass to watch their destruction, standing with Mardonius on his right shoulder. His Immortals fought like madmen under his gaze, but no matter how many of them came against the exhausted Spartan formation, it did not break.

'Stand back,' Xerxes ordered at last. He was appalled at the sheer number of corpses in that place of sea salt and slate.

The air itself smelled of blood. 'Bring them down with spears. Let us not waste any more lives.'

His Immortals had been destroyed, he realised, the elite of all his regiments. Barely half the ten thousand remained and he could not replace them.

From both sides, spears were thrown high. The exhausted Spartans raised shields on arms of lead and some of them fell. Leonidas was one of those, so that his guard took post over his body and would not move another step. They did not have the numbers or the strength to attack those who stung them. Arrows and spears brought them down, one by one, until the last two or three were spitted through with shafts and fell amidst the rest. The red cloaks were bright in that place.

The Persians cheered the victory, a sound that went on and on, spreading to the host behind. It was heard across the sea and it sent a chill through Greek crews as they came on deck to peer at the land and consider what that cheering had to mean.

49

Themistocles gathered the commanders of the fleet on his flagship. He had no cabin of his own below decks. He and his men slept wrapped in their cloaks under the stars. Nor had they much room for stores. They were all leaner than they had been on leaving Athens, after rations snatched in the evenings and nothing but water during daylight hours. The rowers were already looking hollow in the chest, ribs showing just when they needed strength. He wondered if the Persians were suffering as much. They had been at sea far longer. Perhaps the need to feed oarsmen was why they had gone so slowly and kept the land army in sight.

The Spartan Eurybiades ignored an outstretched arm and climbed up on his own. He seemed diminished by the fall of Leonidas, wounded by loss. Themistocles sensed a seething rage in the man, like a pot about to boil over. His instinct was to tread carefully. The commander of Corinth was there, leaning against the prow with his eyes closed, exhausted. He'd spent the previous day in constant battle and had lost fingers and part of his right hand. It was a serious wound and Themistocles thought privately that the Corinthian might not survive.

Xanthippus arrived with Epikleos and Cimon, clambering up with ease from the small boats alongside. It was hard to imagine the first time Themistocles had seen Xanthippus heave himself on board. He moved rather better than he had that day.

Themistocles waited until his men had brought cups of

honey and wine, warmed on the brazier amidships. The morning was cold and they sipped with pleasure, tasting cloves and cinnamon. To a man, they watched the coast, where the Persian army was tramping south through the pass of Thermopylae.

Themistocles too watched the slow passage of regiments. The great army of Persia was a vast enterprise. The mere act of passing through a single spot and assembling on the plain beyond would take days. He could not see an end to them as they stretched back over the plains north.

He had known no small force could hold against them, not even the men of Sparta. They were not gods, to stand immune before spears and arrows, to defy soldiers who stood like stars in the night sky. And yet . . . the days had passed and somehow, each morning, there they were. Leonidas had kept his word, Themistocles thought.

'We have all lost friends,' Themistocles said, his voice low and hoarse after days of shouting orders. 'None of us knew how many the king of Persia could put in the field, at sea, on land. From the first moment I saw this fleet, I thought, "How can we ever stop so many? How can we win?" I took heart from you – from Xanthippus, from Cimon, from Eurybiades . . .' One by one, he named them all, men of Megara, Chalcis, Arcadia, down to the captain from Cythnos who had been able to pledge just one ship. It had survived a glancing blow from a Persian ram. Rough repairs and men baling seawater from below at all hours had kept it afloat. It still held its place in the line, after days of fighting.

'You are Greeks,' Themistocles went on with a smile, 'so you did not despair. You looked at the narrow strait and the Persian ships and you chose this place to stand in their way, with me.'

He looked from man to man and saw only pride amidst the weariness. They had not been broken, not yet.

'I did not intend at first,' Themistocles went on, 'to hold the line, to fight and ram with such ferocity, to risk everything just to hold them here. It was the example of Leonidas that changed our purpose, the news that the army needed time to come out.'

He paused and dipped his head, almost as if in prayer.

He did not say aloud that Aristides and the hoplites of Athens had been ready in the field for three days. They could not move without the Spartans and the men of Corinth and all the rest, that was the truth of it. Not against such a host. Not if they wanted to have a chance. No one alive had ever seen so many soldiers marching. Themistocles shook his head, realising his thoughts were drifting.

'We held this strait to give our people time to gather and to arm. Leonidas stopped them at the pass; we stopped them at sea.'

He glanced over to the coast, no more than three or four arrow shots from where he stood that morning. Ahead of them all, the first ranks of ships were readying themselves to kill and burn, as they had before. The allied captains there knew what they had to do, though it had become a grind of flesh and iron, with fresh ships coming to the fore each day on both sides – and more hulls overturned, and more dead men gazing up from beneath the surface as each sun rose.

'Now they are through,' Themistocles said. 'They can march south – with Athens naked before them.'

'They will be met,' Eurybiades said. 'When the army of Sparta comes out, they'll go fast to cross paths with the Persian host. If your hoplites are quick, you can still join forces and play your part.'

Themistocles closed his eyes for a moment. The Spartan stood on his right side, facing the coast. As a result, Eurybiades

425

did not see the Athenian thump his hand three times against his thigh. It would only make things worse to take the man to task, though it was the arrogance of Sparta that had almost cost them all of Greece. In the face of the battle king's sacrifice, Themistocles kept his own counsel. He chose not to point out that Sparta was the architect of all their losses, that the city's piety and stubbornness had already cost the lives of thousands. Instead, he spoke calmly, seeking to persuade.

'There is a chance now,' Themistocles said, 'that the Persians will force-march south to Athens. Sparta lies much further, beyond Corinth and Argos. They will not be in time to save my city.'

Themistocles took a deep breath, smothering the panic he felt even to say the words. He needed to bring the other faction leaders to his side, not beat them into submission. He glanced at Xanthippus, who at least knew what they had agreed.

'With that in mind, I would withdraw this fleet – and use it to evacuate the city of Athens.'

He went on quickly as Eurybiades opened his mouth, knowing he would be likely to strike the Spartan if Eurybiades scorned the plan – and that would surely end in bloodshed and murder.

'We cannot stop the Persians reaching the women and children in the city,' Themistocles said. 'Not an army like that one.' He pointed to where it still marched through the pass. 'We have ships enough. If we send half our fleet this morning and the rest tonight, we can take the people away before they ever see the enemy.'

'The Spartan army . . .' Eurybiades began.

'Has spent days in prayer, when they should have been preparing for war!' Themistocles snapped. 'Your king Leonidas understood that well enough. I honour him for it! But it will not save Athens. Not now. We had one chance to do that – and that was for Sparta to have come out from behind your barricades two or three days ago.'

Eurybiades clenched his jaw, a slow flush spreading.

'I have not been spoken to in such a way . . .' he started.

Xanthippus was the one who broke in then, trying to deflect both men's rising anger before it overwhelmed them.

'The island of Salamis is closest to Athens – by the port of Piraeus,' Xanthippus said, speaking in a rattle of words. 'With every ship and boat running back and forth, we could get all the people out. If we give ourselves a night's start, we think we can do it – before the Persians reach that part of the coast.'

'Our crews will be exhausted by then,' one of the other commanders pointed out.

'So will the Persian fleet, having chased us,' Xanthippus replied. 'We'll face them again at sea – and we have their measure now.'

'Athens will be destroyed,' Cimon said in a low voice, almost to himself. The young man's face showed grief, but Themistocles chose to hear him.

'A city is not houses, or even temples. All that matters are the women and children we left. If we can get them out, we can rebuild – anywhere.'

'Why the island of Salamis?' one of the other captains asked. 'The people you land won't have ships of their own. They'll be trapped there, won't they?'

Themistocles was watching Eurybiades as he answered, waiting for the man to agree the plan. If he did not, Themistocles was seriously considering throwing him overboard in his armour.

'It is close to the port of Piraeus,' Themistocles said. 'And large enough to take them all. In the time we have, there is

427

nowhere else.' He took a deep breath, his eyes fierce. 'I don't need to tell you that my crews will not just sit by and watch Athens burn. We are the heart of this fleet – and you cannot stand against Persia without us at sea. All that matters now is that we keep our people safe. We'll do it with you – and call you friends – or we'll do it alone, and then face the enemy fleet again. What other choice is there?'

He was looking at Eurybiades and it was the Spartan who replied.

'Are you saying the decision is mine?' he asked.

The answer was in the faces of the men looking back at him. Eurybiades nodded wearily, sick of the world outside Sparta. At home, he had always known where he stood. Here, the damned Athenians would argue every point to death and think they had accomplished something.

'I held the fleet here while King Leonidas fought,' Themistocles said. 'We gave him hope, as he gave us hope. Now he is gone, I must think of all those others who look to us for their lives. Take my hand, Eurybiades. There is only one right choice here.'

The Spartan breathed out slowly, making his decision. If he withdrew the remaining Spartan ships, he would lose the aid of all the rest. He didn't care if the Persians took Athens, not particularly. The city had been a competitor and thorn in the side of Sparta for hundreds of years. He needed their fleet, however.

Eurybiades reached out and took Themistocles' hand, grinding the knuckles together in his grip. He thought the Athenian let him do it, which stole any sense of satisfaction.

'Very well,' the Spartan said. 'We'll save Athens.'

50

Agariste saw the horseman coming as a plume of dust on the
road from the city. She stood on the wall to the estate, looking east and south, her shadow long as the sun began to set
behind her. Her slave Manias had called her to the wall, his
instincts prickling. Other horsemen had gone barrelling
past, heads down and dust choking their lungs. There was
something happening. Manias could read the flight of birds
in the air. He could scent war on the breeze, and when he
looked up and began to worry, she did as well.

When she saw it was Epikleos, she gasped, then let air out
like a sigh or a last breath. He was not meant to be there. He
was meant to be with Xanthippus, out on the deep waters.
She felt her hands flutter against her dress, beyond her control. He could not be dead; she would have felt it. She would
have dreamed it and seen him for the last time. The gods
would not be so cruel as to simply take him and never let
her know. She had spent part of that morning picking
flowers in the meadow. The thought that she might have
breathed in petals and known peace as Xanthippus fell
was a wrench of pain. In that moment, as Epikleos dismounted, she almost wished he would just go on and not
speak to her, that whatever he knew could be held in his
lips and not spoken.

'Agariste,' he said, looking up to where she stood, frozen
in fear.

His tone was dull, his face and hair thick with dirt – and
there was some bloody scrape along his temple, at the

hairline. His left arm was mottled with bruising, she saw. Epikleos had been battered and wore the marks of war under the dust.

'Is he dead?' she asked, her voice choked and high, so that she sounded like a little girl.

'Xanthippus is alive, but we cannot save the city. Gather the children, Agariste. Summon your household. There are ships waiting to take you away – if you come now.'

'Open the gate!' Agariste said.

She ran down the steps and embraced the man who came past Manias and the armed slaves set to guard. Epikleos staggered and she sensed how tired and filthy he was.

'Agariste, there is no time. The Persians are coming. Please call your children. Have your slaves gather up food and tools, weapons. Is there a cart? Horses?'

'Yes, all those,' she said.

Some of the slaves were already moving, though the mistress of the house stood in a daze of confusion. Epikleos seemed to understand she was not taking it in. He took her hands in his.

'*Listen* to me. The Persian army is coming here, to Athens. Xanthippus has ships down at the port, ready to take you and the children. You must come now, as fast as you can.'

'But . . .' Agariste waved a hand. The estate her uncle had built lay encompassed in that gesture, with all the wealth and influence of her family.

'Leave it, please,' Epikleos said. 'Leave everything. The whole city is going to the ships. I have a place for you and the household – with Xanthippus.'

She shook herself and he breathed out in relief at the return of the iron he knew she had in her. With a nod, Agariste looked into his eyes for a moment, then spun away from him, calling orders to Manias and the house slaves.

'Pericles! Ariphron! Eleni!' she called at the top of her voice.

Epikleos heard high voices replying and he began to jog towards them. Xanthippus had given him the task of saving his family. It was a sacred trust and he would not let him down.

Xanthippus stood on the shore of the port of Piraeus. He could see the limestone spire of the Acropolis in the distance and he longed to stand there, instead of shepherding thousands of his people onto the galleys rowing in and out in ceaseless order. The waters were calm enough in the shelter of the port, though he had reports of a galley turning over in the strait between the mainland and the island of Salamis. The sense of panic was on them all since the bulk of the Greek fleet had appeared, weary men at the oars who nonetheless fell into their new duty and began ferrying passengers over from the port. Salamis was visible from the coast, across the sea. It was no safe refuge, not for anything more than a few days. It had one great advantage over Athens and the mainland – no soldier could reach it on foot. The women and children and slaves of Athens would be spared the slaughter and rapine of a marauding army entering Athens. It was all he could offer then. Some cold, still part of him was afraid it was nothing more than a delay. The Persian king had brought so many men and ships, it was hard to see how anyone could do more than just retreat and retreat before them.

Two more galleys came in, backing oars at the last moment so that they bumped against the stone quays, throwing ropes to waiting men there and heaving in the oars to sit, staring in exhaustion. Xanthippus whistled up the water boys he had assembled, sending them on board as soon as the gangplank

431

was tied on. His people had gathered in vast numbers, more and more of them streaming down from the city. They carried valuables in sacks, some of them, clutched as close as the children who peeped out from their legs and cloaks. Some wailed in fear and anger, others exhorted the aid of the gods in their hour of need. The ships took on as many as they could cram onto the decks without risking their lives. The danger was constant and Xanthippus could only pray they wouldn't lose more. Half a dozen women and children had been picked up from the galley that went over. The rest had drowned.

He rubbed his face, so tired he could barely think as his vision blurred. He needed to sleep, to eat, to experience quiet and peace for just a few hours before being thrown back into the tumult. He and his crew had peeled off from the main fleet the morning before, part of a hundred and sixty Athenian ships. Themistocles had trusted him to lead them home, then carry the news to the Agora and the Areopagus. Younger men had made the run from the port into the city, calling the news as they went. It had been chaos from the first moments, but they'd come. His people had gathered up their loved ones and run to the quays. They had trusted in the Athenians of the fleet, their husbands and brothers and sons.

Xanthippus slapped himself on the face with his left hand, keeping himself alert. He looked further along the road, watching for Agariste and the children. He would not leave without them. Yet all the while he stood there, he felt the gaze of many, wondering why his ship remained while others drove back and forth, back and forth. Some old women had tried arguing with his hoplites, gesturing furiously. Those men had glanced back in mute appeal, but he had sent them to another ship, over all their curses.

The crowd was thickening, if anything, though he'd seen

more people than he'd known lived in the city taken to Sala-mis. He imagined every deme of Athens being emptied – the Ceramicus, the council building, the temples on the Acrop-olis. He wondered if the city had been quiet without the men who crewed the ships. He imagined them subdued and wor-ried, waiting for news. They had been given a victory after Marathon. He recalled the cheering crowds then, with gar-lands of amaranth flowers. That day was still a shining memory, he realised. Before his banishment and all the bit-terness of years away. Before the politics of the city had taken on a sour taste. Before the king of Persia had brought an army and a fleet to break them.

Xanthippus swallowed when he saw the cart coming through the crowd. He was not certain for a moment, then he recognised Pericles on horseback, with Agariste and Eleni driving the cart and – there, Ariphron and Epikleos riding horses at the rear. He could hear his dog barking and saw the big mastiff bounding along, wild with excitement. They made a path as those on foot gave way to the strength and size of the horses or were buffeted. Some of the women trudging along must have recognised Agariste, or known it was her husband who waited with the ship. They increased their pace. Part of the crowd there seemed to swell and heave forward, coming in his direction, so that Xanthippus saw they would arrive together, infecting one another with a sort of desperate need. He could hear his dog howling as it ran.

'Let them on,' he called to the hoplites guarding the gangplank.

The crowd began to run and he saw his men knocked aside as women and children abandoned caution, seeing only the empty deck and safety. One of them went right down, vanishing in the rush. Xanthippus felt a surge of panic at the thought of too many pouring on board. He glared at his men, seeing their helplessness. They could not draw blades on women and children, but the crowd had a life of its own and a need that would not be denied.

'Fetch another dozen men out,' Xanthippus bellowed to his crew. 'We can't let them run wild. They'll swamp the ship.'

On board, orders were roared to get out and help as Agariste and the children drew up and reined in. Xanthippus reached up to his wife and took her around the waist, helping her down to the stones of the port.

'It's good to see you,' he said.

Her eyes searched his for reassurance and found none.

Epikleos was there, using his outstretched arms and booming voice to make a path for the children. The horses were left where they stood and Xanthippus almost went over as his dog Conis leapt up at him, tangling itself in his tunic and cloak and slobbering. Xanthippus embraced the animal, laughing as it wriggled and bounced.

'Are you coming with us?' Agariste said.

Xanthippus shook his head.

'Not yet. I wish I could. Keep Manias and the others close. Shall I leave you Epikleos?'

'I'd be happier knowing he was with you,' she said. 'We'll be all right.'

Xanthippus saw his children had come closer, unwilling to interrupt their parents in their conversation. He kissed Agariste quickly and embraced them one by one, feeling the strength in them all.

'Keep your mother and sister safe – your lives on it,' Xanthippus said sternly to Pericles and Ariphron. Both of them nodded, matching his seriousness.

Xanthippus glanced over his shoulder. His hoplites had come out and brought some order to the crowd pressing to get on board. Already they were waving some away and telling them they would have to wait for another ship or join the crowds further along the quays. None of them wanted to risk losing a place and they cried out in entreaty, then anger, as Xanthippus brought his family and his wife's household through.

He pressed Agariste forward with a hand in the small of her back, then his sons and his daughter, pausing only to kiss the top of her head. Manias went too, with no more than an exchange of glances. The old man would look after them, as he always had.

Xanthippus felt the wrench of it, even in the midst of his relief. He had reached them. He felt as if he could faint there and then on the quayside, just give way to complete collapse. There was shouting and crying all around him in the press of bodies, while still more streamed down from the city.

Epikleos was there, at his shoulder, appearing out of the mob.

'I can manage the crowds here. Go with your family. They need you more than we do, at least for the moment.'

Xanthippus nodded, overcome. He pushed through the hoplites guarding the ship and reached the deck. He felt tears in his eyes as his children caught sight of him and hung from his arms and chest, crushing the air out of him. Agariste was weeping, he saw.

'Where is my dog?' he asked them.

They all looked around, but there was no sight of the great beast. Already the ship was being pushed off, the oarsmen settling to their task one more time. In moments, the sail was raised to catch the gentlest breeze, anything at all that might lessen the burden for the rowers. Xanthippus saw the crowds pressing in their desperation. One or two fell into the sea when the crush was too great, shrieking in fear.

He looked up and felt a rushing in his ears and blood drain

435

from his face. The Acropolis seemed to shift in shape as he watched, as if some great hand twisted it. He understood then, feeling the hair on his neck prickle. It was smoke, a great column of blackness that engulfed and smothered the city. The Persians had reached the city of Athena – and when they found it empty, they had set it on fire.

He heard the gasps from those on the crowded deck as they too saw the column and understood what it meant. A low moan of fear and pointing hands made him turn his head to the east. Greek ships were all around him, ferrying women and children. Beyond, a new line of ships had appeared, rowing, rowing, making the sea white. The Persian fleet had come.

Xanthippus clutched his family to him. Looking back at the port, he saw the tiny figure of his dog suddenly fall or leap into the water, vanishing beneath the surface, then appear once again, paddling after him. He swore under his breath at the stupid animal. He could not halt the galley, even if they'd had a boat in tow to set down. The dog would never survive the swim to Salamis.

In the face of the destruction of Athens, it was a small thing, but he felt tears streaming down his face even so. He watched the struggling dog for a long time until he was just a speck on the waters and then gone, lost in the vastness of the sea.

Historical Note

When does a story really begin? When Greek cities in Ionia (western Turkey) came under the control of Persia? When they rebelled, called for help and Greek columns rampaged through the region? Or when Greek diplomats were asked for 'earth and water' – complete submission – by a satrap of the Great King. Far from home and unable to consult, they gave the obeisance required and so became vassals of Persia, at least as far as Darius was concerned.

Or is it before those events, when Athenians were fighting against tyrants like Hippias? When the head of the Alcmaeonidae family bribed a priestess in Delphi to give the same message to any Spartan who came to ask a question, regardless of the subject: 'Free Athens from Tyranny.'

When Sparta eventually sent an army to force the tyrant Hippias to stand down, they were tempted to stay and rule a competitor city – until every street filled with armed men. The citizens of Athens had been promised self-rule and that is a powerful thing. The Spartan army left, though the incident rankled. Men like the Athenian Cleisthenes thought up rules and tribes and laws – a system of checks and balances and responsibilities, designed so that no one could ever rise to be a tyrant again. It is the birth of democracy, an idea of equality before the law that has endured for two and a half thousand years.

The battle of Marathon that opens this book has a number of gaps in the record. We do not know if King Darius was present. No one knows what happened to the Persian cavalry. Cavalry was a big part of Persian armies at this time – and would be present for the invasion with Xerxes later on. Here, though, the horses are reported and then vanish. It seemed to me that after sacking the seaport of Eretria, the beach at Marathon must have been a handy staging post for an invasion of Athens along the coast. It is only twenty miles away and a reasonable spot for the Persian force that day to regroup, repair and give their horses a chance to run off some seasickness. I've assumed the reason the cavalry was not there is because it had gone aboard.

It is true that Xanthippus was present, father of Pericles and husband to Agariste, niece of Cleisthenes. The wonderful Themistocles was there in the centre, to lead the Leontis tribe. Aristides stood with him, leading Antiochis tribe. The 'polemarch', or war leader, was Callimachus on the right wing, though Miltiades seems to have been in effective command throughout. Callimachus was killed in the fighting. A statue in his honour was raised on the Acropolis, though it did not survive the Persian invasion.

As a matter of record, the playwright Aeschylus was also there – and saw his brother killed. Miltiades thinned his own centre and then saw it beaten back. His heavy wings then came down on Persian forces and crushed them with long spears and a disciplined phalanx formation. It was as savage as might be expected from men defending their home. The 'Miltiades helmet' – presumably the one he wore at Marathon and marked with his name – is at the Archaeological Museum of Olympia, Greece. Though damaged, it is an incredible thing.

I wrote the scene with Miltiades delaying the wing to explain a later event. When Miltiades returned from his failed expedition, having lost men and ships, the great hero of Marathon was badly wounded. In that moment of utter shame and weakness, Xanthippus made his accusation. The trial that followed is hard to explain unless Xanthippus had a personal motive. I wondered if he considered the man a traitor and an enemy, based on something he had seen at Marathon.

That sequence of events seemed likely to me as a way of explaining Xanthippus' behaviour. Many Greek states supported Persia. The Thebans were infamous for being present on the wrong side, mocked and scorned for centuries in Athenian drama. Queen Artemisia of Halicarnassus also worked with the Persians. She was presented by Herodotus as a sympathetic character, perhaps in part because he came from the same place. It might look like treason today, but the idea of the nation state had not yet taken root.

Miltiades died a prisoner, in 489 BC, the year after Marathon. Xanthippus was ostracised, or exiled, five years later, in 484 BC, after a public vote. Pieces of pottery, 'ostraca', from that event with his name inscribed survive – one with two lines of verse scratched into the surface. It mentions an injustice in politics as the reason. We cannot know for certain whether it was the trial of Miltiades, though that seems likely. Nor can we know the exact part Themistocles played, though it is true that both Xanthippus and Aristides were ostracised by public vote. With the death of Miltiades, that left Themistocles effectively as first man in Athens. Despite the slow reveal, it does look like a campaign by a man famous for his persuasiveness. Only an extraordinary event would force Themistocles to use his influence once again – to reverse the ostracisms and bring good military men home. That event was the invasion of Greece by Persia.

*

It is true that Themistocles persuaded the Assembly of Athens to use the windfall of silver from a new seam at Laurium to build a fleet of one hundred and eighty ships – a fleet that would be instrumental in evacuating Athens. Themistocles literally saved his city – with three brilliant ideas. This is the story of the first of the three. The Greeks did not take the favour of the gods for granted, but there are times when it looked as if they were rather blessed . . .

I have compressed the timeline between Marathon and the Xerxes invasion – there was only one ostracism vote allowed per year, for example, which is sensible, but it robs a narrative of a little dramatic energy. I've kept the main events as they happened, however. I think it is a fascinating tale and Themistocles was a brilliant man, often overlooked as a key historical figure. The scene where Aristides wrote his own name on a shard of pottery for an illiterate man to vote is well attested – and a fascinating clue to the nature of Aristides.

In Persia, the death of Darius interrupted the terrible vengeance he desired. It is true that he shot an arrow as his vow and had a slave whisper three times each evening for him to 'Remember the Greeks'. Yet it would be his son Xerxes who brought the army and the fleet to Greece, crossing the Hellespont on two bridges of ships to do it. The detail of his wife giving thanks to the god Ahura Mazda by burying children alive is from Herodotus.

Note: the Persian capital was Paarsa. I have used the Greek name for it, Paarsa-polis (city of Paarsa) or 'Persepolis', throughout as it's better known.

Over four or five years, news spread of the huge invasion force being gathered in what is now modern-day Turkey.

When Aristides and Xanthippus were summoned home early from exile, it can only have been with the connivance of Themistocles. Their personal feuds were simply put aside for the greater good, which is extraordinary. Xanthippus took on a senior role in the fleet. Aristides was given command of the main force of Athenian hoplites and took them out to join the allied city-states.

First contact with the Persian fleet was off the island of Sciathos. The Persian sailors seem to have made heavy weather of the unknown coasts, taking it very slowly. However, ten of their scout ships came across three Greek triremes left there to carry warning.

The Persians rammed and sank one Greek ship. They sacrificed a particularly handsome sailor on the deck of his own ship for good luck. The second Greek crew was overcome after a fierce resistance. The final trireme made it to the mainland and the crew took off over land. Meanwhile, three of the Persian ships ran aground on a bank out to sea, which they then marked with a stone pillar brought for that exact purpose – to show the danger to those following. This was the first incident of the Persian war of 480 BC, and it was a complete disaster for the Greeks: surprised, overwhelmed by superior numbers and massacred.

The fleet of Xerxes lost many more ships to storms as they came south, though exact numbers are unknown. In strange lands, they hugged the shore and tried to keep the army under Mardonius in sight at all times. The plan was to reach Athens by land, after crossing a final range of mountains – through the pass known as Thermopylae. At the same time, the Persian invasion engaged the combined Greek fleet at sea for three days of fighting along the strait near the town of Artemisium. (It seems to be just a coincidence that the queen of Halicarnassus was called Artemisia.) The number of Persian ships was reported at around 1,200, though it may have been as low as six or eight hundred.

The battle of Thermopylae took place at the same time, on a strip of coast that was the only way past the range of mountains. The sea has retreated there today, with new land creeping in. It is no longer possible to see what Leonidas saw, not exactly. Yet he would have been in contact with the fleet. For three days or so, he prevented the Persian advance on land, while Athens and her allies fought their fleet at sea. It was a coordinated effort – and the purpose was to give the main Greek forces time to assemble and make ready.

It is true that Leonidas had been to the oracle at Delphi. There he was told that the Spartans would mourn the loss of their city or the loss of a king descended from Heracles – the bloodline of Leonidas. In essence, the king would have to choose between saving his own life and saving Sparta. I suspect that explains why he did not leave the pass of Thermopylae, even right at the end, when he sent most of them away and remained with just his elite guard, and around a thousand others. Interestingly, his helot slaves remained with him, though they would have known there was no escape at that point. Leonidas knew it was the end – and he accepted it. For some reason, that aspect of his thinking does not usually feature when the story is told, though it may be the most heroic part.

In the great strait that runs along the east coast of Attica, ship-to-ship actions went on for three days, dawn to dusk. The Persians had what must have seemed an unlimited number of warships, but the Greeks were better motivated, with free citizens as rowers, men who had families in Athens.

When Leonidas was finally killed, the Persian land army surged through the pass. It was only then that Themistocles made his extraordinary decision – to pull back and evacuate Athens. The Spartan navarch, Eurybiades, wanted to pull the fleet right to the Peloponnese, but Themistocles over-ruled him, saying if he did, it would be without the Athenian ships. In bending the Spartan to his will, Themistocles kept the fleet together. Pericles, son of Xanthippus and Agariste, was part of that mass movement of people to the island of Salamis, the boy aged around fifteen. It would have been a memory that stayed with him his entire life.

In the evacuation, crews rowed themselves to exhaustion, back and forth, crammed each time with fearful women and children. They managed it, but when the Persian fleet appeared, the Greek galleys remained to finish the job – stuck in the narrow strait by Salamis, once again denied the open sea they desperately needed to manoeuvre. On the land, visible to all, they saw the plume of smoke that meant the Persian army had begun to burn Athens to the ground.

Hope died, but Themistocles was there. It is rare to be able to say one man saved a country, on one day. In the case of Themistocles, that is the simple truth – as I'll describe in the next book.

Conn Iggulden, London, 2019

Lennox &
Addington
LIBRARIES